HANDFASTED

Catherine Helen Spence, born in Scotland in 1825, migrated with her family to the new colony of South Australia in 1839. She became a teacher, a journalist, an untiring philanthropist, wrote eight novels, travelled the world twice and worked as a propagandist for proportional representation. She was Australia's first woman candidate for political office (unsuccessful) and, when she died in 1910, was described as 'the grand old woman of Australia'. Spence's life demonstrated that a nineteenth-century Australian woman could achieve a lifestyle which, even in today's terms, could be described as satisfyingly liberated.

Helen Thomson (editor) is a senior lecturer in the English department at Monash University. Melbourne-born, she completed her first degree at Monash and has lived in England and Germany. Her current research interests are nineteenth-century feminism and contemporary theatre. She writes theatre criticism for the *Australian* newspaper. She is married to a fellow academic and they have two children.

Penguin Australian Selection contains lively and enjoyable books which have been lost for too long. Some have been out-of-print, others never published. All have been chosen because of their intrinsic interest now, their readability and the pleasure of discovery.

CATHERINE HELEN SPENCE

HANDFASTED

Edited, with a preface and afterword by Helen Thomson

Published with the assistance of the Literature Board of the Australia Council

PENGUIN BOOKS

Penguin Books Australia Ltd,
487 Maroondah Highway, P.O. Box 257
Ringwood, Victoria, 3134, Australia
Penguin Books Ltd,
Harmondsworth, Middlesex, England
Penguin Books,
40 West 23rd Street, New York, N.Y. 10010, U.S.A.
Penguin Books Canada Ltd,
2801 John Street, Markham, Ontario, Canada
Penguin Books (N.Z.) Ltd,
182-190 Wairau Road, Auckland 10, New Zealand

First published by Penguin Books Australia, 1984

Typeset in Garamond by Dovatype, Melbourne

Printed by The Dominion Press-Hedges & Bell,
Maryborough, 3465

CIP

Spence, Catherine Helen, 1825-1910.
Handfasted.

ISBN 0 14 007505 4.

I. Thomson, Helen, 1943- .
II. Title.

A823'.1

CONTENTS

Preface by Helen Thomson vii

Book One The Lost Scottish Adventurers 1
I My Family and Especially My Grandmother 3
II The Marriage Question 9
III The Lost Scottish Adventurers 14
IV Recollections and Speculations 22

Book Two Out of the World 27
I Found 29
II The Peculiar Institution of Columba 36
III A Columban Bridegroom and Bride 45
IV I Teach and I Learn 50
V An Evening's Amusement 61
VI Voting in Columba 70
VII The Capital of Columba 77
VIII Our Journey 87
IX A Columban Saturday Night 98
X A Columban Sunday 105
XI I Find a New Side of the Intellectual Problem 117
XII Three Fellow Workers 125
XIII The Columban Drama 134
XIV Stories Retold 140

Book Three A Revolution of the Past 149

I	The Columban Library	151
II	Madame Keith's Story – Youth	159
III	Madame Keith's Narrative Continued – Love	165
IV	Madame Keith's Narrative Continued – Marriage	171
V	Madame Keith's Narrative Continued – A Mother's Sorrows	177
VI	Madame Keith's Narrative Continued – Farewell to Scotland	186
VII	Madame Keith's Narrative Continued – The Settlement of Columba	191
VIII	Madame Keith's Narrative Continued – The Origin of Handfasting	198
IX	Madame Keith's Narrative Continued – The Kirk and the Sabbath	204

Book Four Three Rivals 213

I	I Declare Myself	215
II	How Liliard's Bridegroom Took It	223
III	Some Short-comings in the Columban Constitution	229
IV	Two Great Wants in Columba: Lack of Devotion and Lack of Humour	236
V	A Discovery	244
VI	Deliverance	252
VII	Harvest Home in Columba	258
VIII	We are Handfasted	262

Book Five Back to the World 271

I	Communication Restored	273
II	An Unwelcome Intruder	280
III	Jack Barnett's Active Curiosity	287
IV	Liliard's Forecast	296
V	Knowledge of Good and Evil	303
VI	Liliard's First Introduction into Society	310
VII	I Meet Some Old Friends from Melbourne	318
VIII	Mr Campbell's Losing Bet	327
IX	The Result of Liliard's Parliamentary Report	336
X	Liliard's Letters	342

Afterword by Helen Thomson 363

PREFACE

Catherine Helen Spence is one of the neglected women of Australia's history. With a number of remarkable achievements to her credit, she has become little more than a footnote in the chronicles of 19th-century Australian life. Part of the reason for this may be that she was from Adelaide, arriving there from Scotland in 1839 at the age of fourteen, and identifying herself with what, in contrast to the cities of Sydney and Melbourne, was an idealistically planned colony, untainted by convict origins, or by the subsequent uncontrolled mixture of emigrants in search of gold. Adelaide, then as now, was often thought to be provincial, but Spence herself was extraordinarily cosmopolitan. Not only did she twice travel the world, she also read widely in both French and English, writing book reviews for newspapers and corresponding with other writers and reformers in America and Europe.

Spence began her professional life by teaching, supplementing a meagre family income, then supported herself and her widowed mother by writing. Her first novel, *Clara Morison; a tale of South Australia during the gold fever*, the first novel written by a woman about Australia, was published in 1854. Six other novels were published between then and the 1880s, by which time she was a full-time journalist. She wrote on a vast number of public issues, particularly on women's rights, law reform, child welfare, cultural trends, co-operative ventures and trade unions. The last two decades of her life – she died in 1910 – were almost exclusively devoted to electoral reform and the advocacy of proportional representation. With this as her platform she stood, unsuccessfully, as the first female Australian political candidate in 1897.

The manuscript of *Handfasted* was sent in 1879 to the *Sydney Mail* which was offering a £100 prize for a novel. Its rejection on the grounds that 'it was calculated to loosen the marriage tie – it was too socialistic, and consequently dangerous' tells us something about Spence's radicalism relative to the prevailing *mores* governing fiction. Trial marriages of a year and a day (the 'handfasting' practice to which the title refers), no longer have much power to shock, and the feminist utopian novel has become remarkably fashionable. Spence's utopian society of Columba has freed its women from the traditional sexual and social constraints of the 19th century. Handfasting dealt a blow to precisely those social laws which had enslaved women. Chastity becomes virtually meaningless in a society which sanctions changing sexual partners. Illegitimacy is an unknown concept, and thus the power of patrilinear inheritance laws disappears. Women in Columba are land-owners, voters, and usually more highly educated than their menfolk. From a masculine, conservative point of view *Handfasted* in 1879 certainly raised potentially subversive ideas.

However, when Spence sets up in her novel a small social laboratory somewhere in Central America, 'lost' to the world since 1745, described as 'a curious political and social experiment on a small scale under the most favourable circumstances', she discovers weaknesses as well as strengths in her model, and realistically concludes that the 19th-century world as she knew it was not capable of such radical change. Thus she draws back from total commitment to her radical ideal.

All of Spence's novels indicate explicit preference for Australian society, and this unjustly neglected novel is no exception. The hero and narrator returns to Melbourne convinced of the superiority of this colonial city which, if it lacks the socially superior advantages of Columba, also lacks the worst aspects of both the brash new world of America and the unregenerate old world of Europe and England.

Whatever her disappointment at the rejection of *Handfasted*, Spence sensibly decided to transfer her energetic abilities and reformist hopes to the more mundane but rewarding sphere of journalism and public speaking. She wrote only one more novel, and then two polemical works, and became increasingly absorbed in the political movement for proportional representation. When she died in 1910, at the age of eighty-four, she had earned the title 'grand old woman of Australia'. By then her fictional works, only one of which had by that time gone into a second edition, must have been almost forgotten. Seventy years later it is her journalism which seems the mere ephemera of history, while her novels, two of which have already gone into modern reprintings, are seen not only as important social documents, but as landmarks in the literature of 19th-century Australia.

The manuscript of *Handfasted*, which found its way into the archives of the State Library of South Australia in 1922, is a fair copy in another hand which has been amended by Spence, probably after its return from Sydney. As far as can be known, Spence never submitted the manuscript to a publisher, and so it has never undergone any editorial scrutiny. This edition is not a reproduction of the manuscript, but has been edited, hopefully much as it would have been had it been published in Spence's own lifetime. The punctuation has been standardised, unnecessary repetitions have been deleted, and also a considerable part of Book One, where Hugh Keith's grandmother's conversation seemed unnecessarily wordy and immaterial to the novel as a whole, has been omitted. One entire chapter in Book V 'Salt Lake City' has also been omitted because of its unnecessary prolixity.

Helen Thomson

The manuscript of *Hammond*, which found its way into the archives of the State Library of South Australia in [illegible], is [illegible] in [illegible] which has been [illegible] by [illegible], [illegible] [illegible] from Sydney. As far as [illegible] known, [illegible] [illegible] [illegible] the [illegible] not [illegible] published, and [illegible] has [illegible] [illegible] [illegible] [illegible] [illegible]. [illegible] [illegible] [illegible] [illegible] of the manuscript, but has been [illegible] [illegible] [illegible] it would have been had it been published [illegible] [illegible]. The [illegible]

[illegible]

BOOK ONE

THE LOST SCOTTISH ADVENTURERS

I

MY FAMILY AND ESPECIALLY MY GRANDMOTHER

Those who care little for their ancestors will never be very interesting to their posterity. Although I cannot boast of aristocratic birth I have been trained up to be proud of my descent from a good old Scottish family in the old times, and to look back for eight generations to respectable and educated ancestors. As the oldest living link in the chain, I have the highest regard for my grandmother whose knowledge is accurate and whose judgement is excellent. The adventures which befell me lately were doubly interesting on account of her recollections. She had heard from eyewitnesses of the emigration of the Scottish adventurers in the beginning of the year 1745, and I did not meet my distant kin beyond the sea like a stranger and an alien. The long gulf of time in which they lived apart from the great stream of history was less of a severance to me than to others, the laws and customs which they had originated or modified for their new conditions seem to me in these days when all history is looked upon as evolution, very well worth chronicling. At the risk of appearing egotistic, I must begin this narrative with some personal details about myself and my family necessary to give the reader the right understanding of what is to follow.

There had been a traditional rule in our family for many generations that one son, generally the eldest son, should follow the profession of healing. There had been alternately a Dr Hugh and a Dr Archibald Keith who took his degree at Edinburgh University as he came to man's estate, and who practised his profession somewhere in the Lowlands of Scotland, for more than a century. My father had, however, been induced to give up a promising practice in Dumfries to emigrate to Melbourne shortly after the gold discoveries in Victoria. He still held to the custom of the family, and he trained me his only son according to the same pattern as my ancestors in the same University to be his helper and successor. When my father left Scotland, he was accompanied by his mother, who though she had two daughters married and settled in the old country, had one daughter married to a prosperous squatter near Geelong, who formed one attraction to the movement. But my father was her favourite son and his newly married wife was especially dear to her, and as it was on account of the delicate health of my mother that the change was made my grandmother thought she might be more helpful in Melbourne than in Dumfries. My grandmother lived in love and amity with her son and his wife until the death of my mother, which took place when I was eight years old, and after the birth of a third little sister. After this sad event, my grandmother remained the head of the household until my father married again, when she took a cottage near, so as not to appear to interfere with Mrs Archibald Keith's domestic arrangements. There were two girls born of the second marriage, and two boys who both died young so that I was the only male representative of the family.

My father's practice was a good one, and as he was a prudent and sensible man of business, he lived within his income and invested his savings in property which rose in value with the extension of Melbourne and the suburbs. But from the time when I could understand the subject, he treated me with the greatest confidence as to his affairs, and I felt that the prospect of being his partner, and by and by when he was too old for active practice, his successor, was a most enviable one. I liked the idea of studying where he had studied, and of learning all that was new in theory and in practice during the thirty years that had elapsed since he began his medical education.

There were of course great regrets from all my sisters when I had to leave the pleasant house in Collins Street, where as the eldest and the only boy I was somewhat spoiled, but there were letters to be exchanged, and journals to be kept, and various palliations for the sufferings of absence, which this nineteenth century of easy communication furnishes even between two antipodal centres. I was to live with my Aunt, Mrs Semple in Edinburgh, and was to be sure to visit Upper and Nether Keith, which combined formed the old estate of the family sold about the middle of the last century, and also to make a run to the village of Colbrandspath or Cockburnspath (vulgarly pronounced Coppersmith) from the manse of which had come the first Dr Hugh Keith who had graduated in 1750. I had letters to many friends and introductions to many Anglo-Australians, resident either for a time or permanently in the three kingdoms.

My Edinburgh relatives, who had the idea that the modern Athens was still the hub of the universe, took some exception to some of my friends and some of my ways as altogether too colonial, but on the whole I got on very pleasantly with them, and when I left Edinburgh for a year's residence in Paris, which my father thought would show me some of the continental practice, and a larger hospital practice than Edinburgh, I felt that I left very good friends behind. But the Paris air was intellectually keener than that which I had left, and among the thousand various currents which in that centre of European civilisation were playing round me, I felt that there was a great deal for an Australian colonist to learn. The language and the literature of France had always a great charm for me and I greatly improved my acquaintance with them, and thus I delighted my father by writing an article in a medical journal in very passable French. The cultivation of that language was also a tradition in our family dating as far back as the Colbrandspath manse when the minister had brought a French Huguenot wife of good family to preside over his house.

Among my Melbourne correspondents, the most regular if not the most lengthy was my grandmother. In all my pursuits and all my tastes she had taken the warmest interest from the earliest period that I could recollect and my travels in Scotland, in England, and in France during the vacations, were always followed by her on the maps, and the places looked up in the Gazetteer or the Encyclopedia. Her early girlhood had been nurtured on the third edition of the Encyclopedia Britannica which her father who was a tenant-farmer on a large scale in East Lothian had bought for the family reading, when it came out in 1797, and she still had the old desire to get at the bottom of everything, and not to be contented with names or words without the fullest knowledge of what they meant, so that her habitual accuracy put younger students often to the blush.

When I returned to Melbourne at the age of twenty-four with my M.D. degree and some other tokens of a successful course of study, the father's eyes were moist, the stepmother's greeting was warm, the sisters kissed and hugged me, half laughing, half crying, but the old grandmother leaning on her staff blessed me with a patriarchal blessing: a sort of *nunc dimittis*, as if this was what she had lived to see, and could now depart in peace.

However, the departure was of others and not of the dear old lady. My father had waited till my return to take a hard-earned holiday after a quarter of a century's unremitting work, and after a few months' joint practice, in which I satisfied both my father and his patients of my competency, he left me in sole possession of the field. He took with him Mrs Keith and the five girls, and the big Collins Street house felt very empty and very quiet, when there was only my grandmother and myself left in it, for she gave up her own cottage to keep house for Hugh Keith the younger. The old lady liked the society of young people and encouraged me to ask my friends, while she invited girls on her own account to meet them.

Old Mrs Keith, as she was generally called by her acquaintances, was even in her eighty-eighth year a competent housekeeper, and her eye was not dim, nor her natural strength of intellect abated. She was very little over the middle height, but she had still a commanding presence, and sat more upright in her chair than some of her young granddaughters. The widow's cap, that she wore of an unfashionably large size, made a most becoming framework for her comely face with its pure white frillings, tied comfortably under her chin with a white ribbon. She had never had great beauty of feature, but in her youth she had a complexion of roses and lilies, and a beautiful hand and arm; still the soft smooth skin, with the bloom of a winter apple on the cheeks, showed the lastingness of the beauty which is contemptuously called only skin-deep, while handsomer features might have taken on too much of the nutcracker style for beauty. Except that she was a little lame, and walked with the assistance of a staff, she had no other infirmity of old age, and as she could see to read and to knit, and only required people to speak distinctly to her to be heard, she was generally called a wonderful old lady.

But to me it was the youth and vigour of her mind that was more remarkable than the preservation of her bodily senses; the interest that she took, not only in things that happened long ago, but in everything that was going on now; her willing acceptance of all new truths and all new discoveries, and her attitude of mind towards possibilities not yet ascertained as truths, or as practicable methods, were traits rarely found with people twenty years younger. In some ways she thought us young Melbourne folks a little fast. But her criticism was limited to outward things. The science, the art, the literature, and even the theology of her grandchildren's days, she accounted as higher, wiser and better than those of her own youth, and even to be preferred to those of her vigorous middle age. What a wonderful panorama of life and of literature had passed before her since the time when she had written at the foot of her copy book 'Margaret Rutherford 1799'. She had read *Sir Charles Grandison* and *The Vicar of Wakefield* as the only novels of the old school fit for girls' reading, had eagerly welcomed Scott's poetry and had wondered and guessed at the authorship of the Waverley novels, and still somehow looked on Dickens and Thackeray as quite recent authors. She had pshawed at the silver-fork school and groaned over the sensational school of novels. She had learned Burns by heart in her teens, and Byron and Scott later on, and now could appreciate Tennyson and Browning. She had been surprised by a gentleman of her acquaintance somewhere in the forties reading Carlyle's *Sartor Resartus* with the vain help of a dictionary, for somehow it never gave any key to the new hard words. She had moved in religious matters from the moderatism of the beginning of the century through the red-hot evangelicism which brought on the disruption of the Church of Scotland, to find nothing dangerous or distasteful in the pulpit services of the Scots Church in Collins Street in 1879. In political matters, though brought up with the ultra-Tory notions of the long wars with the French Republic and Empire, she was always at heart a Whig, a reformer, and perhaps a radical.

Her youthfulness of spirit made it always easy for me to get on with my grandmother, and she had toleration for all my fads, and welcomed all my friends and even my acquaintances with old-fashioned cordiality, tempered with the dignity which belonged to her years.

II

THE MARRIAGE QUESTION

In one point I disappointed my grandmother. She had a great desire to see me married and settled before she left this world for some new untried stage of existence, and she knew of several nice girls who would make excellent wives. There was one in particular, who followed the changing fashions at a respectful distance, and modified them so as to suit her own face and figure, so that though she was scarcely to be called handsome, she often looked better than people with more beauty and less judgement. She was a sensible practical girl too, of a good old Melbourne family, and likely to have a considerable fortune, and all these good things found favour in my grandmother's eyes. Certainly she said I must be very unimpressionable, very different from the young people in her time, or I should have been over head and ears in love with Florence Campbell long ago, or with some other girl, either in Europe or Victoria.

Of course she acknowledged that it was absurd to think about marrying until you could keep a wife and contingencies, which was the old lady's pet phrase for possible encumbrances; but for her grandson Hugh Keith, with a profession, a practice, and the best of prospects, to be satisfied with celibacy at twenty-five, was a puzzle to her. She could not understand the cause of the decline of matrimony in Victoria, for to her the roots of the thing lay deeper than commercial depression or erroneous fiscal policy, or the idleness and extravagant dresses of the ladies or the expensive self-indulgent habits of the young men.

'Hugh!' said she to me one day. 'I wonder if it is the smoking that makes you young fellows all so satisfied with single blessedness. In my young days in Scotland, no man used to smoke; only poor old wives would indulge in a pipe to comfort them, and I wondered in reading the *Spectator* and other books to see that English men in those days were given to smoking too. The other day when you had your young friends here at what you call a 'small and early' (out of consideration for your grandmother's dislike of late hours) at ten o'clock, there was your friend Mr Jack Barnett lying his full length on the sofa in the smoking room, smoking the rankest tobacco till his clothes were penetrated through and through with smoke. And he came immediately afterwards, and asked my Florence to waltz with him. She might as well have danced with a tobacco-pipe.'

'Jack does smoke not wisely but too much,' said I, 'and beastly tobacco, but he considered it very virtuous and accommodating in him to dance at all. He actually danced twice that night.'

'Yes, and looked out for the best-looking and best-off girls in the room,' said my indignant grandmother. 'I wonder you ask fellows that are no good.'

'He is not a favourite of mine,' said I. 'He has one faculty which may be called a talent if not even a sort of genius; he has an unfailing eye for the weak spot of any of his friends, and he delights to show the seamy side of every fellow's character and family and circumstances. If he were not so lazy, he might make a fortune by a society paper in Melbourne, that is to say if he kept clear of libel. But a great deal that is very disagreeable to ourselves, and very interesting to the gossiping public, may be safely said nowadays.'

'Why was he asked to the house?'

'He was asked for the sake of his sisters.'

'They are both stylish-looking girls. Some people say Eva is prettier than Miss Campbell.'

'So she is, if you go by features and not by expression, and she is taller.'

'But she is not so nice.'

'No, certainly not. Of all the girls of my acquaintance I think Miss Campbell take her all round is the pleasantest.'

My grandmother beamed all over.

'But yet I am not at all in love with her, so don't build on this true confession.'

'As after my father has had his fifteen months' holiday, I am to have twelve months of travelling, I think you should see how much better it is that I should go a perfectly free man.'

'I'm not so sure of that, Hugh; what a honeymoon tour you could have with a bonny young wife!'

I shrugged my shoulders, 'Yes, if I were sure she would keep perfectly well in health, and if she could drag over mountain and wood and river with me and my camera, which I must take with me as I want to show you as much of what I have seen as can be put on record through photography. As a rule, honeymoon tours are a great sell. How any right-minded couple, who have any respect for each other, can step from the altar to a ship or a coasting steamer, and endure the publicity of the situation and the agonies of sea sickness before they have been accustomed to help each other, always passes my comprehension. If it were not for a few awkwardnesses as to getting accommodation in strange places, I should prefer travelling with my sister Loney, who is never ill, and never tired, who can eat anything that is set before her, and who understands my photographic apparatus, than with a bride. You know your rhyme:

A new made wife full of frippish freaks
Fond o' a' things feat for the first five weeks.

I think it is only fair they should be "feat" for that time.'

My grandmother sighed.

'But when I have got through this travelling experience, I dare say that the settling-down fever will come upon me. My father says a medical man should be married, and I shall still be young enough to win some fair lady's heart. Perhaps it is because I have always been so busy, first with study, and now with practice, that I am so unimpressionable. Love in idleness may overtake me on my travels, if they go too smoothly.'

'Well, I hope you will not be led on by a mere pretty face to marry a woman who is no gentlewoman. A rising young man cannot make a greater mistake in life. It is of more consequence for your comfort and your position that your wife should have the manners and habits and thoughts of a lady than that she should be ever so deeply read.'

'Oh! don't think I am going in for a blue; my present notion is that she will be a subdued edition of myself,' said I. 'No doubt, however, when I present my wife to you and the family, you will all think I might have made a better choice. But you must bear in mind that it is my life that is to be spent with her, and whatever blunder I may make of my own free will, I may lay my account with it, and bear it as best I may. Whereas in the French fashion of the marriage being arranged by the parents of the bride and bridegroom, it may be perfectly suitable as to money matters, but an awfully rash partnership in other ways.'

'I never could hold with that, Hugh – never! Far better the worst blunders of your own than that. But in waiting for the electric touch of love, you may wait past my day. I said to your father when I said farewell to him, that it was very likely at my advanced years that I might not live to see his return, but yet that should not hinder nor sadden him. It is a journey we must all take alone, and carry none out with us, and my good son would have my blessing in life and in death here or at the other side of the world. But if it is doubtful that I should see him again, it is more doubtful that I should live to welcome you back – wife or no wife. There are many things that I would fain see the end of, but of none more than of your wooing, that I cannot see even the beginning of.'

'You hear of the wooings and marryings of other grandchildren in all parts of the world,' said I.

'Aye! Hugh, aye! and they are all such dear girls and such excellent young men, and everybody is so pleased, and they send out descriptions and photos, and if you can make out what sort of characters they have from these things, it is more than I can do.'

'And unless I do some stupid thing in the way of marriage, you have hopes of me?'

'Indeed I do, and to tell the truth there is not one of my descendants of the second generation, whom I count up to twenty-six, who is so dear to me as you. As your father has been my best son, so was Mrs Archie your mother, the dearest of all the daughters I won by marriage. I would I may live to see your wife and give her an old woman's blessing before I die. But I greatly fear that you are too fastidious – too hard to please and that like some men I have known, you will choose the crooked stick at last when you have passed by through a whole wood full of handsome straight grown timber. I should not wonder to see you make choice for life of a girl not half so clever as Florrie, or so elegant as Jessie Scott, who cannot tell the difference between a water-colour drawing and an oil painting, and who maybe does not know a note of music. That is a very likely thing to happen when a young man is over hard to please – but it's like enough it will come after my day is over.'

III

THE LOST SCOTTISH ADVENTURERS

My grandmother and I had during the absence of the family many quiet evenings together, though she was very indulgent to me in the way of giving me free liberty to go out as much as I pleased. With her books and her knitting and her good maid Jane, she said she could never feel dull, and indeed she lived over again in memory her whole life as she sat by herself. And more than her own life, the old national and family traditions clung to her memory, and all sorts of hereditary traits were noted in her grandchildren as having come down from this or that forbear or ancestor. She had one old theory that she held out for in the face of all the modern reproach cast upon it, that the marriage of cousins, even of cousins-german, was not wrong or mischievous. She had married a cousin once removed, and her parents had been still more closely connected, and she, though the oldest of the generation, was one of five who had exceeded the age of seventy-five out of a family of eight, and she did not see that her children showed any physical, moral or intellectual degeneracy. Of course the stock must be good, and the conditions of life fairly good, to result thus satisfactorily, but as she said the bulk of the arguments against the marriage of cousins was derived from the marriage of two members of a family strongly tainted by consumption, scrofula or madness, while no one took into account the results if one consumptive family married in another with the same predisposition to lung-disease. Owing to the close relationship of all her ancestors, she was as well informed about her husband's folk as about her own.

I liked to read to my grandmother in the quiet evenings when we were alone. She was especially fond of travels, though she often said that of all the books that we got through the book club, there was a greater proportion of the rubbish in that line of literature than in any other.

But Wallace's *Russia* was a book of another stamp, and the old lady was listening with the keenest interest to all that this competent and thoughtful author told of a country in which he had lived so long. When I came to the passage in the second volume at the 109th page where Mr Wallace visited the Shottandskay Kolonia, and was addressed in broad Scotch by a man who called himself John Abercrombie, the old lady gave a great start, dropped her knitting out of her hands and said, 'Preserve us, Hugh Keith, and they're there after all! I thought they went to America. How in the name of all that is wonderful could they get to the back of beyond in Russia?'

'Who are they?' asked I.

'You know that two ships' loads of our folk left the country in 1745, in the spring, before the rebellion broke out later in the year. They were never heard of after they put in at some port in Virginia, and then again in Jamaica, and took seeds and plants, and livestock on board, and sailed to the continent.'

'Oh yes, and you always said they were drowned; I've heard you and my father speak of it many times.'

'So they said, but they might have been nigh-hand wrecked and picked up by some foreign ship, and carried, some of them at least, to some other part of the world, and thus drifted away even to Russia, which was then more out of our world than America itself. You see it was family emigration, and there was less stir made about their loss than if it was here and there one out of various families, as in the Darien scheme, some forty or fifty years before, when first 1,200 and then 1,300 and lastly 300 out of the flower and the youth of the best families in Scotland went out to perish, from the climate and starvation, and the attacks of hostile tribes of Indians, and the pirates who were worse and the Spaniards to boot. But this later exodus all grew out of the Darien scheme.'

'How so?' said I.

'Well, in this way: there was an Abercrombie who returned from the ill-fated expedition, that all Macaulay's fine words will never make me forgive William the Third for, and he used to say constantly that there was the most wonderful fine country better than Virginia in every way, that he had been driven to in search of game when he was starved out of what they called Caledonia, and that with a fair body of men it could be taken and held against the few Indians that now used it for a mere hunting field; that tobacco and maize and sugar and cotton would grow there to heart's content, but it was ill to get at through mountain passes, and a sort of narrow gorge with a waterfall. He had drawn a sort of rough map of it at the time, but he could not till he was an old man, raise any such band of men. "Burnt bairns dread the fire," and the Darien failure checked the spirit of adventure in Scotland for half a century. But there were bad times in the Lowlands, and a spirit of unrest among the people, so that when his son John Abercrombie (you see the Russian name is the same) proposed an expedition to take possession of this fine tract of land, some that were discontented, and some that were in debt, enlisted on the strength of their bodies as soldiers, while others that had property, sold it to furnish money for the project and they set out with stores of all sorts of needful things, and the old man Ralph Abercrombie as their guide. They took ploughs and harrows and carts and household plenishing, spinning-wheels and looms. They persuaded ploughmen, carpenters, smiths and weavers to go with them, a schoolmaster for the bairns, and for the minister, your own ancestor Archibald Keith formerly of Colbrandspath with his fair French wife Margaret de Launay.'

'Thus they took all the elements of a complete settlement with them,' said I. 'It was a great pity that nothing more was heard of the bold wise settlers.'

'Well I believe there were over five hundred in all, and they must have been close-packed in the two ships, but when they sailed from Glasgow, it was a nine days' wonder then to see the thought and what you would now call the organisation of the party. John Abercrombie and Archibald Keith were the two leaders, the one in matters secular, the other in both secular and spiritual, for he was a masterful man, your great great great great grandsire.'

'But alas! grandmother,' said I, 'this cannot be your Scottish colony, for to return to Mr Wallace's book, which has called forth all this speculation and these eager surmises, this turns out to be something altogether different. Your Lowland adventurers left Scotland long before the time of the famous Edinburgh doctor, by whose name this true Circassian was called.'

And I continued the narrative which told the reader that in the first years of the present century, a band of missionaries went to Russia for the purpose of converting the Circassian tribes round about the Caucasus, and that John Abercrombie was a child purchased from Circassian parents with money subscribed by the great Edinburgh doctor, and received in baptism that gentleman's name. And that of the genuine Scotchmen there was only one remaining in the district when Mr Wallace visited it.

My grandmother looked very much disappointed. She had often thought of the band that had thus gone out into forgetfulness in the first half of the eighteenth century, and had read every book of travels in America with special interest, in the hope of finding some trace of them, and the old hope had burned up brightly at the promising opening in the book with mention of the well-remembered name.

After this delusion had been completely dispelled, she appeared to give less and less attention to what I read. She did not pick up her knitting, or take it from me when I picked it up for her, but sat perfectly still. As I saw that the book had ceased to interest her,

I closed it, and asked for some more particulars about the emigration which had taken such a hold on her imagination and her affections.

'You see,' said she, 'with two long lives, one can go back to the very time. When I was a girl of seventeen I spent a winter with my grandmother who was fifteen at the time of the rebellion in forty-five. She had a distinct recollection of the gathering of the Abercrombies and the Elliots, and the Hepburns, and her kinsman Archibald Keith, and the mickle ships and the fair plenishing they took on board. What beautiful Scotch my grandmother spoke! not like what you hear now, that aye sounds vulgar, but it was soft and full and round in the mouth.'

'I like to hear you get to your Scotch,' said I. 'It quite satisfies me.'

'Oh, it is not to be compared with hers. But as I said, it was the talk of her youth, and made its mark on her mind. The getting no letters was not so much wondered at at first, for they were going forth to a new place, where they had to fight their way, but it was looked for that the ships would come back either to Glasgow or to Virginia to get more supplies, for it would be a while before they grew sufficient for their sustenance. When I read about the Mormons going to Salt Lake, and that some of them sowed and reaped crops on the road, I felt that if our folk had got to their destination, they might make a fend to pull through without the aid from older settlements that they reckoned on. But there was less moan made about the loss because they went in families to thrive or fail together. All America has now been so travelled over and over and through and through, that I sorely doubt my supposition, that they might have made a little Goshen for themselves in the wilderness, is a mere fancy; someone must have come upon them or their descendants long ere this time.'

'But if it was really all family emigration, how do we come to have been left?'

'Ah, that is a long story, Hugh. Archibald Keith had two sons by his French wife, he took the younger with him, but the eldest whom he had cast out as the prodigal, was left behind, and a sore heart the mother had to leave her first-born. But he turned out the best of all the Keiths that I ever heard of. When he was cast out of his father's house, he went to an old friend, maybe an old sweetheart of his mother's, who was a captain in the Navy, and then he was first surgeon's mate and afterwards studied at the Captain's charges in Edinburgh, and was the first of the Dr Keiths of which I am like to see in you the last. And of all the moan that was made, Hugh Keith's was the sorest for his mother and his brother.'

'Not for his masterful father the minister?' said I.

'His father had dealt hardly by him, and deprived him of what should have been his inheritance by selling Upper and Nether Keith, which made Archibald Keith who was the most determined in character, also the richest of the adventurers, and that gave him a great say in the direction of the whole affair. It would be a stricter Puritan settlement than New England itself if he had the ordering of it, at least so my grandmother told me.'

'The estate was not entailed then?' said I. 'And what made the Laird of Upper and Nether Keith take to the Kirk, and a poor parish like Colbrandspath?'

'There is a queer story about it, that is in the parish records. John Keith the eldest brother of your ancestor, and a newly-married man, had a quarrel with a neighbour, a bigger man in the matter of property than he was. I'll not say that there was no ill blood about the lady, but that was not the apparent cause of the quarrel; Sir James taunted Keith with being a mere cattle salesman, for he had taken to breeding black cattle. Keith replied, 'I sell nowte, but you sell nations,' alluding to the bribes his neighbour had taken as a member of the Scottish parliament to pass the Union Act, which though a great blessing to Scotland, was held for more than half a century to have been a degradation of the old nationality, and was brought about by the most shameful practices between the English Government and the Scottish legislature. Well, at this word, swords were drawn, and there was much ado by the landlord of the change-house, where the insult was given, to make peace; and they drank together as it was supposed in amity, but just as Sir James Kerr had drained the stirrup-cup, sitting on his horse, with Keith standing by, he drew out of his belt a pistol and shot him dead on the spot, and clapped spurs to his horse, and took ship at Berwick for Holland. The parish record says, "Sir James did not live long after that foul murder, as he was wrecked off the Danish coast whither the ship was driven by storm, and picked up dead." '

'That was poetical justice, at least; then my ancestor Archibald Keith was the heir,' said I.

'No, it was Hugh who served as heir to the estate, but as John had not been married a year and a day, and there was no child or likelihood of any, the widow, according to Scottish law, can claim her marriage portion or *toacher*. This was three thousand marks – and she had secreted it somewhere, for no trace of it could be found, or any account of how it had been spent. Nevertheless, she sued Hugh Keith for the restoration of the three thousand marks, and cast him into prison for the money. It was not so easy to borrow then as now, and he was like to sell the estate to satisfy this false-hearted woman, but his graver and more determined brother, then travelling on the Continent with the grandson of Lord Seton as his governor, with the promise of the parish of Colbrandspath, when the then minister died, entreated him to hold out, and sent him money for his necessities till some means could be devised to save the estate. But Hugh caught some sort of fever in the riotous living he led along with other debtors in the Precincts of Holyrood, and died childless, leaving the estate to Archibald, who married a French wife with money enough to pay that iniquitous claim.'

'Then I should have thought he would have given up the Kirk. Colbrandspath seemed a very poor place when I visited it. And Upper and Nether Keith must, even then, have been worth a good deal of money.'

'Oh! but preaching was his vocation; he was a minister above all things, and it was the thought that he would be the spiritual guide of five hundred emigrants more effectually than he could be in a Kirk with a patron and temporalities and a cauldrife Kirk, session and presbytery, that as my grandmother told me, led him to clear out of everything, and join and lead the party. And he got into great trouble with his old pupil Lord Seton who was his chief heritor. He led the eldest son Hugh Keith astray into all his wild ways, married him to a worthless woman that he should have married himself, and vexed the minister all that he could, not paying him in money as was the custom, but laying down so many chaldrons of victual at his door or in the street of Colbrandspath, and this did not contravene the law, so that your ancestor had no redress.'

'And these things induced the minister to sell his property and to give up his Kirk, and to go out with the adventurers to some transatlantic Canaan flowing with milk and honey; but as you think, he never reached it.'

'My grandmother never doubted that they were all lost, drowned in the sea, or slain by Indians, pirates, or Spaniards like those who went out before.'

IV

RECOLLECTIONS AND SPECULATIONS

'It is a very interesting narrative,' said I. 'In this brand-new Melbourne of ours, one feels proud of such respectable family traditions and I must, while you are alive, gather from you and write down your earliest recollections.'

'In this life of mine that has been lengthened even beyond my grandmother's,' said the old lady, 'I have heard of so many unexpected things that until I die, I'll not altogether give up hopes of hearing about these folk. What a wonderful eighty-eight years it has been to be sure! My grandmother used to say that I was not likely to see or hear of half as many wonderful historical events as she did. For just think of it! She recollected of the forty-five, and had lived through the American war, and the great French Revolutionary war which closed at Waterloo. She said too that she had seen spinning jennies take the place of the wheel, and the power loom of the hand-weavers craft, and more than that, had once seen a ship go without sails over the water. But the face of the whole world is changed, I think, since the good old woman died in the year 1815. What with gas and railroads and telegraphs and chloroform and photography, and every sort of 'graphy' and 'ology', and the news flying from one end of the world to the other on the very wings of the lightning,

I whiles wonder if it is the same Maggie Rutherford that sat at her feet at Upper Keith and heard her stories, that now sits beside you in Collins Street, Melbourne.'

'In two long lives, wonderful progress has indeed been made,' said I.

'That is true, Hugh; for look you, in the town where I was born, there had not been a new house built within the memory of man up to the day I left it and lo! out here, there is a city of hundreds of thousands of inhabitants, where when I was forty years old, there was only the kangaroo and the native wurly.'

'But Scotland has by no means stood still during these later years.'

'True, quite true, but in country parts, as your father writes, the change is very slow and small. It is in the cities and busy manufacturing and seaport towns that the great growth has been.'

'It is a pity you could not have gone with them to the old country, granny,' said I.

'I am too old to travel now; I would have been a hindrance to all their pleasure. But through the letters they write, and by and by, please God, through the hearing of the ear, I can gather maybe more than I could have strength to pick up for myself.'

'There are great changes even in your native town, as I saw for myself.'

'Aye – a railway station for tourists, a corn exchange, and a cold water establishment flourishing. Indeed the last would have been as queer a thing to the old inhabitants as the telegraph itself, for whisky was the cure for all ailments then, and there was little love for cold water, either outside or inside. But it has aye been borne on my mind what could have become of that band of Scottish settlers if they had alighted on some wild place in America, or say in Russia itself, and had lived out-bye, as it were, from all the great thought of the world, had faced all their difficulties without help or counsel from all who have risen up to guide us, and solved maybe some social problems in a new way. Mind, Hugh they were picked men and women, even more so than those who afterwards founded the Australian colonies.'

'By now,' said I, 'the facilities for communication all over the world have let everyone profit by what is discovered anywhere.'

'And in your case, you have a great advantage over me,' said the old lady, 'you are a young man and in the midst of everything. You have a greater part to play in the world, and a better field to play it in, than ever was set before old woman or young woman. And yet I want to live a few years longer to see the end of some things more likely to come to pass than the discovery of the Scottish adventurers in some faraway plantation. I'd like to see women have votes – though I doubt I cannot live till the bulk of them have learned to use them rightly – but it is the right step. I'd like to live to see Ireland as contented and as prosperous as Scotland. I'd like to see what Turkey will settle down to and above all I want to see some good outcome from Socialism and Nihilism as well as from Irish dissatisfaction and agitation.'

'You believe that there will be a good outcome then?'

'I do,' said the old lady emphatically.

To the ordinary commonplace eye what could the old woman, sitting in the easy chair with her book and her knitting, do to help forward the progress of the world. But the influence of every living human being upon other living human beings, which we cannot see exerted in any way by disembodied spirits, is a real and often a powerful influence. My grandmother had written nothing that could live after her. She had given birth to children of somewhat exceptional talent, widely scattered over the globe, and while she lived she was the rallying point for the family but after her death a whole storehouse of traditions and experiences and observations would probably die with her.

'The spiritualists or spiritists would allow you to come back to us again,' I said, 'and hold limited converse with those who were dear to you in life.'

'Don't speak of it Hugh, don't mention it! Surely there would be fitter occupation for the soul or even an old woman like me when this feeble husk is thrown off, than to be hovering bat-like in the dusk, and giving feeble replies to foolish questions through the medium of raps and turning of tables. Surely there must be worthier waiting than this. Clairvoyance and spiritualism – all are sprung out of the want of faith in this faithless generation.'

'I thought, grandmother, you believed the world was changed for the better.'

'Yes, Hugh in most ways. I think the world is on the whole more kindly and charitable than it was; there is more of what you call the enthusiasm of humanity in it, but there is a sad lack of faith – I see it in yourself.'

'I fancy it is the scientific study, and the tendency to take nothing for granted that leads to this result,' I replied.

'Well, the result is materialism on one side and spiritism on the other.'

'Well I am a good deal of Tom Paine's opinion about the prospects of the human race. Will you not be shocked if I mention it?'

'In my young days the mention of the name would be enough to put any opinion whatever out of court, but I'm willing to hear it. After these last thirty years of bold speculation, it is hard to shock me.'

'Well, his opinion was that the bulk of mankind was not worth either saving or damning.'

My grandmother drew a long breath, 'Very bold, very clever, and may be after all very true. It is not the wicked only, it's the stupid, the conventional, the unutterably wearisome that one does not want the company of in Heaven, and far be it from me to confine even them to the misery of Hell. I have often wondered how many lives it would take for such a man as your uncle's neighbour, the skinflint squatter, for example, to come to any sense of the grandeur of the nature of man, let alone the infinite perfection of God. Oh! the Catholic purgatory, though it should not be trafficked in and made a tool in the hands of priests, has great weight on its side, and there are things St Paul himself says that are a good deal more like Tom Paine's theory than the interpretation given in the Confession of Faith and the Shorter Catechism. Immortality through the gospel but not universal condemnation out of it.'

My grandmother paused for a little. Her liberal views suggested to me another train of thought. 'If the creeds and standards had been lost and only the Bible left, I wonder what the Scottish colonists would have made out of it by this time, without the assaults of science on the one hand, and biblical criticism on the other,' said I, 'and with no French Revolution or German philosophy to undermine so much of the faith of the educated people.'

'So long as your forefather, Archibald Keith, was in life, he could have supplied all the standards from memory, and made the flock over which he ruled act up to them; but of course he could not live for ever.'

'His French wife might not have been so hard.'

'Most likely not, but she was of Huguenot blood.'

'But am I the descendant of Hugh Keith's unworthy wife?' said I, who did not like such an ancestry even at the distance of so many generations.

'No Hugh no, she was dead when he came back from the long voyage with Captain Durham and he then married Bessie Rutherford that was the first connection I know of between the families, but it was by no means the last. Marguerite was the name of the minister's wife, and it has been kept up in the family down to this day, and your second name Victor was one of her introducing too, it was that of her brother, who died young.'

Thus this old story which had been brought so vividly back to me that it almost seemed as if it had happened yesterday, had been the cause of my receiving the names of Hugh Victor, which made me known at school and college and among my familiars now by the appellation of Victor Hugo, and had also drawn me strongly to the novels, the poems and the dramas of the illustrious veteran of the French romantic school of literature.

BOOK TWO

OUT OF THE WORLD

I

FOUND

My father was as good as his word; after his return from his own pleasant tour and his settling down to his old rounds, I obtained my leave of absence for at least twelve months. Absence was to be mitigated by frequent letters, and sending full, true and particular accounts, as well as photographs of the places I saw. I made promises of little gifts and remembrances for all of the home circle, but when I asked my grandmother what she would like, she laid the dear good old head on my shoulder, and said in a broken voice, 'Bring yourself back, Hugh, the same as you are now, even though I may not live to see your return.'

My story does not purport to be a book of travels, for except in one special direction, I saw nothing but what has been described over and over again by various writers, but I can only say that I tried to look with my own eyes and to exercise my own judgement both as to old and new civilisations. I left the too-British town of Hong Kong and travelled into the interior to see John Chinaman, the standing scare of Australia and California at home, and wondered at the patient industry of the people, and their preservation of so many social and family virtues without any sort of religious sanctions. The same thing struck me in Japan, which is marvellously secularised, not that the old faiths have been sapped by the new Western civilisation which has been imposed on it by the will of the Emperor, but that the old faiths had been worn out before.

From Japan I went to San Francisco, which I thought far inferior to Melbourne except in the matter of hotels and tramways. Among a motley crew of all sorts and races who rushed on board the steamer to offer their services, came a half-breed Indian, who fastened himself on me as a likely mark, and offered himself as a guide if I wanted to go to out of the way places in search of adventures or game. He handled my luggage and my camera carefully, and showed a testimonial from an Englishman of good family, dated back some years as to his being an experienced and trustworthy guide. So after a stay of a few days in the city I set out in a south-westerly direction under the guidance of this man Sam Peters, not with any expectation or hope of discovering my kin beyond sea, but for the sake of exploring untrodden regions, and having some good sport.

I meant to push south through Colorado with the intention of working back to Salt Lake City, and there taking the transcontinental railway through America. But my half-breed, Sam Peters, was only a broken reed as a guide. Whether from ignorance of the country, or as I afterwards suspected, from a pre-concerted design, he led me through the blankest and most uninteresting country possible. Still though it was desert and stony, he had some instinct or certain knowledge as to water. He always could find a camping place where there was a spring or a waterhole. He also could carry on his back a load that might have been enough for a horse, and trotted on with it as fast as a Chinaman could do, so that if we chanced on any game, he could carry provisions to the next station, and was very clever in cooking and preserving either fish, flesh or fowl! He gave me as his reason for taking this route that at the end of it, I should come to the most wonderfully fertile valley in the world, where there was every kind of beast and bird.

I remonstrated with him, but in vain, when day after day we passed through this horrible country; he was either too stupid or too cunning to be turned from his own way, but as he saw me take an observation at noon every day, which I had learned to do in my various voyages, he used to say sulkily that if I did not like to go on with him, I could go back without him; that however was not so easy to do with my impedimenta.

We had come near a range of mountains which he said enclosed the valley he had been seeking, and camped as usual at nightfall. It was moonlight and the night was chilly so I wrapped myself in my sleeping bag, and threw something over my face to protect me from the moon's rays, and, tired out, fell sound asleep. When I woke, Sam Peters was gone out of sight and out of hearing. I looked round and missed nothing of all he used to carry, except some tins of extract of meat and other condensed provisions, and the waterbag in which he had carried a supply between our stages. This looked ominous, but there was more than this taken from me; I suddenly recollected my purse, which I had put under my head, but which had been abstracted stealthily, probably when I had first showed signs of unconsciousness. It contained not only a letter of credit, of no use to anyone but to myself, but about forty pounds in American gold eagles. I had paid Sam Peters half in advance, for he said he had a wife and children in 'Frisco to be kept in his absence but he had evidently been indisposed to trust me for the remainder and had thus paid himself his balance six times over, and left me penniless, encumbered with my camera and my other baggage, a long day's journey from the foot of the lofty mountains about which he had no doubt told me a parcel of lies.

I first thought of returning on my old tracks, trusting to my compass and my observations to find out the old waterholes and streams. But my provisions were gone and I could hope for no game for several days' journey, and I felt singularly attracted towards the great range where no doubt there were streams of water, and living birds or quadrupeds, some of which might be shot. I swept the whole horizon with my eye and field-glass in vain, there was no appearance of the faithless Sam Peters. Without my camera, I was without the means of propitiating savage tribes of Indians, and without money, I could not hope to purchase hospitality from any more civilised inhabitants of the valley. But I could only manage to carry my gun and my valise, and must leave the bulkier luggage for Sam Peters to take or leave if he happened to come back on the same track, though I had no doubt he had made the best of his way home to San Francisco with his booty.

I was pretty well worn out before I reached the green gorge on the mountain, whence a little stream ran which lost itself in the stony desert, and if it flowed at all, went underground. There I camped and slept. It was likely to be better country for game as well as for the chance of human help on the other side of the range, so after a night's rest I resolved to push across. I found it very steep and very rugged, for it rose tier above tier, and I went up and down, up and down, without any outlook on the other side. I shot two birds, which I ate half raw, and made a shift to go as straight in one direction as possible, so as not to waste my strength over clambering without progress, but yet I know I fatigued myself more by the steep paths I took. At last I seemed to reach the topmost ridge, and the descent, though even more precipitous than the ascent, appeared not to be tedious. But as I came nearer, I could see that it was no mere fertile valley of grass and trees and wild animals, or even of Indians that I had come upon, but that there were signs of cultivation on a very considerable scale, and smoke rising from habitations, which here and there were clustered thick as if in towns and villages, far beyond anything ever built by the red man in the days when we have known him, though not so grand as the buried cities of a bygone civilisation in Mexico and Guatemala. Footsore and faint, I followed the track of a bright watercourse that danced in the sun from early morning till close upon noon. I ate in sheer hunger some cress or such like herb that grew at the water's edge.

At a turn in the gorge, just as it opened into the valley, I came full in sight of a handsome young woman of apparently twenty years of age, who was walking towards the brook, knitting as she walked. She stopped suddenly and looked at me; I looked at her, and wondered what her nationality might be. She had dark eyes and dark hair, but her skin was not nearly as dark as that of a Spaniard; her colour was vivid, and her large brown eyes were full of softness, and yet of fire. Her dark hair was twisted into a graceful knot with a silver pin stuck through it, and instead of a bonnet or hat she had a very pretty head dress of bright coloured feathers apparently arranged from those of the humming-bird. She wore a sort of jacket or jerkin or what is now called a jersey, of knitted scarlet wool, fitting close to her figure, with sleeves down to her wrist, and a short petticoat of blue and white striped cotton, which showed a well-shaped foot and ankle. She wore no stockings, but her feet were encased in shoes of rough brown leather with silver buckles. Her figure was tall, lithe and shapely, and her head sat on her shoulders with a graceful bearing that would have been fit for a queen. Her fingers had been moving her bone knitting needles quickly, till my appearance had startled her; now they were perfectly still, and I saw on the third finger of her left hand a half circle of gold, which had been made hollow, and was threaded with indiarubber, so that on the back of the hand as it held her work, there was half an inch of gold and half an inch of elastic. She looked at me with curiosity, but without fear, and she was the first to speak. The voice was soft and liquid, but the words were broad Scotch, 'An whaur hae ye come frae? for you seem a stranger in the thae pairts.'

'From Australia,' said I. 'Melbourne is my home.'

'Are ye no frae Scotland,' she asked with an air of great disappointment. 'You speak our tongue and no the Austrian.'

'Yes I am, or at least my family is from Scotland originally. My father was born in Scotland but he emigrated to Australia as your father probably did to America.'

'Not my father or his father or his grandfather either,' said she. 'We've been in Columba for a hundred and thirty-five years. But you are straight from the world, the great world,' and she dropped her knitting and clapped her hands in exultation.

'Are you the descendants of the adventurers who went to found a Scottish colony, that my grandmother told me about that sailed from Glasgow with five hundred souls in two ships, and touched at Virginia and Jamaica and were never heard of more?'

'Deed we are,' said the girl, 'an have you come seeking us?'

'Well, I was on my travels and I thought I might maybe come across you, but everybody thought you were all drowned or cut to pieces by the Indians, or slain by pirates or Spaniards. My grandmother, however, kept to the idea that you might be found yet.'

'Well we were nigh hand all lost, as the old folks said, but we fought our way and made a bonnie hame for oursels here, though nae doubt ye'll think it's narrow.'

I recollected what had been told me about the Scotch of my grandmother's grandmother, who was a young contemporary of the founders of Columba, as being more beautiful than anything to be heard now. And in the tropical climate, a few generations had probably modified even this. No spelling could rightly represent the pronunciation, while it would make my narrative almost unintelligible. Somatimes there were words used which either were archaic Scotch or brand-new Columban, but what I could not understand, I could easily guess, for my new-found countrywoman was eloquent with eyes and gesture. It is likely that she too guessed at my meaning in the same way, for in our ordinary talk, there are many words that are not to be found in the *Spectator* or in Allan Ramsay, and it was so far back in the history of the language that her ancestors and mine had taken each their own departure.

'And what is your name?' she asked.

'Hugh Keith.'

She clapped her hands again in exultation, and laughed till the hills echoed the sound. 'And I was looking out for Hugh Keith to come hame for his dinner, for he's gone to the town to the wrights with a casting he's made for him to see to fit it right, and here another Hugh Keith drops from the clouds to take pot-luck with us. And hungry enough for it you are, no doubt, if you've climbed over these hills that are our fortress.'

'I have been three days without food except two birds I shot.'

'Haste ye, then, haste ye, come wi' me, and I'll give ye what we have got,' and she picked up her knitting, took my valise in her hand, and would even have taken my rifle, but I objected to her burdening herself to that extent, and she moved swiftly towards a cottage about a quarter of a mile off built of sunbaked bricks, and thatched with reeds, with a little vegetable garden at the back and a forge a little way from it.

'This is our dwelling place, Maister Keith,' she said. 'No doubt you and Hugh are kinsmen, though it may be hard to count it. I'll ask the minister, Maister Hepburn, if he can tell about it.'

'I think I could clear it up myself,' said I, 'but I must not be Mr Keith here. My second name is Victor – that will serve to distinguish between me and my cousin.'

'Victor!' said she. 'That proves the relationship stronger still. Victor is a name with the Keiths and with no other of the families. Victor Keith was Hugh's ancestor who landed with the first expedition. Come in and welcome.'

She gave orders to a little maiden to serve the dinner which to me was delicious: soup, boiled meat, delicate vegetables and a sort of milk pudding.

II

THE PECULIAR INSTITUTION OF COLUMBA

My young hostess was delighted to see me eat so heartily, and was pleased that I praised it so warmly. She appeared to me to be fitted for a higher sphere than this homely colonial dwelling. The walls of the cottage were about ten feet high, but there was an aperture of about eighteen inches between them and the thatched roof, which formed a sort of verandah all round the house, and let in a good deal of light and air. The house was not ceiled, the partitions only ran up the ten feet, and across the rafters hung a saddle and some harness, as well as smoked and dried meat. There were also some beams overhead on which rested baskets of seeds and sieves, and some tools of which I did not know the use. The table was covered with a white cloth of cotton and the plates and dishes were some of wood and some of the coarsest earthenware I had ever seen. The knives and two-pronged forks were of bronze, and the Scottish settlers appeared to have rediscovered the secret of the Peruvians of hardening bronze till it was nearly as useful as iron, for the knife had a very good edge. My hostess offered me more and more till I bade her stop, for I knew it was unwise to eat too much after so long a fast.

'Indeed,' said she, 'I know nothing about such things, for we live in a country of such abundance that I never had to do with a famishing man before this day, and it seemed to me that you had a lot to make up for.'

'Yes, but the stomach is not strong enough to digest it,' said I, 'but I'll punish your larder for the next week if you are good enough to keep me.'

'And blithe both Hugh and me will be to do it. It is such a godsend. Oh! there never was such a piece of good luck as your dandering down just at our own hill when there's never been a stranger here for a hundred years and more, and you might have happened on the other side of the valley. I wonder what is keeping Hugh. It's not fair for me to have all this great joy to myself and him nearer in kin.'

'Husband and wife are one, you know, both by law and gospel, Mrs Keith.'

'But I'm not Mistress Keith. I'm only Liliard Abercrombie.'

'The descendant of the John Abercrombie who was one of the leaders of the expedition along with Archibald Keith, my ancestor and Hugh's?'

'Oh!' said she with flashing eyes. 'I see you know all about it, was there ever such a providence? I am John Abercrombie's great-great-great-great-grandchild.'

'Well, Miss Abercrombie, I have no doubt we are related somehow too if we had my grandmother here to set us right.'

'But I'm not Miss Abercrombie either.'

'Oh I forgot, the old word was Mistress for married and unmarried ladies alike. Mistress Abercrombie is your name.'

'But you see I'm neither the one nor the other,' said the girl. 'I'm only Hugh Keith's bride.'

'Oh engaged – betrothed – trysted to be married,' said I wondering at the apparent housekeeping of the young woman for the man to whom she was troth-plighted.

'No, Maister Victor, I'm only *handfasted* to Hugh Keith,' and she looked at the curious ring on her finger. 'Only handfasted for a year and a day. Surely you have heard of such a thing.'

Handfasted! I recollected the passage in Sir Walter Scott's novel of *The Monastery*, which mentioned the Border rite by which a man and a woman bound themselves to mutual fidelity for a year and a day, at the expiry of which time, they were free either to separate for ever, or to be married for life tightly as the Roman Catholic church could do it. I recollected too the indignant denunciation of the preacher of the Reformed Faith, Henry Wardour, of the practice which bound the stronger to the weaker while she was the object of desire, and let him throw her off when she was the object of compassion, soiled, besmirched and despised into a cold and cruel world and how heartily I had agreed with his eloquent protest. And here was as handsome and apparently as virtuous a young woman as I had ever seen in my life, telling me without a blush that she was handfasted to my namesake, Hugh Keith, whose house sheltered me, whose dinner I was devouring, and whose coming home was expected immediately.

'Handfasted, yes,' I said after a short pause for reflection. 'I have heard of such a thing as practised long ago in Scotland in remote districts, where priests were few. The bride and bridegroom took conditional vows first to prepare for the binding ones, and I suppose that is the case with you.'

'Mostly,' said Liliard, 'but whiles folk are glad to change.'

'And it is a year and a day as it was in Scotland in these old times, hundreds of years before your folk left it?'

'Aye that is aye the beginning, but whiles it is lengthened for two and even three such terms before it is made a fast marriage. Though I think, on the whole, the half of the couples are eager for the year and day to be out that they may have no more doubt.'

'Then does everybody take this extraordinary step in the first place?'

'Everybody. We cannot be married in Columba without it. Hugh Keith would fain have made quite sure but he had to hold by the law like other folk.'

'But widows and widowers . . .? Have they to go through this extraordinary ordeal too before they take other mates?'

'Oh! they have to go through the same time to see if they suit, and indeed though they may be older and should have more sense, I think they make as many blunders as the youngest among us, and whiles, if they don't get on well with the bairns, it is better for them to part.'

'But how came you to begin this strange custom? You surely brought the Bible and the Church Standards with you, and certainly you could find no sanction for this thing there.'

'Oh to be sure we brought the Bible, but the minister was lost at sea in a great storm when he was working with the rest, and as for the Questions and the Standards as you call them they were left on shore when we fought our way up to our present abiding place in the charge of some of the party, sailors and others; the pirates that took the ships, slew them or made them captive, and burnt all that did not seem good to them to keep. There was but charcoal and ashes found of the big boxes of the books as well as many other needful things when the waggons returned for them. We had to be a sort of Law and Gospel to ourselves and to order our doings as seemed best to the leaders of the band.'

'And you have no books at all then,' said I looking round the house, which in many points, resembled an old-world country cottage in Scotland, with the spinning-wheel in one corner, and the bink or dresser set up with the store of family crockery or wooden ware in the other, only without the great chimney, for the cooking was done outside, on account of the heat of the climate. There was no shelf for books to be seen, and not even a big family Bible to give warrant of the religious character of the family, and to serve as a record of the births, deaths and marriages of the household.

'Only a few that folk had in their private possession which werena many, if ye leave out the minister's ain, and these had been left as over bulky by Madame Keith, and the son Victor, that in a measure took the father's place.'

'And you have made no new books all these years,' said I, again looking around the room in search of what I could not see.

'What could we do in the way of writing and printing where

there were so few hands and them so full of work? No, the old ones are all in safe keeping at the Town House at Ebenezer, and from them our bairns learn, not on the books themselves, which would be nothing for our big schools, but the masters and mistresses learn, and teach by word of mouth.'

'And then your children do not learn to read. Cannot you read?'

'No, not a word, more's the pity,' said my hostess in a very sad tone of voice.

'Nor of course write either?'

'No – I was not thrown off by my parents, and that would have been my only chance. Though I had such a good father and mother, I have sometimes been sorry to be shut out.'

All this was most bewildering to me. 'What then could you learn at school, if you neither read nor wrote nor ciphered?'

'Well, we learned a great part of the Bible, and question books about right and wrong and the history of the world and of Scotland, and the story of our own Columba and all its laws, and them that liked poetry learned a lot – Shakespeare's plays and *Paradise Lost* and Pope's *Homer* – and some of the *Spectator* and *The Pilgrim's Progress* and *Don Quixote* and some things that have been made in prose and verse here out of our own folk's heads, for though we are out of the world, we are not fools.'

'No, you are certainly not fools,' said I wonderingly, 'if you can learn and recollect such great books. What memories you must have!'

'Well, it is helped with the knitting and the sticks.'

'How so?'

'You see all the lasses learn at school to sew and to knit, as well as to spin and to weave, and all these things can help us to keep mind of what we hear, and the laddies do pin-knitting (crochet) and learn to whittle sticks, and that serves the same turn.'

It dawned upon me that this simple but intelligent people who had thus been thrown upon their own resources when a printing press and types would have been a great waste of labour, must have developed a kind of artificial memory which could be combined with useful work; and as Madame Dafarge and other women, noted as the terrible *tricoteuses* of the Revolutionary times, knitted in the names of the dangerous and the denounced, and their several offences in some occult way invisible to the ordinary eye, so on a large scale on some definite system, a good deal might be done as aids to memory.

My hostess drew out of a drawer a great bundle of little pieces of fine knitting of various shapes and of no apparent use. She then showed in another drawer a regiment of sticks of various lengths notched out and cut in various ways.

'This is all I have in the way of books,' said she, 'and as Hugh aye hated pin-knitting which he said was only fit for women, he has only these sticks. But mine is out of sight the biggest collection. He's so clever with his hands at his business that he cares less for the old-world stories.'

'And his business is at the forge I suppose?'

'He's a smith, and though he's young yet, he's like to be the best in all Columba. I wonder what's keeping him, he's no having his dinner with the wright surely, though no doubt Alison Elliot will be pressing him. She's broken off her last handfasting with John Rutherford, and is at her father's house again, and she has aye had a soft spot in her heart for Hugh – but he thinks nought of her.'

'But I don't understand this strange heathenish custom of yours; surely the Bible gives no warrant for it.'

'Deed the Bible gives warrant for a lot of things a great deal worse than that, if I learned it right,' replied my handsome hostess. 'And it was far from being done in a heathenish spirit. No, the handfasting is a solemn religious ordinance gone into with prayer and solemn thoughts; at least I am sure it was the case with Hugh Keith and me.'

'But both of you would have been glad to have made it as binding as marriage surely – at least you said so.'

'Hugh would, but then he was in a measure beside himself that I consented to the handfasting after long courtship; but for me, I thought then, and I think now, that the year of trial is a wise thing.

Nobody could be kinder and better than Hugh, but he might have been different, and I know I'm provoking whiles, and no just the good house-manager that his mother would like to see me; so it's just as well he should see all my faults, and make up his mind to bear with them. No, you must not call it heathenish,' and she looked so earnest and so good that I felt she was justified by her own conscience in what appeared to me so dangerous to morality.

'But how did it begin? It was such a strange departure from all the Scotch or French ideas on the subject, which our ancestors and our ancestress Madame Keith would take with them to the settlement.'

'It was the Indian women that began it,' said Liliard Abercrombie. 'You see there were far more men than women in our first settlement and there was a tribe of Indians here that we had whiles to fight and whiles to make treaty with, and some of our men took Indian wives or rather no wives, but what in the *Spectator* would be called mistresses, though little mistress-ship the poor things were like to have. Well, Madame Keith and her son and my forbear, John Abercrombie held a council with some other elders so as to give these women some rights, for Ralph Abercrombie had taken one of these daughters of Heth, called Palahna, the very first year, and others had done the same. And they would not marry the redskins out of hand, for they were not Christians, so the Council settled that they should live together for a year and a day, which would give time for their conversion and give opportunity for the instruction of these poor women in the true faith, and then if both of the parties wished it, the heathen woman should be baptised and married. If they could not agree together, they parted and maybe tried another, but if they continued to love each other, as my forebear and Palahna did, then there was a grand solemn marriage. She was baptised by the name of Margaret, and they lived to a good old age together in love and counsel, and had ten sons and daughters. And many did the same, but no doubt there were many who were not so constant. But Palahna was one among a thousand.'

'But this has nothing to do with your Christian people,' said I.

'They needed no term for conversion, no sort of probation in the civilised life like savage women.'

'Maybe no, but then the elders of the plantation and Madame Keith who had a great deal to do with these matters saw it was a good thing for the Indians and with regard to the Christians, they were all disposed to marry so young, before as the elders and Council said they knew their own minds, and so they decreed that it would be well to give them the chance of drawing back at the end of a year and a day. And as the first of the mixed handfastings was that of my forebear Ralph Abercrombie, so the very first of the Christian handfastings was on the part of Hugh's forebear, Victor Keith, and he was all we had for a minister till others were trained.'

'My forefather Archibald Keith's son and successor in the sacred office! And did he show the example of this extraordinary ceremony?'

'Indeed he did, and it was no godless or heathenish thing, but one devised with much deliberation and many prayers.'

'But both these first handfastings were confirmed.'

'Aye, and I'm thinking that this would give folk confidence in it to see that there were no light changes made at first, though the power to change is really the thing aimed at.'

'And this handfasting of yours to my namesake – was it . . .' I hesitated to ask the question as to whether it was a first or a second or a third experiment for that appeared to me like impertinent curiosity. I stammered out, 'was it entered into when you were both very young and likely to change?'

'No,' said she, 'we were both rather old; at least I'm going on for twenty-one, and he is a year older. But it is my first handfasting if that is what you mean to ask and I fancy it's like to be the last.'

'But are there any that never settle, that go from one to another?'

'Oh there's some that go on like that till they pass their youth, and then they settle down with some one maybe the crookedest stick of the lot, as the saying is. But they're not much respected.'

'Then these fickle changeable people are sent to Coventry; I mean that you will not associate with them.'

'Oh no, not so bad as that. It is not given to everyone to be naturally constant, and a year and a day with some men or women is just as much as any one woman or man can put over.'

'Of course if the law allows of these changes, public opinion will be gentle with them, but the Kirk has no rebuke or exclusion for them?' I suggested.

'Oh! no! where would be the use of that. Surely they need the good of the Kirk and the Sacraments just as much as other folk, and if they keep to the bargain they make for the time they vow for, they surely cannot be held as offenders. But I suppose it all seems strange to you. You can get married as soon as you like in Scotland and in the new place I never hear of before, in Austria I think you call it and so fast too that there's no breaking of it.'

'Indeed we can get married in no other way,' said I laughing.

'Well, it seems an awful thing to risk it to us that are used to different ways; it will make folk think longer about it. Are you a married man yourself with a wife and bairns at home?'

'No, though I am twenty-six years old and perhaps you call that old,' said I laughing. 'My dear old grandmother in Australia which you would call New Holland used to say she wondered at the unwillingness of the young men to get married. It never entered into her wise old head to propose such an alternative to lead them on.'

'Oh! but I do not so much wonder at it, where I think there is no remedy if you are taken in or make a blunder, and if you were going on your travels by yourself, you might chance to see someone you liked better than the wife you had left behind. I think you were very wise.'

The wisdom of my determination had never appeared so great as when this half-married woman so gravely enunciated it, but still at the same time the whole arrangement appeared to me not only strange, but probably demoralising. This was an unexpected outcome of the want of the minister and the Standards with people who interpreted the Bible just as they pleased.

III

A COLUMBAN BRIDEGROOM AND BRIDE

Our talk was interrupted by the approach of the master of the house who with quick step, whistling a tune unknown to me and followed by a sort of collie dog, barking with joy, came towards the house. He was tall and fair, as if there had been no admixture of Indian blood in his ancestry. Madame Keith had always been spoken of as the minister's fair French wife, and the Scottish Lowland emigrants were Saxon or Scandinavian. But there was a family resemblance between my kinsman and myself. He would probably as he grew older be a larger man and more powerfully built, but at twenty-one he had not come to his bulk, though he stood the same five feet eleven inches high that I did. He was clothed in rough homespun, little altered from the fashion of a hundred and forty years, only that on account of the climate he had discarded the long waistcoat and wore only a cotton shirt under the long waisted coat with its comparatively short skirt. He wore knee breeches with long grey stockings, with shoes like his bride's in shape, but heavier and stronger, and a knitted Scotch cap with three gay feathers stuck upright in it. He took off his cap as he entered the door, where Liliard met him, beckoning to me to keep out of sight till she had greeted him.

He kissed her, and said, 'I have gotten that crinkum crankum tune that they played last Saturday right at last.'

She made way for him, and then he started to see a stranger sitting at his table, and stared breathless and amazed.

'Hugh,' said the girl, 'you'll no guess in twenty guesses who this stranger is, where he comes from, or what is his name.'

'No, Lil, I'm but an ill guesser at the best, and at my worst before I've had my dinner, so he had better tell me or tell me yoursel'.'

'It's a Hugh Keith, a Hugh Victor Keith, come, no from Scotland, but from some place we ne'er heard tell of, over the mountains, days and nights of clambering, hungry and thirsty, that has dropped down among his own kin. The first that ever came into Columba, and that was really looking for us in a way too.'

The young man seized both my hands and wrung them in a friendly and close grasp. 'Welcome, welcome, though you would maybe mair welcome if you came from Scotland itself, at least to the old folk.'

'But I have spent four years in Scotland.'

'Oh! that's good,' said Liliard eagerly. 'And have you been anywhere else? What have you seen of the whole world?'

'I spent a year in Paris, from which place I made a run across the Alps and had a look at Venice and Florence and Rome and the next spring I went to Germany. This was during my studies. I am a doctor by profession. My father and mother were Scottish born, and I am only Australian by birth.'

'And you'll speak the Austrian tongue at home; it is a good thing you learned Scotch in Scotland, though your speech has a very queer sound with it,' said my namesake.

'Not Austrian,' I said. 'Australian! Out of Europe altogether. In the biggest island in the world, that used to be called New Holland, to the south-east of India in the South Seas.'

'Oh!' said Hugh Keith, as if he did not at all take it in.

'It was the South Sea scheme that brought so much trouble about twenty years before our folk left the old country, and the Darien scheme you mind about more than twenty year before that. Surely ye mind that at the school, Hugh,' said Liliard.

'Indeed, no; it went in at one ear and out at the other. You see cousin, these old stories had no bearing on our life or our work here though Lil delighted in them. Oh, I see she's been showing you her knittings, and I'm sure you can make neither head nor tail of them; I forget whiles my own sticks. But Lil am I to have anything to eat?'

'Directly Hugh. Jenny will fetch you in some warm kail and the pudding; the meat has got a fright for we have had a hungry man to feed. Your mother would have had a better set out, but there's so few of us, the things just spoil.'

'Never mind Lil, we'll make up with eggs or bread and cheese. If I only get plenty, I care little what it is.'

The cheese was a small round one, the bread was made of maize flour and did not look so tempting as the warm broth and meat and delicate vegetables I had devoured, but the young people pressed me to rest my weary limbs on a sort of couch covered with woven matting, and then, on a sort of erection at the head, Liliard threw a large light piece of irregular knitting to keep off the flies and the mosquitoes. Through this veil I could watch this Columban bride and bridegroom. I saw that Liliard who had eaten nothing when I ate, still ate nothing while she waited on her husband, but was evidently too much excited and interested by the arrival of a stranger to care for food. They subdued their voices and apparently thought I must be asleep.

'Now this arrival must be reported at the Town House without delay, and our cousin sworn in to respect our laws, and be one with us so long as he bides and what is to hinder him to bide,' said Hugh.

'Bide,' said Liliard, 'no, he'll no bide. Who that has been in the world would ever think to cast in his lot with us. But for a time I think he will take the Columban oaths.'

'He behoves to do it or we have the power to expel him.'

'And if he is a doctor, how much he could teach our doctors and our nurses. He might find out what is the matter with Mother.'

'Oh! Lil, as usual, you aye think we are not learning here just as well as folk are learning outside. Have not we made great discoveries about herbs and bandages and fresh air since we settled here. The old wives' notions have been just as well scattered to the wind in Columba as in Scotland itself, I'll be bound. He brings little with him but this gun and this valise, and though the gun is a beauty, I'll not give in that it will shoot better than the one I made myself.'

'Ah, Hugh,' said she shaking her head. 'This must be better, see how slender it is in the bore see how fine it is in the workmanship. I'll say nothing against your gun, but what can we learn here like what they can in the whole big world.'

I broke silence for I recollected my surgical instruments and camera left on the other side with my sleeping bag.

'I am not asleep, my friends, and do not think I am likely to sleep, though I am resting luxuriously. But I left on the other side of the ranges not only some clothes and other things needful to myself, but also a case of the best instruments used in surgery nowadays of the very finest steel and also something that prevents people from feeling the pain of operations. The latest discoveries of our greatest scientific medical men have been in that direction.'

'Oh! Hugh,' said Liliard, 'did I not say he was sent by God to us?'

'I was robbed of my money and of what food I had provided by a thievish half-Indian guide who carried the bulk of my baggage, and I was forced to leave a heavy portmanteau behind as well as my wraps and a curious sort of apparatus that will take pictures by the sun. I should like, if you, my cousin, would risk accompanying me tomorrow, to go in search of it, for the things are heavy, if your bride would allow you to go. I am sure it would give you and all the Columban people great pleasure to see pictures of yourselves and your houses.'

'Pictures!' said Liliard 'Pictures! yes surely. But without a permission from the Town Council, Hugh could not go and indeed you must go without delay yourself to give your name and swear fealty to our plantation Government. We've to go to the town at any rate; are you equal to a walk of a mile and a half before sundown? That would give you three hours' good rest.'

I declared myself quite able for the walk but I could not think of sleep. Here was a sleeping palace to awake to all the history and all the inventions of a hundred and forty years, a strange, barbarous, civilised society. There was rough comfort in this cottage, which kept out the rain and the sun, but was not beautified by a flower garden outside, or by any object of art or taste inside. The floor was of clay or of some composition of clay smooth and clean, the walls were neither papered nor whitewashed, there were no curtains or blinds or attempts at drapery anywhere. The windows were of blue coarse glass, and did not show the outside landscape truly; the greater part of the light came in from the space between wall and roof. The table was of a sort of red cedar set on four square legs, and was covered with a coarse white cotton cloth for meals, but left bare when the dinner was over. The bink or dresser was set out with wooden trenchers and plates of coarse crockery ware with an atrocious blue edge.

Six straight-backed chairs which had sloped seats and two three-legged stools and the couch or settee on which I lay, were all that served as furniture, but the absence of books, of pictures, of anything pretty in the way of colour or form except the wonderful beauty of the mistress of the house, made that even more striking than in the tropical luxuriance of the vegetation outside. Hugh said he must go to his forge, as there was work to be done this afternoon if he had to be absent for days, and saying he had no doubt Lil had some spinning to do, unless she had to prepare for the evening at the Kirk, he left the house. Liliard took out her wheel from the corner, and began, but her curiosity about all the things I could tell her was stronger than her desire for work, so she again took out her knitting needles and began a large piece of work like the sort of mosquito net she had thrown over my head which I shook off to be able to talk the better.

IV

I TEACH AND I LEARN

'And now,' said she, 'tell me everything that has happened since we lost all reckoning of the ways of the world, and that was in the year of grace 1745.'

'Impossible,' said I feeling the enormous amount of information that was needed, which half-an-hour before I had been only eager to begin.

'Try!' said she. 'Begin at the beginning.'

'Begin with what? the inventions, or the literature or the history?'

'The history first,' said she, 'and I'll try to take it down.' And she prepared for this novel style of reporting in such a business-like way that I felt more nervous than in a crowd.

I thought that if I had pen and ink in hand, I might have made a better synopsis; I had not been trained as a speaker, and even in such little attempts as I had made in our Edinburgh Debating Club, it had been argument or eloquence, and not narrative that was called for. And it appeared as if it would have been easier for me to work back from the present-day to the earlier, than to take up the history of Europe at that particular point where the Scottish adventurers left it. I really was better posted up in the stirring times of the seventeenth century, the great Rebellion and the Restoration and the Revolution of 1688, than in the middle of the eighteenth century, but my young hostess's eager questioning eyes and waiting fingers inspired me to make a plunge, and I began with the Rebellion of 1745 and the romantic adventures and escape of Charles Edward, in spite of the 30 000 pounds reward put on his head. I then worked on to the accession of George Third which put an end to the hopes of any Stuart, as the young king was popular and respectable though singularly wrongheaded and arbitrary. The increase of the power of the Crown, the rupture with the American colonies, the war, the victory of the rebellious colonists which had resulted in the formation of the great Transatlantic Republic; the interference of France with this domestic quarrel; the earthquake of the French Revolution; the long war first of self-defence and then of foreign conquest; the European coalition against Napoleon, the Peninsular War, the Russian Campaign, Napoleon's defeat, banishment to Elba, the hundred days, the first victory of Waterloo, and the banishment to the lonely ocean rock of St Helena of the disturber of the European Monarchies and Empires.

Here I paused; Liliard covered her face with her hands and was either weeping or praying, perhaps both. I had not been giving her dates. I fancy she thought I had brought up the narrative to the present time.

'Oh what a world to have lived in,' said she, 'and to have taken part in! Did you go to fight at Waterloo, or as a leech to heal the wounds of this war?'

I had to tell her that Waterloo was before even my father's time, that my grandmother, now a very aged woman, was married in that year, and that there were new pages of history opened out, new French revolutions, monarchies, republics and empires to succeed while Britain made up for the colonies she had lost by planting others as flourishing and as full of promise in all quarters of the world. The Great Indian Empire had been built up from a few trading stations of the East India Company, South Africa, Australia, New Zealand had been added to the old colonies in the West Indies and to the British possessions in Canada. The population of Great

Britain and Ireland had been trebled at home since the Scottish adventurers had gone forth, besides having colonised a Greater Britain abroad, and the industrial progress of the country had multiplied perhaps tenfold the productive powers of the population.

As I dwelt upon the modern development and the modern spirit which sought out the miserable and the poor and the ignorant for comfort and help and instruction, I could not but show that the amount of suffering in the world must be great. With moist eyes, she followed me, but the hands never slackened for a moment. She asked questions, some of them the most unexpected, but yet on the whole the most pertinent, as to what I thought of such and such things which I mentioned – were they right or wrong? were they wise or foolish? were they the work of kings and courts, or of parliaments and people?

Three hours had thus passed away, and the master of the house returned to find that no preparation was made for the evening meal, at least on his bride's part. Jenny however had been more thoughtful and had for the first time ventured to make an omelette which we all ate with appetite and pleasure, and, this with wheaten bread and fresh butter without any admixture of salt and the most delicious coffee I ever tasted, made a simple meal. Hugh Keith smiled at the sight of the useless knitting instead of the spinning which ought to have been done.

'I'll have lots of time to spin when our kinsman is gone, but I wanted to keep mind of what I heard,' she said. 'You'll be glad to hear it by and by when you are not busy.'

'Are you ready for tonight?' asked her bridegroom.

'Oh I daresay it's all right,' said she.

I took out a cigar from my pocket when I saw Hugh take his pipe to smoke, or as he called it to blow, as he walked, and struck a match to light it. He remarked upon the rapidity of the process. 'It is the same on principle as ours,' he said, 'but ours are slower,' and he took out a match and rubbed it a dozen times on the wall of the house and got a light for his. The cigar however was also a novelty. 'It's better maybe than the pipies our women like to blow at; let our cousin see one, Lil.'

Liliard took down from a corner of the dresser a cigarette made of tobacco enclosed in a roll, not of paper, but of dry palm leaf and offered it to me, and I found out that in delicacy of perfume and flavour this Columban tobacco was superior to any Havannah or Cheroot I had ever seen.

'We'll go – you and me, cousin Victor,' said Hugh, 'to this Town House first, and you, Liliard may look in at my mother's or yours and tell the news if you like.'

We walked together to the town by an excellent road either for foot passengers or for carts or carriages. It had a good crown to throw off the heavy rain of these tropical regions and was evidently made compact by some good binding stone broken small. The road however was exceedingly narrow, only one cart or waggon could possibly keep on it. Here and there was a broader part meant for a siding, to allow of one passing another or of two from opposite directions crossing.

The industry of the Columbans was turned into opposite channels from that of the Japanese, who made their dwellings beautiful and full of beautiful ornaments and curios but who had not a mile of good road except the short railwayline all through the thickly-peopled country for the conveyance either of passengers or merchandise. In this Scottish colony there were well-cultivated fields of rice and maize and millet, of cotton and sugar and tobacco; careful irrigation of such crops as needed it, and draining of crops which liked dryness such as wheat which was the hardest to grow in all Columba. But the houses were mean-looking and ugly; all built of sunbaked clay bricks or dabs, about two feet square, with verandahs round them, but without any ornament whatever, without carpets or curtains or hangings, and the wooden work unpainted though sometimes varnished.

The town of New Berwick which we approached was not the largest in Columba. The town of Ebenezer was the seat of Government, where the Protector of the Commonwealth lived and where his Council met once a week for the despatch of public business. New Berwick, the second town in the settlement, was an irregularly-shaped collection of houses with narrow streets running in various directions, with only one striking feature, a great central square or rather oval plot of ground, surrounded by fine trees with benches all round in the shade. This broad belt was laid down in close fine turf, but in the centre the ground was as smooth as concrete only much softer to the foot, and quite level, except for a slight fall to throw off the water. At the north end of this splendid open space was the Town House, at the south end, the Kirk. On the east was a pile of buildings that served as the school, divided into several rooms, and on the west a row of ordinary houses. From this open space, the streets led out in various directions. The shops, of which there were many, had no signboards, and no imposing front, or display at the windows. All that betokened the business was: at the baker's, the actual loaf over the door; at the shoemaker's, a shoe; at the draper's, a piece of cotton cloth; at the tailor's, a coat; at the grocer's a few coffee-berries and some sugar-candy. The narrow streets were kept scrupulously clean, and all the people about were well-clothed and appeared to be well-fed and contented and singularly good-looking.

We parted from Liliard at the outskirts of the town, for she was going to her mother's, and as I walked with my kinsman I paid a tribute to the comfortable and orderly appearance of everything and everybody that I saw. He appreciated the compliment; he was thoroughly satisfied with the place and all that was in it.

'That is what I tell my bride,' he said. 'She has such notions that we've been sleeping when other folk have been moving on but we can strike out some things for ourselves even in Columba!'

'Yes, I see that you understand making the arch of a bridge below the road, and not over it, and that has only been found out in my father's time. There are many of the old kind to be seen in country places in Scotland yet, though there are none in Victoria – my own home.'

'Look at our great place,' said he. 'I'm sure they have not the like of it in Edinburgh or London itself for a dancing green.'

'I'm sure they have not,' said I, 'if that is the use you make of it. The seats in the middle are for the musicians, I suppose?'

'Yes, and the benches round for the old folk and for the young when they are not dancing.'

'But to me the strangest thing you have struck out here,' said I, 'is the handfasting.'

'Oh, we did not strike that out, it was done in old times; but we've made it more orderly and more solemn.'

'But I could not say to your – bride,' it was always hard to stumble over that word, and I could not call her either Mrs Keith or Mistress Abercrombie, 'what appears to me to be the great difficulty in these . . . temporary bonds . . . the children. What becomes of the child whose parents separate after a year and a day?'

'Oh! of course the first year it belongs to the mother; after that whiles the father and whiles the mother keeps the bairn, according to circumstances or according to agreement.'

'Then I fancy the mother will get it oftenest thrown on her hands,' said I.

'Well, you see, it depends on who breaks it off. If it is the bridegroom, she can claim the child. If it is the bride, he can claim it and I think the most changeable are the men, but there is not much to draw between them.'

'But a child is a burden for a woman to bring up.'

'Oh no! not here, a bairn is a blessing and a treasure,' and Hugh Keith sighed. 'For the sake of the bairn many will overget little causes of difference and keep together that they may keep the little one. Burden! what is the little a bairn can eat or that it needs to clothe it, compared to the help and counsel you get from your sons and daughters when they come up?'

'And of course,' said I half to myself, 'there is no disgrace according to your laws either to the father or to the mother.'

'Disgrace! What disgrace could there be? No, a bairn is a crown and a blessing, as I said before.'

'And whose name does it bear when the parents separate?'

'The name of the parent who keeps it. Where they take year about as often happens, the name of both, but that of the father is the surname.'

'Do both parents help to maintain the child?'

'That's according to the bargain they make. Whiles one is richer than the other. But there's no trouble about that.'

'No trouble about that!' said I somewhat puzzled. 'But will the law enforce a claim then on the part of the mother or the father for the maintenance of the little one?'

'Oh! to be sure; if they think to go to law, but we none of us trouble the law much.'

'Then in a land of well-being like this, the one terrible difficulty seems got over. In Europe, and indeed in the civilised world generally, a child born out of lawful wedlock is a burden to the mother, which she has much difficulty in partially shifting off sometimes to the father. As for the disgrace, she generally bears it all.'

'Well, I think Liliard herself will allow that we manage things better here,' said Hugh. 'A child born in lawful handfasting is just as well-born as if his parents had been married for a dozen years. There must be hard times in the old world if folk would ever be glad to throw off their bairns, at least in any way that was general so as to make the handfasting work badly.'

'And are they never thrown off here?'

'Well sometimes the father and mother cannot and will not agree about them, and there are some black sheep here as well as elsewhere, and then they solemnly give the children up, and they have to go to the Kirk to do it once and for ever, and then the little ones are accounted as God's bairns, and brought up different from the rest of us.'

'How so? is that what your bride meant by saying she sometimes wished she had been thrown off?'

'Ay, I dare say Liliard might have said so. Up to the age of ten they are taught with the sticks and knittings like the rest of us, but after that the cleverest of them learn to read and write, and them that show the greatest gifts are made into ministers and teachers, male and female, and have the access to the few books we have got in Columba. Some are our doctors and our nurses, and some keep the records of the Commonwealth and do our public business, and judge our offenders and settle our disputes.'

'So then all your professional men and women, and what we would call your civil servants come from these castaways?' said I astonished beyond measure at such a strange social arrangement. 'I should think that a temptation to parents to forget all the ties of blood, and put their children into such a good line of life.'

'Oh! you do not understand what it means to give them up. They have not your name; you have no claim on them. They grow up apart from you, and grow fond of those who care for and teach them, and actually care less for their fathers and mothers than for other indifferent people.'

'Then what names are they known by?'

'Only Christian names till they get married, when they take the names of the wife or the husband they choose. Whatever you may think about it, we have barely enough of such bairns for our requirements, and that made Liliard when she was fifteen years old eager to be let in as a helper. And a brave preacher she would have made, but her father and mother would not hear of such a thing; it would have been to them a disgrace, so she has to content herself with the storytelling and such like.'

'Then your women preach as well as your men?'

'If they show any gifts that way, and in the matter of prayer I think they have often great utterance; Sister Dorothy at Palmtown is a sample of this. But you are not to think that one in a hundred or maybe in a thousand would be glad to part with their little ones on the chance that they might come to honour.'

'Then what may be the population of this little Commonwealth? You began in 1745 with about five hundred, I've heard my grandmother say but you lost some of your number by fighting and hardships before you took possession.'

'But more than half of the sailors came in with us and helped with the fighting; there were but ten slain or captured when the ships were taken.'

'But then there were some Indians that you intermarried with.'

'Aye that is true. I should say there was nigh-hand eighty of them first and last, women and men, gathered into the Commonwealth.'

'That makes say five hundred and fifty to start with. I suppose you double your population in twenty-five years.'

'In less than twenty years, but if you want to ken the number of our folk that is easily told. We are not like David the King of Israel, fearful for the consequences. We behove to know how many there are on the land, and how much land each man has. There was last Martinmas just twenty-five thousand seven hundred and eleven of all ages.'

'Just the population of a country town in England or a large mining township in Victoria. And spread over all this valley of how great an extent, can you tell me?'

'It is about sixty miles long by a middling width of thirty-two,' said my kinsman proudly. 'Although I'm not greatly concerned about foreign things and old world stories like Liliard; I keep mind of my own country's affairs.'

'Just a fair-sized English county but not big enough for Victorian district, and the land as I see is splendid.'

'But here we are at the Town House for though this is not our capital we have our own Council for the streets and the roads and keeping order and such like.'

My kinsman introduced me to the Council of five, who sat in a plain room round an oval table. I declared my name, my birthplace and my avocation, and told the honourable Council that I was willing while I sojourned with them to submit to all the laws of the country, and in so far as I could, to make myself serviceable to the community either by my profession of a medical man and a surgeon, or by my amusement as a photographer or sun-painter. Only I wanted leave to retrace my steps to the place where I had left my photographic apparatus and small case of surgical instruments, and

I begged for the company of my kinsman, Hugh Keith, with whom I would return with the greatest possible expedition.

'What says Liliard Abercrombie to that last proposal?' asked one of the Council.

'She is quite willing that I should go,' said Hugh.

'Will you cast in your lot with us for good?' asked one who seemed the chief speaker. 'We could allot you a share in the town lands of New Berwick and swear you in as a citizen. We like not strangers who come and go; the Indians first and last gave us much trouble till we made them one with us, and those who would not abide, we thrust forth.'

'But I am of kindred blood and name,' said I. 'I have found the descendants of ancestors, of whom I have heard much, in this valley, although all my near relatives, all my friends, and all my interests in life are many thousands of miles away. Surely my request is very reasonable.'

My kinsman had some influence with the Town Council, indeed his father was a leading member, but all the Councillors liked to have their say at Columba as elsewhere on any new matter, and all the more because from the first they suspected it was beyond their jurisdiction. I made another appeal on a different tack.

'Your community appears to me the most interesting place I ever saw in all my travels, and I would gladly stay with you, and learn perhaps more than I can possibly teach.'

This smoothed the troubled waters a good deal. There was nevertheless some hesitation. I was referred to the central Government at Ebenezer, seven miles off, which would cause a delay of twenty-four hours to which I had reluctantly to consent. My desire to take away Hugh Keith, even for a few days only, was a more objectionable proposal than my own to live with them and leave them. The Columban communal Government was one which subordinated each individual to the community, and even though I might teach them some new things, the risk of disturbing the minds of the lieges, and of showing them the way out of this secluded fastness, was an evil which it would need great services to make up for. The wealth of the Commonwealth consisted in its industrious population, and if the young and the adventurous were wiled away it would be a serious loss. These things I only half saw at the time but on greater knowledge of the institutions of the country I understood somewhat of the weight of objections that appeared to me at the time to be childish and unreasonable.

V

AN EVENING'S AMUSEMENT

'And now business being over, so far as we can proceed at present,' said Hugh as we departed, 'let us to the Kirk, and see what pleasure we can get there.'

'You must be a very pious people,' said I, 'to go to the Kirk on week-evenings. That's going out of fashion even in the old country, and on Monday of all days in the week too I should least expect such a thing.'

'Oh! there's not so much piety about that, as you may soon see, and there's Liliard in front, let us catch up to her, and tell her how we've sped.'

She was accompanied by her mother, who was a widow, by her brother and two sisters, one older, wearing a white cap, and one several years younger whose hair was bound with a bright tie, not a ribbon, for there was no silk in all Columba. I was introduced by Hugh to Madame Abercrombie, Mistress Elliot, and Marjorie Abercrombie, and then to Tom Abercrombie. The family were all good looking, but none so strikingly handsome as Liliard. The mother had an expression which spoke of suffering physical or mental.

The building was large and seated with benches to accommodate not far from a thousand people; the walls were of the same character as all the others I had seen, but the Kirk was high in the roof and round shaped and very well supplied with ventilators. It was lighted fairly well with two rows of kerosene lamps, with white reflectors above; the long windows were all open for air. Hugh motioned me to a seat, but Liliard separated from us, and took her place above on a sort of platform at one side of the building, raised about four feet above the front benches. However, the floor of the Kirk was not flat, but rose gradually on all sides, so that those at the back could see over the heads of those who had front benches, an improvement of very recent introduction in the civilised world in churches though long used with regard to theatres.

'So your women really preach,' said I in an astonished whisper to my namesake, 'but are such young women as your wife selected to address so great a congregation?'

The young man's face lighted up at the sound of the word wife. 'There's no preaching tonight; it's Monday and storytelling, and Liliard is the very best hand at that in all the country. She's very clever at the playacting too, but that comes on Thursday, and I doubt we'll no be back from our travels by then.'

'Playacting in the Kirk?' said I.

'Yes, to be sure, there's no other place big enough to hold all the folk that come to see and hear.'

'And what on other days?' said I.

'The dances on the green. It was called a green because it was first laid down in grass, but they found that heavy for the feet and they made the smooth ground that you see now, but the old word green lasts, and at any rate there are green trees all round. We cannot dance in the Kirk, on account of the floor, but we have brave dances out of doors in the evenings and on Sabbath afternoons.'

Surely if Archibald Keith had not been consigned to the ocean, and if his remains had been brought to be buried in this new country, he would have turned in his grave to hear of such uses to make of a Kirk, and such practices on the Sabbath. My face showed my surprise.

'Have you no such things in the world?' said Hugh. 'Surely folk need amusement everywhere after a day's work.'

'Oh!' said I. 'Yes, but then we pay for it, and have lecture halls, and theatres for acting, and concertrooms for singing, and ballrooms for dancing. We keep the Kirk for preaching in on Sundays.'

'Well to my mind that is a great waste. We have not the means to make all these different big buildings, and the Kirk and the green do for all. Only the Kirk's best to hear in; there was a lot of trouble taken about that, and so all the speaking and the acting and the singing goes on in the Kirk. In your new country what called you it? where the folk went out into the wilderness to the place in the South Seas where you were from.'

'Victoria in Australia,' said I.

'Do they make just the one use of the Kirk there?' asked Hugh.

'They would think it profanation to do anything else but preach and pray and sing praises to God in it,' said I.

'Well, I would have thought they might have more common-sense,' said my namesake with some contempt in the tone of his voice.

'Sometimes they may have religious service in a lecture hall or an Institute, but they would never have anything but worship in a church,' said I. 'They sometimes have Sunday School in it.'

'Sunday School!' said Hugh. 'That is the only day in the week that our brains don't go to school. Surely the poor little creatures need a rest as well as grown folk. I was aye glad when Sunday came round for the dances when I was a scholar. But whisht! the minister is going to ask a blessing.'

The large white-faced clock in the Kirk had just struck seven, and an old man with a few silvery locks of hair, who had entered after Liliard, and who sat in a chair beside her, rose, and the whole body of people rose with him, to ask a blessing on their evening's amusement to which the flock said with him, 'Amen'.

Then Liliard rose from the chair on which she had been sitting, and broke into a narrative of the early Columban days, which was marvellously clear, picturesque, and connected, and which was accompanied with the greatest modulation of voice and the use of every gesture to show surprise, terror, joy and despair. Sometimes when the subject matter of her tale was of rapid action, she walked up and down on the platform, as if to carry with her words the idea of progress, of flight, or of search; sometimes when the crisis was imminent, she stopped short, and gazed intensely into vacancy as if there was no help for the situation, then as if some hope dawned, she started off with a few quick steps as if towards deliverance. Sometimes at the pathetic passages, she seemed to have tears in her voice, and to pause till she recovered, and often again with clasped hands she sat down, and the words came forth as from some deep source beyond her own control. Often there were old words that I could not tell the meaning of, and new ones coined as by every living race, and especially by a transplanted race to supply to exigencies of changed and changing conditions, but her natural eloquence was great and it was genuine. The broad vowels, the tender diminutives, the racy graphic phrases of the Northern vernacular, seemed in this narrative to take more dignity than in the common talk, and to lend itself to the grand and to the pathetic with as much force as to the humorous and shrewd, to which I had been accustomed before this new experience.

The subject of the story was one of their old legends. It was the tale which told of her ancestor Ralph Abercrombie's captivity among the Indians, who were in possession of the valley, and how a daughter of the tribe, Palahna by name, cut his bonds and escaped with him. It was the account of the wooing of an intelligent and affectionate savage by one whom Liliard Abercrombie conceived as a gentleman. It was the story too of the first handfasting that had ever been entered into, and that with the wish on both sides for such oneness of faith and love as would lead to the bond being ratified. But the year of handfasting had not been without its perils, for in the absence of the brave Ralph, Palahna's father and brothers had stolen away the bride, and hidden her in the woods. There the little son was born whom the parents had hoped to rejoice over together, and Palahna prayed to the God she had learned to worship, over the little one that her brave white warrior might come to their rescue.

As Liliard uttered the simple words of the prayer, her voice seemed choked with sobs; the soul of her ancestress appeared to have passed into her. I found my own eyes filled with tears as I looked and listened.

There was a desperate chase to find her out, and all sorts of ambushes and ruses practised on both sides, till at last Ralph found his beloved Palahna, and taking his infant in his arms, he led her through dangers and hardships to a place of comparative safety, when the poor Palahna felt that she could move no further, but lay down exhausted. Wrapping her up in his own coat, and pillowing her head on the moss, he carried his little son on till he laid him on his own mother's knee, and then went back for Palahna, whom he carried in his strong arms, reviving her with kisses and fond words, till she reached the home from which she had been taken. How tenderly he watched over her till she regained her strength, and waited impatiently for the day when the appointed time expired, and then they went together with their friends to the Kirk, and mother and child were baptised together, and the half ring was taken off the finger, and the marriage ring put on, and they vowed love and fidelity till death; and long they lived and well they loved ever after, and they had twelve sons and daughters whom they brought up in the fear of God and for the good service of man.

All this story was told with the greatest profusion of detail; conversations were given minutely and characteristically; descriptions of the places, all of which the storyteller had seen with her own eyes, were fairly though not artistically given. There was a young brother of Ralph Abercrombie's, a sort of mar-plot, who did not want his brother to marry the Indian woman, and who had connived at the abduction. There was a sister, however, who clung to her affectionately. Madame Keith and her son who suggested the handfasting, were introduced and worked into the whole texture of the narrative, along with Ralph Abercrombie's father, John Abercrombie, and his grandfather the old Darien adventurer. The Indians and their counsel were laid bare too, and they were not on the whole such interesting savages as Fenimore Cooper describes, though the storyteller admitted that they had a fair grievance against the white settlers, who at first were aggressive and cruel, though Ralph Abercrombie was a true hero who had only fought in self defence.

My cheeks glowed, my eyes I'm sure flashed; I was carried out of myself by this vivid improvisation and I could see that though most of the audience had some quiet occupation, the interest was very generally felt. The women had knitting or needlework; some of them were mending children's clothes; many of the men were whittling sticks, though my namesake and I were simply absorbed, never taking our eyes off the speaker. All my recollections of the conventional full-dressed white-gloved reciters and singers and declaimers of the old world had no parallel here. Liliard wore the simple dress in which I had met her. Her uncovered hands had an eloquence in their every finger, which would be impossible in any human hands tightly covered in white kid; they were large though well-shaped and their strength and power fitted them for effective movement where the tale was swift and strong and vehement.

'Truly,' I said to myself, 'we have lost a great deal by the practice of writing and reading books.'

For an hour and a half, Liliard kept on with her story with no slackening of power, the building was certainly made on good acoustic principles, for even in spite of the little rustle of fingers all round, her clear penetrating voice was heard all over it. When she came to her conclusion, there was no round of applause and no curtseying to the audience. She simply stopped and sat down, and the white-haired minister dismissed the assembly with a blessing.

'Well,' said Hugh, 'what to you think of our use of a Kirk on ilka days? Have you better things than this in your halls and theatres?'

'Nothing so good. I never saw anything carry me away so much; but all your storytellers are not like this.'

'Well, not just so quick with their words and so grand with their hands as Lil, but there's three or four not far behind her here, and she says the minister is better than her when he gives us a chance to hear him, which is not often however.'

'And this is all given to the people for nothing,' said I.

'To be sure.'

'And everyone who is called on must do the duty?'

'Certainly.'

'And who settles the order of the entertainments?'

'The Town Council that you saw sitting, settle it from week to week.'

'With us, such crowds as these would pay for their admittance and that would pay not only rent for the theatres and music halls, but all the actors, or reciters or singers very handsomely for their trouble.'

'Then Lil's useless gifts, as folk call them, would make her a rich woman where you live.'

'No doubt,' said I.

I could scarcely speak to Liliard herself I was so full of surprised admiration, but a slight dark man who had watched the whole with as much attention as Hugh, but with an expression of fiercer delight in his eyes, stepped eagerly forward on to the platform, and thanked her for her glorious story, and especially for the subject.

'I thought I did well tonight,' said she.

'Them that pride themselves on what they call their pure blood have got rather a downsetting,' said he. 'You showed them the beginning of the mixed race, from which you and I both spring.'

Liliard drew back with a little surprise.

'You must have been thinking of me?' he insisted.

'No,' she said, 'I was not thinking of you more this day than any other day, but the old story was borne in upon my mind because Hugh's kinsman Hugh Victor Keith, that you see in strange attire sitting beside him, dropped in upon us as if from the clouds, out of the great old world, and he asked about the handfasting and how it began and what good purpose it served, and I thought the old story would tell again to all of you, and would be new to him, and help to explain how we were led to it.'

There was another restless glance at me as I sat by Hugh. There had been a few before both from him and others. My coat and waistcoat and trousers and felt hat were of a very different fashion from theirs, and my close-cropped hair had not the picturesqueness of my kinsman's fair curls, which fell a little way on his neck.

'Oh!' said he. 'Another, no doubt. You're free of your will for three months to come, but I'm free to do what man can do to break the bond, and till the last moment, I'll not draw back a hair's breadth.' This was a new phase of the Columban domestic institution. The bride was open to be courted, and probably the bridegroom was liable to temptation too, even if he did not go to seek it. Disappointed or aspiring rivals had full liberty given them to reverse the temporary union until it was made irrevocable by marriage.

My namesake looked at me and whispered, 'I have little fear of what Ninian can do after his six handfastings, with my Liliard who, please God, will be my wife in three months' time. And all his brag about her story being in favour of the mixed blood is nonsense. Her story was of the right kind; it was in praise of constancy and fidelity to bride and bairn.' And Hugh sighed as he had done before under the influence of the same idea and then broke off on another subject. 'Did you take note that the handfasted wear feathers; there were some sitting before you that you did not seem to notice, and May Abercrombie that is not handfasted yet, wears a ribbon in her hair.'

'She looks shy,' said I.

'Oh she has not got out her head yet but her time is coming no doubt. She is more like Lil than the rest of the family, and I'll warrant she'll have sweethearts enough.'

'You cannot like the way this half-Indian behaves,' said I.

'Well, I cannot say that I do, but our folk give the greatest freedom of speech and place for all manner of courting till the time is out, for they say it is far better that we should find out we like someone else better in good time before the thing is past mending. And you see at these gatherings it's the handfasted couples that are aye brought to the fore. And though I cannot tell the stories like Liliard, I can do the playacting, and sing and whistle. As for her, where there's singing, she's out of it. She cannot sing a note, though she has a face like a flower and a speaking voice that just goes through you. Whatever the Council decides on, you'll see you will be quartered on us or on some other handfasted couple; they would not send you to married folk. As our kinsman we have the best right to entertain you. Your ways are not our ways, and no doubt at your age you've left someone behind that you're either married or promised to.'

I answered my kinsman lightly in the negative. It was only as a curious intellectual riddle that I was interested in this beautiful young woman who was all but married to Hugh Keith. With so little education as we should account it and with so much genius, as a listener she had called the very best out of me, and made me feel that I had almost done justice to my great subject; as a narrator she had held me in breathless suspense such as I had never before experienced, during the whole course of her story. Still their ways were not my ways and I did not imagine that I took much greater interest in Liliard Abercrombie than I might have taken in her brother Tom if he had shown the same eager curiosity and the same picturesque dramatic talent.

VI

VOTING IN COLUMBA

Ninian, for that appeared to be all the name he had, accompanied us on our homeward way as far as the house of Hugh Keith's parents, talking eagerly to all three of us, but especially to Liliard, all the time. Master Archibald Keith we had seen at the Council, but he and his wife had preferred a quiet evening at home. Perhaps they did not care that their son's bride should make herself so conspicuous. Several of Hugh's brothers and sisters, however, had been in the Kirk.

'Here is our kinsman Hugh Victor Keith, mother,' said my cousin as he led me in. 'My father would tell you of his arrival and his application. We are going to call him Victor, to make a distinction between us. Does he favour the family do you think?'

'I buried my Victor five years ago. He is not to equal what he would have been by this time but he is welcome,' and Madame Keith gave me her hand in greeting. 'And chance or Providence led him to your very door, I hear.'

'All my father could do, we could get leave from the stupid Town Council for me to go with Victor over the ranges to get some wonderful things he could not carry, and we behove to appear before the General Council at Ebenezer tomorrow. They have sent a special messenger to warn them of the important business – have they not father?'

'Indeed they have,' said the elder Keith 'I wish you well out of this, for if there ever were folk to make a mountain out of a molehill, it is Protector Elliot and his backers.'

'It would have been different if it had been Protector Keith no doubt. Well, Father, you'll have better luck next time.'

'It is not such a molehill after all,' said the old lady. 'I wonder at Liliard letting you go on such a wild errand. Nobody that ever crosses the ranges ever comes back. It is a desert full of wild beasts and savages, I have heard my grandmother say.'

'But there are two of them, Madame,' said Liliard, 'and what our cousin left behind are wonderful things – all sorts of cutting instruments for the chirurgeon made of iron, nay of bright steel, and a framework of something that will make pictures by itself. Oh! I have no fear of Hugh's safety.'

'If folk want to get back,' said Hugh, 'they are sure to find a way. Victor, who is quite a stranger, made his way by himself and can show me the safe track. He too will bind himself to the Council to return forthwith, and tell us all the wonders that have been found out in the way of healing.'

'He says he can take off a man's leg without his feeling it. What say you to that Madame?' said Liliard.

'That would seem to me a very perilous gift,' said Madame Keith. 'Take good heed that he plays you no trick.'

'Nay,' said Liliard, 'we've no cause to suspect him. And to think that he of all the people in the world should drop upon us, not from Scotland direct but from that great waste place that used to be called New Holland. Oh! I've heard such wonders this day, I'll not sleep a wink.'

'Smoke a pipelet to quieten you, Lil,' said the old man, her father-in-law. 'As for you, cousin Victor, I'm thinking you are ready for bed. If you tramped o'er the ranges and then had to tell all the news that has upset my good-daughter, and to come to the town, you must be sore of foot and gey tired in the headpiece. We must have all the ferlies that you bring and can tell us of when you come back. But what think you of our plantation?' The father like the son was more anxious to hear my opinion of their country and institutions than to learn what was going on elsewhere.

'I think Columba should be called the Happy Valley,' said I. 'I never saw so much apparent comfort and happiness anywhere.'

'And you have travelled by land and sea?' said Liliard eagerly.

'We are none such fools after all you see,' said Hugh.

'Even with such a set of blockheads in the Council, the people have plenty of commonsense,' said the elder Keith.

'I hope to learn all about your laws and your settlement on the land when we have our few days travelling together. There are many things absolutely new to me that are done nowhere in the world but by this handful of Scotchmen.'

'No such handful,' said Madame Keith. 'There are seven town lands and a new one about to be laid out. Hughie, mind to wrap up at night when you are on your travels; it's bitter cold on the heights, and see that you keep by the watercourses. You can take a drink of the burn, but you canna take a bite of the brae and carrying water is cumbersome.'

'The other side is a stony desert,' said the old man, 'with no end to it as I've been told by them that had it from the Indians.'

'Yes but my half-breed Indian always managed to get water to the last and made off with my provisions, my water bag and my purse full of gold when I was a long way from the foot of the range. I'll take my rifle - my gun - with me, and we may provide a little food for ourselves to eke out what we carry for that saved me from utter want.'

'Well, God speed you, but it seems a venturesome journey,' said the worthy parents, who were by this time surrounded by several of Hugh's brothers and sisters who came in hopes of seeing more of the stranger.

We went our way for a short time in silence. My own thoughts were in a tumult; and Liliard said she did not know whether she was on her head or her heels. Hugh whistled to his dog now and then the new tune he made out, and then broke out into a description of our meeting with the Town Council and the difficulties and objections they made. 'Is the General Government compounded of the same class as the ministers and teachers?' said I.

'Oh no, there is a Councillor for everyone of the seven town lands the plantation is divided into and every householder votes in his own district. None of the Kirk's bairns can serve in the Council, either for the town or for the whole Commonwealth, and none of them have even votes.'

'How long do they keep their seats?'

'The Town Councillors are voted in every year for the town lands but the General Councillors are voted in every two years.'

'And the President or Protector?'

'He keeps his place for four years. My grandfather had a term of office, and Liliard's grandfather too, and her grand-uncle once. Her father was in a fair way to be made Protector when he took ill and died. It is the south that was so strong last election or my father would have been in.'

'Do the Councillors get anything for their service but the honour?'

'What should they get? It's but an hour a day one day in the week that they behove to attend, though they may sit for hours or have bye meetings when they think there is any business of consequence.'

'We may not hit on the hour or the day for their meetings,' said I.

'There will be a special meeting tomorrow, as I said, for this is special business.'

'The less delay we have the better so I hope it may be summarily settled. But your Protector is paid for his services?'

'Oh, yes, while he holds office. He has the right to six town lands.'

'You mean six allotments such as other people have to make them voters for the town lands.'

'Yes, that is what I mean.'

'Are there any of your poor people who have not land who have not a vote?' 'Oh they have all votes for the General Council, but only them that have town lands have votes for the Town Council.'

'Have you open voting or the ballot?'

'We vote by the voice; we cannot write, if that is what you mean.'

'But I suppose most of your heads of families have land.'

'Everyone may have land that likes if he applies for it and pays the fen-duty to the Commonwealth every year and that is a groat an acre. A town land pays twenty shillings a year; that is a twenty shilling piece that you got as arles or earnest-money.'

So this little piece of gold elsewhere worth five shillings represented the land taxation on the average estate of a Columban citizen, and was a very important part of the general revenue.

'But if people take out land, and do not cultivate it, what is done with them?'

'Oh, they may pasture it or they may get somebody to cultivate it for them, or it will go back to the Commonwealth if it is left to lie waste. The clearing of the wood is the heaviest part of the work.'

'But there is a limit to what each man may take.'

'Only one town land to each but folk buy from each other. No man may take out from the Commonwealth more than the one, after that he must buy. Whoever buys, buys with the perpetual rent to be paid.'

'Then by dummying,' said I smiling, 'as in Victoria, I suppose you have some large estates.'

'Yes!' said Hugh. 'John Abercrombie has as much as ten town lands, six hundred acres of his own, and there are estates three times as big as that.'

'And your Protector has only three hundred and sixty acres to enjoy.'

'The Protector's land is the best in all the Valley, worth more than John Abercrombie's and that is prime. It is free of fen-duty too and that is something. But then he loses it when he is put out, and another man takes possession when he is chosen.'

'And who chooses the Protector?'

'Oh I forgot, there are seven town lands in the place, and when the Council is elected, they choose one of their number to be the Protector; that is to say every other election, for there is one that is missed, till four years are out and that town needs no election, but behoves to be satisfied with the Protector, and indeed is proud of it.'

Thus the excitement of a Presidential election was saved to the citizens of this miniature Republic, who seemed to manage their affairs with the greatest economy of excitement, and with little risk of friction.

'Do not these things seem small to you?' asked Liliard.

'No,' said I eagerly, 'not at all. I feel like a disciple or scholar trying to learn some first principles, and to unlearn some old prejudices.'

'Then you will come back if you get leave to go?' said she in a low eager tone, while Hugh was whistling for his dog which had got away.

'Yes no doubt, I will bind myself by a solemn promise to return, the only thing that grieves me is that my father and sisters and my old grandmother will think me lost, and I have no means of letting them know that I am amongst good and kind friends.'

'I thought you could. I heard you say that the lightning carried your messages, and an iron horse your letters. Surely over the ranges you can speed the news.'

'True, but there must be the machinery. We are hundreds of miles away from a railwayline or telegraph wire, so I must delay my communication till I have fulfilled my time with your Government for without that I am told that I cannot get leave for Hugh to accompany me, and without his aid I am sure to come to grief.'

'And how long would you like to engage to stay here?'

'Three months with the power to stay longer or to settle for good.'

'Oh! that you will never do, but in three months I must learn much.'

'Could you learn to read?'

'No, no, Hugh would not allow it, nor his people, nor mine. And what is the use of being able to read when there are no books but those I know by heart. No, but you must tell me everything – everything.'

On reaching home after this most exciting day, Jenny served up for our supper a dish resembling haricot beans, well-seasoned, which had been simmering by the fire during our absence for the maiden had been at the Kirk with others, and Liliard drew from a cask some very pleasant light ale in a wooden quaich or beaker. We smoked a pipe, and she joined us in that soothing performance, and then my host showed me into a clean bare bedroom, where a truckle bed was made up for me. The bed was of cotton flock, the sheets were coarse but soft and warm, as was the cotton quilt. There were no blankets in Columba for from May to October there was no need of them. Hugh promised to call me in time for a comfortable bath before we set out on our journey, but not too early, for after the fatigues and the agitations of the day, I stood in need of rest. I fell asleep to the rhythmical sound of grinding coffee, in which my beautiful hostess was engaged.

VII

THE CAPITAL OF COLUMBA

Hugh made a holiday to go with me and his bride to Ebenezer. It was not often that they went abroad, but this was a grand occasion. He managed to get someone to take his work, he borrowed from his father a strong horse, which would carry double, and his own lighter horse was given to me. I had never in my life before seen such a thing as a woman on a pillion, but here was a youthful Darby and Joan, as handsome a couple as you could see on any summer day, travelling in this old-fashioned familiar and confiding manner. I kept alongside, full of interest in all that I saw and all that I heard. Ebenezer was a larger town than New Berwick, but not a whit handsomer. It had a still larger space in the centre for the dances, and the Town House was larger and more imposing; on the south side, where there were ordinary houses in New Berwick, was a range of buildings which might be called the public offices, where the land registers were kept, where the students were trained, where the money was coined. The central building in the Town House was used as a court of justice. To the right was what served them as a House of Parliament, the modest room appropriated to the sittings of the General Council; to the left was the presbytery hall where the clergy of the seven parishes, those in the outlying districts, with an elder from each parish, met one day in the month. Here were kept the registries of births, deaths, handfastings, and marriages on rolls of parchment and connected with this was the meagre library of the settlement to which no one but 'God's bairns' had access.

We started early, for my friends wanted me to see all I could, and while Hugh went to put up the horses at his cousin's and to inquire about some bronze work that he thought he might get to do, as he had a high reputation beyond his own neighbourhood, Liliard took me through the school. This happened to be the school where she herself had received instruction, for it was not till after her father's death that the family had removed to New Berwick where her two brothers had taken out town lands. The school was very well graded and each class was under a separate teacher in a separate room. But a school without books, copy books, or slates, appeared to me the oddest thing imaginable. The only scholastic thing about it was a large map of the world as known to the early settlers, copied from an original drawing by Madame Keith and her son. It had a very shapeless Australia with Tasmania attached to the mainland, and there was a great deal of blank interior unexplored in various parts of the old and new world. There were no names written on it, but some mountain ranges and rivers were roughly defined and there were crosses and circles for large and smaller towns. In fact it was a rude attempt at the blank map of our modern schools. There was also a map of Columba with the natural features of the place rudely drawn, and the boundaries of the town lands brought up to the present date by which I could see where the bulk of the waste land lay. The schoolrooms were provided with benches but no desks, and there was a good playground outside.

The teachers were of both sexes, and the classes were of boys and girls mixed. The first or lowest class learned to count and to sing, and to repeat rhymes, and indeed the two lower classes were worked up almost exclusively in Columban unwritten literature. I recollected that children's books were not in existence at the time when the emigrants departed from Scotland, neither books to make the first steps of learning easy, nor books which are at present the great incentive to the youthful mind to acquire facility in reading. Even the fairy tales which had been put into literary shape out of the folk lore of the Aryan races were written for courtly ladies and gentlemen, and not for children, and the Arabian Nights with their tales of marvels were the delight of Eastern men long before they were diluted into the form which has for more than a century amused Western children.

My grandmother had shown me the ABC and the Shorter Catechism and explained to me the use made of the single page containing the alphabets large and small, and a few unmeaning syllables for sound. This elementary page formed the only introduction to that first reading book for the use of the schools in Scotland a century ago, when the children plunged from *bla ble* to '*What is the chief end of man*' in Italics, and the answer in Roman letters, 'Man's chief end is to glorify God and to enjoy Him forever,' a sublime question and answer, but scarcely to be called milk for babes. From the Shorter Catechism with its 106 questions and answers the young readers were advanced to read the Proverbs, and afterwards the New Testament and after that the Old Testament; and no other reading books were heard of in the parish or National Schools of Scotland in these eighteenth-century times.

The natural evolution in this kindly child-loving community was a perfect wealth of rhyme and ballad, suitable for the understanding of the little ones, and each new teacher tried to introduce something of his or her own among the little ones. They learned to count in rhyme; they learned the history of the colony and part of the history of Scotland in such simple rhymes before they were advanced to such literature as was got from books. I asked Liliard if all the teachers could read and write; she said no; only those who took the highest classes, those who were to be ministers and those who were employed in keeping the records of the Commonwealth were allowed to handle the few precious books belonging to the community. Each of the teachers might have had the chance, for it was according as they showed talent or capacity that at the age of twelve they were especially instructed. But even those who could read, never used a book or even a blackboard. It was the ear and the memory that was especially educated except in the little geography they had to learn; from the maps I have described there was no appeal to the eye.

In the second class mental arithmetic was taught dealing with simple numbers, and also the Gospel history. Here the knitting for girls, and the crochet hook and sticks for boys were first used. There was a sort of catechism taught to this class about the miracles and the parables, and about the duties of children at home, at school and in society.

In the third class, money tables and weights and measures and the ordinary four rules of arithmetic were taught as far as this could be done without slate or pencil. The memory was exercised on Scripture History and on General History so far as it had come down. Here began the learning of great books such as Pope's *Homer* or Dryden's *Virgil* – and *The Pilgrim's Progress* with some shortening of the theological portions was a favourite study. A more advanced catechism or system of questioning on the Bible narrative and children's duties was taught.

In the fourth class there was instruction in the rights and duties of citizens, some lessons given about the animals tame and wild, the plants and the mineral productions of Columba, arithmetic applied to measurements and strength of materials, and some crude agricultural chemistry as they understood it.

This class all children were bound to go through, but after that the boys fell off, as they generally wanted to go into some practical way of life, but the girls, particularly if their parents were in good circumstances, continued at school and learned there to sew and cut out, to spin and many of them to weave. And owing to the practice they had had from a very early age in helping their memories by means of various modifications and variations in their work, they were generally the better informed and the more fluent of the two sexes in expressing what they knew or what they imagined.

In the highest class of all, the sixth, there were no boys at all; the girls loved to rival each other in verse-making and in storytelling, and though Liliard Abercrombie was especially gifted from natural genius, I was astonished to hear how well this class expressed themselves. And as all sorts and conditions were educated in the same way in a body, there was no vulgar dialect known throughout the plantation. It might sound a little vulgar to an Englishman, who considers a broad vowel a mark of under breeding, but to me it appeared remarkably pure and racy speech. And the manners of these young Republicans were good. They moved in and out of their seats without hurry or tumult, and though they were a little excited by the sight of a stranger in strange clothes, they did not stare rudely, nor did they as far as I could see make remarks to each other as to what a 'Guy' I was.

All classes from the youngest upwards were taught to dance and a great variety of gymnastic exercises besides. The way they walked out and in was very different from the alternate pounding of the right and left foot which we in our State schools call on visitors to admire, as drill and marching. It was free and graceful and as swift as it could be without disorder. I had observed on the previous evening what a fine looking race the Scottish colonists appeared to be, but now as a medical man, I was lost in admiration of the splendid physique of young Columba, the open chests, the strong straight limbs, the steady eye and the firmly closing mouth. That some were richer and some were poorer could be seen by their clothes; the whole young population of Ebenezer from five years old and upwards were there; but there was not a low type of face amongst them all.

There did not appear to be one child in the school of pure Indian blood though there were many who had a very large admixture of it with the Anglo-Saxon or Scandinavian. To English eyes, the absence of stockings and frequently of hats would look like poverty, but the universal use of the simple parasol made of palm leaves was a sufficient protection from the sun, and they all wore shoes, some home-made, and some evidently of better workmanship. Stockings were worn by neither rich nor poor in youth, and only in winter by the women and the prevailing garment for girls was somewhat like part of the bloomer costume, or like that worn in the Sandwich Islands, resembling a yoked nightgown of striped or checked calico coming half way down the leg. The boys wore wide breeches and a tunic - both of cotton - home-grown, home-spun, home-dyed and often home-woven as well as home-sewed.

Liliard looked a little sadly on the classes; it reminded her that she had been shut out from teaching. All the teachers wore on their sleeves the badge of Columba - a dove rudely-sewn in coloured wool. To me, accustomed to think of the children of the State as the lowest class in the community, only recently taken up with a conscientious effort to absorb them into the ordinary working population of any country, it seemed strange to see them in places of authority over the children of well-to-do parents. There were only five scholars with the same badge, which showed that they were meant for the public service.

But this visit was only too soon at an end; we were summoned to the Council, and detained for three hours, while the matter was seriously discussed whether my services should be accepted, and whether the dangerous experiment of allowing a citizen to leave Columba should be tried in the case of Hugh Keith. I claimed for myself, not only the rights of hospitality, which every stranger might reasonably expect in a Christian land, but also that I was the lineal descendant of the elder branch of Archibald and Marguerite Keith, the chief among the early settlers. I also said that I could serve the Commonwealth in various ways which I mentioned, but that without the property which now lay in the desert, I could not serve Columba half so effectually and that alone and unaided I could not hope to bring it back.

Owing to the constitution and laws of Columba, each citizen who was represented in the Council was secured in his rights and property. There was in ordinary circumstances exceedingly little for their representative government to do, so that this was a splendid opportunity for the Columban Council or Parliament to air their eloquence. We must recollect too that the power of expression had been cultivated to the utmost among these people from their earliest days, so that they had far more excuse for making a mountain of a molehill than some of our Australian legislators, who make havoc of the Queen's English in season and out of season. The Protector, Master Elliot, felt that it was a great constitutional question which had cropped up in his time and, as there was a standing jealousy on his part of the Keith family, he wished to treat it sternly. He was conservative to the backbone, and could make the excuse that he dreaded the innovations which such a wandering young man as myself might introduce. I heard afterwards that he dilated on the fact that if I was a descendant of Archibald Keith, it was through his outcast son, whose disgrace had led to that Godly minister turning his back on his native land, and as for what I had said about painless surgery, and pictures taken without hands, it savoured more of the black art of their forefathers than of Christian doings.

Hugh and Liliard were called in separately, and questioned as to all that I had said and done, and another long discussion ensued. At last I was called in, and somewhat grudgingly allowed to take an oath of fealty and engaged for three months to serve the Commonwealth in any way that the Council might from time to time point out. Permission was given to Hugh Keith to go with me, and to return with the shortest possible delay, and for the first month of my residence in the Plantation, I was appointed to be the guest of him and his handfasted bride, Liliard Abercrombie.

I received a small gold coin, a fifth part of a guinea in weight, but worth twenty shillings in silver as earnest-money to show that I had made the engagement and the clerk of the Council made me sign and seal the contract which he drew out on parchment. Hugh put on his seal to his engagement to return without delay, which if he forfeited, his town land in New Berwick, as well as his house, his forge and some other property could be seized by the Commonwealth.

The first duties imposed on me were to give instruction in medicine and surgery to the doctors and nurses of the plantation, according as the Council should hereafter signify for they appeared to wish to occupy the time of my necessary absence in devising some plan for this object. With regard to the sun-pictures, that was to be a private venture of my own, only I found that I was granted the privilege on one condition, that of taking the likeness of the Protector and of each member of the Council for nothing and also a general view of the hall in which they sat with the present Council in session.

I left this solemn audience with a feeling of surprised amusement. This sensible, intelligent, well-bred people appeared in every way to be superior to their rulers. Was this really the outcome of democratic institutions? Nowhere in the world was there such equality of conditions as I saw here in Columba, but as we have seen in America and in the Australian colonies, democracy does not choose the wisest and the best of citizens. Democracy thoroughly carried out, as we have hitherto seen it practised, tends to abridge the sphere of Government action, and to make people fussy in a narrow sphere. All opportunities for patronage and for influence in the civil service were denied to these representatives of the people, by the law which settled that the business of the country should be administered by 'no man's bairns'. All they could do was to promote by seniority or by merit those who had the prescriptive right to fill the various posts, and to punish with extreme severity any of them who might be detected in dishonesty or other evil doing. My kinsman Hugh said they were a very poor lot at present in power, and that his father had been the strongest opponent of Master Elliot at the election, and therefore that there was a little personal spite in the difficulties that were made about a very simple matter.

'A Keith's word is as good as his bond,' he said, 'and there is too much to bind me to my home for them to dread that I should be unsettled by going over the ranges to a stony desert.'

'As for you, Victor,' said Liliard, 'they should have gone on their knees to ask you to do for them what they made such a favour of accepting. But never mind; the people will be glad of it.'

I saw that among the democratic habits of this people, there were very few titles of courtesy. All the young people were called by their Christian names, and generally by both Christian and surname; for among these twenty-five thousand inhabitants of Columba there was a very short supply of surnames; and the intermarriage had made the people generally more or less of kin to each other. And my grandmother's theory was borne out in the very fine physical appearance and the high average intelligence of the race. I was Victor Keith to everybody - not Doctor Keith or Mr Keith - for there was a Doctor Keith in the settlement already who being one of God's bairns, and therefore having no name of his own had taken the name of his wife, a second cousin of Hugh's, who lived at Palmtown. The old married women were addressed as Madame, and their husbands as Master, but the custom in Columba as in provincial villages in Scotland to this day, was to speak of people by their names without prefix and sometimes as a distinction by their farms or properties.

After we had left the Council, Liliard took me to see the Kirk; alas! not the original Kirk, the first built in the valley for that had been absorbed in the school, but built on the site of the original Kirkyard, where two plain slabs showed where Marguerite de Launay or Keith and Ralph Abercrombie (the elder) had been buried. The burial ground was now out of the town, and we followed a funeral train carrying the remains of a little child to be interred. The coffin was not covered with white flowers; there was nothing beautiful but the sorrow of the parents who were married people, and the prayer offered up at the grave by Sister Dorothea, who though the minister at Palmtown was in great request for sick and dying children. Partly a teacher, partly a preacher, partly a nurse, and wholly devout, she was at the beck and call of all the little ones in Columba and she followed the remains of this her last charge to its final resting place. She was much older than Liliard and might be called as handsome though in a different style, with a fair face and dove-like eyes and angelic smile. Accompanying her was a girl of seventeen who called her 'mother', and to whom my friends spoke. She was going to make her first appearance on the platform of the Palmtown Kirk - St Marks - on the following Monday as a storyteller, though only for half the time allotted; another young woman was to take the remainder. Sister Dorothea had been handfasted in her youth to one Neil Scott and after two years of trial for she had extended the time at her bridegroom's request, had come to the conclusion that she was happier and more useful free from such bonds. From a teacher she had risen to be a preacher, and was very much esteemed by old and young.

The burial ground lay rather high, and was full of fine trees. Liliard showed me her father's grave, and not far off the last resting place of her ancestors Ralph and Palahna. It was not long after the death of Madame Keith that the inhabitants of this tropical valley discovered that the dead and the living should be kept apart, and there had never been a churchyard round about any of the other churches which were built after that of Ebenezer.

The schoolchildren were dispersing when we returned from the funeral, and taking their several roads homewards. The more I looked at them, the more I admired them. Sunburned they were, and as I have said with regard to the elders, a shade or two darker naturally than their kin in the old country, but clear-skinned, lithe-limbed and bright-eyed. When one considers that these children had never had, nor needed to have measles, whooping cough, scarlet fever or smallpox; that they lived a very natural life; were all well-fed, sufficiently clothed and wholesomely lodged, and that there were none of the population checks of poverty, drunkenness and vice which exist even in our happy Australia, I did not wonder that according to my friend Hugh's account, the population more than doubled in twenty years, and I felt quite sure that the universal industrial training had kept up the standard of health. The colonists of Columba did not look on themselves as exotics who could not thrive in a tropical climate; they found work to do, and no one to do it for them, and they did it.

It was a lovely ride home; Hugh was never weary of showing me their modes of cultivation, and the wonderful tropical growth which rewarded effort; we looked in at the place or green of New Berwick as we passed in the twilight and saw the dancers footing it to the sound of somewhat harsh music. We called in to see Hugh's parents as well as Liliard's and got home all pretty tired, though perfectly satisfied with our day's work.

VIII

OUR JOURNEY

Long before sunrise Hugh woke me as he had done the day before for a bath, which was a short way from the house in a pool formed by damming up the stream, and sheltered all round by shady and ancient trees. From this dam also ran little channels for irrigating the maize and the rice which were grown on Hugh's land, and it also turned a wheel that served him in his bronze work.

After a refreshing bath, we returned to breakfast which was abundant though it had little variety: coffee, wheaten bread, hominy cakes, butter and boiled eggs. My hostess was packing up a dozen of eggs in cotton wool in a grass basket when she suddenly asked me, 'And what about Spain? In all your story of the history of the world, I think you scarcely mentioned her at all, except that Wellington helped her in her sad straits when Napoleon's army had seized on her, and when our folk settled here she was the power they dreaded most. Indeed it was to protect themselves against invasion from the Spaniards, either of Mexico or the Spanish Main or from the old kingdom itself, that they built up the road they came through with a high wall that none can scale from within or without. There is no pass in the range where soldiers could bring their guns or their baggage waggons, and we have dwelt in safety ever since. But Spain is still in the map of Europe, and no doubt strong on this side of the ocean too.'

'No, not strong,' I answered. 'The feeblest in Europe, no longer one of the great military powers and in America; it seems only a question of time when the United States, the old English Plantation you know which extends from the Atlantic to the Pacific and number fifty millions of inhabitants, will take in Mexico and stretch to the Isthmus of Darien. The great Republic may annex Canada too which was conquered from France in George the Second's time and that I should be sorry to see.'

'Millions!' said Hugh. 'We don't deal in millions in Columba. Fifty millions do you say in the American Plantations from which we got our tobacco and other needful things?'

'Everything is so vast in the world that I feel as if I was less than nothing,' said Liliard.

'Are you not making it out greater just because Liliard is so eager for wonders and so humble about our own doings?' said Hugh.

'No indeed!' said I. 'But extent does not always mean well-being. The vast empire of Spain has fallen to pieces through lack of wisdom and lack of care for her subjects.'

'Well I hope you are satisfied for the present Lil, for we must set off,' and Hugh kissed his bride and said goodbye. Dividing our burdens unequally, for he insisted on taking the heavier share on account of my previous over-fatigue, we took the way up the same valley down which I had descended and made a good day's march resting for the night in a sheltered nook at a high altitude. My pocket compass was an object of curiosity to him, for in the circumscribed limits of the valley there was no danger of losing one's way, and no need of any scientific rectification by compass or sextant. Hugh was astonished at the practicability of the route which I retraced. He said he was sure that the Valley was almost inaccessible at any other point, and when we got on to the top of the range I was satisfied that by accident my guide had struck for the very easiest pathway for me. If he had not robbed me of money and provisions for his return, I might have fancied that he was making for the Valley himself.

During the first day, Hugh told me much about the methods of agriculture and the division of land which was held in trust by the central government, and portioned out to the people unimproved with a fixed fen-duty or rent, but which when improved was bought and sold very freely. The great disproportion in the value of the two precious metals caused the prices to appear very different when reckoned in silver and in gold but by a little thought I managed to carry this in my head. There was actually no iron to be found in the valley at all, and the remains of old ploughs and pots and other ironware, had been carefully preserved and wrought into steel for special purposes, as well as the meteoritic stones containing iron which were here and there to be found. But there were silver mines, in which there was an extremely small proportion of gold, copper mines in great abundance for their needs, and tin and lead.

Hugh Keith, though what we should call in England or Australia an artisan, was in Columba as good a gentleman as any there. It is evident that if the servants of the state and the professions were recruited from the children thrown on the public by the solemn abandonment of their parents, almost all the paths for talent and ambition were closed to the young of all ranks, who lived in the normal condition with their parents and brothers and sisters. There was no emigration possible, and considerable limitations of landed estate. Hugh's handicraft was reckoned among the highest in the Commonwealth. No doubt in early historic ages, the smith who forged the armour and the weapons, and who made the tools of the community would have been the best man in the village, if the warrior who used those weapons had not proved himself the stronger. Here, where there was no profession of arms, and no aristocracy at all, most men who wanted to be something, practised some handicraft in addition to the normal avocation of cultivating the ground, and indeed often paid others to cultivate for them while they worked to more profit. Hugh was exceedingly practical, and though he was as destitute of taste as his fellows, he knew the temper and the strength of the material he worked in; he put good honest work upon it, and was always fully employed. He confided to me that at odd half hours when Liliard was not looking in upon him, he was making silver spoons for her birthday, and he had hit upon the conceit of putting a whistle at the end of the shank, which he said would be sure to please her much.

All the mines belonged to the Commonwealth, and this along with the fen-duty on the land made up the revenue on which the churches and schools and government were supported, as also the roads and bridges. The roads had received very great attention from the Government of the Commonwealth, and the perfection of shape and consistence had been reached by much tentative experiment. A sort of concrete, which bound closely and which lasted without any repair for ordinary traffic for very many years, had been formed of a volcanic stone mixed with soft limestone, and some vegetable solvent, and this had come into general use, but when it began to break up, it was hopeless to patch it, the whole had to be picked up and a new layer superimposed. The irrigation and drainage were done in main lines by the Government, and were very complete, but this was an innovation. Originally these were all done by associated enterprise, but with the growth of population, the revenues of the Commonwealth became larger and in order to open up new lands for what we should call selection and settlement, the people were tempted by the offer of this improvement. Although at first the town lands were only taken out by young men, latterly partly for the sake of the increase of revenue, partly because the sexes were in reality growing more and more on a level, where there was no war and where the women were more highly cultivated educationally than the men, the young women also claimed their town lands, and with the town lands the right of voting. Much of the work of the minute cultivation necessary for the most valuable of their crops was done by the women, and even by the children of the family because there were no tasks out of school, though school attendance was enforced pretty strongly. For the sake of revenue the Government allowed land to be taken out at an earlier age, and then when the revenue was large, the land-holders demanded a good deal more to be done for it.

In addition to any land which might be bought or inherited every young Columban thus had a right to take out a town land of his own, and this led to their scattering to where the new land was best. There was a standing rivalry between the north and south, a sort of bidding for the new blood on both parts. The cemeteries, as I had seen, were laid out far from the towns, and the towns themselves kept very clean and well-drained. Pipes conveyed water into the houses in towns; this was done at Government expense, and there was no water rate levied. As there was one considerable stream fed with lateral tributaries all the length of the valley, there was no want of water. But the course of the river was rapid and there was a great fall, so that every here and there it was dammed up for special purposes. At its outlet at the south end of the valley a great fall of sixty feet sheer down made any thought of navigation quite impossible. The brave band had got through the pass indicated by the first Abercrombie, who was a leader of the expedition, but as the Spaniards were threatening and dangerous, one of the first steps they had to take was to fortify the place, and finally they thought it wise to build with stone, which was at that point pretty abundant, a wall without a door. This showed an amount of faith in the resources of the place which was in time justified. No doubt, as I thought, if they really wanted to get out they could knock down the wall or at least knock a gateway through it, but such a thing did not present itself to my kinsman as possible, or if possible, as advisable.

Hugh was the youngest son of a large family, and as he said, he had had his choice of a business. Liliard was the second daughter of a family of five, for her father, a man of exceptional abilities and fine character as I could gather from Hugh, had died young, but the widow had never married again and had not even been handfasted. She was not strong and lived with her eldest son and her unmarried daughter. Archibald Keith had been a wright or rather a cabinet maker, for his specialty was such plain furniture as the colonists used and he was still able for a good day's work.

There was abundance of mahogany in the valley, but it was so hard that bronze tools could not work it, and the people made their furniture of softer and inferior wood; the woodwork, though serviceable enough, was neither beautiful in form or polished as to the surface. And the women had little of that elaborate work in the way of beautifying the house and polishing furniture which had occupied their ancestresses, though they spun all the thread which made all the garments of the people and some of them did the weaving in looms at home and also took a large share in the field work on the farms.

This little community though it had settled in the tropics, had never taken into its head the notion that white people cannot work in a hot climate; as I have already said their physical health was very much better from their full occupation. I have never thought that a climate where people cannot work is a climate in which people ought to live and after seeing what white men can do in an Australian harvest field, when well-fed and temperate with regard to intoxicating liquors, I feel doubtful of the fact that Europeans cannot work anywhere. It is the presence of a numerous inferior race who are glad to work for low wages, that makes the Englishman think he cannot work in India and the Southern states of America. Here in Columba there were no negro servants to be had, the few Indians whom they had come in contact with were not the sort of people to be enslaved; the difficulty with them was to induce them to work at all. In slavery, they would simply have died there as they did elsewhere, but in the truce that succeeded the first years of desperate war, the women first and afterwards the men, settled down to peaceful pursuits. First as hunters and trappers of game, and next as keepers of sheep, cattle, pigs and goats, which gradually came to multiply and to be a constant resource in the way of food, next as clever with horses and carts and ploughs, the Indians took a respectable position. Latterly the miners and workers in metals were greatly drawn from the mixed race. There were very few full-blooded Indians in the place for they were originally but one to six and they turned out more delicate than the settlers though the mixed race was perhaps the wiriest of all. But there was no fire-water in Columba. Even the sugar growers made no rum but a light kind of beer from their refuse, and the manner in which people of all ages and sexes were amused as well as instructed at the public cost, made the craving for spirituous excitement, which many of the early settlers probably brought with them and which the later colonists might have inherited, die out. There was no such thing as a public house in the whole valley, the communal Government from the first had prohibited it and as for prostitution, I think my friend Hugh did not understand what it meant. Handfasting was easily entered into, and was held solemnly binding while it lasted, but the power to change in case the pair did not suit each other physically, or if their tempers clashed, or if they had not the element of constancy in their natures, did not drive those who were discontented or unhappy into vice, but only made them look forward to some legalised change for the better.

There seemed to be little or no wealth as we would account wealth, but on the other hand there was no poverty.

'There is as you say a territory of sixty-five miles by thirty-two – or in round numbers rather over two thousand square miles – but a good deal of that is I suppose waste still?' I said to Hugh.

'Yes out of the million acres, there is only 375 000 that we use for arable and pasture together, but that is a good share for the number of folks.'

'I suppose you plough with oxen mostly?'

'Aye, and there's a lot of hand work in the cotton, and the coffee, and the sugar growing, and I think I'll show you as good hoes and weeders and drain cutters in shape at least, in bronze as you have in iron.'

'Your land is very different from ours in Australia. In places it takes five acres to keep a sheep.'

Hugh laughed at this. 'Then they will not want for exercise to work off the fat they lay on in such a hungerly country. How you can keep them as flocks, poor things, I cannot imagine.'

'In England they speak of a sheep *walk* and in Australia of a sheep *run* for that very reason no doubt.'

'Here they may call it a sheep *rest*, for it's little exercise they need to take.'

'Don't your adventurous young folks sometimes cross the ranges,' said I, 'to see what is outside your happy valley?'

'Well no, there is plenty of work and plenty of fun going on, and all our old stories tell us of a world of trouble and injustice and fighting, and some few at the top trampling on a poor lot of slaves at the bottom, and besides, we are in the midst of a great stony desert. What would be the good of going forth to the certainty of worse at first, with the merest shadow of a chance of being better in the far future. So long as the old folk lived, they told us our condition was what all the world would envy. And indeed we had such work to get here and to fortify ourselves safe here, and to get and keep the upper hand of the Indians that were in possession, that we never fash to think what may be going on outside.'

'Ninian has much more of the Indian blood in him than your bride.'

'Aye a lot more – and far more of their disposition. He is the only one that I suspect has crossed the ranges for he is whiles away for a week, but as he always comes back we can only fancy that he sees little to tempt him to stay. His father was a Graeme, but he has no right to the name, and as he has never been married, he cannot take that of his wife. He would fain take the name of Abercrombie; at least he says that if he could win my Liliard, he would never change again.'

'Then he is one of your foundlings or castaways?'

'Yes, he is, and employed in the mint. Very clever, they say he is, in melting the silver ore and such like; and I must confess that he is very knowledgeable with the copper and tin mines, that I am myself most concerned with.'

'And did both father and mother give him up?'

'The mother was half-Indian and she died, and the father had to work for ten years for the family of Simon Paterson whom he maimed for life in an unprovoked attack, so he behoved to give up Ninian.'

'And is there no disgrace to the son?'

'No, what for should there be? Only Ninian would like to have a name, and he can never settle so as to get one.'

'Did you tell me he had been six times handfasted?'

'Aye no less than six, several of them for two years, but up to this time, never with a day's space between one and another, except with the one who died.'

'And what about the children, or are there any?'

'He had one by his first bride whom she kept. He lived with her for two years but after that he set his heart on another and so they parted. She has been since handfasted and married happily enough.'

'And his second?'

'He lived with her too for two years, but she had no child and that was the main reason why he parted from her. She is not married, but handfasted and like to be married when the time is out.'

'And the third?'

'Oh their tempers did not agree, and there was a terrible quarrel about the child at the last. No one could say which was most eager to part, so neither had the least right to claim the laddie. However they settled it that he should live with his father and his mother year about, till he came to the age of fifteen when he can choose and do for himself.'

'And what became of the bride?'

'Oh! in spite of her temper after abiding a space in her father's house, there was another man willing to try her and William Scott says she is none of your soft ones, but a right good manager. I fancy she'll be married when the time comes round. Every woman Ninian fancied was sure to be good looking, and that goes a good way with some men.'

'And the fourth?'

'Oh! poor thing she died with her first child. He was sorely downcast for a while, just as if he would go mad, but he got handfasted in three months to Elspeth Rutherford who was a widow woman and seemed greatly taken up with the bairn but they soon began to quarrel and parted. And then he took up with Jean Anderson who was more carried away with him, more wild and jealous about him than any of the others.'

'And this was his sixth and probably not the last?'

'He has set eyes on my Liliard,' said Hugh bitterly, 'and Madame Abercrombie, that ought to know better, does not discountenance him, and he hangs about at her house for the chance of seeing her, as well as puts himself forward as you saw yester evening whenever she is in public. When he tells his stories or strings his rhymes, for he has the gift of the gab, I'll not deny it, he tells them at her, and praises her up to the skies as his glowing Lily of Columba.'

'Is he richer than you,' asked I, 'that might make Madame Abercrombie favour him; at least mothers are accused of that in other places.'

'Well he may be. He has a good post under the Commonwealth and has bought town land after town land from them that are willing to sell. But I have a town land of my own that I think is the best in Columba of the new ground, and my father will leave me at least one of his that has been well done to for a hundred years, and my trade is the best paid one that is going here. When I am as old as Ninian, I'm like to be better off than him. And to do Madame justice, I don't think she is greedy of gear any more than Liliard is herself. It is ferlies and wonders that carry the day with Liliard. But to hear the outside world from you may put Ninian's pipe out with her.'

'It cannot be family, for certainly he appears to have no family to boast of, and folk of the old Scotch blood think much of descent.'

'No, it is not that surely; it is his quick eager ways and his determination. I may be slow, but I am sure, and as determined as he is, especially where Liliard is concerned.'

'You have no fear of what he may do in your absence.'

'No, for Liliard says she will not leave the house, and it is not the custom to come to a man's house to woo his bride. And I have faith in Liliard at all times, though if there were a bairn or the prospect of a bairn, I'd feel my mind much easier. When bridegroom and bairn pull one way, there's few women can stand against it.'

That appeared to me to be true and I could not deny that the handsome sensible affectionate young man, who was on his trial, had every right to Liliard's undivided heart.

IX

A COLUMBAN SATURDAY NIGHT

The camera, the sleeping bag and the heavy portmanteau were found where I had left them, and we retraced our steps heavier by that baggage, but lightened as to the carriage of provisions. We made very long days for our journey both ways, as we wanted to be home for Sunday. I cannot tell which of the two was the most eager, Hugh to return to the home and the Plantation which he was familiar with, or myself to return to the Plantation where everything was new and strange. Mindful of the necessity for my return I planted a sort of flagstaff at the camping place, and watched the bearings carefully.

'Next time you travel you will be alone,' said my kinsman.

'So I fancy,' said I, 'for you Columbans seem great home-lovers and not possessed of an adventurous spirit.'

'We have a proverb here; maybe you've not got it. "Let well alone" and I must say there is not much tempting here,' said Hugh. 'How or why should your half-Indian guide have led you through such desolation as this? If he had meant robbery from the first as is most likely why should he not have done it earlier.'

'He certainly had as much opportunity on any night. Perhaps it was a sudden temptation or a temptation which took all this time of our journey to gather strength.'

It was early on Wednesday morning when we set out and it was

Saturday evening when we returned. The journey was not so rugged and did not appear half so long with Hugh's good company and with the certainty as to our route. Hugh had solaced himself with a sort of rude flute which he played badly enough at intervals on the way, and we had the best of Columban tobacco in the shape of pipelets which Liliard had prepared on the evening after our excursion to Ebenezer and supplied us with for the journey. One long shrill whistle from Hugh gave warning of our approach, and Liliard ran to meet us with overflowing joy.

'So you've come back; you've both come back,' said she taking from her bridegroom's hands the portmanteau and from mine the sleeping bag as if eager to give some help for the short remaining distance. 'I've cooked you a good supper though I feared you would not come so soon, if you came at all.'

'How should you doubt our coming back?' asked Hugh. 'Did you think I was tired of you, and wanted to leave you to Ninian.'

'No, but then when you got into the world, I feared that it would look so grand and so wonderful, that you would never demean yourself to be shut in here.'

'Tut, nonsense Lil, outside there is the same sky with the same sun in it by day, and the same moon and stars in it by night, but as for the land, it is not to be mentioned in the same month as ours. Land that would take ten acres to keep a sheep – nay twenty – without a hill or a tree or a sheltering bush, and nothing but stones to stumble over and tussocks of grass that would need to halloo to each other to have any sort of intercourse, is no way tempting to me, let alone that everything and everybody I care for is in this, that our kinsman Victor calls the "Happy Valley".'

'Do you indeed?' said she. 'I thought you would not come back, for it is so little and so backward, but you promised; I should have kept mind that you promised.'

'We must have a wash in the pool together before supper,' said Hugh, 'for four days' travel and long days too has not improved our looks or our comfort, so let us leave our belongings and refresh ourselves with fair water and clean clothing.'

Liliard gave her husband what he wanted and offered me a change from his stock, but I had what I needed in my valise. Supper was a cheerful meal, to which we all did justice and when we sat under the verandah in the evening our hostess joined us, and she too took a pipelet, and joined our peaceful smoke. She did not do this often, as I afterwards discovered, but she was so happy over our successful expedition and our safe return, that she said she needed quietening, and this would help towards it. This was a thing that my grandmother could not abide, and against which I myself had a strong prejudice, but nothing that Liliard ever did appeared to me unbecoming to her. As we sat talking, and to tell the truth, I had the largest share with Liliard, as I had the lesser share with Hugh, for her curiosity was even more eager as to the things outside the valley than mine as to the things within it, Madame Abercrombie came accompanied by Ninian, to inquire if we had returned and to make further acquaintance with the new inmate whom the Council had billeted on the family for a month. They did not enter the house; Hugh did not invite them and etiquette required an invitation, but they sat down on a bench beside us.

'Two Hugh Keiths, Liliard, you will be well watched now. This is bad news for Ninian here,' said Madame Abercrombie, half in earnest and half in joke.

'Let them do their best and their worst; I'm a match for both of them,' said Ninian.

'Marjorie Elliot and Jean Anderson would say that you have been a match for six women, and you may well be a match for two men,' said Hugh.

'And how are we to distinguish you? There's very little mastering goes on among us for young men, so we'll call the stranger Mr Hugh, and you Hughie as of old,' said Madame Abercrombie.

'Pray call me by my second name Victor, Madame,' said I. 'My cousin does so already and I hope that his wife will do so too and her friends.'

'Not his wife yet,' said Ninian. 'Only Liliard Abercrombie.'

'So much my wife,' said Hugh, 'that I will have no one courting her either inside or outside my own door.'

'Hugh is quite right,' said Liliard quietly. 'Mother should have brought one of our own family here tonight and not you, for you have no discretion, Ninian, and no good manners. I'm sure you ought to know that Hugh's little finger is dearer to me than your whole hand.'

'I never knew it before, Liliard! Thank you for your plain speaking,' and he turned on his heel and went his way.

'I wonder at you, Mother,' said Liliard with some emotion, 'starting him off when you know his temper with the idea that I am watched. I need no watching as you may see for yourself.'

Madame Abercrombie excused herself by saying that she was on her way alone, as the young folks were both out, when Ninian fastened himself on her and would accompany her. She tried to enter into easy conversation with me, and singularly enough, at least quite contrary to my expectation, I found her to be a clever and original woman. As I came to know her better although I did not at all share her good opinion of the half-Indian Ninian, I learned to understand her dissatisfaction with her daughter's first tentative choice.

In spite of Ninian's varied experience, in spite of his six handfastings, she fancied that some qualities in him would make him more likely to satisfy her Liliard's heart and imagination than Hugh Keith. She had discouraged the handfasting, which had been conceded to his devotion and his pertinacity. She had no fault to find with the good, steady, affectionate fellow, but that he was too young to be Liliard's master, and not of sufficient superiority to be her guide. She would be happier with a man who was less perfect, but more interesting, and Ninian's skill in improvisation, which his many handfastings had given him great opportunity of practising, had always had much fascination for Liliard. It was not till she had been handfasted to Hugh, and thus in a fair way to be altogether out of the range of his choice, that Ninian had fixed his wavering fancy in a manner which Madame thought quite other from any of his previous experiences on her beautiful and brilliant child.

Indeed her beauty and her brilliancy had never appeared so great in the days of her maidenhood. Although there was little or no repression in this simple society for people of both sexes, and certainly nothing like the vigilance of French parents over their unmarried girls, there could be no question that with the handfasting there was a distinct step taken towards liberty of speech and action. It was a 'coming out', as the English would say; it was equal in its scope and boldness to marriage in France, though as it was not preceded by conventual seclusion or watchful chaperonage, and was not irrevocable, it was infinitely less dangerous. I had myself more than once seen the girl who was thought nothing of either for beauty or wit apparently so transformed by a happy or even by a brilliant marriage, as to make men who might have been suitors, wonder why they had not seen the promise or the actual presence of these qualities. So that as I listened on this evening and on many succeeding occasions to Madame Abercrombie's talk I gathered a good deal of information indirectly as well as directly from it.

As in most cases at least at first there is one who loves and another who is loved, the cheek was there for Hugh's kiss, but it was not offered to receive it. Hugh had ardently loved his bride and though he had swerved for a while, he returned to his courtship with redoubled ardour, and she not having then seen anyone whom she liked better, had consented to the handfasting which she considered as we in ordinary English and colonial society do an engagement, which it might be painful and not altogether creditable to break, but which ought to be broken off if the feelings changed. With most people, especially with most women, love both as a passion and as a sentiment increases after the perfect union of interests in a fairly well-assorted marriage. Her respect for her husband, and that deep and anxious, because not absolutely secure, love he felt for her, would in ordinary circumstances, have been a sort of guarantee that the half-ring would be exchanged for a whole one. But Madame Abercrombie thought Ninian had never had a fair chance to settle. She saw deficiencies in every one of the brides he had chosen, in temper, ability or sincerity, which quite warranted his fickleness, but now when he was old enough to appreciate Liliard's beauty, spirit and genius she would have a pride in making a man of him. Whereas Hugh Keith could neither be made or marred by any woman. He was safe to do right and to be respected whoever took him in hand.

It rather jarred on me that Liliard could allow such bold speeches to be made to her by this questionable interloper, and that her mother took many opportunities, though generally out of Hugh's hearing, to speak in Ninian's favour, but it appeared to be the custom of the country. As I said to myself, it was only like an engagement with us, a thing which in fact and in fiction, public opinion is against enforcing if there is any change of feeling. The very stir made by the Woman's Rights advocates against the law for recovering damages for breach of promise of marriage, shows that those who think most of women's claims, prefer that she should often submit to serious injury to prospects as well as to feelings rather than that she should take any step towards the enforcing the fulfilment of a promise which only continued mutual affection can sanctify.

Why was it that Liliard's declaration that she loved Hugh's little finger better than his rival's whole hand, while it satisfied my sense of fitness, nevertheless gave me some pain? What was Liliard Abercrombie to me that this natural expression of regard to her affectionate bridegroom should somehow give me a shock? Or was it that it was not a strong enough expression to denote absolute love? If the heart of such a woman as this had been really stirred, she would have made use of a more forcible metaphor and expressed it, not calmly as she did, but passionately and indignantly. Ninian's departure though in dudgeon, was not at all in despair. Are not clever women often attracted to a man of varied experience and of faulty character out of curiosity and generosity – and was not Liliard Abercrombie just such a woman?

'Have you not any books in your packings,' asked Liliard, 'new books that we have never seen nor heard tell of?'

'Only some half dozen,' said I. 'I wish for your sake that I had more, but where one can buy new books at every railway-stall, one does not care to carry many from place to place.'

'Ah! are they really so easily got all over the world?' said Liliard with a sigh. 'I should like to see some books; even half a dozen would give me great delight.'

'Have you any Scotch books,' asked Madame Abercrombie. 'There is only *The Gentle Shepherd* and some ballads in the real tongue that we speak, among all the books that we have in the Town House.'

'Yes! I have *Poems, chiefly in the Scottish dialect* written by Robert Burns, but not new; they were published about the time my grandmother was born, and she knows the most of them by heart.'

'Do you?' asked Liliard. 'I should like to hear some of them.'

'No, only scraps here and there cling to my memory which is not like yours. Let me have a light and I'll read you what I like best which ought to be very appropriate to the time and place – 'The Cotter's Saturday Night' – Liliard lighted a lamp and put it into the window at my back and I read the poem through.

'That's better – far better than *The Gentle Shepherd*,' said Liliard. 'Ah, there's a depth and a pathos in that that goes to my heart, and I like to hear you speak more like oursels. "But now your weary toil is at an end" and after all this tramping I'm sure you'll be fain to get into your bed. I'll go with Hugh to see mother home if he's not overtired.'

'Tired?' said Hugh. 'What has there been to tire me in four days' tramp in the best of company? But Victor is scarce used to the country, and had days of it before.'

So while the young pair escorted the older lady home, I turned into bed and forgot my fatigues and anxieties in a long deep sweet sleep.

X

A COLUMBAN SUNDAY

Sunday morning in Columba broke bright and warm as was to be expected in those latitudes in May, but the sun was pretty high in the heavens before my kinsman called on me to rise. 'Liliard and me have had breakfast hours syne, but we would not rouse you, only I fancy you'll like to be in time for the Kirk.'

'Of course I would,' and I dressed in haste putting on a white shirt in honour of the day and occasion.

'Your things look finer every way than ours,' said my host, 'though I cannot say I like the fashion and the cut of them. What bow-legged man invented these long breeches and short stockings, and who could work with things stiffened and glazed about the neck and wrists. You'll get the starch out in the dancing this afternoon I'll warrant.'

'I've done that in Melbourne before now many a time but we dance in great rooms by lamp or rather gaslight, and never on a Sunday.'

'Well, every place has its own ways, and ours suit ourselves,' said my host who noted my clothing from the guernsey to the pocket handkerchief with the eye of one who knew the quality and value of his country's own produce.

'Victor Keith has finer knitting than you can do, on his clothes,' said he, 'and finer spinning and weaving, Liliard, and finer sewing too, than you put on mine.'

'But there is no handwork on it at all,' said I. 'The woollen cloth and cotton and linen is spun and woven by machinery, the socks and undershirt knitted by machinery, and the shirt and clothes put together by sewing machine. The steam engines in Great Britain alone can do as much work as all the inhabitants of the known world could do by hand.'

'Oh that must save labour in all directions, but can that be good for the poor folk that live by their work? What do your people find to do when all these things are taken out of their hands? I could fancy this machinery, as you call it, would be a good thing for us with so few folk. But where you count your hungry population by millions, one is sorry to have the work taken from them.'

'That is the very reason. These millions must be fed, clothed and all their wants provided for at the very least cost of labour.'

'Well, that is very puzzling,' said Liliard. 'I must try to understand it.'

'You tell us,' said Hugh, 'that there are three times the folk in the old country that there was when our forebears left it, forbye them that have gone to the ends of the earth like you. How can they all live in such a narrow space?'

'They live mostly on coal and iron,' said I.

'Hard fare I'm thinking; they cannot surely eat these things.'

'No, but they make such goods as go out of the country and they buy food of various kinds with the price of them. They get wheat from Russia, from America and even from Australia and New Zealand. I don't think the last was found out when your people left but it is as near half round the world as may be.'

'Wheat, said ye? Wheat from so far? It took our folk about three months to get here stopping at Virginia and Jamaica. It would take a year to travel with wheat from such as faraway part of the world.'

'No, not a quarter of it if you go by steamships.'

'Steam, steam, steam,' said Hugh. 'I fancy you must be for ever in hot water in your country if the sailing and the casting and the spinning and the weaving and the sewing no doubt is done by that. There will be blistered hands no doubt if folk have to wait upon steam as you say they have, just to see that it works aright.'

Liliard examined my wristband, and I turned it up to show the elastic thin guernsey below. 'It's all too wonderful,' she said. 'I'd like to get the spinning done any way for that is a terrible taker up of good time.'

'Liliard likes things that she can put out of hand fast,' said Hugh. 'She has not got my patience and solidity.'

'Nay,' said Liliard 'your work has change in it; it is now a hoe, now a plough, now a knife, that you make.'

'And now and then a spoon,' said Hugh smiling to me. 'But the spinning is a never ending thing, hour after hour the same, every yard like another.'

'Now,' said she when I had finished my breakfast, 'we shut up the house for the day. Jenny goes to her own folk, and we take our dinner with Hugh's father and my mother Sunday about, and this is mother's day. Everybody that has friends in the town goes to them or carried something to eat under the trees in the green – for it is overmuch fatigue to travel back and forth again.'

I took note of the people who went to the Kirk, and as we were early and stood by the door, I was well stared at as a foreigner. My differently fashioned clothes and boots, my white shirtfront, my watch and chain with its bunch of charms hanging to it, and the report that had spread in our absence that I could do many wonderful things, and that I though a stranger and an alien was to serve the Commonwealth as only the deserted children were allowed to do, made me a mark for general observation.

On the whole they all looked very well in their Sunday clothes, darker as a rule by two or three shades than a Lowland congregation in Scotland, slighter of build, and quicker of movement and with a great deal more gesture and effusion in manner. There was little or none of the stolidity of the Scottish peasant about old or young. The education which had been all addressed to the memory, had certainly made them more attentive. They were from childhood trained to listen; I expected to see a much more attentive congregation than that of an average county town parish in Scotland, and I was not disappointed.

But I wondered above all things what sort of doctrine should be preached. If the course of 155 years had so altered some so-called presbyterian dogmas so much, in spite of subscription to confessions and creeds, that we heard in the Scots Church in Collins Street the most uncalvinistic and unorthodox sermons and prayers, what would be the extent of the falling away of this easy-going people in a tropical climate without any Church standards at all? The first noticeable variation from public worship as I had joined in it was that till now I had never before seen a congregation absolutely without books; prayerbooks, Bibles and hymn books were associated with Church and Chapel all over the world; though no doubt in the dark ages there were none and in missionary work at first there must be none.

The next striking departure from all previous experience was that all the service was in the vernacular. Even the English Bible was pronounced as to the vowel in the Scottish manner, as it had developed on Columban tongues. There being no English nation at hand to fix the pronunciation of the literary language, it took its natural form. But not only was the congregation without books, the preacher also trusted to his memory and to his extempore powers of speech. The few Bibles that had been brought would have been worn out in the course of five or six generations of pulpit handling, and as yet there had been few fresh copies written out - at least complete ones - though as a test of fitness for the sacred office, each probationer was made to write from memory one book of the New Testament and one of the Old on parchment.

So there was no book in the preacher's hand, not even a Bible or a hymn book. The hymn, which was quite new to me was given out verse by verse; it was a paraphrase of the 23rd psalm in the ordinary vernacular. The singing was exceedingly bad, but it was congregational. There was a precentor, a leader, but no trained choir and everyone sang, well or ill as the case might be.

Next came a prayer which was chiefly one of adoration and of thanksgiving for the many good and pleasant things the inhabitants of Columba enjoyed. Then came a recitation from the Scriptures – not exactly word for word – of the Creation from the first Chapter of Genesis.

Then followed a hymn for children in which they only took part. It was pretty with regard to the words, but the voices were shrill and not subdued by any stronger deeper notes.

Then the white-haired minister announced that George Hepburn and Jessie Rutherford sought to be handfasted on the morrow; that James Elliot and Helen Marr gave notice that their handfasting would be confirmed by marriage on the same day; and that John Scott and Violet Keith sought to break off their handfasting on the following Wednesday. The Monday was the regular day for the marriage and handfasting matters and the year and day of probation demanded that the breaking off or the ratifying of the contract should take place on the Wednesday.

After this there was a short prayer for all these couples that the coming together and the parting should be done reverently and in the fear of God.

Next came a simultaneous utterance of the Lord's Prayer, not the minister first and the people afterwards, making a sort of confused murmur, or sometimes something like a race, which to those unaccustomed to the service is anything but devotional, but absolutely true with short pauses between the versicles. There was an excuse for the repeating after the minister in the old days when no one could read, which does not hold with ordinary congregations now but here all knew the words and accompanied Master Hepburn. Then followed a sort of liturgy, a few words by the minister and something more by the congregation in which there was a petition for the dear land of our fathers, and them that rule over her and another, perhaps more fervent, for our native land of Columba, the Protector and all the constituted authorities.

Next came a recitation from the New Testament from which the minister took his text: 'The Sabbath was made for man and not man for the Sabbath.' He had been to see Liliard during our absence, and had heard from her of my astonishment at the use that was made of the Kirk and of the different ideas of the Sabbath which obtained in all English and Scottish communities.

He went back to the original idea of the Sabbath; he had no speculative doubts, nor had any member of his congregation as to the literal six days of creation, and he took the institution as intended to give that rest and refreshment after six days of continuous work, which the old story supposed to be needed, or at least to be desired by the Almighty Creator himself, and he traced down through the Jewish dispensation that rest from labour was the only thing needed. And that it was not till the time of the later prophets that the idea of the exclusive devotion of the day to religious exercises had taken hold of the Jewish people. Here in Columba the people divided it into a half day of worship, and a half day of enjoyment and the holiday was no weariness.

He quoted from an old father of the Church, Tertullian, whom I had often heard quoted on widely different ground, that Christians could indulge in any sort of amusement that they could pray after and this, though it fatally cut at such fights of gladiators and of wild beasts with criminals and Christians, as were the favourite amusements of the populace when he wrote, had no deterring influence upon the storytelling and the playacting, the dances and the songs of the people of Columba. 'These,' he said, 'we ask the Father of the families of the whole earth to sanctify with His blessing in the same way as we ask that blessing on the food we eat, and the partnerships and the unions we enter into. We not only pray after but we pray before our innocent amusements, and therefore whether in the Kirk or out of it we never lose the sense of His presence or the desire for His approval.'

He said moreover that many of the Christian churches all over the old world, as had been told to them of Columba in the old days by their greatly honoured sister Margaret Keith who was to them as a veritable mother in Israel, had held to this use of Sunday, and therefore wherever our Christian liberty was called in question, we had both precedent for it in the past, and expediency in the present to back us. The Sabbath, or the Sunday after all was not so different from other days. On every day of the week, we could worship God and serve our fellows. To work has been accounted as good as to pray by many sainted men and women of old, only it was well that in resting we should all rest together, in worshipping that we should have fellowship in devotion, and in our rejoicing and merrymaking that no one should be shut out.

The sermon was of the length of three-quarters of an hour, which in other places would have appeared to me to be over-long, but it was full of movement, of illustration, and anecdote, and even showed considerable exegetical skill. He did not move about so much as Liliard did in her stirring story, but there was much of the art of the actor to aid his eloquence. The practice in a long life of always speaking extempore, and trusting altogether to his memory and invention, had made this venerable man a perfect master of oratory. He described such a Sabbath as might have been held in the manse of Colbrandspath in the main very correctly, and with a considerable amount of scorn for people who thought this serving God. He described on the other hand a Sunday without worship as a grievous mistake and enjoyment without thought of God or man as bestial or devilish.

There was little or no weariness among the listeners, even the little children appeared trained to good behaviour. We stood in prayer and in praise also. The preacher at the close of the sermon gave a benediction, and the congregation dispersed but he joined us in the street. He was dining with his own family, and therefore declined the warm invitation of Madame Abercrombie to come with us, but he promised to meet us at the green in the afternoon.

'Your Kirk is large and has plenty of fresh air,' said I.

'It is a bonny building,' said Madame Abercrombie. 'It was not the first that was put up. St Andrew's in Ebenezer was the earliest, and they say the old folk wept for joy when they first worshipped in it. But that has been built over and over again for it gets over small. This of St Matthew's was put up when I was married, and the old Kirk turned into a school.'

'Do your sunbaked bricks last long? I hear they do in Egypt but there is little or no rain, and here you have much.'

'The good roof and broad eaves save the walls, and you see the lower portion is all cemented,' said my kinsman Hugh.

'Here you see there is no Kirk-yard,' said Madame Abercrombie. 'That the old folks say was always round the Kirks.'

'I saw the grave of our common ancestor Marguerite Keith at Ebenezer,' said I.

'They say she was the grandest and the fairest woman that came out with the party,' said Liliard, 'as well as the kindest and the best.'

'We may hold our heads high,' said Madame Abercrombie, 'for we are all in a straight line from the first leaders of the adventure, who brought the most goods and gear, but one man is as good as another in this country. At Kirk and at market, at dance and at funeral, in the Town Council and the Common Council, there is no difference made. Liliard there will be dancing with her maiden Jenny's brother if he asks her.'

'And a capital dancer he is too,' said Liliard, 'but I hope to dance with our cousin Victor too. I'm thinking you can dance.'

'Perhaps not your dances,' said I. 'Have you the old reels and strathspeys and jigs – or is it the minuet that you like best?'

'We've new dances forbye that we found out oursels. There is the courant, that is like running, and the chase, that is like pursuing, and some that are like the Indian war dances, only not so fierce. But you'll learn them in time, if you are a taught dancer at all. We have dances here all the evenings that there is nothing on in the Kirk and every Sunday afternoon.'

'Who is the Violet Keith whose handfasting is to be broken off?' said I addressing my kinsman. 'Is she a near relation of ours?'

'No, only a fourth cousin,' said Hugh. 'Her bridegroom is a nearer relation, though he has another name.'

'And what is the cause of separation?' I asked.

'Violet has not had a day's health since she was handfasted,' said Madame Abercrombie.

'That is not a common thing I suppose,' said I, 'and is that her only reason?'

'Well it is the only one she gives out; she says it would be hard for John Scott to be tied to a sickly wife all his days. She'll not be out, nor him either this day. It is not considered fitting for folk that have been "cried" in the Kirk on any sort of footing to be either at the worship or the dance.'

'Do people ever go back to their old loves?' I asked. 'After trying one or two others, do they not, sometimes find that the first love was the best?'

'Oh yes,' said Madame Abercrombie, 'there is an example just before you in Richard Hepburn and his wife aforetime May John; Richard tried another, but he was glad to tie the bond for life with her again.'

We did not take long to reach the house though it was a little way from the town, and Madame Abercrombie gave us an excellent dinner. I may have tasted finer meat, and meat more elaborately cooked than I got in Columba, but in the matter of vegetables and soups, I think they were the most consummate cooks I ever saw. I had to learn the names of many, and the properties of most of the vegetables we ate. In the line of puddings, they made a great many preparations of milk and eggs and farinaceous food which were both quite new and excellent. The cheese was indifferent and the butter only good when freshly churned. We had a dessert of the earliest fruit which ripened then, a sort of wild berry which had been cultivated, and a fruit resembling the loquat, only pink in colour instead of yellow. As sugar was abundant, the Columbans were also great in preserves of all kinds. They did not refine their sugar to any degree of whiteness; it was brown but very bright.

There was indeed a great gathering at the green. There were

benches, as I have said, three tiers round under the outside shade of the trees, and within the benches groups danced in the afternoon under the inside shade, though as the sun declined, they moved towards the centre. On a platform in the centre, thatched overhead, sat the orchestra, which had both stringed and wind instruments, and was powerful enough to be heard all over the place. But the music was like all the Columba music, very bad, except with regard to time, which was strongly marked. It had all a Scotch style; the melodies whether from original defects of instruments or not, had the same curious intervals which make people say that Scotch tunes can be all played on the black keys of the piano, but there was no idea of concerted music.

The band played together that they might play loud enough to be heard, and marked time by ear without the baton of the conductor; indeed the simple character of the instrumentation made this unnecessary. No doubt many new tunes had been discovered, but there was a great sameness in their character. But the dancing was wonderfully fine, full of variety, full of spirit and full of grace. There was none of the close quarters of the modern ballroom; the partners occasionally took hands, or one put a hand on a shoulder or a pair took hold, hand to elbow, but there was no hand round a waist. Under the trees also danced the children in groups by themselves, and one could see how the whole people had been trained to grace of motion and rhythmic step from their earliest years. Mingling with and overlooking the children were a few grown-up people of both sexes who apparently were the teachers, with the Columban badge on the arm, but there were also their parents watching their movements and grandparents and great-grandparents, all apparently taking delight in their skill and their mirth. Here too was the headquarters of gossip where all the news of the week might be discussed, and no doubt I had a very large share in the subjects of conversation for that Sunday.

The dance was begun like the storytelling with a short prayer for God's blessing, and the old minister who had taken his wife's name of Hepburn, moved from group to group of sitters to talk to each in turn, but he had his most permanent place beside me. His eagerness to learn what had been done and written and thought in the great world outside, was only less than Liliard's, while his curiosity as to what I thought of Columba and its people and its ways was as great as Hugh's. He was not so self-complacent as to all things being the best possible, though he shook his head as to the practicability of any suggestions I might make as to a change. But to me the assemblage of old and young for pleasure on this Sunday afternoon was the most striking thing that I had ever seen anywhere. It was not as on the continent, a thing permitted and winked at by the church, but one countenanced and hallowed. The minister seemed as much in his place there as in pulpit or rather platform, and I heard grave words of consolation fall from his lips to a bereaved mother whose surviving children had tempted her out and to a poor cripple who could no longer join in the dance, but who still liked to look on, and share in all the sociability of the scene.

I was not allowed to remain a quiet though a deeply interested spectator, for I was called on to dance and acquitted myself fairly enough in a reel with Liliard, Hugh and her young sister. There was more figure and more variety in this dance than I had seen either in Scotland or elsewhere. But my attempts at the courant and the chase were but lame affairs, though, as Hugh said I had no lack of ear or agility, so perhaps I would be able to manage it in time.

In this Republican gathering, I saw Hugh take a dance with his maiden Jenny, who was not a little proud of his notice, and looked over her shoulder at a youthful swain who evidently was somewhat smitten with the fair-haired girl of sixteen. And on the other hand Jenny's brother Peter Borthwick had a courant with Liliard, and as she said, he danced very well indeed.

The twilight shades deepened, but the full moon rose, and the dancers continued to foot it till half past eight o'clock when the minister dismissed them with a blessing, and I walked home with my host and hostess in the pleasant freshness and coolness of an early summer evening in these lovely latitudes. All sorts of flowering trees and shrubs sent out double fragrance; the wind swept over the beautiful cotton plantations in full flower, and I could not help thinking that Johnson's conception of the Happy Valley of *Rasselas* was poor in comparison with this, where toil sweetened pleasure, and where all ranks and conditions of the inhabitants met at Church and market, at polling-booth and at dance on a footing of equality.

XI

I FIND A NEW SIDE OF THE INTELLECTUAL PROBLEM

I had said to my grandmother that I had hitherto been too much occupied to have time or inclination to fall in love with any woman, however desirable she might appear to my friends and acquaintance to be. If business and hard work were to protect me from falling in love, I certainly had enough of them now. Not even when studying hard for my degree in Edinburgh, or when taking my father's whole practice in his absence, had I ever had so busy a life as I had now. I was asked to be at the Town House from ten to three to teach the doctors and nurses of the plantation all that I knew, but I found that this would not suit my other engagements, and I obtained the concession that they should come to me at certain hours. I rigged up a photographic studio, a sort of tent, and in this I gave lessons to them three days in the week; the other three days I travelled about as a consulting surgeon and doctor with the Columban practitioners to show the new methods. I analysed the medicines in use, mostly preparations of herbs and other vegetable products, and found that they had discovered healing qualities of considerable value.

Their worst foe was fever and ague, and they had not the cinchona tree, from which quinine is prepared. However, I had been provided by my good friend Baron Müller with a liberal supply of the seed of the eucalyptus or blue gum, which has been found so valuable in similar climates, and this was sown in places where there was most marshy land and vegetable malaria.

The beautiful cleanliness of the beds on which sick people lay, and the thorough ventilation of even the poorest houses pleased me much and did much towards cure. They had also discovered the healing qualities of cold water. In surgery however they were very backward, and the antiseptic cure was quite unknown, though their bandaging was very dexterous. There was no school of anatomy, and the dissection of dead bodies was not studied any more than the vivisection of living animals; but the faculty of Columba took my word for many facts which I had ascertained, and were willing to act on my suggestions. There were of course one or two exceptions among the older members of the profession, but the weight of the majority strengthened my hands. The female nurses as well as the female teachers were a shifting body, for after marriage they generally left the business, and were absorbed in household cares, though during handfasting, it was common for them to continue in the line of life to which it was possible that they might return. The career of the men who were the preachers, the teachers, the doctors, the civil servants and the musicians of Columba, was fixed for life. Their payment for their services was not in any way extravagant – only the average income of a small farmer; there was no difference made in the rate, except for length of service, there was a small increase every five years except in the case of the heads of departments, who were supposed to be advanced by merit and not by seniority. I was engaged at a sum that measured in gold was ridiculously small but in silver handsome enough, being three times that of a civil servant of twenty years' service.

If my rascally half-breed had not stolen my purse with my gold eagles in it, I might have figured as a man of some wealth but I landed in the secluded community absolutely penniless and had to work for my living. I could however make a handsome income through my other profession of photography, and the early morning hours and some of the afternoon were given to this. Owing to the limited quantity of chemicals, and especially of prepared paper which I had, I could not undertake to supply cartes or cabinet portraits by the dozen, for a population of twenty-five thousand, all eager for the immortality of a photographic likeness for although this simple people were singularly inartistic, they could appreciate the imitative though not the decorative arts. The sun-pictures were so essentially reproductions of what they saw that they recognised them, though at first with some hesitation.

Hugh and Liliard helped me to rig up my photographic studio of the thick brown calico which was made for threshing some of their most valuable seed crops on, on the very first Monday of my stay, and my first attempt was a likeness of Liliard herself and of my kinsman. I think their first impression was more of surprise than delight, but Liliard gradually took in the exact points of resemblance, and more slowly appreciated the effects of light and shade. Hugh, like Queen Elizabeth, would have liked to take away those black things, the shadows, which he said were not to be seen either in his bride's face or his own. I showed them in the little locket which I wore the coloured likeness of my mother in her youth, and of my grandmother in her old age. They liked the colouring, though at first Liliard was bewildered by the exceedingly small scale of the pictures, but when I showed the effect of a magnifying glass on them, she continued to gaze with increasing satisfaction.

Hugh was far more interested in the magnifying glass and its effects than in the object under it, and indeed all along cared more about understanding the process than the result. It was an art that he might learn to excel in himself, and he therefore was eager to be allowed to help me, and when I considered how little scope there was for ambition for the average Columban citizen, I did not at all wonder at this desire. I felt I could repay his hospitality by teaching him the whole process and presenting him with the apparatus when I took my leave of the Happy Valley.

When I took out a little bundle of unmounted views which I had taken of the country through which I had passed, forests, mountains, rivers and lakes, Hugh said, 'What made you take all this trouble for the like of these?'

'Because they are beautiful.'

'Are they?' said Liliard thoughtfully, as she continued to look at them.

'Don't you think so?'

'Indeed I've never wasted a thought on the matter,' said Hugh. 'I don't wonder at your liking to have a sort of picture of the folk you care about, especially if they are far away, and the thing is wondrous clever – to get the sun to do the work and you only to wait on him – but what good can there be in making pictures of the like of trees?'

'I wanted to keep in mind the look of the country I have travelled over and to show it to my people when I got home again, and I think these views very beautiful.'

'Maybe they are,' said Liliard slowly. 'I whiles feel my heart swell when I look at the hills where they touch the blue sky and the part in the Plantation that has not been settled by our folk, and left just as God made it, with the great woods and the trailing plants and the feathery ferns and the undergrowth of flowers and grass and brushwood, I'm thinking would please you much. When you make a picture of that, keep mind to stamp off one for me'.

I had a few views in my little portfolio which pleased Hugh and interested even Liliard more than the landscapes. Edinburgh the traditionary capital of their forefathers, Melbourne the modern growth of little more than a generation, and San Francisco the very latest metropolis I had visited, furnished great food for inquiry and explanation. The houses so close and tall and handsome; the churches with their lofty spires; the public buildings, and above all the photograph of the Palace Hotel in San Francisco where I had spent a few days, which looked as if it would hold the population of the whole town land at New Berwick, astonished them both.

'And this you say is a new place like your own Melbourne,' said Liliard, 'only some forty years won from the desert and the savage, and us with a hundred and thirty-five years to work in what have we done to compare to this?'

'All the difference was made by the constant and close contact of the newer colonies with all the civilisation and progress of the world.'

'Oh! why have we kept apart then?' said Liliard a little impatiently.

'If we had not,' said Hugh, 'we would not have had our own ways.'

'Your isolated handful of Scottish settlers,' said I, 'had everything to discover, and everything to modify for themselves, and in many respects they have discovered wonderful things, and wonderful modifications.'

'Surely what we think out for ourselves must be better for us than what we just copy from other people,' said Hugh.

'The discoveries of the old world have been forced on it through the necessities of crowding millions,' said I. 'The new ways of Columba have been brought through the desire for the well-being of every individual in the community.'

As we were looking over the photographs in the tent, Ninian approached, bringing a brace of birds shot in the old forest which he presented to me with considerable natural grace and with a request that I would try my gun with his, some day. His eye, quick as that of a savage, at once fixed on the likeness of the woman he was courting, and he despised it as inadequate, and objected more to the black shades than Hugh had done. Taking up a piece of charcoal, he drew on the calico walls of the tent, what he considered a better likeness of Liliard Abercrombie and, although altogether unskilled, the first attempt showed considerable spirit. Not only was he himself surprised at this success, but Hugh looked a little crestfallen at the display of this new accomplishment on the part of his rival. Liliard, however, saw more in the sun-picture when it was contrasted with the charcoal sketch. I offered to take Ninian's own likeness if he thought it worth having, and although but the minute before he had made disparaging remarks as to the whole concern, he now eagerly accepted the offer. He composed himself to such rigidity of attitude and expression that the usual cautions to sitters were quite unnecessary. Of course the effect of this was that he looked much more like one of his own ancestors nerved for the torture or the stake, than like the mobile, versatile creature he was. The Indian characteristics came out strong in every way, but he had not got such an exaggerated opinion of his own person as he had of Liliard's, and he acknowledged the accuracy of the likeness.

Hugh almost entirely left off his bronze work, and engaged an assistant for it in order to help me with my photographs, and he inquired carefully as to the constituents of my chemicals so as to be able to imitate them and increase the supply. Paper was not in the colony or cardboard, but the pictures were mounted on thin pieces of wood or sometimes on calico. With very little instruction, Liliard learned to mount the photographs very nicely, and she even suggested the substitution of calico for paper for the proofs. Spinning and even knitting was neglected, and Jenny was left to her own devices in the way of cooking, while her young mistress busied herself from morning till night in assisting her bridegroom and myself in this fascinating work. Of course I could seldom keep any negative, only those which I most highly valued such as the likeness of my host and hostess, Ninian and the old Master Hepburn, who next to Liliard interested me most.

Thus all three working together for several hours every day with so much of the work mechanical that it allowed great scope for conversation, I learned ere long that it was not as an outside problem that I regarded the result of my kinsman's handfasting, that it was not how it would affect Ninian and his latest bride Jean Anderson, who felt sure that if he had no hope of Liliard, he would go back to his love for her, but as it affected myself. It was no mere intellectual riddle as to the wonderful development of genius in new and strange conditions, nor as to how what I had thought and observed would strike a mind so strong so receptive and so just; it was the happiness of my whole life that was on the cast of the die. Yes, the electric current had touched at last the capacities for affection and passion which hitherto had lain dormant in my soul; the great reservoir of love which had hung idly overhead like the clouds in an Australian summer sky, and had hovered now over this woman and then over that woman, had at last been set free. When all sorts of recommendations and suitabilities had had no effect, here in a strange land among strange people with strange ways, my every pulse was thrilled and my whole nature transformed by the image of Liliard Abercrombie, handfasted for only two more months to my confiding kinsman, Hugh Keith.

My grandmother's prediction seemed to be fulfilled to the letter even beyond the letter. Here was a woman who had never seen a drawingroom or worn a bonnet or a pair of gloves in her life, who did not know a note of music, who could not distinguish between a water-colour and an oil painting who could not draw, could not sing, could not write a polite note, nay who did not even know her letters, and yet who, in the spirit of my grandmother's desire, was a worthy mate for the best gentleman in Christendom, for she had the charm of a true gentlewoman and the capacity, the intensity and the devotedness of the only woman of genius I had ever met with.

In the whirl of a newly-awakened passion working amongst altogether strange conditions, everything that I had seen, everything that I had heard, and everything that I had read on the subject of troth-plight of marriage and of divorce, presented itself to my memory with startling and painful distinctness. The vague ideas that I had entertained and even sometimes partially expressed, as to the necessity for some relaxation of the marriage laws in England, and especially in France, took dominating and distinct shape here and now. Freedom of contract had never seemed to me so just and fair in this momentous personal matter as it did now when I saw the singular elasticity up to a certain point of the Columban marriage laws, and the apparently satisfactory working of these laws among this simple and sincere people.

I said to myself over and over again that it was just like an engagement, and therefore no sin to woo Liliard; only my conscience smote me that it was dishonourable to sap the foundations of plighted troth when the sufferer was a host and a friend. In this instance, there had been long wooing and ten months of the common household companionship which ought to endear a good man to a good woman. Nevertheless all the difficulties, all the inconveniences, all the reproaches I might encounter, only made the winning of Liliard Abercrombie more absolutely imperative for my happiness.

XII

THREE FELLOW WORKERS

As the weather grew warmer, Liliard threw off the tight-fitting scarlet jersey which her bridegroom thought her most becoming attire and dressed in the commoner fashion of the country, the long tunic of cotton belted round the waist. There was no printed calico in the plantation, all the fabrics were dyed in the thread, so that there were only striped, checked and speckled stuff worn; the dye-stuffs were excellent but the designs were necessarily monotonous. Nor were there muslins worn at all; even the caps of the matrons were made of thick cotton, snow-white, and bordered with some sort of knitted edging like coarse lace. The men too wore cotton garments for six months in the year and took none of the precautions in the way of flannels which we are accustomed to think absolutely necessary in a tropical climate, except for a bandage below the waist. There were no sudden falls of temperature such as we have in the hotter season in Australia, and even a thorough wetting from a tropical shower did not seem to strike any chill.

I soon got into Columban clothes, which were cheap and strong and very comfortable, and as Hugh said, I looked not only more like other folk, but a far better-made man altogether in the garb of the country. Columban shoes, made by Hugh Keith's cousin William were the most comfortable things I ever had on my feet, as they followed the exact shape of the foot, and pinched me nowhere, and my first pair of long stockings had been knitted by Liliard's own hands. I asked her what story she had knitted into them, and she said only some fancies of her own of no account, which did not much interfere with the uniformity of the fabric. Home work was so universal for all sorts of things that when I proposed to give out my washing, there was no professional laundress to be found in Columba. Madame Keith at last discovered a woman who was glad to take it for money along with her own family washing.

In my various capacities, I became acquainted with a wonderfully large proportion of the twenty-five thousand inhabitants of Columba. From far and near they travelled for likenesses, and I travelled to the farthest limits of the settlement to visit the sick when there was any special call for my exceptional skill. Their own doctors and nurses give their services for nothing, but I was allowed to make a fixed charge, and had a horse or horses belonging to the public service at my command for journeys of any distance. But the demand for photographs, and the eagerness of my sitters to look their best, let me in to quite as much of the characteristics of the people as my visits to the sick and the dying.

One day as we were all together in the tent, Sister Dorothea and her daughter came with a request that I would take them together and with the elder woman I was very successful, though the younger was harder to take.

'Let Liliard tell a story and then I will look my best,' said the girl, when the first attempt had been pronounced a failure and Liliard with the help of her knitted record told them something of the history I had told her the first day of my arrival, of all that had happened while the Columbans were shut out. This had the desired effect, but the narrative did not cease when the likeness was taken and while I was engaged with other sitters, I could hear the voice that to me was music itself repeating my own version of the story of the world with here and there a remark of her own and here and there a question from one of her listeners.

When I was again at leisure, Sister Dorothea was gone. 'That is the woman I used to envy most of all,' said Liliard, 'before I knew how small is the place anyone can fill here.'

'Why did you envy her so much?'

'Because she could read and write, and teach and preach and pray and because she had one little girl all to herself; aye, and maybe because she had to fight hard to get her.'

'How so?' I asked.

'You see she broke off the handfasting, because she felt that she had another vocation, and she had ceased to feel that love for her bridegroom that could sanction marriage. So she had no right to the bonnie lassie she loved so dearly, and Neil Scott thought she would change her mind if he held to his rights. She offered to redeem the child with money, and for the first fifteen years she gave half of her substance for the privilege of keeping her and he took it. Now of course Grace chooses her mother.'

'Then Neil Scott was very fond of Sister Dorothea. She is a lovely woman, in my opinion; I don't wonder at her exciting strong affection.'

'Her face is just like Heaven,' said Liliard, 'but it was not just that entirely that made her bridegroom so eager to keep her, for Neil Scott is a good deal more for this world than for a better one. Sister Dorothea was just a wonderful clever girl at the schools, and was paid so much for it that Neil thought her worth keeping, for he was eager to lay field to field, and any wife that he might take that did not belong to the sisterhood, could only do the housework, the spinning and such like, that is all very good in its way but brings in no money.'

'He got the money out of her at any rate as it appears. But how could such a man captivate such a woman as Sister Dorothea?'

'Well, she was young you know and everybody here gets handfasted and married. The account you give of so many people living single all their lives I can partly understand, but I don't think there is many others of our folk that could. And Neil Scott has a very clever tongue in his head, and will not lose anything that he is set on for want of the asking. But I am sure Grace was all the dearer to her mother because she cost her so much.'

'What sort of terms is she on with her father?'

'Oh, civil enough. He is rather fond of her, especially as her mother had no name to give her, and she is forced to go by his.'

'If two of your children of the State get married what do they do for a surname?' said I.

'They have a right to choose one for themselves, but it must not be one that is in Columba before. It is generally picked out of the Bible or out of some other book. Matthew, Mark, Luke and John were the first favourites, but no name can be taken up twice, but there are not many of such marriages. You see there are two things these children have not got, a family name and the right to take out land, and I think they set more store on these things than they really are worth. There's Ninian, for instance; he is greedier of land than anyone of us, and he would give a good deal even of that for the right to call himself Ninian Graeme.'

'But is the hard-won possession of Grace the chief thing you envy in Sister Dorothea's lot?'

'Oh no – it is the work: the influence she has with old and young; the way she can advise and comfort. When she found out that she had no true mate in Neil Scott and felt that there was no one else to lose herself in, she had her work to go back to, and went to it all the stronger and the wiser and the tenderer for her experience, and may be for her mistake and her struggle. Don't you think that is likely?'

'Very likely. The preachers, perhaps like the poets we know, "are cradled into poetry by wrong, They learn in suffering what they teach in song" and the highest preacher may be perfected in the same way.'

'Now for me,' said Liliard, 'if I find out that my vocation is not marriage and I have often and often before my handfasting and after it too, had my doubts of it, what is there for me to go back to? Only to my mother's house to do the things that everybody else does better.'

'You would still have the storytelling and the acting. If you were in the world you might develop into an author.'

'An author! Think you so?' said Liliard with an eager flush of pleasure on her cheeks. 'What could I write that would give pleasure or that would give profit to a world full of books?'

'I can scarce tell what direction you might incline to, but I think you could write novels and poetry and even dramas.'

'I would need a wider sweep for my mind than I have here,' said she thoughtfully. 'Our folk most of them can make verses, but though they run smooth, they're not like the great poets of the world. The only thing I ever heard that could be placed beside them was a little piece of Sister Dorothea's.'

The same thing had struck me with regard to Columban poetry. It was perfectly beautiful in the way of nursery rhymes and the school rhymes were neat and terse. There were some pretty love songs, and a few connected with the domestic affections but as there was but little eye for natural beauties and little exciting in their history, as the picturesque contrasts between power and weakness, between innocence and crime, were all but unknown, the poetry was tame as the history was dull in this happy community.

'So you see,' resumed Liliard, 'that here in Columba there is nothing for a woman to do but get handfasted and married unless she has had the special training that Sister Dorothea had through the faults of her parents. And I am not clever at the things our ordinary folk do. I like this helping of Hugh and you because it is interesting, but yet I could fancy better things still – don't laugh at me, Victor.'

'I do not laugh at you,' said I; I had only smiled to think that the cleverest woman I ever saw in my life should consider it a promotion to be mounting photographs. 'I think there are much better things to be done.'

'But not to be done here,' said she with a sigh as she adjusted carefully the state picture, the particular one which I had engaged to do in consideration of my permission to practise the art; the Council Chamber with all the members in session for which there had been several sittings, and of which no less than twenty proofs were required.

Hugh was only sorry that they were such a set of maunies whom we were immortalising. This was a pure Columban word of which I could trace no derivation, but I think it corresponds in meaning with our Victorian word *duffers*, probably of mining origin. The forthcoming election would probably make an alteration for the better, and he hoped if I took a likeness that his own good father would fill the Protector's chair.

As he moved to and fro occasionally joining in our conversations but generally so much absorbed in his work as rarely to speak on subjects apart from it, there was never anything said between Liliard and myself to which he could take any exception. He had thoroughly accepted the idea that we belonged to different spheres, and that I was going to leave Columba for ever at the end of three months; and as he had visions of constructing a photographic apparatus for himself, and getting both profit and credit by it, he was very glad indeed that Liliard was so thoroughly interested in the process. Neither Ninian nor another aspirant who had shown unmistakeable signs of admiration, could offer her such a sphere of usefulness, or work that could give so much pleasure to everybody as well as to herself.

I often wondered that my kinsman's jealousy was not aroused to the sense that his half-wife was more to me than all the world. And what was I to her? Perhaps not much in myself, but in what I knew and had seen, a great deal. All her eagerness to know about the world from which she had been cut off – the life, the death, the joys, the sorrows, the sins and the virtues of that huge confused mass of humanity to which I alone could give her any clue – made her delight in asking questions, in drawing inferences, and making comparisons, and my growing reluctance to leave the Happy Valley of Columba was less from the pleasure of studying the primitive manners and the arrangements for the moral and material well-being of the community, than because I could not endure the idea of going away and leaving her behind.

At intervals I felt ashamed of my passion, but in the normal state of my mind, I felt that if all is considered fair in love in other countries, surely it was fair in Columba. But my heart smote me when I saw that her bridegroom's simple narrative of what he had done or seen in his narrow range had no zest, and that she would turn to me to ask about European, American and Australian ways and people. Whatever was done at home she asked me how it would be done elsewhere. So far as my limited library and my own memory could serve, I introduced her to the new poetry and the new fiction of the time. I shall never forget the rapt silence with which she listened to the *Ancient Mariner*, to some of Browning's *Dramatic Idyls* and his wife's sonnets, to passages from the *Morte d'Arthur* and to George Eliot's 'Choir Invisible'.

She was always particularly sensitive to the sublime and the heroic and to self-renunciation and sacrifice for worthy objects. This impressed me the more because there was little or no religious enthusiasm among the people, and she did not appear to have more of it than others. The religion of love had been preached for a hundred years and more, and the religion of fear with its striking contrasts and its imperative demands had been kept in the background. The Fatherhood of God was accepted by this well-to-do and cheerful people without question or doubt, and the easy rule under which the children lived made that very word Father convey a sense of indulgence which their forefather's could not have realised. There was no dissent in the colony, and as the laity had no Bibles and no books, no difficult questions cropped up for solution. No discoveries of science were made here but for strictly practical purposes; the age of the world was fixed for the Columbans by the narrative of Genesis, and the creative action was limited to the six days. There were no doubts as to miracles and prophesy as existing in Scriptural epochs, though the people were absolutely free from all superstitions ideas and practices with regard to the present. Custom had sanctioned a few departures from the practice of Jews and Christians, but the record was on the whole believed not with eager passionate faith, but with complacent acquiescence.

I had no desire to disturb this comfortable frame of mind. I recollect once going to a small church not a hundred miles from Melbourne in a newly settled district, and hearing a young curate deliver an eloquent sermon on the modern speculative difficulties of belief to a congregation of three men, six women and nineteen children, who probably none of them had experienced any difficulty at all about belief, though they might about conduct. I certainly could not offer anything better as very much of my own belief appeared to be held in solution, and to need some strong agency in the shape of emotion or experience to give it any consistency. In fact, for the ordinary run of people, the faith seemed good enough to live by and die by, but there appeared to be in Liliard Abercrombie a capacity for some deeper spiritual experience than she had ever dreamed of, and it seemed as if through Master Hepburn and Sister Dorothea she was groping after it.

All the clergy continued to take a share in the teaching of the schools, in which each of them went through a probation of four years before ordination. The single sermon on Sunday was no great piece of preparation where the memory and the invention were so well trained. And as for what we call pastoral work, they visited the sick and the sorrowful, but as a rule, people were at work all day, and at some sort of amusement in the evenings, and the minister came into contact with them there. Morning and afternoon calls were not Columban institutions. Greetings were exchanged in the marketplace or at the Kirk door, and if there was any occasion for visits or any invitations given, visits were paid but there was no routine in the way of exchanging calls or paying debts of hospitality. As in every country where food is abundant, the people were overpoweringly hospitable, and I might have had every meal every day in a different house and welcome for the pleasure of my company. But there was one house where the meals were sweeter than anywhere else, and from which nothing but absolute necessity could make me absent myself. Hugh said it was a great compliment to Jenny's cooking that I should refuse an invitation to sup with Protector Elliot, and hurry home to be in time for the evening meal with humble folks like himself and his bride: The Protector and his wife and family might be stupid people, but in the way of a change when I wanted to see everything in Columba, I might have put up with their company for the sake of the best of victuals cooked to perfection.

XIII

THE COLUMBAN DRAMA

The first play that I saw acted was *The Gentle Shepherd*. My kinsman took the part of Patie which he studied by means of sticks. Roger was impersonated by a cousin of Hugh's, two fair damsels acted Peggy and Jenny, and the minister himself was Gland. Here and there a coarse expression or allusion was dropped out, but the pastoral was very faithfully rendered. As for scenery there was none, the little rhyme describing the scene was repeated by the prompter, and the audience had to construct it from their inner consciousness. Liliard sat beside me, watching how it would go, and wondering what I would think of it. It had not the recommendation of perfect novelty which had characterised her improvisation, and besides it had no feature of surprising interest to me. I had always been amused at my grandmother's excessive admiration of Allan Ramsay's masterpiece.

'Do you ever act Shakespeare's plays?' I asked in an interval between the acts, which was very short as there needed to be no shifting of scenes which were not.

'Sometimes, but I think whiles that it is beyond us. We want all to be first-rate to act Shakespeare, and there are so many actors needed. I like *The Tempest* and the *Midsummer Night's Dream* and oh! I do like *As You Like It*.'

'Do you ever act in them?' I asked.

'Yes, I have done Rosalind four times and every time I seem to see more in it. The others are like life, I dare say, but not like our life. I can scarcely explain – I like some of our own plays that we make up ourselves better than many of Shakespeare's, that is I mean for acting. If I could read them I dare say I should like *Hamlet* and *Othello* best of all.'

'How do you make up your plays when you do not write? By sticks, I suppose?'

'Aye, but we have great freedom of speech without the sticks. There's the story set down by the sticks, and when the actors have to come in and go out, and what each scene is to incline to, and how it is to end but we are put upon our mettle whiles for we scarce know what to say when something we ne'er bargained for has to be answered.'

I had acted in improvised charades with clever people more than once, so I could form some idea of the difficulty, and also of the sharpening of the wits through such practice.

'And what is your most common subject?' I asked. 'Is it the Indian wars, which before the recent great Civil Wars in America were the great subject of all school boy games and dramas in New England?'

'They used to be our favourite plays but they have somehow gone out of fashion, though they aye rouse me. There is one of our plays about the march of the first folk up the valley and another of the onslaught of the pirates on those left in charge that I like much.'

'But in the last case, there would be no woman.'

'There were really no women, but we cannot act without them. Nobody would feel any interest without some sort of love story in a play. So we put three women in as mounting guard with the others, and I like to take the part of one of them.'

'I suppose,' said I, 'you know about the battle of Liliard's Edge, where a maiden disguised herself in armour to fight the English by the side of her lover, and was found dead on the field while he was safe.'

'Aye, I have heard the story.'

'I never knew or saw a Liliard but yourself, but you often bring to mind the old story, for you look as if you were capable of the action.'

'Fighting days are over, at least with us,' said she with a sigh, 'and you tell me that there now is scarce any opportunity for personal courage even on the battlefield, when such mighty cannon and fearful engines of war work such havoc at a distance. But as I said the most of the young folk care little about the old times that I care about. No, I think the handfasting is the great subject matter of our plays, for there's aye the chance of its being broken through, and yet it is thought the right thing to stick by it.'

'Oh!' said I. 'Then the very object for which it was instituted is rather discountenanced.'

'Aye,' said she, 'for of course constancy is really the best thing, and for one man and one woman to cling to each other from youth to age without change or regret as you say they do in the world is what would build up the family most perfectly. But you say yourself that the first choice here in Columba is made too young to be often the best choice.'

'No doubt!' said I eagerly. 'I see that every day. Why your Jenny has got a sweetheart I see, and is thinking of being handfasted forthwith. But it is not at that early age that courtships are so interesting as they are in later life.'

'Maybe so,' said Liliard. 'I myself feel ten years older since I was handfasted to Hugh and he says it is the same with him, though that is maybe because I said it first.'

'It is perhaps since you thought so much about the world outside that you have felt older.'

'So it is,' said she thoughtfully. 'You are quite right there.'

'But in your stories, and your plays, most people try to make the bride and bridegroom true to each other, as your ancestor was true to Palahna.'

'Yes, they mostly do, though there are some of our young folk that go the other way. Jeanie Matthew made a sort of stir with a story she told about six months back, where the bride broke off sudden the last day, after making as if she and the groom were all in all to each other for the whole twelve months. All the more was it spoken about because Jeanie married her bridegroom Christie Johnstone a fortnight after. If I had been in her place, I could not have stood his sulky temper for a week, but they say he shows his very best side to her, and she will not hear a word against him. My Hugh had an outcast with him about some work he did badly, and they have not made it up since.'

'Do you go to law here to settle your disputes?' said I. 'For the law in its myriad shapes, criminal and civil as well as that of marriage and inheritance, with its police and detective officers is a great stock from which our novel and play writers draw. So much so that several of them consult a skilled lawyer as to their plots, so as to fall into no technical mistakes, and those who do not are often told of their mistake by the critics in a very painful manner.'

'What sort of mistakes may they be?' asked Liliard.

Here I was reminded as I had often been before, of the great change and growth of the language which had been identical five generations before. Not only had none of the words derived from our modern machinery, invention and travel reached Columba, but the modern language of culture with its accurate definitions and nice distinctions was quite unknown to a people who had only inherited the book-English of Addison and the Bible, and the Lowland Scotch of Allan Ramsay.

'Technical mistakes in the cases I spoke of are mistakes as to points of law, and forms of procedure, when there is any question either about the guilt of an accused person, or the rights of a disputant, or about the order of inheritance or the validity of a marriage. Then in an old populous country there is a complicated machinery for the finding out of criminals.'

'We do not trouble the law much at any time,' said Liliard. 'As for births, they are all registered like the handfastings and marriages, and the property is equally divided among all a man's bairns or a woman's bairns (if she has property) whether they were born in wedlock or in handfasting, all but them who are given up, who have no sort of title to inherit from either father or mother. Land is all registered too, and all the sales, and there can be few disputes about it. But of course some folk do go to law, or the judge would have little to do only trying offenders. Neil Scott has gone to law three times, once about a piece of land, once about a bargain that he thought the other man did not keep by, and the third time to get back some money lent on usury.'

'Usury – do you call interest or rent of money usury?'

'Aye, what else, payment for the use of it – and there was some dispute about the nick sticks, that the borrower said had been altered – but Neil Scott gained his case, and the man had to sell his town land to him to make his claim good.'

'Does such a case ever last over months or years?' I asked.

'Oh no, it is very soon disposed of. What is the good of wasting time like that?'

'In England people often keep a dispute unsettled for many years with new trials, and appeals to higher courts.'

'Oh! our ways are different,' said Liliard. 'I think it is better sometimes to put up with a little injustice than to waste time, and no doubt money, to get one's rights.'

'Your ways are wonderfully good ways,' said I. 'I am sure I learn far more than I can teach from the order and happiness I see around me here.'

'Aye may be,' answered Liliard with a sigh, 'but to my mind, the days when men carried their lives in their hand, the toilsome tramp of the first settlers, with their whole substance, their wives and their babes, in peril on every side, were grander than these piping tunes of peace. And in the great world in which you live, there must be dangers and adventures, rapture and despair. You must tell us one of your new-world stories, and wake us up a bit. Do not shake your head and say you cannot, for you have gone through and through me with what was bare history and there are things that move more than history, when you see what is thought and what is suffered, at the back of what is done.

'With regard to our law,' Liliard resumed after a pause, 'I think it is very simple, but maybe Hugh, or better still the minister, could explain it better than I could. We waste no money in prisons and no labour in idleness. If a man has done wrong against the law, he has to work on the roads – if he has done wrong to his neighbour, he has to work for him till he makes it up.'

'Then do you not take life for life?'

'They did so in the earliest days, but even that has been made milder since. We take a man's life's work, but we let him shorten the sentence by good conduct. There have only been four murders here these hundred years, I hear them say. Gilbert Elliott's father had a near miss of murder, but the man got better, and forgave him. It was sudden passion that led him on, so he had only to work on the roads for two years.'

'And is there no disgrace to the son of a man who has been thus convicted?'

'Well no, that would scarce be fair. Gilbert was a good son to his mother, and though he is whiles passionate and violent, he aye interests me, and so does Ninian with all his faults, and his father was an evildoer too. You see our folk are all on the same pattern, and one likes a change, even though it may not be for the better.'

XIV

STORIES RETOLD

Although I could satisfy Liliard's curiosity with some books of poetry and one newspaper, a Melbourne one, which astonished her more than I can set down in words, with regard to novels, I possessed none. I told her some of the stories, and though I had none of the vivid genius she possessed, or the practice in improvisation, her interest in the subject was so great, that she filled out my narratives and made them live. I never was so struck with her talent in this way as after my first public appearance on the platform of St Matthew's Kirk, which I felt was a failure, in spite of notes taken beforehand. *The Heart of Midlothian* was my subject, and as it was the story of a time quite within their traditions, for the Porteous Mob was about the last public event of which they had any historical record, and took place in Edinburgh, the capital city of the kingdom. As this had created a strong national feeling in Lowland Scotland from which the pioneers had gone, I thought that this story would give a good idea of the genius of Sir Walter Scott. However my execution was not at all equal to my ambition or to my subject; I boggled, I stammered; I tried to explain manners and customs which were different; I hesitated because I believed I was making use of words unknown to my audience, and on the whole I made a complete mess of the story.

I had not the eager, quick apprehension of the single listener, which had made me intelligible and at times eloquent, when holding forth to Liliard or to Master Hepburn. In spite of the tolerance granted to a stranger and a foreigner the reception of my story was decidedly discouraging. But even my inadequate presentment of the tale had affected Liliard greatly, and much to my surprise, when she was asked suddenly, on account of the illness of the person appointed to take up the tale on a particular day, to fill his place, she said she would do so, if allowed to tell Victor Keith's new story in more Columban fashion.

So I had to sit and hear my tale retold with some alterations and modifications, with very few attempts at explanation as to different customs, but with a picturesqueness and a realisation of character that carried the audience, myself included, away with her.

The effect of the tale told in Liliard's sweet penetrating voice, with the narrative and the conversations in the same dialect, was very different from what it had been in my hands. Lady Suffolk had been kept out of my narrative, and of course could not appear in hers. With all their handfasting arrangements, the presence of a wife and a mistress together was a thing quite unknown. In the words of the old song, they held it necessary to be off with the old love before they were on with the new. Courtship of a handfasted woman was open, but public opinion forbade any secret meetings or the least approach to a caress until the term was out. And a handfasted man was bound by the same unwritten law.

Their peculiar institution was brought in by Liliard telling her audience that Madge Wildfire had first been handfasted to George Stauntan or Robertson, and that Effie had been handfasted subsequently, but that this was disapproved both by his rich noble relations and by Effie's strict father and sister, as somehow disgraceful, as it was not then and there recognised by law or gospel. In fact the tragedy of the story seemed by this showing to arise from the hard judgements of these stupid people. It was very curious how plainly she spoke, without in any way appearing to transgress any Columban known law of decorum. I had boggled a little over my story as a little risqué for a young man to deliver before a mixed audience, but Liliard went on unhesitatingly and appeared to satisfy everybody.

I was full of praise, but scarcely of words when she thanked me for the framework on which she had built. 'There is so little here to tell about that is new, and your things are so different.'

'They say happy is the people whose history is dull.'

'Dull enough!' said she. 'Your history is not dull either in England or your big Australia.'

'No, it has not been dull lately. Party spirit has been very hot in my own colony of Victoria.'

'Oh! so your newspaper showed that you read me such astonishing things out of. And only to think that you are going to have an Exhibition of everything that is produced and everything that is invented all over the world in a place that is farther from Europe than we were and that was a wilderness when my father and mother were alive.'

'But fine feathers do not make fine birds, nor do all these wonderful things always turn out wonderful people. I am not to be compared to you as a storyteller. At any rate you improved much on my story for your audience.'

She could not deny my comparative failure.

'You will do better next time, Victor,' said she to me on the following day. 'Try what you told me of a story of Dickens, *A Tale of Two Cities*. I think you would do that better. But both of these are not only written by dead men, but relate to a time long past, I would fain hear a new story, the very newest – such as the young folk like you and me in the great world would delight in.'

Now the very last novel I had read was on board the steamer coming across from Hong Kong to San Francisco, Besant and Rice's *My Little Girl* and I told her so.

'Written by two people?' said Liliard. 'Oh! I understand – one thinks it out, and another man writes it down. That is what sometimes wish for myself, that someone would put in black and white a lot of the things that come into my head – for' said she as she took out of her drawer the pieces of knitting that were her whole library 'there is not a back stitch nor an open stitch, nor a double stitch nor a twist nor a knot that does not tell something to me, but there is only a vague notion of what it is about that anyone else, even the cleverest of our knitters could gather; and your books are so exact they tell the same to everyone. Look for instance at this little square that I knitted at school eight years ago; to me it says "on the fifth day of the moon, which according to the custom of my forefathers I always keep holy, I climbed the mountains of Bagdad to spend the day in thought and prayer" and she went on with the Vision of Mirza with a few verbal alterations, and a few little omissions from its original from an Addison paper in the *Spectator*.

'Into this,' she said as she took out a thin spider's web looking and much larger piece, 'I have put a great part of the story of Troy; the *Iliad* in English verse, but the rhyme helps me there but no one else could find it there. Sister Dorothea's daughter Grace has been trying hard to follow my stitches, and where she knows the story before, as in these, she can make it out fairly well. Here too are some of the stories I tell on the Monday evenings, and they are still harder for strangers to make out; nay they are impossible to be read by any but the one who thought of them.'

'Then your work and your knowledge will die with you,' said I. 'Wonderful as is the memory you have cultivated, and wonderful as is the invention you possess, the pen and the printing press would fix the results of these gifts for ever – at least comparatively speaking. Some books of course die.'

'Do they? Do people let them die?'

'Yes, surely they should die if they do not take hold of the mind of the public. But one copy is kept in the British Museum of every book that has been published in England.'

'Ah! what a sight that must be,' she said with a sigh, 'to them that care about books. It must be filled with people from the length and breadth of the land, and the far parts where the tongue is spoken. But what I was saying was that these two men, what did you call them?'

'Walter Besant and James Rice.'

'Well, the one would think and the other write. Which is the greater of the two. Thinking to my mind is the easier.'

'We in the old world have a very different opinion of the relative merits of the two; but in point of fact, though I do not know the authors, I have no idea that such was their method. One might take the plot, and another the conversations, one might do the grave and another the lighter parts, one might take the main plot and another the secondary one, but these literary partnership have always puzzled me.'

'Are they common?'

'No, not at all common. They say that Mr Wilkie Collins helped Mr Dickens with *A Tale of Two Cities* and it is known that they wrote some Christmas tales together. Perhaps the combined authorship is most common for theatrical authors. One might understand the literary part and another the action and the spectacular part of a drama.'

'Aye, that may be so. Here we have no spectacle at all and no attempt at scenery.'

'But you have a more vivid way of delivering what you have to say,' said I, 'and you make use of gesture which seems to me in the highest degree dramatic. In the old days when Shakespeare himself saw his own plays, I am sure there was little attempt at the costumes, the scenery and the furniture of the place and time. The actors trusted to the power of their speech to convey the idea of reality, as your people do.'

'But this has carried us far from the story, that I wanted you to tell me what these two people wrote; *My Little Girl* you called it.'

Perhaps no tale in the world could present a greater contrast to the ways and the moral sense of the Scottish settlers in the valley of Columba than this one. When I told of the poor scholar Hartley Venn adopting and training a little girl Laura Collingwood, and telling her he hoped she would marry a gentleman, and then described how the inexperienced but beautiful Laura falls in with a scamp Philip Durnford who deceives her with a false marriage, which he binds her to keep secret, whereas her great object in consenting was that her guardian Mr Venn would be pleased. After showing himself not only a scamp, but almost a brute in telling her that she was no wife at all, and that he was tired of her, the girl fled and hid herself in the great city of London but was discovered by her guardian. Instead of rejoicing that the bond, which on her side had never been one of love at all, was null and void, and that his dear little girl was actually free to marry a better man, free to marry himself, Hartley Venn stirred heaven and earth and worked by threat and promise to induce Philip Durnford to do his victim what the world calls *justice*, and marry his own darling legally and irrevocably. Of course, the novel writer cleared the way for the true marriage of guardian and ward by putting an end to Durnford by suicide or perhaps by an accidental overdose of some dangerous narcotic, so that the blunder was not so bad in its results as might have been expected – but the false principle was the same – that the valid marriage was forced on both sides, and had not love as its sanction on either.

Liliard's face grew graver and graver as I went on with the tale. 'Is that the way folk think and behave in the world?' She asked. 'Such folk could not comprehend our handfasting. Is that the kind of thing you approve of? If it is it must be very shocking to you to see our fashion about marriage.'

'No, it was strange, but not shocking. Indeed it was very shocking to me to read this story, because it is the love that sanctifies the marriage, and no amount of prayers or of ceremony could sanctify such a marriage as the second one. If there had been any child whose rights of inheritance would have been lost through the illegality of the first marriage, there would have been more excuse, but if I had been the child, I should have preferred to lose them. And though the novelist can make the scamp die, in real life, he would have outlived the Guardian whom Laura Collingwood loved.'

'And in real life people would not be so wicked?' said Liliard eagerly.

'So wicked as to deceive with a false marriage? Not very often I think.'

'So wicked as to try to mend matters by a falser one,' said she gravely.

'Not often exactly in the way of this story, I think.'

'But every marriage is false if there is not love in it,' said Liliard.

'I fear there are many loveless marriages made all over the world. Money, connection, and parental influence often come in to make true love retreat to the background. And in the middle and higher ranks there is a terrible dread of poverty and of losing position by a rash marriage.'

'Losing position?' said Liliard. 'I scarcely understand that.'

'In a country of such equality as this is, it is most difficult to explain to you the nice gradations of society elsewhere. Where even the children of criminals do not seem to lose caste, you could not understand that if people marry to be too poor to mix with their old equals on an equal footing and have to give up dinner and evening engagements because they cannot afford sufficiently rich and varied dress, or the necessary cab to drive to them in, and cannot ask their old friends in the same way because their domestic appointments are on a different scale, this is often felt to be too hard a price to pay.'

'For love and perfect union of heart and soul?' she asked 'I think that is very cowardly and petty. But then I do not perhaps make allowances for how your young people are brought up. You in the world I thought would care more for real greatness of character and less for money.'

'You will see whole long novels made up of nothing else but the difficulties of overcoming obstacles where there is money on one side and none on the other, but I must do the sentiments of the English reader and writer the justice to say that the obstacles are generally overcome often by an opportune legacy, and sometimes by magnanimity on the part of the relatives of the richer party.'

'But how if there is no money on either side?' asked Liliard.

'Then they must wait till they have money or at least a competent means before they can marry with any degree of prudence.'

'Well here people go into handfasting so early that there can be little money. There you see my Jenny is wooed by Hugh's lad at the forge. And I believe they will be handfasted ere long, but she will stop with us for the year I doubt not, and he with Hugh, and both can lay penny towards furnishing a house in case of their being married. When he is twenty-one he will take out a town land, and when she is the same age she will take one too, but they would never think of waiting so long before they were handfasted or married.'

'There seems little or no fear of absolute destitution here. There should be little in our Australian colonies for young industrious people but yet there is fear of comparative poverty.'

'And that is what you call losing position. But is that all the story?' said she after a pause. 'If there is nothing in it but this idea about marriage that seems to me false and immoral, I think very little of it.'

'No, there are much better things in it, and some very good social pictures. These authors generally take something very improbable for the main plot, but fill in with very probable and lifelike details.

'I don't think I should like to tell that story to our folk. I have at times wondered if the common notion that handfasting should be made marriage, does not work mischief; but that is only opinion, it is not law. And if you cannot do the right thing when it comes to the test, you must abide the consequences. If Hugh had confirmed his first handfasting, he would have rued it all his life.'

'Oh, then you are his second?' said I. I had already heard the fact from other lips, but this was so tempting an opportunity of getting at Liliard's own feelings on what was a subject of such vital interest to myself that I feigned ignorance.

'Aye, and he has been so contented and happy with me that he thinks more of me than I deserve.'

'And what became of the first?'

'Oh she was ten years older than him, and a widow with four bairns.'

'Too much for Hugh, poor fellow.'

'No, he liked the bairns, but she had a weariful tongue, and had no sense of what was fitting. He broke it off, and then he courted me for two years, and then I consented. I'm not much of a manager, as his mother says, and he might do better, only he does not think so.'

'But was he not an old suitor of yours before he was handfasted to the widow?'

'Aye, but I could not give a thought to him then. I was then so eager about the storytelling, and thought I might get taken on at the schools through Sister Dorothea's good word. And then Hugh seemed to me so young.'

'And it was because you would not listen to him that he turned for consolation to the widow?'

'It is likely enough, but Hugh never says word to me of the matter, and if he were to do so, I would discourage it – for all that is between him and her, and I have no business to intermeddle with these memories.'

BOOK THREE

A REVOLUTION OF THE PAST

I

THE COLUMBAN LIBRARY

The conversation narrated in the last chapter took place when I was busy with my negatives, and Liliard was mounting the photographs. We were interrupted by Master Hepburn, who came in the first place to have his likeness taken, and in the second to say that he had, with some difficulty, obtained permission for me to go and see the collection of books in the Town House, and the parchments in which the records of the plantation of Columba were registered year by year. Statistics were kept by one or two of the foundling civil servants, and all the inhabitants could, like my kinsman Hugh Keith, at any time know the population, the area of inhabited and waste lands, the amount of stock and the revenue though they had not the knowledge to enable them to check the figures.

My friend Master Hepburn, though his special vocation was spiritual, took a great interest in the temporal affairs of the colony, and I was only sorry that the incessant work on which I was engaged did not allow me to have more conversation with him. His age enabled him to go farther back in the traditions than Liliard could do, and he had the same comprehensive view of the tendency of different institutions to produce different kinds of character which struck me so much in my kinsman's bride. But when I had pleased myself with his likeness, of which more copies were to be struck off than of any private person in the valley, I accompanied him to what was called the Columban Town House.

I had already learned a good deal of the details of the administration from Hugh and others. Everyone in the valley was well acquainted with the general affairs of the Commonwealth but the Library was the Sanctum Sanctorum which needed special favour for even a civil servant to enter. But this at last was conceded to me.

There were some departments of our ordinary colonial returns conspicuous by their absence. There were no customs duties to collect and no ports to collect them at. There was neither army nor navy, nor even any volunteer force for defence, there was no post office or telegraph department, no newspaper press, no statistics of religious denominations, no loan account for public works, no public houses in all the valley to inspect, no compulsory standard of education, though public opinion made school attendance regular and it was free to all. The roads were made partly by the criminals and partly by free labour paid out of the ordinary revenue. There was only one judge and a jury of twelve, a majority of two-thirds to decide as to the guilt or innocence of the accused and as to the right or wrong of a civil action. The judge sat every day in the most central township as a sort of police magistrate, and two days in the month there was a jury for the trial of offences and of disputes between the citizens. The jury was changed every month. There was a public prosecutor, of course also one of the caste of civil servants. People pleaded their own causes, and employed no lawyers but the Columbans were all ready with their tongues and I had been very much interested in the clever defences that were made. Until the day came round for trial, the accused went on with his ordinary avocations, but two of his friends guaranteed his appearance when called for. The police force consisted of ten men who had other employment when not needed.

The most elaborate Government department was the mint, and it was singular that Ninian, who was half-Indian or nearly so, should have worked himself up to the chief position in it. The metals which were most abundant in Columba were copper, tin and silver, there was no gold to be got at all except very small quantities in the copper and silver ores and he had divined some process by which this was more easily separated. The dies used were very rough; on one side was the Scottish thistle as a mark of the original nationality, and on the other an attempt at a dove as a type of the peaceful state of Columba. The only silver mine was Government property, copper and tin paid a royalty, but were worked by private enterprise. There was little silver or gold used for ornament: the richer had half and whole marriage rings of gold, the poorer of silver. The currency was kept up to the requirements of the community, called in when worn and replaced by new - there were no bank notes used and no bills of exchange given - but there was a good deal of barter and of occasionally sales on credit, registered by tally sticks, the old fashioned nick sticks mentioned in Scott's novel of *The Antiquary*, which were brought into court and compared in case of dispute. Sticks were used in keeping accounts by the ordinary population, who could not read or write, but the accounts of the Commonwealth were kept with pen and ink on skins of parchment cut into long strips and paged and dated.

I was now for the first time introduced to the Training College where in point of fact the strangely selected body of civil servants were marshalled for future use, so that the headmaster of this establishment had the direction of all the Government patronage for a generation or two, and in a large room where about thirty students were at work under two teachers, I saw the whole literary possessions of the community.

There were a good many Bibles still not worn out with yellow paper - long S's and compound consonants connected together - almost all copies including the Apocrypha. There were as many New Testaments in separate form, and a few Psalm books also separate. The paraphrases as I knew, were of later date than the departure of the adventurers. There were five copies of Shakespeare very much the worse for wear, and single copies of the following works:

Bunyan's *Pilgrim's Progress* and *Grace Abounding*
Don Quixote
Robinson Crusoe
Pope's *Homer* and *Odyssey* and an odd volume of poems containing *The Essay on Man*
Dryden's *Virgil* and 'Alexander's Feast'
Spectator, three copies
Tatler
Addison's *Cato* and his poems
Gentle Shepherd – three copies
Paradise Lost
Paradise Regained
Milton's whole works
Several bundles of Scotch Songs and of English Ballads
A book in manuscript of History partly of the World and more fully of English and Scottish history

There were also some political pamphlets against the Union bound up together; a few Latin books, Caesar, Horace and Buchanan's *Psalms* and one single Greek Testament.

'Do you learn any of the foreign languages?' I asked.

'No,' said Master Hepburn, 'we are content with our own, but I have often wished to know what is the original text of the New Testament. I fear I am too old to learn, and at present you are too busy to teach me. But there is a book in the French language that I have a still greater curiosity about. It belonged to Madame Keith, and as it is bound up with blank leaves, she was wont to write in it in her native tongue, but whether it was pious reflections, for this seems to me to be a religious book by one Pascal, or any of our early history, I cannot tell. And as she was your ancestress, Victor Keith, it is well your part to try and find out what she wrote. After the death of her son Victor there was no one in the plantation that knew aught of the French tongue, and this has been lost to us altogether. It should be of interest to all the Keiths as well as to yourself.'

It could not have been of half the interest to anyone that it was to me, and when Master Hepburn took it out of the box of perfumed wood in which it had lain so long, I opened it with the greatest curiosity. It was indeed the *Pensées* of Pascal and a fine and rare edition interleaved and bound in vellum with silver clasps, now tarnished with age. It had evidently belonged to some other before it passed into the hands of Marguerite Keith, née de Launay. I was not long in discovering that most of the pious notes were by some Jansenist woman, whose life of self-renunciation found its reason and its solace in the maxims and exhortations of Blaise Pascal. In this book there was shown neither the scientific side of the great mathematician nor the polemic side of the masterly author of the Provincial letters. The thoughts are those of the Augustinian or Calvinistic Roman Catholic, and with few exceptions would be echoed in the Presbyterian Church of Scotland. But the expression of this faith was more gentle than in the Kirk standards, and some of the most unlovely dogmas were rather inferred than declared. The original owner of the book was an aunt of my ancestress, who had brought her up until she reached womanhood in a country château near Fontainebleau, while M. and Mme de Launay had been forced to retire to England with their other child, a boy several years older, on account of the persecution of the Huguenots after the revocation of the Edict of Nantes. It was evident that though a thorough-going member of the Reformed faith would not choose a Romanist to educate her only daughter, there were family reasons for Marguerite being left, and the aunt belonged to the best side of the church, that which opposed the Jesuits and the Grand Monarque almost as strongly as the Huguenots. For the sake of the little Marguerite, her aunt had never taken the veil, but had kept her own appanage for a *dot* for the child. It was not until the aunt's death that Mademoiselle de Launay joined her family, or discovered how much she was indebted to the saint-like woman who had worn herself out with austerities, but who made the maiden's life bright with the few innocent pleasures she could procure – for there is in the Catholic Church a distinction made between the higher and the lower-religious life, the first full of many voluntary asceticisms, and the other treated indulgently with great allowance for human weakness.

It was to the writing of Marguerite herself that I turned most eagerly. Neither of the hands was easy to read. The very letters were much more different from ours than is usual in modern French; the spelling was antiquated; there were many abbreviations and even sometimes a cipher, and the subject at first was so new that I had great difficulties in helping my apprehension of the meaning with the context. But I was a good French scholar, and had a turn for verbal puzzles. I begged leave to take the book home with me for a week, and I transferred to my own notebook, which was now getting greatly filled up with new and strange things, this most interesting narrative. It not only gave a sketch of Marguerite Keith's early life, and an insight into her character, but went on to explain much of the early history of the colony of Columba, and the modifications of old laws and customs, which had appeared to me so inexplicable for Christian people wherever and however situated, to frame and to obey.

As I sat over this book every spare moment of the following week I was absorbed and agitated in various ways – for I felt the meanness of continuing to be my kinsman's guest while I was daily becoming more conscious of the strength of my love for his bride, and felt also that she was falling under an influence disastrous to his hopes and yet quite unable to tell him the truth. This story seemed strangely near to me: all the intervening generations appeared to be swept away, and the mother whom I had scarcely known seemed to be speaking to myself through the pen of Marguerite Keith. All her yearnings after the dear lost son the first Dr Hugh, all her prayers for his restoration, all her faith of the good that she knew was still in him, which the world and his father could not see, but which his subsequent career proved, seemed to have a living and personal bearing on myself. When I contrasted the easy régime under which I had developed – the mirthful childhood, the eager ambitious youth, the school full of interesting work, the home full of kindly toleration – with the hard life of Marguerite and her boys, I felt that times had indeed changed for the better. Only in judging from some of the results I felt that I personally was scarcely worthy of my ancestry; such discipline often produces strong men and resolute women, whereas our easy-going generation would fain go easily from the cradle to the grave.

This widowed woman, as I had heard from Liliard and Master Hepburn, had had greater influence in moulding the little Commonwealth in its earliest days than John Abercrombie himself, and passages in her life gave the key to the handfasting, to the Sunday half-holiday, to the use of the Kirk for all social purposes, as well as to the criminal and civil law as administered in Columba. Although Madame Keith was Hugh's ancestress and not Liliard's, her interest in the story was tenfold what his was. As she went about her work in the house or in my studio, which with the advancing season, was now excessively hot, she could think of nothing but this revelation of a sad life and of a beautiful nature.

The religious reflections of both aunt and niece were a good deal beyond all of us, but Hugh smiled and almost laughed at their futility and their unreal visionary character. He was unconsciously a sort of materialist, though he went to church and believed himself to be a good enough Christian. I had passed through a period of intellectual struggle approaching to a spiritual experience and had come out with a creed rather pantheistic than otherwise. I did not deny the possibility nay the reality of spiritual life and kinship with the Divine, but I myself had no strong pullings in that direction. Morality was the only religion that I had any tangible hold of, and the service of man appeared to be the most safe and profitable way of serving God.

To Liliard those eager prayers, this introspection, this confessional to the blank leaves of a book for want of a human priest appeared like a revelation. The devotional side of her nature had not been developed as her sympathetic, her imaginative and her emotional sides had been. But now trouble was entering her mind and with trouble and perplexity came prayer for guidance, and views of self dedication. But the narrative must speak for itself.

It would be perhaps tedious and, to the ordinary reader, too much like a sermon if I gave it in full, but I shall endeavour to give the reader those parts which have the greatest bearing on my own story, and on the institutions and manners of Columba. It had not been meant at first to be an autobiography at all, but only a repertory of pious thoughts on the part of aunt and niece. After the latter had been married to a man who could not understand French, it was a safety-valve for her to set down in these blank pages in her own tongue such thoughts as he had small sympathy with. The pious reflections were exchanged for questioning doubts, notes of interrogation were added to previous comments, and it was evident that a mental and spiritual revolution had been experienced by the minister's wife of which he took little cognisance.

The autobiography was begun when the sudden resolution of her husband to go to America as minister of the colonists was likely to sever her from her eldest boy for ever, and I gathered that it was to have been left behind for his reading, but the messenger had somehow betrayed her and she found the book among others when the emigrants were in mid-ocean. Thus the first part of the book belonged especially to me as the descendant of that dearly loved son, while the later part of the narrative was likely to be more interesting to the descendants of Victor Keith who alone had been able to read and understand his mother's story. But as Hugh Victor Keith I seemed to represent both her sons, and although I was a native and a citizen of a (to her) unknown region, I had travelled over all the scenes which she described, where her life had been spent. I had visited the home of her childhood and youth at Fontainebleau; I had lived in the Paris she had wondered at; I had spent some time in London in which she had loved and married; I had visited the Scottish parish in which she had been buried alive and the family estate her husband had inherited and sold. And now, by a strange chance, I had reached the place where her life's most interesting work had been done, and where she lay at rest.

II

MADAME KEITH'S STORY – YOUTH

From the aunt's prayers recorded in the blank leaves of the old book, even more than from the niece's narrative, I could gather that Marguerite in her childhood and youth had been beautiful, spirited and imaginative, all these qualities being to the recluse, qualities full of perils and temptations to the soul. She had been careful to rear the girl in those principles of passive obedience and submission to intellectual and spiritual direction in which she herself found repose. Her Jansenism led her to object to the direction of the Jesuits or of the worldly and ambitious branch of the Universal Church, but it did not lead her to think of standing by herself, and having no mediator between her own soul and God. When Armand de Launay left France in haste and fear with his wife and son, Marguerite was but a year old, and was out at nurse near Fontainbleau. The aunt promised to keep the little one till she could find safe escort for her, but she grew so attached to the child that she did not seek such escort, and she brought her up as the daughter of a noble house, though a poor one, was brought up in those days. As a Jansenist, Mademoiselle de Drouin was under a cloud, and had some difficulty in obtaining the service of a confessor of her own way of thinking, but her quietness and her obscurity was her protection. Although she would have preferred that her niece would show some vocation for the convent, she did not press it on her, and allowed her great freedom with her good natured nurse or bonne who took her much out of doors, especially on saints' days, Sundays, and fête days to see how the peasantry enjoyed themselves, and whose ordinary family cares were a little counteraction to the fascination of her aunt's austerities and pious speech and reading.

If there was one lesson above all impressed upon the young Marguerite it was the subjugation of the will; in youth, to those placed by nature and providence above us, and in mature age, to the higher religious motives which ought to govern the life; and these for women ought to be interpreted and laid down by the Church speaking through its priests. Free choice of life, free choice in marriage were things absolutely forbidden to a well brought up young woman in those days in France, and even now there is not much more choice given. The only circumstances in which the will of parents might be withstood without blame was when the religious vocation was so clear that to the soul marriage was a sin. Humility, acquiescence, patience in all possible walks of life, were the virtues which crowned woman most gloriously, and Mademoiselle de Drouin practised what she preached. Christian piety with her as with Pascal, annihilated the *moi* or the *ego*, and the perfect manners of a gentlewoman in which she educated her niece, went far to suppress and conceal from the ordinary eye the natural individuality and strength of character which the girl possessed.

Poverty for herself Mademoiselle de Drouin would have preferred, for she thought wealth and even comfort full of temptation, but after her sister had been exiled with her husband, and the family were in straitened circumstances in a foreign land she rather rejoiced that she could not only bring up Marguerite in true Catholic principles, but could aid her other relatives in England with her money.

However, at the time of her last illness, there were such glowing accounts of prosperity from England; M. de Launay had invested all he could lay hold of in South Sea Stock, and was, according to his own showing, likely to be a rich man for the rest of his life.

The aunt altered her will, and left half of her property to the Church and the other half as a *dot* to her dear child Marguerite. The good lady was rather *suspecte* by the authorities as a staunch, though a quiet and obscure Jansenist, but through the good offices of a kinsman in favour at court, Marguerite's money was secured and settled on herself under his guardianship until marriage. While these matters were pending, Marguerite had spent a month in Paris in the splendid hotel of her friends, and had there seen something of the great world under the chaperonage of the only worldly people with whom she seemed to come in contact during her whole life: pleasure-loving, pleasure-seeking, and eager for social distinction. In spite of her recent loss, they took her everywhere with them, that she might have a sort of carnival between the asceticism of Fontainebleau and the gloom of London, and as she had been trained to obedience, she submitted. Here for the first time, she discovered that she was beautiful and received those very direct compliments which are inadmissable nowadays. She also was surprised to find that she was accounted witty, and for the time highly educated. All this gave her natural pleasure, and she hoped that her hitherto unknown parents would be satisfied with her person and her mind.

Marguerite was just eighteen when she landed in England. She knew by letter that the bubble had burst, and that the anticipated fortune was lost, but she was not prepared to find her father in the Fleet prison for debt to an amount far beyond discharging with her money even if the control of this had been in her own power. All she could do was to draw the interest of her 30,000 livres and maintain the family in the Liberties of the Fleet. This slender income was slightly increased by means of some lessons in French and in the classical languages which her father could give to pupils who sought him out in their poor lodgings. Victor de Launay, her only brother, who had studied medicine, was at sea as surgeon of a man-of-war going round the globe on a voyage of discovery. The parents had missed their daughter much, but on the whole thought she had been happier and better educated under her aunt than if she had been sharing their precarious fortunes. The first step to be taken now however was to effect her conversion to the Reformed Faith – and this was not a very long process. In these efforts they were aided by one of their most frequent visitors, Archibald Keith, who of a good Scotch family well-known abroad, had made his way even to the Fleet Prison for purposes partly friendly and partly politic. He was much disquieted by the precocious vice and strong will of the young man whose governor he was, and also found that he was held at arm's length by the English divines with whom he desired to associate as a member of a democratic and unlearned church.

'Medieval Latin was my father's strongest point,' wrote Marguerite whose narrative I shall for the future follow with some necessary omissions, 'and Mr Keith had a desire to see how the corruptions in doctrine and in ceremony had entered the once pure early church. While in London, he picked up old copies of the Fathers at bookstalls and sought my father's help in getting at their true meaning, becoming at every step more rigidly presbyterian than before. His horror at the idea of my dangerous condition as a member of a church full of soul-destroying superstition, was much greater than my father's, and his zeal for my conversion was more earnest. All the lessons of submission and subordination to authority which I had learned from my aunt's teaching made it easy for me to throw that teaching off, and to see the force and logic with which two strong men like my father and Mr Keith, overthrew the dogmas of an infallible church, priests, and sacraments, and asserted the rights of private judgement. I had always thought that my aunt's asceticism was a mistake, and now when not only these able men, but my own sensible mother, beset me with arguments and with ridicule, I was not long in forsaking the modified Catholicism which I had blindly followed, and felt that both my understanding and my conscience guided me in the change. Mr Keith was proud of his convert, for he naturally thought his arguments had the greatest weight with me, and became more and more interested in me.

'The death of an old minister made room for him in his own Church, for Lord Seton, the grandfather of his pupil, had promised him the living, and what was more, in addition to this presentation he was pressed by urgent private affairs to return to Scotland.

'The family estate was burdened by an unjust demand of the widow of a murdered brother for the repayment of her *dot* or *tocher*, which she had secreted or made away with, and Mr Archibald Keith had pacified her and prevented the sale of the estate by paying partial interest on her claims until he could raise the money to clear it. The money market was very hard at this time and the tenants to whom lands were let were in arrears, while Hugh Keith, the nominal owner, was spending more than his income in the prison into which this woman threw him. Hugh was unmarried, and was not likely to live long, so that Archibald Keith as heir presumptive even of an encumbered estate as well as the minister of a county parish in Scotland might be considered to be a match in point of age, birth and circumstances for a girl whose parents were living in the Liberties of the Fleet with small hope of ever getting out. When therefore he formally asked for my hand from my parents, and made the generous offer that they should enjoy half of my income so long as they lived, they joyfully accepted the proposal for me.

'I had never thought of Mr Keith as a lover and even now he did not look like one. Although only twenty-nine, he looked much older, he was grave solemn and austere. I had never had much that could be called pleasure in life, except with my doll, and in the woods with my *bonne*. But some instinct told me – I certainly had not been taught by anybody – that there was happiness to be found in a marriage of affection. I objected that my parents' comforts would be seriously diminished but they eagerly disclaimed any consideration of that kind. It was the dearest wish of their hearts to see me settled in a worthy marriage. What would become of me if they died? And what suitor whom I could ever meet with could behave so generously as to my dower as Mr Keith? A protector was absolutely necessary for me, and in every point of view he was the best man in the world for their Marguerite.

'I suffered myself to be persuaded to consent. It was the whole lesson of my life to submit and I could bring forward nothing against my grave wooer. I had never seen him angry but once, and that was with good cause. The young heir whom he had the charge of, had been all but entrapped into one of those Fleet marriages which were a scandal to Christendom, and was just rescued in time. I had seen some of these disgraceful scenes where parsons as bankrupt in money as in character, married for a bottle and five shillings any couples, drunk or sober, who came to ask their offices, and these marriages in spite of their informality, in spite of the horrible cheating and bullying that attended them, were as irrevocable as if they had been entered into soberly, honestly and in the fear of God. There was so much that was beautiful in the Roman Catholic marriages I had seen at Fontainebleau, that I was shocked beyond expression by what I saw and heard daily in this wretched neighbourhood and I was not surprised at Mr Archibald Keith's blazing indignation when he rescued his ward, and flung the greasy prayer book at the parson's head, and knocked down the drunken clerk who had tried to bar his entrance. The fighting blood of the Keiths came out there in action, as it did elsewhere in controversy. My aunt had always told me that marriage was a snare, and here I saw it, but my parents and my suitor pointed out how different such a marriage as they urged on me was from those Godless vows. I pleaded for delay, especially as Victor was on the point of returning from his long voyage, and I wished to make his acquaintance. So Mr Keith returned to his own country and was installed as minister of the little parish of Colbrandspath near St Abbs Head on the East Coast of Scotland, which I afterwards knew too well.'

III

MADAME KEITH'S NARRATIVE CONTINUED – LOVE

'And now for me life seemed to begin. Victor and his friend Paul Durham, a lieutenant in the *Dauntless*, took lodgings near us and we spent every hour of the day that was possible together. I breathed a different air; I learned what youth and hope and vitality really meant. The poor home resounded with laughter. I joined the young men in many cheap pleasures: excursions, rides and sails, which called the healthy colour into my cheeks, and the light of youth into my eyes. I was no longer the pale grave Marguerite, who had nothing more interesting or amusing than a theological argument in the parlour, or a pot-au-feu in the kitchen to fill her thoughts, but a girl like other girls, laughing at little jokes, eager for little pleasures, gratified by little attentions.

'Victor loved me, rallied me, teased me, but his teasing was pleasanter than Mr Keith's wooing, and as for his friend, he watched what I said, watched for what I was going to say, defended me from all Victor's attacks, and recollected and satisfied any wish I might express or that he might guess at, always for things within reach, but not within my reach alone or unaided. They took me to such public places as were frequented by good society or respectable people, and somewhat scandalised my grave parents by taking me several times to the play, but Victor could do almost anything with them after his long absence and his hardships; and after all this was only once in a way, I should see and hear nothing of this kind at Colbrandspath, under the guardianship of the Rev. Archibald Keith. They could not resist laughing at the accounts we gave of all we heard and saw, and almost weeping when I described what had moved me on the stage.

'My mother as well as my father remarked that I seemed another girl since my brother had come, and I myself wondered at the transformation. The bashfulness of the virgin which, as Mr John Milton has it, may conceal stupidity or bad temper by neutral silence, and which had had its charms for Mr Keith, quite departed from me; I seemed to expand like a flower which has grown in the deep shade of the forest, when the stalk has raised it so as to catch the sunshine. My voice surprised myself, it was so fearless and so free; I seemed to feel its music and its various intonations. My laugh went back to the careless laughter of childhood with a clearer ring and a deeper source than it had then. My face, as I caught its reflection in the little mirror over the mantelshelf, looked no longer like my own, and my very raiment seemed to have put on an unfamiliar lightness and grace. It would have been the same in a great measure if Victor had been alone. I had never had any real childhood at all, as I had had no young companions, and had been always living with old, sad, grave people. My *bonne* was kind and good but she was scarcely a companion. My brother, eight years older than myself had really lived, had travelled by sea and land, had mixed with foreign peoples and been associated with his fellows in age and in tastes at school and at college while I had stagnated or vegetated until now.

'It was my brother's being mixed up with this changed condition of things that concealed from me so long the fact that his friend counted for still more in the result. The joy of being ashore, the delight of this orphan sailor in finding even in the gloomy Liberties of the Fleet the family life he had missed, as well as the old comradeship that had bound him to Victor through three years of hardship and danger, blinded Paul Durham also. He had been told that I was betrothed, but as my fiancé was out of sight, he was also very much out of mind. I myself used to forget my engagement till I went to bed at night, and then it seemed to come to me like a blow. I sought to drive away the unwelcome recollection which would prevent me from sleeping, by going over and over again the talk and the movement and the badinage that had given zest to the day, and the fatigues from which I needed repose were forgotten in the delightful retrospect.

'I had now learned to speak English very well, and as neither of the young men would speak French, I was forced to use a great many words quite unfamiliar to me before, a whole vocabulary of fun and also of description of natural scenery, and of human characteristics was opened out to me. I had learned as a part of a gentlewoman's education to make lace, and also to mend it beautifully from my aunt, and when Paul Durham asked me to mend a rent in a Steenkirk which had been once his fathers, I acquitted mysef to his satisfaction, as well as to that of my mother. In his best clothes, and with a few guineas in his pocket with which to fee his lordship's valets, butlers and retainers, the young man was going to wait on the First Lord of the Admiralty, a distant relative of his own, to beg for promotion to a second lieutenancy on board a fine ship just being fitted out for service. With a jest on his lips and hope in his heart he left us, and when he came back with the great man's promise in his favour, he gave to the imposing cravat the credit of his success. For the First Lord was a very fine weather sailor, and only a judge of the outer man.

' "But what will become of Victor?" said I. "I fear this will separate you. He has no friends at court."

' "I trust not," said the young lieutenant. "I believe he has the best chance for the appointment on the *Invincible*. In fact I was bold enough to name him. And his appearance too will win him favour. He was the handsomest fellow on the *Dauntless*."

'I tried to laugh for joy, but instead of that a strange revulsion of feeling made me weep for something like sorrow. The floodgates seemed opened and I could not check my tears. All this good news would bring separation from those whom I loved, and banishment for myself to the new home which had never before seemed so unattrative.

'"Marguerite," he said and the only French word he ever used was like music to my ears, "Marguerite, my Marguerite."

'"Nay, nay," I stammered out. "I am Mr Keith's Margaret, not your Marguerite. You know I am betrothed."

'"Nay say not so – some idle words misunderstood. Some chaffering on the part of parents, but no true betrothal. You are the life of my life," said Paul and his eyes were as eloquent as his lips. How different had been the grave solicitation I had heard but a few months before.

'"I have given my promise to Mr Keith and thus confirmed the promise of my parents," said I, but my voice faltered and belied my assurance.

'"What, my Marguerite, does the promise mean? That you will at some appointed time vow to love honour and obey your father's friend? Obey you may, honour too perhaps you may, but Marguerite you love *me*."

'It was true, I was silent. He resumed with the rapid impetuous speech which carried me along with it.

'"Look you, Marguerite, it is the happiness of two, nay of three, that is at stake. Will he be satisfied with the husk and not the kernel, with the body and not the soul? If he is so mean as to be satisfied he ought not to be. Will you be at ease if in order to keep one promise made ignorantly, you break your heart and mine, and spoil the life you are supposed to bless. What did you know of love or marriage when you bound yourself by this promise?"

'"My father, my mother thought it best."

'"Your father and mother have not to live the life that they plan for you."

'"And he is a good man – I dare not wrong him."

'"Why what wrong can be so great as what you propose to do to marry him without love?"

'"If I marry him," I said with repressed passion, "I will do my duty by him. By God's grace I will."

'"Duty! Duty!" said he with passion unrepressed, "if you married me would you think of duty? But it is not for myself that I plead, it is for you. Oh! my dear love, pause, think, and break off this unhallowed match."

'"Unhallowed!" said I angrily, catching at some point of defence, "Mr Keith made it a matter of prayer, and so did my father and mother and so did I. Can it be unhallowed to obey my parents and sacrifice myself?"

'"Yes it can," said Paul eagerly. "It is not like anything else, Marguerite. If you worked your finger to the bone for their sakes, if you starved that they might have enough, if you went cold that they might go warm, all that would be good and right and heroic. But that at their bidding you should vow love and duty, that you should merge your name, your opinions, your very existence in those of another, is a very different thing. I may be presumptuous in saying that you love me. But you do not love Mr Archibald Keith. When you change colour at the mention of his name it is the pallor of fear and not the blush of conscious love that comes over your cheek."

'His vehemence frightened me; I made believe that it offended me, for it revealed to me only too clearly the state of my own heart and how I dreaded the coming of October when I was to be claimed by my betrothed. He urged me further, he could even brave my anger that he might put the matter before me with all the force and all the logic he was master of. He swept away every vain subterfuge under which I hid myself from myself and made me confess the whole truth. I cannot now remember those words, those passionate appeals without the old emotion though so many years have passed away since they were uttered.

'But what could we do against the elder and stronger powers. Paul had to join his ship in six weeks, and might be absent for eighteen months or two years, and the proposal that he pressed on my father that he should be married at once, and that I should remain with my parents till he should return with pay and prize money to claim me, was put aside as the dream of a love-sick boy, more worthy of consideration in a public house back-parlour by a disreputable parson than by a pious and prudent parent. It was only as Victor's friend that Paul had been acceptable to my father and mother, and this monstrous proposition turned the tables completely on him. Besides a de Launay's word was his bond, and I had been promised to the Scottish minister as solemnly as possible. This had weight even with Victor, from whom I had hoped for sympathy and help. He could not see that we could get honourably out of such a promise, and he thought as the case was hopeless, that Paul would soon forget me if he was once fairly out to sea, while I, as a well brought up young woman would naturally get over this temporary fancy as a good man's wife, helping in the parish and occupied with family cares.

'I can scarcely now looking back on it after this long lapse of time recollect how I was led or driven or shamed into dismissing the man I loved, and marrying the man whom I feared yet respected. I think shame had the most to do in the business, and that the appeals to my honour were the strongest. And here if self-renunciation is really the highest law and obedience to superiors the greatest moral virtue, my conscience ought to have supported me in this crisis. But somehow the appeals of my lover stung me through all the subterfuges I could marshal in my defence. I think I fell into a sort of lethargy after Victor and Paul sailed in the *Invincible* for an American station, from which I was only roused by the arrival of my bridegroom to claim my hand. If our marriage had not been delayed on account of Victor's return, I should have felt less of a sinner than I did. I should not have known how false I was.'

IV

MADAME KEITH'S NARRATIVE CONTINUED – MARRIAGE

' "To be weak is to be indeed miserable" and though Mr John Milton puts the speech into the mouth of a fallen angel, it is true for all of us. The feeble opposition I could make was of no avail. I was married to the man to whom I had been promised and was bound to follow his fortunes for the rest of our joint lives.

'I bade farewell to my parents. My father I never saw again, and took my passage with my husband in a ship bound for Leith. I was wretchedly sea-sick and wretched altogether. I think the sight of the ship made me more miserable, for all that I knew about seafaring was learned from Victor and Paul. The sailors' songs as they pulled at the ropes, the quick orders of the skipper, the flapping of the sails, the swish of the water put me in mind of the day when I saw the *Invincible* sail with all my youth, with all that seemed to me worth living for in it. We had baffling winds and a calm, we were fourteen days on the voyage, and as I lay on the deck with my husband's greatcoat and a shawl round me I tried hard not to live over again those five happy months. My husband was concerned to see me so ill, and had no idea of anything wrong but the temporary *mal de mer*. My parents had told him about Lieutenant Durham's frantic passion and my constancy, and he had taken it as a matter of course that I should be the object of boyish adoration, but nevertheless should prefer him and his paramount claims. When he spoke of my lover, it was with contempt, and as much ridicule as was consistent with his own grave character.

'My husband's position was better when I married him, than when we were first betrothed, for his brother's death had put him in possession of the family estate and my *dot* or the share which by agreement with my parents I retained as my own, went partially to satisfy the claims of the woman I have already spoken of, and with our moderate desires, there appeared to be comfort and indeed wealth for us in this obscure parish. My husband, however, hoped for promotion to a city church, and was eager to take a stand in the General Assembly so as to check what he called the growing Erastianism of the Scottish Kirk. All that he had seen in England of the subservience of the clergy to their lay patrons and to the secular power, made him eager to fight the battle of spiritual freedom, which if gained, would with men of his spirit and temper, have resulted in spiritual tyranny. He had written some books of controversial divinity, and his greatest grudge against the Union was that secularism had encroached on the Headship of Christ, and that there had been granted sinful toleration for both popery and heresy.

'Archibald Keith was fitted admirably for the church militant, but he had no relish for the church quiescent, and he would have been a dangerous leader for the church dominant. What a covenanter he would have made, what a hillside preacher, carrying his life in his hand, and ready to draw the sword of the Lord and of Gideon on the minions of a persecuting government! What a victim of the rack and the thumbscrew he would have been, calm imperturbable and defiant of all that men could do against the truth as he saw it! But for quiet times in his country parish, he chafed at trifles, he fought like the knight in the ingenious romance of Miguel Cervantes, with windmills for giants, and with puppets for flesh and blood adversaries. And his own sense of personal sin was always with regard to the attitude of his soul to God, and never with regard to his conduct to man. The scrupulousness of his conscience questioned the strength of his faith and his complete absorption in divine things, but never troubled him with doubts as to whether he had been fair in his judgments or gentle in his dealings with his flock and his family.

'It never seemed to occur to my husband that I, a young girl thrown into a society of strangers, foreign in all my manners and my ideas, with a round of new duties to fulfil, would need counsel help and sympathy. His own natural love for me seemed to be a thing against which he had to fight as tending to idolatry, instead of encouraging it as the only means of winning and keeping my love for himself. In every way he hurt my feelings. The Shakespeare which Paul Durham had given to me he burned as a book full of profane stage plays. The *Don Quixote* I wrote of, which was a French translation given me by my French guardian, shared the same fate, when he discovered it was not true. Every book I had in my possession was read partially and contemptuously, and some on account of their Romanish tendency, and others on account of their frivolousness (or what he called viciousness) were destroyed. This book alone escaped condemnation on account of some passages which I read to him with which he thoroughly agreed, and as it was the dying legacy of the aunt to whom we both owed so much, he was not disposed to hunt out heresies in it.

'It has been said that every woman learns to love the father of her children if he is not a brute, but though he was no brute, but a man of many good qualities, my husband did not win upon me after I became a mother, not even to the extent of that quiet household affection which could have made life so much easier for us both. I had lived years in those five months in the Fleet Liberties with my brother and my lover, and now in this remote dull place, I felt a woman in experience, compared with the ignorant and unpolished country folks with whom I was compelled to associate. Although my aunt had had narrow views, and my father and mother were somewhat bigoted Huguenots, they were all people of gracious manners and even temper, while my husband, though he watched for temptation through the senses, always thought he did well to be angry, and whenever he was zealously affected, considered it was in a good matter.

'The death of the old grandfather, Lord Seton, put my husband's untowardly ward in possession of the large estate of the parish, and shut us out from any visiting at the Hall. He led a life openly vicious, and did all that was in his power to annoy my husband and to hinder his work. But that did not take place till my own family bereavements had been overwhelming.

'My father died just after my eldest boy Hugh was born. His health had been failing since the losses through the South Sea scheme, and I saw that my husband was not unprepared for the fatal result. My mother came up to Scotland to live with me, and received but a chilly welcome from Mr Keith. She was but barely reconciled to the change when she heard of the death in action of her son Victor in a long letter from Paul Durham. This seemed to crush her utterly; Mr Keith had reproved her for her excessive grief for the loss of her husband, and described the glories of the blest which he believed he was enjoying, but he never tried to comfort her in this way for the death of Victor, who had had no serious thoughts, and who had led me into haunts of iniquity and vice which had perilled my soul. Though my dear mother had turned in distaste from the consolation in the one case she was now struck to the quick by the absence of it, and by a few stern abrupt speeches which showed that the faithful minister reckoned Victor as lost, and in private talk with me she spoke of my brother's generous, frank and candid nature, of his love for his parents, and his loyalty to his friends. It did not need such representations from my mother, such going back on his old childish days, such treasured memories of his cleverness and his kindliness to make me feel that my brother was more fit for Heaven than his censor, and the letter of my lover – mine no more – had called up more strongly than ever the terrible mistake of my life to my accusing conscience.

'My mother loved my Hugh because he reminded her in his looks and ways of her own firstborn son, and we comforted each other in the best way we could for a year, after which time she too passed away to join her dear ones in Heaven. This was to me a terrible loss, and my husband lost all patience with my sinful repining at the chastening hand, that as he said "breaks our idols to our faces".

'Although my *dot* was substantial, it was not my own to do what I pleased with. I had no right to anything; all my rights were merged in those of my husband. He at once appropriated it to paying off the widow of John Keith, and this done, he felt himself to be the absolute master of Upper and Nether Keith. This however was the inheritance of my Hugh, and I did not grudge it, but I did regret that I was but as my husband's housekeeper and upper servant, that I had no power to do a kindness or to bestow a charity. Scotland was then greatly overrun with sturdy beggars, and for them I had no great amount of pity, but there were hard lives of honest working people whom I thought our superfluity might help, but it was strange how many excellent reasons my husband always brought forward against such charity. There was however one instance in which I had my own way and I thank God for it every day of my life.

'It was two months after my mother's death, and I had been brought to bed of a little girl whom I had called by her name of Clarice, but I took a bad turn, and went off into a fever. When I got better I found my old nurse at my side, and not far off my baby in the arms of a young woman whose sad story I knew well, but who was supplying her wants as I could not now do. Violet Anderson had been troth-plighted to a young man in her own station, and the banns had been put up when a malignant fever came into the village, and she was attacked by it, and subsequently her parents. She was given over for death, but recovered after a long sickness to find her mother dead, and her sweetheart married to another woman. Violet would fain have turned her face to the wall and died too, so as to be done with her grief and her shame, but her father needed her and even in her misery the child to whom she would be the only parent, seemed to claim that she should live. In the straits of our household, she came and offered my baby a share of the milk which was given for her own, but would not give up her boy for any bribe that my husband could offer.

'My little one did not trouble her long, but I grew to love and even to respect Violet, who had learned tenderness through her sorrow, and who wept over my darling as my own mother would have done. I therefore proposed to keep her as a permanent servant, and let the child be brought up in the manse. There were many scruples to overcome on the part of my husband, especially as I was so greatly set upon it, but as Violet had stood the rebuke of the Kirk session, and had been readmitted to church privileges, and was a sincere penitent, there was no logic in his saying that we could not look over her transgression and forgive her when in his capacity as a minister of Christ's Church he had forgiven the sinner. Two years after Clarice's death I became the mother of a second boy, whom I called Victor; I had afterwards two daughters who died young.

'In my grief at the loss of these little ones, I had one sullen source of satisfaction. It was hard to be a woman; to have no will of one's own and no career, to bear children in sorrow into a world which was all thorns and briars for tender feet, all stabs and blows for loving hearts, was no enviable lot, and though I sometimes longed for the sympathy and help of a daughter, I said to myself that it was well for them to be laid under the turf at Colbrandspath at an age when even their father believed their souls were safe, and neither sorrow nor remorse could trouble them.

'In all my troubles, Violet was the most faithful, the most affectionate and the most devoted of friends. To have her own boy brought up in a godly house under the minister whom she reverenced, and the mistress whom she loved, seemed to her to deserve the service of a life, and I knew that her genuine admiration of my husband was helpful to me in making me bear better my earlier trials. But when things grew worse, she became my partisan and especially Hugh's partisan against the minister himself.'

V

MADAME KEITH'S NARRATIVE CONTINUED – A MOTHER'S SORROWS

'How can I tell how dear my first born was and is still to me, and how here in the wilds of Columba I long for him with an exceeding longing? How can I tell to this senseless paper and to the son who alone will read this, how my children, instead of being a bond of union between father and mother, were a constant cause of difference, of sharp words and hard rules on one side, and of deep sullen defiance on the other? Somehow I had learned from experience that self-renunciation does not lead to happiness or even blessedness; for I had a constant sense that what I had done because other people said it was my duty, and that I could never be in the wrong if I sacrificed my own inclinations, had been cursed instead of blessed. Not only was I a worse woman, but my husband was a worse man because I had been so weak as to be persuaded to marry him without love.

'I wanted to make my children happy as far as I could. The rule of children all over the world was very different from what it is in our happy Columba. My eyes fill with tears when I see at their play and their dances my Victor's children, who never keep back a thought from their parents, or fear that they will be chidden for levity or unreasonable talk. In Scotland, and in a Scottish manse in particular, the rule of life was painfully rigid, and my husband grew year by year more and more narrow in his sympathies; my boys would have had indeed a joyless childhood, if in his absence I had not relaxed the discipline, and allowed myself to play and romp and joke with them. In their father's presence, they only spoke in answer to question, and they lost the opportunity of boyish games and childish talk at the parish school, amongst children of their own age, because he did not think the schoolmaster was a good classic scholar, and he undertook to teach the boys himself. He considered himself a good father because he did not spare the rod. When I suggested that whatever Solomon might have done, his son did not turn out well, he said I was jesting on sacred subjects, and it was probable that Solomon who was only inspired as a writer, had not practised what he preached.

'For my own part I know not now whether boys over-indulged or over-repressed run the greatest risk when they come to the liberty of young men, but at that time I was sick of my husband's severity. He chastised for mistakes and blunders as severely as for disobedience and other grave offences. I remonstrated with him, but I might as well have sought to break through a stone wall with my slender fingers. I was unwise perhaps, for I let the boys see that I took their part against their father, but he considered it to be his duty to disregard my entreaties, and to be all the more severe because of my weak indulgence. When what one chooses to do takes the imposing form of duty there is no excess that one will not commit. As Pascal says in this book, "Never do we do evil so thoroughly or so cheerfully as when we do it through a false principle of conscience."

'I on the other hand thought it my duty to make my children happy, and the result may be imagined; the boys loved me and dreaded their father. He too gradually came to see that not only did my blind maternal love come between my soul and God, which was the danger he ostensibly dreaded most, but they weaned my heart from himself. If he needed and demanded anything at my hands, I walked with the deliberate pace of obedience and duty, but at a cry or a word from Hugh or Victor, I flew on the wings of love.

I had no idea myself, nor do I think he had either, of the capacity for good and for evil that was within me till this standing duel began. The negative feeling of indifference and distaste which had been checked by my respect for his character in the earlier days of our marriage, was now changed into an active mental and moral antagonism. And his feelings too changed; he became more sharp and critical; even in the most indifferent things he found cause to give and to take offence, with this difference, that he entrenched himself behind his religious dogmas, and bewailed the corruption of unregenerate human nature which made me and his sons struggle against the pure Christian doctrine and discipline as understood and practised by a minister of the Word; while as for me, I was without chart or compass. The dry husks of Calvinism in which I had been brought up, for Jansenism was as uncompromising as to human nature and Divine sovereignty as the Shorter Catechism itself, had now no savour or nourishment for my soul. The monstrous structure which had been built on a few assumptions, a few texts disjointed from the rest of Scripture and strained to the uttermost seemed to show injustice, cruelty and blind partiality on the part of the Creator, and did not in any way solve the great riddle of the universe.

'Even this book to which I clung as a relic of the past and of happier days, did not help me. There were some beautiful thoughts in it, but still the idea of human duty that ran through it was that we should hate ourselves in order to please God. I did so want to be loved. If my husband did not love me, if I had lost through submission to my parents the love that might have made my life happy and honourable, why should I not love myself, think of myself kindly and tenderly, make excuses for my own faults which no one else would make, appreciate my own good qualities, compassionate my own sorrows? Did not Hugh's dark eyes glow when I said he had done well; did not Victor's dimples play when I heard him his task and told him it was perfect; did not a word of sympathy dry their tears and a pleasant smile divert their thoughts from the punishment that was past or that might be anticipated in the future?

'The strictness of Sabbath-keeping in England as compared with

France had always seemed to me of doubtful expediency, but here in this manse of Colbrandspath it was carried to the extreme. There were family prayers morning and evening on every day of the year, but on Sundays they were of extra length. There were two long services taken at once, occupying three hours and a half between 11 a.m. and 2.30 p.m. There was catechising in the evening of the servants and the household, and no book but the Bible and some volumes of sermons allowed to be read by young or old all day. A walk in the fields or in the romantic glens of the neighbourhood or by the seashore, where the surf beat on the crags and rocks of St Abbs' Head, was absolutely forbidden as desecration of the holy day, and talk on any secular subject was rigorously checked. My boys hated the Sunday, and so did I, for I recollected a great amount of freedom with my *bonne*, while my aunt carried on her private religious exercises, and at meals even she had always relaxed for my sake, and allowed me to talk of the things that interested me. And I had been taken every afternoon to the village, where I saw the country people from the neighbourhood assembled for a dance on the grass. Almost all of them had been to Mass in the morning, but the afternoon was given over to social intercourse and amusement. Here I thought the Roman Church wiser in its generation than the English or the Scottish, and I believed that this holiday, this break in a laborious life was altogether good for the French people, while as for our Scottish peasantry, they had no idea of amusing themselves in this way.

'My brother Victor used to quote from the Latin poet that if you try to drive out nature with a pitchfork, she will return too strong for ten pitchforks to expel. At least there was much more drunkenness and licentiousness in this country parish of Colbrandspath than in the little village near Fontainebleau, and there was a sombreness even in the voices of this repressed people.

'They were generally very poor and hard working, and as such, free from many of the temptations of wealth and ease, but their few pleasures were warred against to the death by my conscientious husband. Dancing, in spite of censure from the pulpit and the Kirk session, was practised by the young men and women and courtships were conducted at windows and in many a quiet rendezvous with all the perils of darkness and secrecy. No merry-making, no mourning was conducted without the accompaniment of ale and whisky; at wedding, at christening and at funeral, the bottle was produced even by the poorest as a necessary piece of hospitality.

'There was a religious stir in my mind in reading the works of Samuel Law and a copy of Thomas-à-Kempis bequeathed by my mother, but afterwards I fell back on the old iron necessity in which I had lived so long. I had had no free will all my life. I had been surrounded by a network of traditionary duties and overmastering superiors, in whom I had been taught to see the hand of an Omnipotent God, who had thus led me through hard paths, but into no peace. Oh! who would care for the hill Difficulty and the Valley of Humiliation, or even the Valley of the Shadow of Death, if only there was the prospect of the Delectable Mountains on this side, and the Celestial City on the other side of the River of Death.

'I used to read Mr John Bunyan's parable and his account of his own life with some notion that the giants I had to fight, and the doubts I had to dispel were very different from those he encountered with the weapons of All-Prayer and the sword of the Spirit which is the word of God. All human nature cannot be changed by a petition or an apt quotation from Holy Writ, and my spiritual foes took on the appearance of angels of light. It was the awful majesty of Justice and Mercy that forbade me to say of this sadly disjointed world that its Almighty Maker had made it good. Mr Pope says, "One truth is clear, whatever is, is right." It may be true, but to me at that it was by no means clear. Now the scales have fallen from my eyes in great measure, and where I cannot see clearly I have faith to trust.

'One cannot expect sympathy from children, dear as they are; they exact it but they cannot give it. If it had not been for my good Violet, I think I should have lost my senses, but she gave me what comfort and cheer she could, and somehow I got strength from the weak and wisdom from the simple. Her boy was a good steady fellow who applied himself to his work with diligence and zeal. My husband made him useful in the stable and garden, and sometimes reproached me that this child of sin was much more towardly than either of our own boys – but Violet, though satisfied with her Gavin, was curiously ambitious for her nurslings, Hugh and Victor.

'But the hardest time of all came. Hugh was clever, and could learn anything, and at the age of seventeen he was sent to the care of his father's sister in Edinburgh to attend the university course. His father had his worldly ambition and meant Hugh to be an advocate who should rise to be a Lord of Session. About this time, his own hopes for church preferment had been baffled. He had been Moderator of the General Assembly for two years, and had carried matters there with such a high hand that the burgesses of Edinburgh from whom he hoped for a city church, thought him rather a dangerous firebrand, and the growing secular temper which seemed to affect Scotland, made his translation even to a better and more important parish more doubtful. For he was not satisfied with preaching the supremacy of the Kirk in the pulpit, but in the presbytery, in the Synod, and in the General Assembly, he carried his principles into active practice. He had never doubted that he would have had his home in Edinburgh when his boys were ready for their university course, and his disappointment was intensified by the manner in which Lord Seton behaved to him. In every manner in his power, he made his presence as the most considerable man in the district and the county felt, and we were not very sorry when he took himself and his ill managed household to Edinburgh for the winter.

'But evil came of this to our Hugh, for he disliked the strictness of his aunt's household. It was even worse than the manse, for there he had a fond mother and a devoted Violet to make amends for the severe discipline of his father's rule. As the most bitter and cruel stroke Lord Seton could lay upon his old tutor and his present adversary, this profligate man pressed the boy to come to his house in the Canongate, where there was dicing and drinking and music and dancing, and where all sorts of reprobates of both sexes were always to be found. This first taste of freedom and wild licence fascinated my boy, and there was one of his lordship's hangers on who had the gifts of a fallen angel to lure the unwary to destruction.

'Hugh was kept very short of money, not so much from penuriousness on his father's part, though if he could be charged with any sin which was not of the spirit, perhaps it lay in that direction, but from the idea that wealth in the hands of the inexperienced is a snare; and this Lord Seton, who kept back our rightful dues in the matter of stipend, supplied his wants with gifts and loans, introduced him to tradespeople and money-lenders as the heir of Upper and Nether Keith, put the dice-box and the winecup in his hands, and even led him into worse haunts than his own evil house. My boy was handsome of his person and ready with his tongue; the old blood of the de Launays and of the Drouins and of the Keiths which in the later generations had been repressed by religious convictions came out strong. He was hungry for pleasure, fun and freedom. It was during the second winter session that he fell into these evil ways, and when his father heard of it, he mounted his horse and went straight to his sister's house, and though I would fain have accompanied him, he told me cruelly that it was to my foolish indulgence that he laid the blame of all this, and said I should not have the chance of doing so now. He was all the more indignant because his sister had been hoodwinked by excuses and pretexts, and what he called lies, as to Hugh's frequent absences.

'I never knew what happened between the two, but I gathered that the father had been shocked at the reckless air, the audacity and the free speech of the son, and when he had repeated to my boy his anger at the sinful indulgence he had always met with from me as the main cause of his failings and vices, Hugh shook the dust from his feet, and took up his abode with his father's enemy. Enemy he was indeed to both father and son. When the lad was excited by wine and fun and jolly company, Lord Seton got Hugh to acknowledge as his wife a girl whom he had himself deceived, and from whom he feared trouble, and there was my boy at twenty, bound irrevocably to a low, shameless woman, five years older than himself in years, and ten years older in knowledge of the evil world. After that there was a severance from Lord Seton on Hugh's part, but there was no drawing to his father. The estate was not entailed, so that the money-lenders ceased to advance, but did not cease to press, and Hugh came of age to find himself loaded with debt, married unworthily, and without a friend in the city of Edinburgh that seemed to him so full of kindness and brotherhood.

'I had little speech with my husband on the subject of our boy, but I wrote to Hugh from time to time, and sent what little aid I could in his straits, and implored him to come back to his father's house; but alas! I could not say that while he was yet a long way off, his father would see him, and go forth to meet him or that the fatted calf would be slain, and a feast made in his honour. Nor could he humble himself as would be needful to bring forgiveness. His only wish was to go abroad, to leave the country altogether, and I had only one friend in the world who could help him, and that was Paul Durham, now Captain of the *Triton*.

'I had not thought that anything my Hugh could do would have moved his father after the rupture in Edinburgh, when his son deliberately preferred Lord Seton to himself, but the marriage was gall and wormwood to him. After what he had saved his ward from at his own peril, that this indignity, this horror should be put on his own eldest born, the heir of an old and honourable house, the child of a decent and godly home, struck him to the heart. His countenance changed. At night when he supposed me to be asleep – asleep! I did not sleep for many nights after that crowning sorrow! – I felt the bed shake with his sobs. For once I believed that we were in sympathy. I spoke through my tears, but he repulsed me. He said he was ill in health, but needed no service which I could offer. He never would allow to me that it was his father's heart that was cut to the quick.

'I saw my boy once after this. Our good Violet got us a meeting at her father's house. He spoke wildly, defiantly, despairingly by turns, but he softened at my sorrow, and laid his head in my bosom, and wept for a long space. When we could gather strength to speak of what was to be done, I gave him a letter to my old lover, begging him for the love of God, and if he had any compassion on the most unhappy woman in the world, to befriend Hugh Keith and if possible put him in some situation in his ship where he might begin a new career for himself. Hugh brightened up at the idea of a change, but alas! Captain Durham was not in port. He was on a Mediterranean station, and it needed money to take Hugh there. I had none, and no means of getting any, and I knew that my husband's worse nature would be aroused at the idea of the lover, whom he now knew I had preferred to him, being asked to befriend my son. And here came out our good Violet's generous heart. She had saved money in our service and so had Gavin, and they poured into my lap the whole of their joint stock, and slender enough it was, to take Master Hugh to his mother's friend. Hugh and I vowed that it would be repaid with usury if we lived. We lived – at least I know that Violet, Gavin, Victor and still live in Columba and I feel as if Hugh still lives on the other side of the world – but that money was never repaid, though thank God they have now a fair estate in land and stock, and are held in high repute in the Commonwealth.'

VI

MADAME KEITH'S NARRATIVE CONTINUED – FAREWELL TO SCOTLAND

'Things went on worse and worse between Lord Seton and our household at the manse. He took advantage of some legal right to refuse to pay his tithes in money, but laid down the quantity of barley and oats which were in other parishes only the measure of the stipend which was paid in money, in bulk in the street before our door, regardless of weather, which we had to sell at a loss. He sent some of his idlest and most dissolute servants to fill the family pew in church, with instructions to behave as irreverently as they could without being expelled; he went outside of his rights in enclosing a great part of the glebe for his own, and making our horses and cows go short of food, and altogether he set himself down as our watchful and powerful enemy. My husband was tried in various ways in both his spiritual office and secular matters at this time. He had likewise felt humbled in his own Kirk session and his own rebellious presbytery after the awful fall of his eldest son, and was disposed to lend a greedy ear to the proposals of Ralph Abercrombie for a settlement of Scottish families somewhere between the French colonies at the mouth of the great Mississippi river, and the Spanish settlements in New Spain or Mexico. Ralph Abercrombie was an old man who in his youth had joined the Darien Expedition, and was one of the few who returned. And in his journeyings through the hostile country of the Spaniards and the Indians, he had fallen in with a valley of the most marvellous fertility, where he evermore maintained that a plantation of Scotchmen could make a paradise, only they must be strong enough to contend with a tribe of Indians who had possession.

'There were some of our Scottish borderers then very little satisfied with the Union on worldly grounds; they thought England got all the advantage in getting peace and prosperity, while Scotland had lost national honour and seemed to have no profit. My husband's chief discontent with this political change was on account of the subjection of the Church to the State, which he said was taking all the life out of the Kirk of Scotland, and when the Abercrombies pressed him to go as their minister, saying he would be a presbytery and a synod and an Assembly, a patron and a minister all in one, he thought there was a great field for his energies in the founding a pure Kirk in the wilderness, and just after Hugh had left me for the Mediterranean, he gave his whole heart to the scheme. My mind was more at ease, and I did not turn against it. I feared for Victor, who would have the same gauntlet to run as his brother, and fancied that in a new country, he would have more freedom of action and of thought.

'My husband's joining the party was just the turning point between the impossible and the difficult, for by the sale of Upper and Nether Keith to the price of which was added other funds from savings much larger than I had been aware of, he put more into the venture than anyone else, and this gave him a right to have his say upon every matter. This was not a religious movement like the departure of the Pilgrim Fathers to New England. It was not an adventure like the Darien Scheme from which young people thought to return with large fortunes. It was simply a plantation for the sake of bettering the condition of the people that went, and it was composed for the most part of whole families, and the more my husband thought of it, the more necessary he felt it to be that he should go to found it on true religious principles, to bring up the children of the settlement in the fear of God, and to see that there the Church should be superior and not dependent for temporalities on a reckless child of the devil like Lord Seton.

'I had never rightly admired my husband's qualities before. His sermons were hard though sometimes vehement, and his prayers public and private, were more like sermons than prayers and absolutely destitute of the spirit of devotion, but in the arrangements for the plantation, he showed the greatest shrewdness as to money matters, and powers of organisation of his human instruments, and an adapting of means to ends such as I had never given him credit for. Perhaps if he had had the larger field in the Church of which he had been disappointed, he might have left me more to the guidance of our house and our family. I could not but wonder at the manner in which he subordinated to his own will men of less logical minds such as the two Abercrombies, and men of more passionate tempers, like Mr Hepburn and the Elliotts.

'As for myself, I was as nothing in his calculations, but he felt for a little that by the sale of the lands of Upper and Nether Keith he had deprived Victor of his inheritance, for it was no longer looked on as Hugh's. Still he said to himself that the few hundreds of barren acres near the Lammermoor hills would be exchanged for thousands of acres of the rich soil of the new world, and the completeness of the equipment was sure to bring success and of course those who ventured most should reap the largest profits.

'We in Columba now reap the benefit of his wise foresight and the people cherish his memory still. No such expedition had ever left Britain, let alone Scotland. It was not that the numbers were so many, but the equipment was thorough and all trades were represented. This valley had never been taken possession of by France or Spain, and as for Indians they must either be fought or treated with, probably first the one and then the other.

'I had hoped to hear from my Hugh before we sailed from Glasgow in the beginning of the summer of 1745, but there were some political troubles in the wind, and though I believed he had got on board the *Triton* that ship sailed under sealed orders; we knew not whither. Violet and her son accompanied the expedition, but I left a letter for my boy at her father's house and also had meant to leave this book in which I write, with some of my life and some of my prayers for him in it, but by some mistake it was brought back and packed up by an over-zealous servant, and I did not discover the mistake till we were all out at sea. Thus my son could only receive the letter when he returned – if he returned – to see his old home now deserted. I had wanted Hugh to know what was the bond between Captain Durham and myself; I had also wanted him to see my own struggles and questioning doubts as to whether all that I had been educated in was true or wise. Often women disclose difficulties which men alone can solve. In their narrow lives they are thrown much on themselves and they discover things that are wrong, but which they are powerless to set right. But this wish was not granted.

'I have been in Columba now for twenty years at this present time of writing, absolutely shut out from the world. Sorrowful I often am, when I think of my youth and of my son Hugh, but I am not miserable in this new country as I was in most of my life at Colbrandspath manse. But to justify myself to myself for various things that I have done and have left undone in this plantation of Columba, I must write down not only what happened to me and mine before we set forth on our adventurous voyage, but also the circumstances which led me, and the council with whom I worked, to make such great changes. Especially do I wish my son Victor to understand that I did all for the best and that new emergencies called for new rules.

'And now I see around me a little community of more than a thousand souls – we were but five hundred when we left Glasgow – where there is no want, no drunkenness, no profanity, no licentiousness, where there is food for all, work for all, love for all, and amusement for all. I only long with an unspeakable longing to receive my son Hugh into this cheerful circle, and to see him as happy and as honoured as his brother Victor now is. Has the hateful bond into which he was cheated been dissolved by death? Has he now a good wife? Has he loving children round him? Ah! it is all unknown. I cannot know the truth until I die, and then things may look very different to us when we see them afar off from the Heaven we hope for.'

VII

MADAME KEITH'S NARRATIVE CONTINUED – THE SETTLEMENT OF COLUMBA

'We had rough weather across the Atlantic to Virginia, but things were strangely reversed with my husband and myself. On our short voyage from London to Leith, I had been miserably sick as well as heart-sore, while he was only moderately sea-sick, whereas now in the six weeks on board the *Scotia*, I was tolerably well, and he was deadly sick. In his sufferings, my heart turned towards him, and he did not repulse me, though he was not grateful, at least in words, but he sought for my help, and both Victor and myself waited on him dutifully. I was surprised to see how my younger boy grew to manhood in this short time and how when his father was too ill to be consulted about things on board, the Captain and Mr Hepburn spoke to Victor and to me.

'The Abercrombies were in the sister ship the *Berwick Lass* which was never out of sight. She was rather the slower sailor of the two but we trimmed our sails so as to be always within hail. We had one alarm through a Spanish privateer, but we got our guns ready and put on a bold front, and as we did not seem to be an easy prize, they clapped on sail and made off. On the approach of this danger, my husband shook off his sickness and came on deck and moved about among the men with exhortations, and with wise suggestions, but when the enemy turned for flight he crept again into his narrow berth, and appeared worse than before.

'We stopped a week at Richmond on the James River. The ships lay in harbour, and we went over the country to see how they cultivated the tobacco and cotton and Indian corn and other products in that beautiful plantation of Virginia. We took from there all manner of seeds and plants, and also some livestock, for we only took a few draught-horses from Scotland. But this implied the buying of another ship, and Mr Hepburn and John Abercrombie were taken with one that was to be got very cheap. My husband rallied a little on shore and he objected to this, as it seemed to him scarce seaworthy, but he was overborne, and as we had fine weather to Kingston in Jamaica, all appeared right. There we laid in those other seeds and plants that were fitted for our warmer settlement, and also some more livestock especially pigs.

'But now our perils began in good earnest, for we had something more like a hurricane than a storm, and the newly-engaged ship could not stand against it like our sound vessels. We reached a sheltered bay on the coast of Cuba, and there we managed to discharge all the livestock and valuable cargo from the battered hulk which we had to leave with its captain and crew, and sorely over-freighted and crowded, we essayed to make our way to the mainland. Again my husband rose when there was need of his services, and took his share in the hardships and the hard work and the perils with which we made our toilsome way. In contending with the elements, in making the best of all our stores and all our men so as to get as much out of them as possible, and to expend no strength in vain, he showed himself at his very best – and in the end his death was heroic and I doubt not happy. For it was in trying to save our good Violet's son Gavin, who had turned to the seafaring life with great zeal and success, and who was as good a sailor now as any we had taken from Glasgow with us, that my husband met the death he had been all his life prepared for.

'Gavin Anderson was trying to lash more firmly in its place a beautiful cow, the finest in our possession, when a great wave swept him off his feet, and but for my husband's intervention he would have gone overboard. Both were driven sharp against the bulwarks, and my husband held tight to the body of the rescued young man. When they were separated, it was by force and it appeared as if my husband was in a swoon. Something had snapped in the region of the heart; he never breathed again. He had ailed, I know, more or less for years. The troubles with his son Hugh and with Lord Seton, and his disappointments in the Kirk, had fretted him inwardly. I had noted that he could not rest well at night except in an upward posture, and that his colour had changed, but this sudden death was not only a shock to me; I was almost glad to feel it a grief. He had been tenderer with Victor than he ever was with Hugh and he was lost when he was missed by me and by all our party as he could never have been before.

'I know not how it came to pass but when he was to be committed to that troubled ocean that had caused his death, though in the Kirk of our voyagers there was no funeral service obligatory, there was a feeling that someone should pray, and there was none in either ship who seemed to think themselves equal to it. There had been one death before on board, and the minister had got out of his berth to lead the devotions of the people. Calvinistic as he was he felt that that was an occasion to be improved.

'The schoolmaster was applied to, but he said he had no gift that way. They asked Victor if he would not take his father's place, and utterance was given to him, and he spoke the thought of our hearts. It now appeared to me that my husband had foreseen that his life would not be long, for he had had much talk with Victor on sacred subjects. It was, as I have said, not a religious but a worldly adventure, and he had groaned over the carelessness and indifference of the flock he had taken in hand, but he trusted much to the schoolmaster, whom he believed to be doctrinally sound, if not eloquent, and he would himself see that the rising generation should be brought up in the nurture and admonition of the Lord. When his health failed so much on board, he still hoped to rally on land, and that he might be spared till he had trained a worthy successor, but now it looked like as if his young son of twenty was to be the people's choice.

'Old Ralph Abercrombie was now our guide to his wondrous valley, and his son took the active command of the party, but as Victor and myself represented the largest sum of money that had been put into the concern, we were consulted on everything. I was now a free woman as I had never been in my life, and not only had I the liberty to think for myself and to express my thoughts, but I had the aid and the sympathy of a son of good understanding and kindly temper. The weight of years, and experience, and of property gave me influence over all the band among whom my husband had cast my lot. We had indeed perils of all kinds before we reached the place where Ralph Abercrombie thought we might make a safe landing. The two ships were slightly out of repair, but they must be left till we had reached the place to dwell in. The coast was rocky and dangerous, but we made our way to the river-mouth that would lead us to the place we now call Columba. The poor horses needed a few days' rest before they could travel, and then we loaded our waggons with our implements and our various kinds of seed corn and of other seeds and we drove our flocks and herds with us under Ralph Abercrombie's guidance. Some things we left behind, furniture, books and indeed great part of our stores of food also, under an escort of six men from the ship's crew, and two stout men of our own, and with the schoolmaster in charge provisioned for a month, but the most needful things we took with us. On our toilsome march, we were attacked by the Indians in rear and flank, but at last we got into this valley by the single approach which was open for our waggons. The weather was fortunately fine, and we saw that Ralph Abercrombie had not been mistaken in his account of the country. It was beautiful beyond everything I had ever seen. Virginia and Jamaica were not to be compared to it for natural capabilities; there were wild fruits and other vegetable productions in abundance, but of game not so much as we had expected. But our guide had under-estimated the strength of the Indians, who were not here scattered as in the hunting fields of the English colonies on the Atlantic

Ocean but were living in villages with cultivation of maize, tobacco, potatoes and several other eatable roots. At first they were disposed to trade with us, and we were glad of the opportunity. We hastily rigged up huts for shelter, and prepared for cultivation on the low flat that spreads out round our first town of Ebenezer. This was the name my husband had proposed to give to our first settlement. "Hitherto the Lord hath helped us," was the feeling we had when we made our first home in the wilderness.

'As soon as we had unpacked our waggons and rested the horses for a night, they were despatched for the rest of our goods, and their comrades, for these sailors had purposed to take up their abode in the plantation too, but when the waggons reached the roadstead, our messengers found that the ships were gone, the escort probably slain, for there were the dead bodies of two to be seen on the place, and some of the clothing of others. As for the goods, whatever was worth taking, had been carried off by the pirates, and whatever they did not account of value had been consumed by fire. The latter was the case with the books, for the charred remains of some of them could be seen. We had brought all my husband's theological library, and also a supply of books for the schoolmaster to teach the children by, but all these were lost as well as the schoolmaster himself. It was with sad hearts that our people returned with their empty waggons to say that we had lost our ships and our goods and we had to live for years without much that we had been thoughtful enough to provide.

'Now came the stress with the Indians, who after they had got what they wanted in the way of trade, became alarmed at our preparations for settlement. Our weapons were better than theirs, and our numbers, though thinned by the accidents of the voyage and the landing and the journey, were still greater than they could bring forward in a body, but they harassed us perpetually, for they knew the country better than we did, and were full of clever ruses and surprises. They robbed us by night and waylaid us by day. Mr Abercrombie proposed exterminating them as the only course, but Victor and I had some misgivings as to whether we had done right in coming to this peaceful valley to take their land from them. We had years of attacks, defence, skirmishing and fighting and our first crops were put in under great difficulties, and harvested under greater still.

'A common danger led to union with our sometime enemies. All over central America there was a great horror of the Spaniards, and the Indians got scent of a proposed invasion of the valley by a strong party, who had heard somehow that there was an English settlement rich in money worth pillaging. The Indians sought to make truce with us, that we might aid them to repulse this dreaded foe, and for the first time we stood together, and made a successful defence at the pass through which we had brought our waggons. This being the only vulnerable point we walled up and palisaded it on the top. We keep it clear on our own side, but there are tokens that on the other side it is covered with the rank tropical growth of the surrounding country, and will now look more like a thicket than a wall. In this work the Indians aided us, and we made a treaty and allotted to the Scotch settlers and the Indians each their several bounds. We had thinned their numbers far more than our own by the wars we had carried on for more than two years, and in the fight with the Spaniards, they had suffered most, though they confessed that we had taken our full share of the danger, so that we were surprised to find that there were no more than about eighty of them in all when we made our treaty, a number that, as Mr Abercrombie said, we could have easily disposed of. Our own numbers were near six hundred at that time, for though we had had many deaths we had still more births during the two years, and as war ceased, we went on our several ways without any differences that could not be settled by our own Council and the Indian Council. I should not wonder if the whole of the Indians will by and by be taken in as members of our own Commonwealth.

'We had hard enough times for the first two years. We had to plough and sow and reap and fight, as well as build houses and make for ourselves everything that we needed in the way of furniture. The worst thing about the settlement was that we had no iron, and we had to mix our soft copper with softer tin that seemed to make it harder. During the war, our guns and cutlasses were the most valuable things that we possessed. Our spades and harrows and ploughshares were the most precious things we had after peace was made. We had to fare hard for years before we had bread enough and to spare, and to keep our teeth off our domestic animals, but there was always enough of potatoes and maize, and of an Indian bean, and also of many kinds of fruit in the season.

'In the midst of our hardships and troubles I was strangely happy. There was so much to do, so much to plan, and so much to refrain from doing, and to one who had led such a passive existence as mine, this sphere for activity was exhilarating. No one knew how deep had been the dissension between my husband and myself, and Victor and I were supposed to be guided by his spirit. At times I was called on to pray and even to preach and it is strange how a different sort of religion from any I had been taught, entered my soul. In my troubles heretofore I had found no help or refuge in prayer – the attempt had always made me feel more rebellious – but now when prayer could be followed by working to the best of my judgement and to the utmost of my ability I found it helpful and inspiring.'

VIII

MADAME KEITH'S NARRATIVE CONTINUED – THE ORIGIN OF HANDFASTING

'Except for a few odd books that had been out in the cabin among which were many Bibles, we had no literature. We were also almost destitute of pens and ink. The schoolmaster would have no doubt stared aghast at the idea of teaching under these circumstances, but the poor man was not spared to make the experiment, and as every able-bodied man was needed to plough and to fight in our early days, my offer to take on myself this, to me most interesting task, was cheerfully accepted by the people. I fell on the way of teaching them by word of mouth, as our few books would soon have been worn out by their little hands. I think I learned more of human nature from these little ones that I could have done from all the books that were ever written or printed. All the Catechisms, larger and smaller, were destroyed, and I made the Gospels my manual, and found out how differently they could be interpreted when they were not considered under the benumbing influence of tradition.

'One book I compiled myself with the help of my son Victor, and wrote down in a blank book which my husband had brought for Kirk session purposes. This was a sort of history of the world and a history of Scotland, for tradition would change the facts if they were not written down. I found my scholars took great interest in this, and I devised helps to memory through knitting and notching sticks in which they grew very clever.

'There was in the Church to which my husband belonged no religious ceremony connected with marriage. There was this difference between the Fleet marriage from which he had saved James Hay, afterwards Lord Seton, and that into which his sometime pupil had entrapped our son Hugh, that in England it was its celebration by an ordained minister (though an unworthy and disgraced one) of the Church of England according to the form set down in the Book of Common Prayer and the signature or marks of the contracting parties attested by him and his clerk in a book of registration that made it valid, whereas in Scotland it was the declaration of marriage before witnesses that bound the parties. In the one case, the clergyman was liable to censure by his bishop for irregular proceedings, in the other case the parties were liable to being publicly reproved for an irregular marriage by the Kirk session, and denied church privileges until this had been endured; but in both cases the marriages stood good in law, and the offspring of such marriages were legitimate. In our small community, Victor took the part of the preacher at the united request of the heads of families, and therefore he was the person to whom those who sought to marry made their solemn declaration and their vows. Young as he was, he had discretion beyond his years, and I believe the whole of our people had confidence in him.

'But there arose very soon a difficulty with regard to the Indian women. In spite of the battles with the men, our young Scotch settlers found favour with some of the redskin girls, and they were living with them openly without any bond, and indeed the heathens could not understand our Christian marriage. I recollected having heard of the handfasting, practised in remote parishes before the reformation on account of the scarcity of priests, and the impossibility of celebrating the so-called sacrament of marriage without a priest. We called a Council together, as was our wont when any new matter had to be considered, and there I had had my place in from the first, and I proposed that the Indian women should be handfasted for a year and a day, during which time the bridegroom should do all in his power to win over his bride to the Christian Church, and should take her if she was willing to the Kirk on the Sabbath, and during which time she should be honourably treated by all our men and women. If by the end of that term, the bride was converted, and they were both willing they should be married as solemnly and irrevocably as our own people. If they did not choose to be thus married, they were free to part, but in that case the man had to make gifts to the woman whom he had ceased to delight in. The child, if there was any, became the property of the mother, unless it had been at her wish that the parting took place, when the father could claim it, and in that case it should then be brought up like one of our own children.

'The first case in which this was carried out was that of Ralph Abercrombie, the younger, whose Indian wife Palahna was as good as gold, and their love for each other was proved by many dangers, much courage and great endurance. It was a great day in Columba when Palahna was baptised by my name of Margaret, and her infant son by his father's name of Ralph, and they were married. This all took place on the same day and they are now alive the parents of twelve noble children.

'On that marriage day, Victor and I sat together thinking of what had been done with great satisfaction, for we hoped that by the just treatment of the Indian woman, as well as by the fairness of our dealings with the Indian men, and the absence of fire-water in our whole plantation, that friendly relations with our red brethren might be firmly established. He had handfasted three couples after Ralph Abercrombie, and they seemed to be most of them likely to end well. We had not enough of Scottish maidens for our youths, and it seemed a good step to secure these poor ignorant women in some rights as against the stronger and cleverer men.

'It was strongly borne in upon my mind that this was no godless wanton experiment, but one which might be good for Christians as well as Indians. I recollected my own marriage, pressed upon me by the authority of my parents, and my Hugh's marriage into which he had been tricked by a false friend, and no escape from either by law or Gospel. When I also saw how trivial are the motives which led to even marriages of liking among young people, how slight the knowledge of each other that they had before they entered into a bond from which there was no escape, I felt that the old Border rite might be made useful for others as well as in the mixed unions. After a year's experience of each other, if they were disposed to make a lifelong vow, there was far more prospect of its being kept sacred.

'Victor was first startled at the proposal, but the matter cost him, as well as me, weeks nay months of thought and prayer. Truly we both travailed as in birth with this idea, and shaped it out in all ways before we let it see the light of day. And he himself of all our Christian folk, was the first to practise it. He loved Helen Elliott, and he told her his plan. He said he believed he was sure of himself as of her, but yet he would like them both to have the trial of a year. If a child was born or like to be born, and they made up their minds to part, the one who made the first proposal of severance was to give the first choice of keeping it to the other. Of course, the first year the mother perforce must keep it, but after that if she had moved for separation, the father might claim it. In the case that the parent who had the right to the child was not able to maintain it altogether, the other was bound to give help in money or in money's worth. In no way was there any disgrace to fall either on the child or the parents, provided they had been faithful to each other during the term agreed on.

'So Victor and Helen were solemnly handfasted in the Kirk we had put up by that time at Ebenezer, and as was likely to be the case with such a loving and serious couple, they both only longed for the day for the real binding marriage to take place. But the example of the young minister had been followed by young folks of lighter character with different results. Now eighteen years after this first experiment, nobody thinks of anything else. It would be considered very rash and imprudent to bind oneself for life without knowing the temper, the capacity and the physical constitution of one's mate, and what to old world eyes would seem wantonness and fickleness, is in our little Commonwealth considered right and honourable. There was one concession made some few years after this fashion of handfasting had been introduced and this was that when the pair did not want to part, but yet were not quite sure that they loved each other enough to vow fidelity for life, the term of probation could be extended for another year and day at joint request, and again for another similar term on a further and larger payment but after that they must either marry or part. So far however as we have seen, it is generally settled at the end of the first year whether they part or cleave to each other for good. The outcome of the experiment so far is that prostitution is unknown and also such cruel seduction and desertion as my poor Violet suffered from. Handfasting is easy and respectable, and no child is born out of it or out of lawful marriage. Nor is anyone cast out of social intercourse and church privileges because he or she has been fickle and changeable. Even James Hepburn who was handfasted four times before he settled at last, is not disgraced. It is not given to everyone to be constant.

'But with him and such as him comes the difficulty with the children. He has four by different mothers, and as he was the fickle one, the three mothers all had a right to claim them. But this right one of them gave up at his request, for he wanted the boys though he was tired of the mothers, and with regard to one they could not agree. There were about the same time three instances of the parents saying the children were a burden, and the determination of the council was that such children should be solemnly renounced and given over to the Kirk, that they should be looked on as God's bairns and brought up to serve the Commonwealth either as preachers, as teachers, or as judges or other public officers. These therefore were the only children who learned to read and write and cast accounts on paper, so as to keep note of the outgoings and the incomings of the Commonwealth. They had no surname, but were called merely by their baptised names. They lived by themselves and after they had received the ordinary teaching of our schools for some years they were taught by themselves quite differently from the other children of the place. Their parents had no claim on them, and they were brought up to consider God as their father and Columba as their mother. They are all young as yet but are promising. Victor sees two who may be preachers, and as our people scatter and increase, they may take outlying charges and relieve him.

'Children are wealth and not poverty to our young plantation and it will always be rare to have them thrown upon our hands in this solemn and irrecoverable way. And as there is not the least shadow of disgrace on their birth, it does not prevent a woman from being sought for handfasting, which is likely to lead to marriage, that she may have one or two children already. Among industrious people settled in a large fertile territory, children are soon useful, and I have been surprised to see how much the hard discipline of a Scottish home is relaxed in the abode of sunshine and plenty. Schooling costs nothing, and as there are no tasks to be learned at home, the little hands are useful about many things. The girls learn to sew and to knit and to spin at school; the boys are not so long there on account of there being little work that they can do indoors, and they are needed for the field work, and from this cause I think the girls show the best results in the way of knowledge.

'Perhaps the love of children which has increased greatly among us, and the easiness of parental rule generally, partly results from our plantation being not of fanatical sectaries, but of somewhat wordly ordinary people. If my husband had listened to the promptings of his own heart, or cared about the peace and comfort of his household, he would not have been so harsh a father, but he not only held it as an abstract doctrine of the Church but as a real and terrible truth that the nature of a child was evil, and therefore that to give way to it was sinful compliance. Our laxer people were not now stirred up to their duties by earnest exhortations and warnings. Victor's sermons and prayers were as unlike his father's as they could be, and he himself shows an example of ruling his household in love, where father and mother are of one heart and one mind, and their children do not know any fear or concealment or diplomacy in their intercourse with either parents or grandparents.'

IX

MADAME KEITH'S NARRATIVE CONTINUED – THE KIRK AND THE SABBATH

'When we first built our Kirk, we made it also our schoolhouse. There was no sacredness attached to buildings among our people in the old country as there is in France and England, and it was a great difficulty overcome, and a great triumph when we had put up the four walls and the roof of a Kirk that would hold all our people. At first we used it for the Town House too, but by and by that was moved to the present building opposite.

'As we grew in numbers, all our conditions of life became more comfortable and pleasant. We had provided for a great square or place in the centre of the town for a marketplace, and when things got easier for us we planted trees all round, but before we got into the habit of making full use of this for our present out of door amusements, we had found out that the Kirk might be used for other purposes besides worship and school.

'My children – for I looked on myself as the mother of the seventy or eighty children whom I taught, with a little help from Victor and his wife – were so bright in all sorts of ways that I found I could train them to exercises of memory, such as delighted them as well as instructed them. Foremost among my recollections of the old happy days in London was the theatre, and when I saw how dramatically they caught the spirit of what I told them, I made an experiment, and taught to some of the cleverest the second part of *The Pilgrim's Progress*, adding somewhat and keeping out somewhat for their more ready apprehension. There used to be a sort of examination on the breaking-up day before the harvest, to which the parents and the Town Council were invited, and I made the little ones go through their little drama before their elders. This gave great delight to all, and encouraged me to try again. The young men and young women were eager to do the same or to do something better, and gradually we came to have sort of evening entertainments in the Kirk. Sometimes it was storytelling and sometimes little plays, but it was always begun and ended with prayer.

'I recollected hearing my father quote something from an ancient Father of the Primitive Church, Tertullian, to me when I came from the theatre, saying that a Christian knew when his amusements were not sinful if he could pray after them, and I had been somewhat conscience-smitten by the feeling that I could not pray with any comfort. But then my conscience had been made uneasy by the rigidness of the rules laid down for my life, and besides it had on it the great burden of a loveless betrothal, and a new love springing up which ought not to have been allowed. But when we began with *The Pilgrim's Progress*, prayer seemed quite appropriate, and when we came to more secular plays, such as *The Gentle Shepherd*, Mr Addison's *Cato*, and Shakespeare's *As You Like It* no one appeared to see any incongruity in the blessing asked on our innocent amusement or the thanks offered up at the end. All were in the habit of saying grace before and after meat, and that appeared on reflection to be as secular a thing as the other.

'Sunday keeping at first was lax through the eagerness of our people for work. There was so much to do and so few hands to do it with, that the saving clause in the old Shorter Catechism with regard to works of necessity and mercy was strained to its uttermost. Victor and I in reading the Bible by itself, as now we were forced or rather privileged to do, from the want of any theological library, could see that the Jews only abstained from work, that in the early days there was no synagogue for them to worship in, and no religious services anywhere but in the temple, to which only those who lived in or near Jerusalem could go. It was a day of rest, but not a day of penance or restriction – God had *given* them the Sabbath not *taken* it from them. It was not till after the Captivity when the efforts of Ezra towards the keeping up of the orthodox faith, had devised the powerful instrument of weekly public worship in the synagogues all over the length and breadth of the land, that anything like the idea we now entertain of the Jewish Sabbath had arisen, and even then, without good books to read at home, and without the power of reading any books at all, the synagogue service must have been all except the morning and evening prayer of the head of the household – that could have answered to our ideas of religious exercises.

'Here we were a community without books, and until our numbers are increased twenty or thirtyfold, it will never be worth our trouble to print new books for ourselves. Long ere that time, our retreat no doubt will be discovered, and we may again have relations with the rest of the world. But for the present, our people have no books to read in their homes any more than the Jews had in the time of the Judges and the Kings. God's word may be read in other revelations of himself in the beautiful country in which we are shut in, in the family relations in which he has bound us together and in the kindly offices of friends and neighbours. So long as we have public worship and reading of the Bible in the Kirk every Sunday, and instruction in the Scripture in our schools every day, their sacred lessons can never be said to be forgotten or neglected.

'In these early days however of which I write, the largest half of our people gathered pretty faithfully every morning for worship, but after that they were disposed to work as hard as on other days of the week. I recollected the Sunday afternoons at Fontainebleau where our unlearned peasantry danced on the turf, and I believed that was more in accordance with the spirit of the Christian religion than either hard work or wearisome religious exercises.

'Victor's children played on Sunday afternoons before the door of his home. Gradually as the trees grew shady, the young folks used to gather on the place, and exchange greetings and news, and arrange plans for the week. It is only within the last two years however that the dances have begun, but it is now as if it had always been, and not even the oldest inhabitant says much against it. My Violet whose grandchildren are among my cleverest scholars, says that it seems strange to her, but still that the open way in which lads and lasses meet together under the eye of their parents and their minister for diversion as well as for worship, keeps them out of much danger. As for the handfasting, she had always thought it good, from the the day of Ralph Abercrombie's marriage for the Indians – but she had many misgivings as to its use among Christians, till use and custom showed her how it worked.

'With regard to the land, we divided it all round Ebenezer among the heads of families, and the young men as they grew up had to go further afield. But as the land was the only source of wealth for us, we did not give it to our people out and out. Each town land as it was taken out was liable for a perpetual rent charge for the expenses of the Commonwealth, and as the people increase and need more expense for churches and schools and justice and so on, there will be always more land taken up and more money coming in. The longer it is cultivated, it seems to me to produce more and our folk are growing very clever in all sorts of tillage that suits the soil and the climate.

'The mines of silver, copper and tin we kept in the hands of the Council to help the land tax in the keeping up of Kirk and school and other public expenses. The Council were chosen by the male inhabitants including those Indians who swore fealty to our Commonwealth. They were chosen yearly, and served for nothing, but their duties were light. The town of Palmtown has asked leave to have a council of its own, to deal with the land about it. The whole population of the plantation is now double what it was when we came here and in all ways we seem to prosper. We called our settlement Columba chiefly in honour of the great navigator of Genoa who gave a new world to the kingdom of Castille and Arragon, whose merits were neither rewarded by the sovereign, nor acknowledged in the name of the great continent. It was but a little refuge in the wilderness but it was a settlement of free men who lived in unity with the old inhabitants, and this was a plantation more according to his notions than those of the Spaniards heretofore. To my own thinking too, it was a good name for us. Many a time in my old bitter days when I struggled against the hardness of my lot, I had said to myself in the words of Scripture: "Oh that I had wings like a dove (colombe) that I might flee away and be at rest" and here at last I had found it, not the rest of inaction, but the rest of healthful unhindered work, where my conscience and my life were in harmony.

'The old laws that we recollected seemed to us not suited for our small young State, and so as an exigency arose, we had to settle it as it seemed to us best. What good was done by hanging a dozen men at Tyburn, or shutting up hundreds of poor debtors in prison for life, as to my grief I had seen in my stay in London. We wanted all the work of all our people in Columba always. Any man who had wronged another was on proof of it compelled to work for him till he had made up the loss or compensated fairly for the injury, and this we found put a great check on crime and dishonesty.

'The only crime that did not seem to us could be compounded for in this way was murder. The murderer forfeited his life and as we made no difference between the injuries done to an Indian and those to a white man, our red brethren had perfect trust in our justice. But in case of murder not premeditated either arising out of a quarrel or in self-defence - for which in Holy Writ cities of refuge were appointed - we had another law. In the first case of this kind the widow of the slain man loudly demanded justice and revenge, for there was little doubt that though the quarrel was hot, her husband had been the victim of over-mastering strength, and had right on his side from the first. The life was given to her if she would take it herself, and the offender was bound and set as a target for her aim. She was used to the handling of a gun, but her heart failed her when she saw the wife and children of her enemy weeping and lamenting. She threw down the weapon and said she would give him time for repentance, but hoped God would forgive him as she forgave him. So he was unbound, but he made his escape out of Columba over the ranges and was never heard of more. After this case manslaughter was always commuted for service to the widow and children, or to the parents of the slain man, longer or shorter according to the provocation or other excuses.

'Thus it has come to pass that in this refuge shut in by high hills, and so far as we know inaccessible by any foe, we have a little Commonwealth with different laws and different customs from any in Europe or perhaps in the world. If my husband had lived, his force of character would probably have impressed his own convictions as to what was right on the community; his own severe code of morals and of manners might have counteracted in great measure the worldliness of the older and the levity of the younger members. He would have made them feel his weight both of character and temper and means, though no doubt it would have been a harder matter than he thought to carry into a new country among colonists, the authority once in the hands of the ministers of the Kirk of Scotland, the decline of which he had deplored.

'Nothing but his disappointment with his son, the ill offices of Lord Seton and the difficulties with the presbytery would have induced him to cast in his lot with so self-seeking a crew, but as it happened this very selfishness made them now pliant as to changes and modifications of old laws and customs. We were a little band thrown out of the pale of Christendom, forced to make a law and government for ourselves of a republican or perhaps rather of a communal nature. We had only our own wants to supply. After the pacification of the Indians we had no enemies to fight, and we have no trade with other people. We have no costly courts to maintain, no pressure on the conscience from a state church, no cruelty sanctioned by the law of the land, there is food and work and love and amusement for all. On the other hand there is not, and there is not likely to be any architecture, any music worthy of the name, any art or any literature.

'In Columba we have no giants and no dwarfs – no elevation of the greater and down-treading of the lesser. When I see my Victor with his children, the united love of father and mother always looking out for their happiness, and never repressing their playfulness or frankness, I feel what I and my children so sorely missed. Even the love of my aunt and of my parents was always directed towards making me what they wished, rather than what I wished myself. If they ever yielded to my desires, they suspected themselves of sinful weakness. And if this was the case with them, it was so to a much greater degree with my husband towards his boys, especially towards Hugh. All my remonstrances had no effect when he could entrench himself in principle. But I have gathered hope for the afterlife of my Hugh from seeing how beautifully his brother has developed when away from the soul-benumbing superstitions from which we all suffered, and the faith which is springing up in my heart that there is love for us all in the Almighty Maker and Governor of the world, makes me bear the uncertainty to which I am doomed more patiently and hopefully than I could have supposed possible.

'I am now getting to be an old woman, and may not have long to live. The only thing I shrink from in eternity is the meeting with my husband – but all will surely be seen more clearly. If I do not shrink from meeting my God who can see the motives of my actions, surely I need not dread confronting a fellow creature. I write this in an unknown tongue as a relief to my own mind. I would not that anyone should read this narrative except my son, because our people have accepted the changes as they have been made, and are now accustomed to them, and they need not be told that they arose in my own single mind as the fruits of my own sad experience.

'I sometimes think of trying to get out of this valley of Columba to seek my son. If opportunity favours me, I may go, and this book will explain all to Victor, but the length and the perils of the way seem too great. I would not take anyone with me for there is none who has such ties as I have outside and there never was a happier or more prosperous people. Violet would leave her son and her grandchildren for me, but she is even weaker than I am. Victor is of the greatest importance to the community and I would not move a finger to make him leave it on so wild a hope.'

BOOK FOUR

THREE RIVALS

I

I DECLARE MYSELF

As I have already said, this is an abridgement of what I found written in the blank leaves of Madame Keith's book. There were many details and very many reflections which would be tedious in a narrative of this kind though it was all deeply interesting to me. I read every word of it to Liliard, and would have read it all to Hugh if he would have stayed to listen, but he was busy with his experiments in the art of photography, as well as his own old avocation, and went out and in, and said he would be sure to hear it all again from Lil. She recollected everything, and what she did not recollect, she could invent – or supply some way or other – so that for the most part of the narrative she was my only auditor. Although she was familiar with such literature as had been saved by the colonists, the difference between the life outside which Madame Keith had left, and the life inside the valley which Madame Keith had in a great measure brought about, had never been brought before her except by my tales of a world which had been transformed since by other causes. Things contemporary are taken for granted in books; it needs the experience of a change to show how different are the conditions and the tendencies then and now. My coming had been to her a revelation of wonderful things and beautiful things which were absent from the happy valley, but this narrative showed her that there were many sad and hard things from which Columba was a refuge. Besides, in the very narrow library of the Columbans there was no such account of the struggles between the soul and its surroundings. Madame Keith's story was wonderfully modern in its bearings. No doubt there were many such experiences in that apparently uninteresting half of the eighteenth century but they had found for themselves no voice which the world could hear.

Here and there Liliard made an exclamation; here and there a sob escaped her; here and there in the religious experiences many of which I have not reproduced, she looked puzzled and expectant.

'Do you understand that Victor? It is an unknown language to me.'

'I partly understand this,' said I, 'but not fully, for I have not gone through such mental and spiritual struggles, but I have known many who have done so.'

'Is that so,' said she. 'Among us I'm thinking there are few that are very bad, but there are none that are very good. We have not so much to try our metal and to purify us as silver is refined.'

When I came to the passage about the man slayer being set free she said, 'That was James Graeme, one of Ninian's ancestors. He came of wild blood on both sides and I fancy that is what draws me to him in a way.'

'But if this ancestor escaped, I wonder he did not betray the secret of your dwelling place.'

'It is most likely he died in the wilderness, which you tell me is vast and barren. But Madame Keith never left the valley; she died soon after she wrote this narrative, for she was not an old woman at her death. And you are the descendant of her dear son Hugh. But what of the wife he was deceived into marrying?'

'She must have been dead when he came back from his long voyage with Captain Durham, for he then married Bessie Rutherford who was a good wife, at least this is my grandmother's account of it.'

'How strangely near this story seems to me,' said Liliard. 'It is more than a hundred years since the writer of these words was laid to rest, and here it seems as if she lived and breathed and wept and worked.'

'It seems to me as if it were my own mother, or as if I was her own Hugh whom she was addressing,' said I.

'Aye,' said Liliard, 'you are more like her son than my Hugh is: at least your mind has been more cultivated, your life has been wider and has had more changes in it of place and of circumstances. And your ancestor was a physician like yourself. It seems more fitting that Madame Keith's descendants should be healers of the body or of the soul rather than wrights and smiths.'

'My kinsman Hugh represents the outcome of the happy community which it was the pride of her heart to have founded here – frank, fearless and contented.'

'Aye, but you surely take note of what she says after her description of the good points in Columba, that there is no architecture and no music worthy of the name, no art, no literature – no sense of beauty such as you have. What a world it must be outside!'

'Does this narrative make you wish to plunge into the midst of it? You see how hardly Madame Keith was tried.'

'Yes, I see that, but things are very different now. You were not brought up as she was, or as her sons were.'

'No indeed not at all,' said I, as I recalled the easy régime of the house in Collins Street, my father's cheerful temper, my mother's love, my grandmother's pleasant ways, my stepmother's kindness, and my sisters' idolatry.

'It is strange,' said Liliard after a pause, 'but when I hear of misery and anguish, I want somehow to go beside it, to comfort it, nay more than that, I want to go through it too, and feel what it is like. I don't feel as if I have half lived here with so little trouble.'

'Misery at his worst
Has one poor grace of tragic interest
Proud pleasure vainly envies at his best,'

said I quoting from Owen Meredith.

'No, Victor, don't call it *proud* pleasure. It is humbleness; it is the feeling that I have not had my share of the burden of the world. None of our Columbans seem to have that.'

'There surely is pain of body here, and the sorrow of bereavement.'

'Aye, we could not be human if we had not these, but you say yourself that we are the healthiest folk you ever saw, and that even accidents and ailments do not cost us so much pain as you were used to see elsewhere. And as to bereavement, that is God's sending, and we behove to bear with it, and death is not embittered to us by the terrors of the hereafter. Fancy Madame Keith's husband telling her and her mother that their Victor was lost. It is the trouble and the perplexity and the anguish that you folk out-bye have about your own conduct, and the behaviour of them that are dear to you that seizes on my mind. There are no martyrdoms at the stake now, and maybe the thought of them is fading out of your minds even as it does out of ours, but there are other silent martyrdoms, I'm thinking, all the world over, that we have no notion of.'

'And of all the unborn people whose happiness my ancestress was thinking of, you are perhaps the least contented.'

'Maybe, maybe!' said Liliard. 'It no doubt seems to you ungrateful and far from gracious, but when I hear your story of what went on in that great French Revolution, with its grandeurs and its horrors, and the Civil war in America when slavery was put an end to at our very door as it were; I was living at the time, and I never felt the thrill of the strife, or the tramp of the conqueror, or the shaking off of the chains that might have stirred me even in my cradle; and later, in that great war and the siege of Paris that you yourself seemed to be alongside of when a lad, and heard the news as it crossed the half of the world with held-in breath, and never a word of it to come to us, who were going on in our daily work and pastime as if that were all that concerned us.'

'Well, we in Melbourne, and indeed all over the world, did much the same. We were eager to hear the news no doubt, but our own affairs were in no way interfered with.'

'Then,' said she slowly, 'is history when it is a-making, not the concern of all the world? Is it only the soldiers that feel the war-spirit and only the statesmen that are eager about the honour of their country abroad, and such things as concern the good and the happiness of the people at home? Surely not! surely every man in a country should feel as fond of it and as proud of it as Hugh Keith is of Columba.'

'This is not so common as it should be,' said I. 'I admire Hugh's pride in the country and the institutions he and his ancestors have as it were created. I do not think you appreciate the good things you possess here sufficiently.'

'But surely even where the thought of the world has free course,' said Liliard, 'every citizen should feel a pride and an interest in his own corner of it. In an old country because so much is inherited; in a new country like yours because so much is to be done.'

'Well, this is by no means a common passion with the average citizen. If it were not for the claims of my good father and grandmother and sisters, I should like to cast in my lot with you here, and spend my whole life in this Happy Valley.'

'No, Victor, no!' said she emphatically. 'You say it is for them, but it is really for yourself. Your life in that new country, in that big city which in itself holds about ten times the dwellers in our Happy Valley, with its stir and its quarrels and its ambitions, and its receiving and echoing all the news and knowledge of the world, is better than any life you could lead here. Even your grandmother would despise the idea of being set down with us.'

'Nay,' said I, 'you teach me more than I can teach you and that my grandmother would acknowledge with gratitude. If I am henceforward a more complete man with larger and higher and better aims and desires, I owe it to you Liliard Abercrombie.'

'To me!' she said, with a little shiver of delight. No one was so transparent as Liliard. From her childhood accustomed to show her feelings by look and gesture as well as by word; whether she was speaking or was silent, I seemed to be able to read her like a printed book.

'I suppose my discontent is what would be called sinful in your old world Christian talk,' she resumed after a pause. 'Sin frets us little here; we take things as they come, and make the best we can of them like some of the Japanese you talk of. But it seems to me now as if I knew what temptation and struggle and failure may be. It is not only ways and fashions, but the whole root of conscience and honour which is different with us here from what you have in the great world outside.'

'Nay, nay,' said I 'you misunderstand me if you fancy so.'

'Say not so, Victor Keith. I guessed it before but Madame Keith's story makes it clear. There are few of our ways in which we are brought up that could be gone into by our fellow countrymen at home and abroad with an easy conscience. I seem to understand now better than I could do at the time your surprise and horror at the handfasting. Madame Keith and her son were brave in their time. Well after you have gone, I may settle down to my old life, but meantime I must learn – learn all I can.'

She sat for a few moments lost in thought; then I resumed the conversation from a new point. 'Hugh is learning to manage the camera wonderfully well. He shows the greatest aptitude and he is now trying to make paper for the purpose and to mix chemicals. Before I go, he will have got to the bottom of all the process and I know he has been thinking of making an apparatus of his own. The lenses are the most difficult part with the poor glass you make.'

'Yes he is clever with anything that is to be done in that way,' said she. 'His training to a handicraft helps him.'

'He will not need to put his skill to so hard a test for I intend to leave him the whole thing complete to work at or to copy. I shall not take it away from Columba if I leave the place.'

'And I can save his time as I save yours by the mounting of the pictures, if' – and she paused, 'or even if not, I could perhaps still work for him unless he objected.'

'If' – said I. 'I suppose you mean if you broke off your handfasting.'

'Yes,' she said slowly, 'that is what I meant.'

'And in that case, Liliard, you will marry me,' said I eagerly.

'You, Victor? Ah, no!'

'And why not, do you not know that you are the life of my life, the one woman in all the world for me? Have you not seen from the very first that I follow you with my eyes, that I treasure your words in my heart that you are above me in genius, in all ways? But I love you.'

'Love *me*, Victor? me, ignorant, me unpolished, me in your old world eyes in a disgraceful position. Ah! it is because you are shut in here, and see no better.'

'You satisfy every desire of my heart, every ambition of my mind, every longing of my soul. You do not know your own value. Nobody in this valley, nobody all over the world can appreciate you, honour you and love you as I do.'

'Oh!' said she shaking her head sadly. 'Old as you are, you are blind as a boy of seventeen, eager for a first handfasting. Out of kindness to you, I will not let you speak so again – out of very love.'

These last words seemed wrung from her against her will. She looked me full in the face with an expression of pathetic baffled ambition and renunciating love that thrilled through me.

What other people would think of my choice was of no account; she was the arbiter of my fate; she held in her hands my happiness or misery. There was no bond which should prevent her from giving her dear self to me. To any other woman, such as my father and grandmother thought a suitable match for me, I could offer a competence and a position much the same as what she already occupied, but to this woman I could offer a whole world. This was what I held the keys of to her awakened curiosity, to her ardour and her zeal. I did not murmur at this, and say that it was not myself, but what I could give that she loved. I felt like Ulysses, that I was a part of all that I had seen, and like Walt Whitman, that all that I had seen was a part of me, and therefore I was only glad that I could endow Liliard so richly if she consented to become my wife.

'I must speak to Hugh,' said I, 'and do nothing underhand. He was saying today, that we must make a joint petition that I should continue here, because he wants so much to learn the whole art, if not the whole theory of photography, and as my intention has always been to leave him the apparatus in return for his help it would be well if he were made perfect. But when he hears that I am his bride's most resolute suitor, he may quite change his mind – and then I must leave this place, and lose the daily sight and hearing of you.'

'Stop, Victor, let me think! If you were quite sure that I would never be your bride, would you be content to abide with us and to teach Hugh what he takes such mighty pleasure in? That might make up to him, at least in a measure. With such as him, his daily work is his life. Would you be content to stay and do him this service, if it were indeed for naught?'

'Yes, truly,' said I, 'for with hope or with no hope, your presence is what I live in; for joy or for sorrow it may be, but it is my life.'

'That may well be,' said she, 'but in that case, what for should we disturb Hugh?'

'Because I have no right to speak to you in his own house without his knowing it. I should not have betrayed myself even now.'

'You are right, Victor. It is me that's wrong. Only if we have to part – but it will come to that at last. Well go and God speed. He is at his forge and I believe he is alone.'

II

HOW LILIARD'S BRIDEGROOM TOOK IT

I do not think there was ever a worse quarter of an hour for any man to undergo than this which I had to face with Hugh. My kinsman, eager about his new work which was to him a plaything as well as an engrossing occupation, had been planning all sorts of successes for himself when I had gone, and he saw that it would not only bring him distinction but money, and not only these things, but would be a constant interest and occupation to Liliard. There had been always a few little remarks made about her being no housekeeper, and that all the work she cared to do, her knitting, she defaced and spoiled by the inveterate habit she had of working in her thoughts, her fancies and her recollections, so that there was not a single stocking or jersey or other article of the kind that was fit to be seen by critical eyes. But now if she could help him in printing and mounting the pictures, which he only in all the valley could take by the sun, she would be of more use than any wife in all Columba. I had that morning told my zealous coadjutor that I meant to leave him the camera and the chemicals, and he took all the tender interest of a prospective proprietor in the concern. Now I had to tell him frankly that I loved his bride, and the announcement fell on him with a terrible shock.

'I must say what is on my mind Hugh,' said I. 'On the expiry of the term for which you and Liliard are bound, I want her to choose between you and me. She is free and so are you.'

'As if *I* could make any other choice,' said Hugh bitterly. 'And *you*, what will you do with her in your world? She is not fit for your fine fashions. She knows nothing of your ways; she cannot even read and write as you say every beggar can do where you come from. If you stayed here it would be different, for if you tired of her, I would take her back; I could not even be handfasted to anyone while there was a chance of getting her. But you will go – go over the ranges, and whether it is for weal or woe – whether my Liliard's bones are whitening on the desert or whether she is crushed under the wheels of what you call civilisation, I shall hear none of it!'

'I will stay if she wishes it,' said I.

'If she wishes it, and is that likely?' said Hugh with a disdainful laugh which was more bitter than his invective. 'Man for man I am as good a man as you. It is the world she wants to see, the world you have turned her head with, with all its noise and its glare and its wickedness. Columba is a humdrum place, not worth living in now that she has heard about all the kingdoms of the world and all the glory of them, and I feel as if you were the devil himself come to tempt my hard-won bride from me.'

I remained silent for a while, while he went on with his work in the forge furiously, but yet not without some method in his madness. 'Then Hugh, I fancy you are not disposed to go on with me as we have done up till now, and that you will allow the Town Council to billet me quietly on another handfasted man.'

'Let me speak to Liliard first before I answer,' and he strode towards the house. 'You need not hang back. Come with me, Victor Keith.'

I followed him into the house where Liliard sat just as I had left her, with her hands folded in her lap, and her eyes looking inward.

'Our kinsman tells me that he, as well as the scoundrel Ninian and that fool James Anderson, means to try to sunder our bond of handfasting when the time comes, and to carry you away with him to his fine people. Consider, Liliard, before you listen to his idle tales. Have you any fault to find with me? If you have I'll do my best to mend it.'

'No fault at all Hugh,' said Liliard pitifully, 'and I know that you have many to find with me. Before our kinsman came, I was satisfied that I had got a good and true bridegroom, and thought that we need never change. I fancied that the feeling I had for you was the love of a wife, but I know differently now. It would be the kindest thing to say to Victor, "Go, leave us for ever, disturb no more our quiet life. Go back to the stir and tumult, the ecstasy and the anguish you tell us of, and leave us to our little cares and pleasures." Hugh is right as he always is. I am no mate for you. But Hugh,' and she looked on him with pathetic eyes, 'with this turmoil in my soul, I am no mate for you either.'

'Patience,' said Hugh, 'patience, the old feeling will come back when Victor is gone.'

'Never Hugh never. I must dree my weird,' and she took up the thread of her spinning wheel, and turned it as if the dull mechanic exercise would deaden the pain at her heart.'

'In your customs,' I said eagerly, 'neither the one nor the other of you need give any reason for your change. I never meant to do anything dishonourable. Ninian and the young Anderson court your bride openly in the face of day, while, I with every opportunity have never spoken a word to her till today, when it was wrung from me by a chance expression which Liliard let fall.'

'What has it all been but courting,' said Hugh impetuously, 'from the first day you met her by the burn when you came, hungry and weary, for food and rest to this aforetime happy home? Courting by your wonderful talk about the things she cares about, courting by your breathless listening to the stories she is so clever at telling. Ah! Liliard, after all your fine tales about constancy, and the half ring that was but an earnest of the whole one, and now without a fault to find with me, if you take up with this stranger you will be a proverb all over Columba!'

She quivered from head to foot; a tear gathered and fell, and turning her wheel abruptly to divert attention from her agitation she broke the thread, and then fastened it hastily in an imperfect knot which slipped. Hugh moved forward, and reunited it in a perfectly secure knot of his own. 'Aye Liliard,' said he, 'in haste and flurry you snap the thread that binds you and me, and in more haste and flurry you fasten a slippery knot with a stranger, but if I am only at hand when it slips, I hope I may be allowed to fasten it past slipping again. Let him go and it will all be as if it had not been.'

'Never!' said she. 'What I mistook for love is what you should not be contented with. You will win a better woman's heart.'

'I'd rather have half of yours, Liliard' said Hugh eagerly.

'Half!' said she and she plucked at her handfasted ring. 'What a poor return to make for a good man's love.'

'If I'm satisfied,' said he eagerly, 'that is all that is needed.'

'Nay, Hugh – I too must be satisfied. And – could I not go home to mother's to think this over.'

'No!' said Hugh emphatically. 'Whatever you may decide to do, you are bound to me for the term of your vow.'

'Aye, that is true,' said she, 'but it is hard.'

'Hard!' he echoed. 'Could I have ever dreamed of your thinking it hard? It is law and custom and honesty besides. Such a thing was never heard of unless the handfasted couple have quarrelled so that they cannot live in peace. It takes two to make a quarrel, Liliard. I have none with you. Why should you not go, Victor Keith; go forth from among us to your own people, where maybe this sort of thing is counted honourable.'

'As for going I cannot in honour go till I have served the appointed time for which I engaged to the Commonwealth, and it would be a pity for you not to learn the photographic art thoroughly from me while I am here.'

'Do you call that amends,' said Hugh bitterly.

'No, by no means, nothing can be amends for that. But as all your laws, all your customs, give perfect freedom of choice to man and woman for the year and day of probation, I do not see why I should be singled out for so much indignation, because I fell in with your ways. This is the first love of my life and I loved her the first day I saw her, though I did not know it at the time. Before I was fully conscious of it I was oceans deep in love. I loved her for all the useless things you say she is so fond of. She never can be half so much to you or to any one in Columba as she will be to me, and therefore in every honest way, I mean to press my claims on her love. But at the same time, you are the master of your own house, and can keep me out as you do her other suitors.'

'Liliard,' said Hugh, 'would you think better of me if I let our kinsman remain here?' The tenderness in his voice cut me to the heart and had its effect on his bride. She took Hugh's hand and kissed it.

'I'd like you to go on with him with the work you do together in a friendly way, and if I cannot go back to mother's as I should prefer to do, I'd like to go on helping you both, but he had better live in another house. Let the Town Council settle with whom he is to abide for the second month, provided it is not over far off. Dear Hugh, dear Victor, let nothing be done in hate but all in honour.'

'Liliard is right!' said Hugh. 'Leave me alone with my bride in my own house till our handfasting is over. Court her as others do. Meet her at the Kirk on Sundays and weekday evenings, watch her at the storytelling and the playacting, dance with her on the green but do not witch the heart out of her under my own roof with your wild stories and your clever tongue. There's Nicol Elliot not half a mile off, handfasted this last six months, and his bride, most folks say is bonnier than mine. Let her go through the fire too; let him see what it is to entertain a stranger unawares.'

As Hugh said, so it was settled. There was no ill blood between us, though there was little said except on the business in which we were engaged. We worked together for some hours every day, but there was no intercourse between me and Liliard then. He took to her and he brought from her the work she did for us, which she did both quickly and well. And in spite of our declared rivalry with regard to this beloved woman, we were helpful and courteous to each other in this work. I met Liliard as others met her, but we had little of the old interchange of ideas, though no doubt we thought of each other all the more.

It was now generally noised about that I was a suitor of Liliard Abercrombie's. There was a curious jealousy on Nicol Elliot's part that I had no eyes for his bride, though no doubt he would have been seriously annoyed if I had really admired her. She was very fair with flaxen hair and small, regular features, but she fancied she could sing, and it was terrible to listen to her songs. She was one of the women who thought Hugh Keith's bride very impractical, and that he was a great deal too good for her. Now that he was becoming an adept at photography, he was held in greater esteem than ever. Even though he had often an aching heart, he manfully applied himself to what as he thought brought him up to my level in one direction. He certainly was at this time much sympathised with by both young and old, and by no one more thoroughly than by Liliard's young sister Marjorie or May. Madame Abercrombie however was not displeased at the possible rupture of her Liliard's handfasting, though it had taken a different course from what she had anticipated.

III

SOME SHORT-COMINGS IN THE COLUMBAN CONSTITUTION

There was one result of the peculiar domestic arrangements enforced in Columba which Madame Keith and her son and the early Council probably never anticipated. In their eager desire to give perfect freedom in matters of love and marriage to every member of the community, and their determination that the children of separated parents should in no respect suffer, they had erected side by side with the simple representative institutions of a pure democracy, a sort of irresponsible bureaucracy, superior in intelligence, in education and in administrative ability to the people's choice through election. As we have seen, all the professions, religious, medical and legal, and what we should call the civil service, were recruited not from the ranks of the ordinary citizens, but from those children who were solemnly renounced by their parents and given over to the State.

Therefore such a man as Archibald Keith was a cabinet maker and his son Hugh a worker in bronze, in addition to the usual position of a land-holder. It was like the old condition of the papal dominions in a much more simple state of society. There was no public service open to any but ecclesiastics in the States of the church and therefore the rich and the noble were condemned to ignoble ease, if not to worse and more mischievous courses. In Columba as we have seen, it was not only the government service, but the whole of the clergy, the teachers, the judges, the doctors and the musicians who were supplied in this unusual way. It had none of the evil elements of a hereditary caste, nor had it the mischievous effects of a body like that in the United States liable to be changed at each presidential election but it had a great influence in stifling ambition. The people generally were quite indifferent to the matter, for they paid nothing for the services of the phalanx of God's children. They did not have to subscribe to build churches, or pay for seat rents. There was no money paid at the door for the storytelling or the dramatic entertainments. The dances were free as the air of heaven. When any of the inhabitants of Columba were ill, the doctor of the town land attended them free of cost, and if a nurse was needed, she came without fee or charge. The children were taught and trained in schools built by the Commonwealth, and by teachers who charged nothing to the parents. Land measuring for the state, and for private people as well, was done by the government surveyor. The land was originally allotted to the first settlers on the old Scotch system of a perpetual fen duty to the superior, the superior being the Commonwealth itself. I had often thought that the Australian Government might have reserved some such dues, and not have been so eager to part with the fee simple of their magnificent real estate, and it was very interesting to me to see how with this handful of people, the land revenue was elastic enough to meet and even more than meet the requirements of an increasing population.

The revenue of the State was quite sufficient without what we call any direct or indirect taxation whatever. It also made the excellent narrow roads which opened up the country as it was settled. The irrigation and drainage were however originally left entirely to private enterprise, and the manner in which the small proprietors had united for these purposes was admirable. Of late years, as the revenue increased, there had been both irrigation and drainage works begun on the main lines by the government, the direction of which invited settlement. Although the extension of cultivation was not stimulated by immigration, it was induced by the general well-being of the community and its rapid natural increase. Where everyone of the people had much more than a bare living, it took a greater extent of land to supply their wants. In every way the people were better off in every generation. The food was more abundant and more various, and the clothing better as the people became more numerous, though the division of labour was not carried out as we understand it.

There was a considerable amount of waste in all directions; cotton being preferred for clothing, the wool was neglected; there was no care taken to improve the breed of wool-bearing sheep, and the people composedly took it for granted that nature provided that in such a climate the wool should be thin, poor, and brittle. After the discovery of kerosene, there were few candles made and the fat only used for soap manufacture; but this last article the Columbans used largely, and it was of good quality. There was nothing done with the waste fat, bones, rags and other debris, but to bury them, and thus to fertilise the ground; and feed for stock was so abundant, that there was little utilisation of waste from sugar works or other inferior agricultural produce for their use. Machinery and steam power and railways would not have been of any profit to this small community: their own simple processes were probably more effective for their small demand. If there was little difference in the way of living between the so-called rich and poor, it was because the poor were in all ways better off than anywhere else on the face of the earth. Even in our prosperous Melbourne, I had again and again met with cases of heart-rending poverty and distress, and the poor quarters of Edinburgh and Paris had shown me lower depths of misery. In all these cities, destitution was most frequently occasioned by vice, but still not seldom by bad luck and simple misfortune. The curious arrangement that the State provided so much, and yet did not provide for destitution at all was accounted for by the very small amount of it that existed in Columba, and the willingness – nay the eagerness – in a country of abundance to give aid to the needy. All the common benefits given by Government were bestowed on rich and poor alike, and exceptional need was left to

Christian charity. Another anomaly of the same description was that though the State took care of all children of handfasted couples who gave them up, real orphans were eagerly adopted by others.

The administration of the land and mineral revenue was supposed to be under the control and direction of the elective Council, but it may easily be imagined that the bureaucracy, which even with free competition is so strong in many European states, and also in the colonies, would be almost irresistible in Columba. We know that the permanent and irresponsible heads of departments have great power in the shifting ministries in Australia, and that any exercise of power against routine is resented not only by the class itself, but by the whole community; and how could a body, not a ministry, but only a single feeble Chamber, oppose a guild like the Columban civil service. The representation was purely local, each town with its surrounding town lands sent in a member, and roads, bridges, churches and schools for the district were the chief things each representative cared most about. The towns as I have said before, were seven, and the following was the order of their settlement: Ebenezer, Palmtown, Fontainebleau, New Berwick, Westlands, Southfield and Burnside. Each had a church and large school, but there were seven smaller churches, used also as schools, in outlying districts. There was no hospital for the sick or any sort of asylum for the destitute all over the plantation. The sick were attended in their own homes by the Commonwealth doctors and nurses. That want was extremely rare, so rare as to be a sort of wonder, may be accounted for partly from the facilities for all the labour of the country being utilised on an abundance of fertile soil, and from the absence of monopoly in any shape on the part of individuals. But still more in a country where there were no public houses and no pawn brokers, and where sickness involved only the loss of work and not doctors' and chemists' bills, and consequently was not so costly as in other parts of the world, it was likely that want should be a very exceptional condition.

The office of Protector, being not only the highest position in the State, but the only paid office within the reach of the ordinary citizen, was very eagerly sought for, and the chances of being made Protector for four years lent a great zest to the canvassing at the alternate elections. I was told by the Keiths that this was the poorest set of legislators who had ever been gathered together, and probably they were in the right. But as I have before said, things were in such a position that there was very little of what we should call legislation proper in their power. The rights and the privileges of the citizen and of the government employee were so secured to them by law and custom, that the main duty imposed on the General Council was to see to the expenditure of public money, and as they were all ignorant of book accounts, they were very much in the hands of those who could read and write.

Certainly anyone who was discovered to be wronging or cheating the Commonwealth met with the most summary trial and the most severe punishment. I believe that in some instances great injustice had been done, from the difficulties in the way of bringing sufficient evidence against such culprits, and from the practice of jumping at conclusions. But this was a check on wrongdoing; the chance of being disgraced from an honourable employment, and forced to labour on the roads for a long period or even for life, was a terrible one even though detection was not easy. On the whole, I thought that the Commonwealth was very well served, and could not help admiring the exceeding lightness of the public burdens. The perpetual rent, which on cultivated lands was a mere trifle, no doubt greatly tended to prevent land from being taken up speculatively, but still from its abundance and cheapness, there was a good deal of lazy and careless farming.

There was no great desire among the people to make a fortune; what would a Columban do with his money if his income was ten or twenty times multiplied? There was nothing to spend it on – no articles of luxury to be bought – no hirelings to be obtained for the swift and silent service which our millionaires desire. Neither was there the sharp spur of necessity to goad the young to extraordinary effort. The only thing that appeared to act in that way was the very early marriage preceded by handfasting. The desire to have a house of their own if they made the union permanent and the necessity to provide for a child in any case unless they took the extreme step of giving it up for ever, very frequently spurred the young of both sexes to industry and economy very early in life. The very large families which were born under the very favourable circumstances of the Commonwealth were in no case either considered a public or a private infliction. The average families were larger than anywhere in the world; sixteen was quite common, and five a very small family. The proportion of childless couples on the other hand I thought a little larger than elsewhere, as if nature would have some compensation somehow. Perhaps family affection was a little weaker between brothers and sisters, and the common schools and the frequent social gatherings led to friendships as well as love affairs according to choice. The nature of the climate too, led to out-of-doors life and not to assembling round the family hearth and probably to less care about the beauty of their dwellings.

I could have wished that the people had turned to more decoration of their houses, churches and schools, and to landscape gardening, where the soil was so rich and the climate so favourable but all their attention had been turned to the physical and material good of the people, and not to either beauty or grandeur in their surroundings. Hugh Keith spoke truly when he spoke of the excellence of the agricultural tools he made, and there were also great improvements in the spinning wheels and the hand looms.

I do not think that winnowing machines had been invented in England before the colonists left, though Sir Walter Scott introduces this invention in *Old Mortality* in order that Mause Headrigg may express her opinion that raising the wind by human art instead of soliciting it by prayer was an impious thwarting of Divine Providence, he himself in a footnote confesses it to be an anachronism. In this tropical country, where wind at most times was slight, the people had devised winnowers of admirable construction, though they still threshed with the flail, and the appliances for cotton ginning were also excellent. All this utilitarian development formed such a contrast to the development of the American and

Australian communities, where handsome buildings and fine pleasure grounds delight the eye of the visitor. No doubt the want of impulse from without accounted for much of the backwardness of Columba in these things, but there could be little question that the restriction of individual ambition to a single class, and that class from the nature of the case, not a hereditary one, discouraged any taste for show and decoration. And the curiously communal and social character of the Government, and the method of raising the revenue, quenched that greediness of individualism which in other countries leads to monopoly and thence to magnificence.

IV

TWO GREAT WANTS IN COLUMBA: LACK OF DEVOTION AND LACK OF HUMOUR

Master Hepburn was the only member of the guild with whom I became very intimate, and when I pointed out to him that a great deal of the life was taken out of the political institutions by the impossibility of the ordinary citizen finding a career other than the industrial, he acknowledged that there was much force in the argument. None of the children of God and of Columba had a vote for that representative assembly which was ostensibly their master, but in reality very much their servant, and this was supposed to form a sufficient check on them. I thought, and Master Hepburn agreed with me, that it was because the General Council were hemmed in by their own laws and customs from interference with their own citizens and employees that they so thoroughly enjoyed domineering over a stranger like me, and took a delight in sending me contradictory and impossible orders. So far as I could disturb and weaken the old fixed staff of doctors, nurses or any other of the civil servants, they were satisfied to give me full authority, but any suggestions to the Council itself, such as one I had thrown out for the establishment of a hospital, were treated with contempt.

I said to my wise old friend that I thought the time had come which was anticipated by Madame Keith, when the plantation or colony should begin to have a literature. I spoke of the early days of Melbourne and Adelaide, when a mere handful of people inaugurated a weekly newspaper for everyone to read, and explained how the advertisements and public notices helped to pay the cost of printing. I was quite sure that my friend Hugh could make the types, and that from a newspaper the people would soon rise to better things. No people appeared to me to have the literary faculty so much, and it seemed a pity that the wonderful power of expression which such as he himself and Liliard Abercrombie possessed, should die with them.

'These things do not altogether die,' he replied, 'for they have their effect on their hearers, a stronger effect, you say, than reading printed books. You have also told me that before reading became general in England, the stage and the pulpit were the great instructors. Are you quite sure that the newspaper and the silent book are teaching the world better lessons than our people learn here?'

'I cannot be sure certainly, but I feel quite convinced that Madame Keith and her friends took to oral teaching as a necessity of their circumstances and not as a better thing in itself.'

'It appears to me, friend Victor Keith, that you would like our little Columba to have two contradictory things. With books and literature, our people will be more restless and discontented, they will break the old bonds, and leave the place and other people will come into it, and then all our laws and customs, under which we have been so prosperous and so happy, will be broken down. The great devouring republic which, when our forefathers left Scotland, scarce numbered more than two millions of inhabitants but now as you say has grown to fifty millions, will sweep down and swamp us utterly. You may think it progress; I cannot but think it would be ruin. Leave us to our old ways while we are so contented with them.'

'Liliard is not contented,' said I.

'No, even before you arrived with your wild and marvellous stories, she was not contented, and I confess that if there had been any opening for her such as there might have been in any other part of the world, she would have been more satisfied. However, there was one safety valve for her and such as her in the storytelling and acting, which before you came had very great charms for her. And she is still so young that her career in that way was only beginning.'

'This platform business seems to me like the office of the prophet in the old Jewish Church, a standing protest against the exclusive domination of the priests, and like that not forbidden to the officials,' said I.

'There were only two priests among the prophets that I can be sure of,' said Master Hepburn, 'and Ninian is the only one except very rarely myself, belonging to the Kirk's bairns, who comes on the St Matthew's platform. Well, that is an outlet for such talents as Liliard's, and she would have improved year by year, and even after she had married Hugh Keith, which she would certainly have done but for you. So that we would not have lost her.'

'But you are to lose her,' said I, 'and the great world and I myself are to gain her.'

'It will be a heavy loss to me,' said the old man. 'Hugh Keith in the bitterness of his heart, thinks he is the greatest sufferer, but his wounds will be all healed long ere Madame Abercrombie and myself have got over our sorrow. A further loss is that just latterly I have thought Liliard Abercrombie was touched by some spiritual influences which would have made her a valuable helper, and I have been moving among my brethren to make an opening for such to speak. But if you take her away, that is a mere vision of what might have been.'

'Then you think there is much deadness in religious matters in this Happy Valley.'

'I do,' said he. 'I was reading but yester-even John Bunyan's *Grace Abounding to the Chief of Sinners*, and it occurred to me that not one of my people could form any notion of what it meant.'

'That is very likely,' said I, 'and a very good thing too. I think John Bunyan was an ingenious self-tormentor. But my good friend to quote from *The Gentle Shepherd*, "Take your own tale home." You are aiming at two incompatible things: the pleasant easy life when the law and the conscience, and the inclination and public opinion are all in harmony, and the stormy and difficult life where there are clashing interests and new temptations, and perplexity at many times, and remorse mayhap after all. Liliard would distinctly choose the other, with me at her side to go through it with her, and holds that the Columban life is too easy and sheltered for her aspirations. With the struggle comes the higher ideal. Our world may be worse, but it contains the greater souls.'

'But, recollect, you told me or read to me that Madame Keith found a new religion came into her soul when she shook off the old bondage.'

'So she did, but it was what John Bunyan and her own husband Archibald Keith would have called no religion at all – all too vague – a mere sense of dependence without fear or awe – a mere faith in a strong presence to help her best thoughts and bless her best endeavours. No, my friend we cannot have the two things.'

'Have you then in the world?'

'Some have one and some have the other. It sometimes thrills through me to go to a Gospel meeting as they call it, and see hundreds of people touched by a spirit that I envy in some ways, but which I cannot command.'

'Well,' said Master Hepburn with a sigh, 'I feel my own devotion flag sometime by the coldness of my people. And such a Gospel meeting I suppose could not be called out by any Levite of us all. If only we had a prophet to arise in our Israel.'

'On your people's deathbeds,' said I, 'I see no fear for the future. They are honestly sorry to die, and leave a life which to them has been pleasant, and the friends and kindred in whom they take delight, but there is none of the apprehension which I have seen occasionally or the doubts which I have seen often about the hereafter.'

'Oh no,' he replied, 'there is little or no doubt, but there is little living faith – and no longing for Heaven. Even the very best of us cling to the earth – "to the dust" as the Psalmist calls it.'

'Well, my friend, as it is God's earth in which he meant us to be happy I see no harm in clinging to it. In order to do life's work we must love life. The Indians and Chinese, who hold life so cheap, do not improve their condition.'

'But the greatest good has been done to humanity by those who were willing to lose life that they might find it again,' said Master Hepburn.

'You cannot tell how much heroism there is in your people, when there is no cause for which to sacrifice oneself. Only let us see an invasion of armed enemies, or a hurricane, or an earthquake, or a great flood, and I feel as certain as I am of my own existence that there will be no coldness or selfseeking. We see in such times of straits and stress, even average humanity rise to greatness. Common sailors and soldiers are heroic in times of peril and extremity, and your people are morally above the average. Surely the best condition for any community is that in which there are no such calls for sacrifice.'

'The best perhaps for the mass, but not for the individual, as you say, and it is my own soul's health that appears to me to droop and languish.'

'I think we must take you with us,' said I, 'if you are so dissatisfied with the Happy Valley.'

'Nay, my friend Victor, I wish to die among my own people and, even if I see their deficiencies, I am not any the more willing to let my work fall into the hands of someone who is quite satisfied with the Columban type of character.'

'There is one thing that strikes me very much. None of your people commit suicide.'

'Wherefore should they?' said Master Hepburn wonderingly. 'It is a sin against God and their own souls; surely your churches teach that.'

'True they teach it, but suicide grows more common even among Western nations who love their life; they love other things more, and cannot bear to live disgraced or impoverished. Even a sudden disappointment or grief often leads to suicide.'

'Suicide I should say' said Master Hepburn 'must always be preceded by madness.'

'So most of our juries, who are called on to give verdicts, say, but that is mainly caused by the harshness of the law as to the burial of a self-murderer. From my experience in the world, I think that is a great mistake. But you have scarcely any madness here in Columba from the same reasons that prevent suicide: the general comfort and security of your people. It is wonderful to see a community so happily circumstanced.'

'All without printing and newspapers and books,' said Master Hepburn triumphantly. 'I suppose I must resign myself to the lack of devotion.'

'There is another very different deficiency in your people,' said I, 'in all of them, even in my beloved Liliard. You have absolutely no sense of humour. I never laughed so little in my life as I have done here.'

'You have met here with the great serious passion of your life and that is no light or laughing matter. And there have been difficulties in regard to your relations with Liliard's bridegroom which have been painful.'

'But that need not in any way have hindered me from laughing at other things and at other people, but laughter ought to be an infectious thing, and even the cleverest humorist would feel his powers languish if his best hits were always received with grave surprise or with contempt or disgust. Under all circumstances, until now, I used to see the absurd side of many things.'

'Well what of that,' said the old minister, 'we are very happy people, you do not deny that. And you know what Solomon says that the noisy laughter of the fool is like the crackling of thorns under a pot.'

'But there is other laughter than that – laughter with tenderness as well as fun in it – and some of that only a wise man can evoke and a wise man join in.'

'That I can scarce understand,' said my friend. 'I think that to ridicule man is cruel, and I do not see how anything human can be ridiculous.'

'I do not know how to account for it, but I have seen some of the most hardly-tried people, both bodily and mentally, in whom the sense of the ridiculous was the most conspicuous. It was not always, nor indeed often ill-natured laughter, though sometimes it was.'

'But what had they to laugh at?'

'Anything or nothing. Now I observe that the comic parts of any tale I have told to Liliard take no hold on her, and that they do not amuse her. Whatever is either grand or pathetic she appreciates as I never saw any other human being do, but she says that Shakespeare's humour is distasteful to her, *Don Quixote* she looks upon as a woeful tragedy and she simply loathes the tricks played on the hero. I have tried her with modern humour, English, Scotch and American, without her being in any way pleased, though she is sometimes puzzled.'

'Our children laugh heartily enough, Victor Keith. Even at school they are in no way depressed,' said Master Hepburn stoutly.

'Yes, and so do your young men and young women, but that laughter is only the exuberance of youth and high spirits, and is very good as far as it goes; but what I mean to say is that they do not see the comicality of the absurd and the incongruous. There is of course cruel and heartless laughter in the world, but there is also thoughtful laughter, which is a great pleasure and hurts nobody. When I told Liliard of the pun made for a wager by a celebrated wit when he met a man carrying a hare on his shoulder and asked him gravely, "Is that your own hair or a wig?", she said that it was a very ill-considered question, and very ill-bred besides.'

'Well I quite agree with her,' said the minister. 'If that is the only thing you miss here, I think we are quite as well without it.'

'I feel rather sorry for Liliard in going out with me into the world if she is not able to laugh at one side of our civilisation, for I feel quite sure she will weep over the other.'

'It is not like a lover to pick holes in Liliard Abercrombie,' said the minister rather jealously. 'Not that anyone is absolutely faultless, but that seems so little a thing to bring against her.'

'It is not against her at all, Master Hepburn, for I believe it is a consequence of your wonderfully comfortable conditions. The sense of the ludicrous is a sort of compensation for hard luck which you seem to stand in no need of. As for picking holes in Liliard Abercrombie, no hole could I make that my heart may not be found in, and please God I hope to teach her to laugh when we get out into the mad, troubled and absurd world that she so longs to see.'

V

A DISCOVERY

There were calls on my time and attention all over the valley, so that I was very glad when my kinsman could alone and unaided supply the people with photographs. I spent much time as I have already shown with Master Hepburn. He was my friend with Liliard, and so was Madame Abercrombie, who now preferred me greatly to Ninian. I had been called in to see Liliard's mother and I discovered that she must go through an operation quite unknown in the colonial practice. She hesitated because the practitioners for female complaints in the valley had been women, generally the cleverest of the nurses promoted to that class of practice; but at last in great measure at the instigation of her daughter and her minister she let me try my skill. I succeeded even beyond my own hopes, and she was grateful beyond my deserts.

I saw Liliard a few times at her mother's sick-bed and thought she looked a little worn. But I met her at another sick-bed where I did not so much expect to see her.

Ninian's last handfasting had been with a certain Jean Anderson, whose brother James was also a great admirer of Liliard Abercrombie, and though he was really nowhere in the race, she had a great grudge against the woman who had cast such a glamour round the two men in the world whom she loved most.

The Andersons were lineal descendants of that Violet Anderson of whom Madame Keith spoke, and whose savings had enabled my ancestor Hugh to join Captain Durham and begin afresh a new successful and happy career; and therefore, after the reading of my ancestress' narrative they were next to the Keiths and Abercrombies, the most interesting people in the valley to me. Ninian had broken off his handfasting at the end of the year and day, a month before my arrival, very much to Jean Anderson's grief and disppointment, because he had been captivated by the beauty and the talents of Hugh Keith's bride. Jean expected to become a mother, and of course had a right to claim the child as her own after it was born. She went back to her father's house to live, and watched proceedings pretty keenly. Nobody was so glad as she when the news came out that I was not only Hugh's rival, but likely to carry the day, and therefore likely also to quench the hopes of Ninian and of her own brother. She felt that both of these wooers might be saved through me from any alliance with a woman she disliked, and hoped, as she had a splendid boy, of whom Ninian appeared to be fond, that when Liliard was out of reach over the ranges, he would come back to her. After the expiration of the handfasting, there need be no further probation, and the ceremony would then be a binding marriage. But her own recovery was unusually slow. Something went wrong that the women could not fathom, and they called me in to consult and advise. Jean was indeed in the greatest danger, and she seemed quite sensible of it but fortunately the remedy was within the pharmacopoeia of the colony, though the nurses did not know how to use it. She therefore thanked me for her recall to life, and hoped that I might be the means of her reunion to the man who in her eyes was the only one worth living for. She sent for Liliard to come to see her, and managed to make the time suit so that she might see us together. Then she said to me that she was quite satisfied that there was no chance of Ninian ever winning Liliard Abercrombie.

Ninian's old love for Jean had revived at her dangerous illness and he was also very much interested in his boy. But whether it would lead to marriage or not, or whether the marriage would lead to happiness were both quite open questions to me.

I however chanced upon a strange discovery arising out of his attendance on Jean Anderson. Ninian was richer than the Andersons, and he was always very liberal with money. In parting from his bride, he engaged to pay for the support of the little one until it was old enough to do for itself and now he thought he should give me some payment for my services towards Jean herself. I had a tariff of charges fixed by the Council, large in silver but very small if reckoned by gold, and he pulled out of his pocket a little leather bag, and took out of it some of the small gold of the country. I allowed him to make the offer of payment, for I wanted to see how he would do it· for he had always a somewhat magnificent manner and would especially delight in posing as my patron or employer. Mixed up with the silver, I caught sight of a coin such as had no counterpart in Columba. It was an American eagle, the same as those I had been robbed of by Sam Peters. I absolutely declined all payment for I said that my patient had hereditary claims on me that my best services could never discharge. He put back the money into his pouch with precipitation and left me wondering at this strange coincidence. I knew that this man was employed in mines and in the mint, and that he was supposed to do well both for the Government and surprisingly well for himself. What connection could there possibly be between him and Sam Peters? Was the curious certainty with which my half-breed made his way to the valley the result of business visits made over and over again? I had often thought that a limited supply of gold could be most profitably disposed of here, where it had five times the relative value to silver which it had anywhere else.

The quick-eyed Ninian saw that I had observed something and said that through his connexion with the coinage, he was the fortunate possessor of two old English guineas which had not been melted down, and reduced to the small size which now bore that value, and showed me one which he took out of the same bag, as if it was the one I had seen. But I knew the colour and the sharp milling of the edge of American gold, and was in no way deceived by his substitution of the dull guinea.

I thought over the matter, not once but many times, and made inquiries of Hugh Keith, Master Hepburn and Nicol Elliot and discovered that for the last eight or nine years, Ninian had been getting richer and richer, and now, although there appeared to be no greater amount of silver taken out yearly, there appeared to be a good deal more gold in circulation, and yet the only man in the service who was capable of testing the ore for the Government, saw no change in its quality. It was sometimes supposed that Ninian had discovered gold in the old creek beds, but he was never seen at work there and no one else could find any. It was now somewhat strongly impressed on my mind from these circumstances that my roguish guide Sam Peters might have been in the habit of travelling from the gold country in California to this valley, and that there might have been a profitable exchange made, in which the difference of value was halved between the two accomplices. He had been glad to undertake guiding me and was thus provisioned and paid for his southern journey, and he had stolen as much gold in addition to his earnest money as would give him a pretty heavy load of silver to return with. Whether Ninian was an accomplice in the robbery, or indeed knew anything of the matter at the time, was uncertain, but it had been sufficiently published that I had been robbed and deserted by my guide. I felt sure that the gold eagle he had in his possession had not been honestly come by, my old suspicions were confirmed, and I felt that the matter was worthy of investigation. I had no reason to believe that Ninian had any liking for me, indeed I believe he had become jealous of my being near Liliard long before Hugh Keith had any suspicion.

While I was thus engaged in speculation as to this matter as well as the various other things that from day to day and from hour to hour claimed my attention, I was suddenly removed by a decree of the General Council from Nicol Elliot's and billeted on the Protector, who was an old married man of about fifty of the same name of Elliot. Master Elliot had been nearly four years in office, and was very desirous of re-election. He had been very liberal in his demands on my photographic apparatus for he had sent a great many likenesses of himself to his political friends by a messenger. There was to be a new Council and probably some of his present supporters would be cut, though he felt quite sure of his own re-election. He thought he might also learn incidentally through me, who had come in contact with many of the citizens of Columba, what his chances were, and also the idea had at last struck him that he might also learn something from me. I have already said how grudgingly I was received into the Commonwealth, and how little account was taken of what I might teach. The public feeling was much more carried away by the likenesses than by the skill I had in medicine or my knowledge of chemicals and in the first department Hugh Keith was no unsuccessful rival. If Master Elliot had not had a chronic jealousy of the Keith family, he would have been disposed to say that a Columban could beat an outsider at anything he chose to try for.

All the Council objected to the idea of my being a bird of passage but now that it was confidently rumoured that I sought to win Liliard Abercrombie, and probably wished to take her quite away from the Valley, I was looked on as more dangerous still. I was summoned before the Council and questioned as to my intentions which I confessed frankly. They turned me out while they discussed the subject, and on my readmission, they said that if I was willing to serve the Commonwealth on a somewhat weighty and difficult matter, they would connive at my taking with me one of the subjects of the State. Then they opened the question that they had reason to suspect that Ninian was not dealing fairly by the Commonwealth and that he was having some dishonest gains. They therefore made me alone a sort of commission of inquiry as to the condition of the silver mine from which the currency of the plantation was supplied, and I was to watch the whole process, and report on it within a month.

I was inexperienced in actual mining and said so, but my protest was in vain, for I could not say that I did not know something about ores and assays. The rule of the Council was arbitrary and it was fortunate that they could not interfere much with the ordinary life of the citizens. As I had dropped as if from the clouds to disturb the plantation, I must needs do all I could, and more than I could, to further its interests. It was no pleasant and no safe thing for any man to be placed as a spy on Ninian, and knowing and guessing as much as I did, I was particularly obnoxious to him. But I had the office conferred upon me of temporary colleague of the master of the mine and the mint, and unless I chose to go out of the valley altogether, I could not disobey.

In order to blind Ninian as to the purpose of my mission, it was given out that I was to see if his processes could not be improved and I was also to go with him to a new place where it was believed that silver ore was to be found. This last we discovered not to be worth working, but in our travels through the hills, I found some ore which I was satisfied contained iron. Not iron that it would pay to work in Australia, or even perhaps in England, but in a place where all tools and metal work were made of bronze, where, though there was no coal, wood was in the greatest abundance, this was a valuable discovery. Ninian seemed to care little or nothing about this, but to be more eager as to indications of gold. The Council on the other hand were apparently very grateful for this hint about iron, and employed Hugh Keith and his foreman at my recommendation to try the first smelting. This succeeded as well as I could have expected. Iron was not to be kept exclusively for the government, but everyone who could or would make use of it was to take what he would on the payment of a small licence fee. A road was laid out by the government and made, leading to the iron country. I was amazed at the decisive action that was taken by the road surveyors, and to see that within a fortnight, a few houses were actually built close to the first workings.

There was apparently a very good understanding between Ninian and the men whom he employed, especially with regard to his foreman. I wondered if Sam Peters could have been a refugee or absconder from Columba who knew the ways of the place, and the unusual discrepancy between the value of gold and silver, and in the course of talk with the men at work discovered that a youth who had been employed in the silver mine, had disappeared about ten years before and was supposed to have perished on the ranges, which at this particular point were very steep and very extensive, or on the stony desert beyond. Such a lapse of time would have changed even an Indian half-breed especially when one took into consideration the change of dress, but I had taken the likeness of my guide, and once showed it suddenly to Ninian who by this time had become experienced in recognising photographs. In spite of his command of countenance, I could see that he knew the face and I then came to the conclusion that Ninian had habitually for many years given the silver of the Commonwealth in exchange for what amount of gold Sam Peters brought.

Of course, there was no doubt that this was cheating in the full sense of the word, and also that if I gave the hint to the authorities they would proceed upon it with swift severity, but at the same time I had no proof that in any court of law in the world would be sufficient. The momentary glance at the gold coin and the momentary expression of a face were not evidence that I thought ought to ruin a man for life, and yet the difficulty was to get anything further. On the night after I had shown the photograph, I felt that I ought to think it over and devise some plan of operations but contrary to my usual habit, I was oppressed by sleep so heavy that I felt sure I had been drugged, and recollected that Ninian knew the use of some old Indian herbs, not through his parents, but through the constant intercourse with his work people. I struggled with my drowsiness and got at my medicine chest, and took what appeared to myself likely to be an antidote in the shape of an emetic and after that had worked its effect, I again felt sleepy as one does after being exhausted.

But my mind was made up; I would leave the place and report that I had been practised upon. Collecting my belongings together, I was starting off on a midnight walk when I met Ninian and four of his workmen, mostly Indian by race, and as I thought the most ignorant of them all, who evidently were prepared to carry me out – bed and all – in a state of unnatural sleep. Ninian started to see me standing up somewhat dazed and weak, but still quite awake.

'Where are you bound for?' he asked.

'And what are you bound for?' I asked in my turn.

'Oh there is a panther started, and we are going out together to take it dead or alive, and my gun is in the house. Will you come with us. I thought you had heard the alarm and had got up.'

'Oh no. I was ill at ease, and could not stay in bed.'

'Then come with us,' said Ninian. 'There has not been a panther in this valley for years.'

I could see that one of the four attendants thought the panther story a grand fabrication, for he was grinning from ear to ear. I wanted however to get out of the house into the fresh air and pretended to go along with the party. As I got outside the door, Ninian called out, 'There he is, there he is,' and turned his gun barrel to me, and shot at me. I just escaped by a little from a serious wound, but it grazed me on the thigh and I fell down with the shock. With a sudden movement they all fell on me, and carried me over to a deep ravine at the back of the silver mine, they threw me down with violence in spite of my protestations, and left me to live or die. No doubt Ninian thought the wound which bled profusely was deeper than it was, and trusted to the action of the drug which he thought I had only partially recovered from, but I felt certain that there would be a hue and cry after me on the morrow, so I had only to endure for a while in patience.

VI

DELIVERANCE

My chances of escape were slenderer than I thought, for at daybreak someone unseen by me, perhaps Ninian himself, came with a wagonload of rubbish which he tilted on the top of me. Fortunately no very heavy load could be carried over these heights and I escaped being crushed, but I dreaded a repetition of the operation. I could not clamber up the sharp sides of the ravine with my wound, which was painful, besides which I felt a strange heaviness in my limbs. I made some desperate struggles after escape, when to my great joy, I saw Jean Anderson standing at the edge of the cliff with her infant in her arms.

'Victor Keith!' said she. 'Is life sweet to you? What will you give for help to escape?'

'Much!' said I. 'Money and gratitude.'

'I ask for neither,' said she 'but I only ask that you will take Liliard over the ranges and say nothing of what has befallen you here, and then I will save you.'

'I scarce see how you can,' said I. 'You are but a woman encumbered by an infant.'

'The bairn will lie still where I put him. I have the means of saving you, but you will ruin Ninian.'

'He has tried to murder me, who have done him no harm,' said I.

'That may be, but he accounts it harm. He treats you as a rival and a spy. But for me, you saved my life, and I owe you mine – only if I die, spare Ninian.'

'You owe your life to little Gavin,' said I, 'if you can save me without peril to yourself.'

'That is impossible,' said she. 'I run the risk of being shot through the heart if I am the means of letting you loose to tell the Council what you know.'

'But I can give you time to save him and to let him make his escape. He has such relations with the outside world through Sam Peters.'

'Yes I know,' said Jean.

'Well once over the ranges, he is safe and he is clever enough to make a way for himself. If he were only honest, I could guarantee him success. And to tell you the truth even if he killed me, and thus stopped my mouth, there is no safety for him in Columba.'

'He will say you have gone over the ranges with stolen treasure.'

'Who will believe him?' said I. 'Liliard Abercrombie knows I would not go without her, and the Council gave me a commission to enquire into his management of the mines and the mint. Whether I am found or not, Ninian will be held responsible and his fate be far worse than if I had told my suspicions.'

'Is it so?' said Jean distractedly; she released her child from her arms to lay him on the ground and untwined a long sort of scarf of white cotton, which women wore to help to carry their infants, which she tore into thin strips, and was engaged in knotting together when she heard the wheels of a waggon and saw Ninian approaching.

He looked scowlingly at her, and looked down on me. She said over again what I had told her, that he only made his position worse by practising upon me, and that the Council would send to seek for me dead or alive.

'They are a parcel of old women,' said he. 'I have outwitted them for years and do not fear them now – and as for this sneaking spy, I'll do for him once for all.' He took from the waggon his gun but Jean caught hold of his hand.

'Harm him not,' said she, 'but make your own escape for, old women as you call them, the Council will be on your tracks before the sun has set.'

'I was bound to give in a report,' said I, 'this day, and if I do not appear I will be sent for, and all these proceedings will be discovered. Suspicion is already strong against you for tampering with the money of the Commonwealth for your own advantage.'

'Fly!' said Jean. 'Fly, as Victor Keith advises. Seek the path at the back of Hugh Keith's house, which is the easiest.'

'As if I did not know that well enough,' said Ninian.

'What can I do for you – to help you?' said Jean.

'Come with me,' said Ninian doggedly.

Jean's face lighted up with joy. She picked up her child and made ready. But suddenly turning to me she said 'But what will become of you, Victor Keith?'

'Oh never mind me,' said I. 'I will be found no doubt. I must have patience.'

And they went on their way and I was left alone. But only for a few hours for ere the sun was low in the heavens another voice, the sweetest to my ears in the world, was heard and another woman gazed down upon me.

'Victor,' said she, 'I have come with Master Hepburn; Hugh was unluckily at Ebenezer, busied about the forthcoming elections, but we have brought ropes and a ladder. I could not trust the men whom Ninian employed.'

'Who told you of my state?' said I.

'Jean Anderson passed like a fire-flash, and told me to save you, and I was going forth alone when I met Master Hepburn. The sides are steep; are you not much bruised by the fall? You have been bleeding I see.'

'Yes and wounded slightly besides.' I struggled to my feet and crawled to the place where my friends let down the ladder which they held steady by the rope, but it was not long enough and I had some trouble in making the final spring. I was caught by my two hands in hers as she reached them down to meet me and the old minister gave his help too. Neither Jean nor Liliard has supposed the difficulties of extrication would have been so great, and when I saw the height from which I had been thrown I wondered again that I had not been killed, but I had fallen on some soft moist soil and not on jagged spurs, such as were on the top, so that I had got off with bruises and a terrible shock but no broken bones. When at last I got on to a level with my deliverers I threw myself into Liliard's arms. For a moment she allowed me to cover her face with my kisses, but she recollected herself and the unwritten law of Columba. 'No, Victor, not yet – you forget that I belong to Hugh. Thank God you are safe now, but you need nursing and care.'

'Now,' said Master Hepburn, 'we must have some sort of litter made and get you carried home to the Protector's. It is a long way but it will be easier travelling than in a cart.' Some of the mining hands were summoned by a shrill whistle and came up scared and terrified, but among them I saw none of those who had carried me away. I spoke to them saying that I had been wounded and thrown into the ravine; they said that Ninian had told them I had plotted robbery of the gold and murder of himself and his foreman, and therefore no doubt the four men had obeyed him in all that he ordered. They were surprised to hear that he had gone away for good, and that I had been authorised by the Council in all that I had done. I was laid to rest in the now-empty house, and Liliard and Master Hepburn nursed me till they could get someone else, and by good luck Sister Dorothea was not engaged with any sick child, and came to my aid without much delay. Liliard then bade me farewell, with such evident reluctance, with such repeated efforts to go and repeated returns to say something to me or to suggest something to Dorothea for my comfort, that I knew she was just as loath to part as I was.

Master Hepburn charged himself to inform the Council fully and minutely with the facts of the case on the following day. We thought that would give Ninian and Jean a sufficient start.

On the next day when the Council was informed, sentence of outlawry was pronounced on Ninian who had forfeited all rights of a Columban citizen by his defalcations, and on Jean Anderson who had gone with him without leave, forth from the plantation, and had assisted him in carrying off the spoil, for, though burdened with her child, Jean had helped him to carry out all the gold and great part of the silver that had been made into ingots for minting. What amount of provisions they had also burdened themselves with we did not know, but it was a bare cupboard I had come back to, and both Liliard and Dorothea had to beg and borrow for my first meal, as well as for their own.

But there was more than a sentence of outlawry pronounced in the first instance. Hugh Keith as the only citizen who knew the road, was ordered to follow and to shoot Ninian as an outlaw. Hugh did not like the dangerous and thankless task of avenger and besides said very justly that singlehanded he was no match for Ninian and Jean. But it was contrary to all the laws and customs of Columba to order any other citizen, even any member of the police force to go with Hugh, and so to show others the possibility of escape. Archibald Keith who was making a strong party for the coming elections, made such a protest against the conduct of Protector Elliot that he withdrew the order and Hugh was allowed to rest in peace.

As for me I was not allowed much credit, because I had allowed Ninian to escape with his ill-gotten booty. Of course they did not take into account the probability that if he had been tried and sentenced to work on the roads, he would have escaped over the ranges before a week had elapsed.

The subordinates excused themselves by their habit of implicit obedience to the head of the department and were let off with moderately light sentences. The judge somewhat eloquently laid down the principle that they served the Commonwealth, and not the officer employed by the Commonwealth and that though Victor Keith was a stranger he ought to be treated honourably by all Columban subjects.

In the course of three days, I was sufficiently recovered to be moved not to Protector Elliot's, but to Madame Abercrombie's, who entreated that I should make her house my home. Here I might sometimes hope to see Liliard when I could not go forth from the house to the gatherings. My recovery however was so rapid as to surprise myself. I hoped to be well enough to be present at the Harvest Home festivities where there were to be Columban athletic sports and a competition for a prize poem and of course a great dance on the green to wind up with.

VII

HARVEST HOME IN COLUMBA

I do not think I have mentioned that the dances and the story telling and the drama were not all the amusements in Columba, but that the children had many toys and games. I had seen some athletic sports on breaking-up day, which preceded the harvest. There was no cricket or anything like cricket as it is played in England, but there was a sort of hockey played with a ball and hooked stick. There was the old game of knuckle-bones or as my grandmother called it 'chucks' played with four shells or pebbles and a marble; there were marbles and hoops, and spinning-tops, and kites or dragons as the Columbans called them. Children also blew soap-bubbles from tobacco pipes, though they had never heard of balloons, and there were a great many more talking or patter games, and beginnings of little plays than in the old country because their early education was so full of rhymes and stories. The children had six weeks holiday at harvest times because they helped with it so much – they did not reap corn but they gleaned and they picked cotton and coffee berries and drove flocks of fowls and geese into the stubble – and relieved the hard workers of many light jobs during the busy season. There were two other times of the year when they had holidays: seed-time and the time of weeding and hoeing up the crops that were drilled.

The sugar crop gave the hardest work of the year, but in Columba as it was not a crop for export, there was not the drive of night and day work under which so many of the negro slaves in the Southern States and elsewhere used to break down.

The harvest included so many and such various crops where the country was absolutely self-supporting, that a protectionist would have held it forth as an example to the civilised world, and it was of course the great event of the year. The season had been most propitious. There was therefore a thanksgiving service in church for the bounties of providence more appropriate than it often is in Australia where drought or red rust or some other untoward circumstances thwart the farmers' toil and although this was held on a weekday, the attendance was very general. Thanksgiving day or Harvest Home was the favourite time for putting on new clothes – and I could not help admiring the effect. My Liliard had on a new jersey of brown with gold collar and cuffs and facings, which in a high art sense was more admirable than the scarlet one I first saw her in, but Nicol Elliot's bride was arrayed in pale blue. At first I had thought the dresses one and all unbecoming because unusual, but now I had an eye for all the little differences and saw who had some taste and who had none.

The games were many of the old Scottish ones: throwing the hammer, putting the stone, running and wrestling, jumping and hopping. There were also some fine pole exercises and tilting at a ring on horseback but there was no grinning through horse collars, no running in sacks, no climbing up greasy poles for a leg of mutton at the top, no three-legged races. The deficient sense of humour among the Columbans made such things unattractive either to competitors or lookers-on. I watched to see if there was any betting going on as to the winners but I could observe none and on inquiry I learned that there was no such practice in Columba. The prizes were products of the harvest. A large bag of wheaten flour was the highest prize given, a smaller bag of sugar followed next; a still smaller bag of coffee was the third – raw cotton, beans, peas, maize, barley, potatoes also had a place as prizes. The prizes were all given by the government and each prize was accompanied by a wreath of various foliage, according to the nature of the trial of strength or skill. This mixture of the simple rewards of Greek and Roman republics with the solid prizes of Columban industry rather amused me. The maidens and handfasted women wove the wreaths or garlands and I was only sorry that I could not put in for one of them, which I knew Liliard Abercrombie had devised and fashioned.

It was given for throwing the hammer, and was won by Hugh Keith, and when Liliard with her own hands, as was the custom, placed it on his head, where it mingled with his abundant chestnut curls, I could see from the look exchanged between them that he was proud to do well before her for the last time, and she was pleased that she could do him honour.

The first dance with her on the green belonged to Hugh of right, and though I was well enough to appear, I was not well enough to dance, except one minuet with Liliard, and one with Sister Dorothea. The minuet was a little quicker in Columba than under the ancient régime in France and was always interspersed with a lively movement. When I sat down beside Liliard at the end of our dance, I reminded her in a whisper that her term of handfasting would be over in ten days. I knew that a month was considered a proper time to wait between one handfasting and another, though there were some impetuous people who did not wait more than a day.

'I am glad Hugh has had this success,' said I. 'How handsome he looks in his new clothes.'

'The last I shall make for him,' said she. 'I thank God that we shall not part in bitterness. I have hopes that he will turn his thoughts on Marjorie. Do you note how her eyes follow him everywhere. She is younger and more to be bent to his ways than ever I was and he is so good and true, he will make her happy. If you had not crossed my path, I might have thought I loved him.'

'Then in a month from the rupture of your present tie you will be mine. Could not Master Hepburn make it a real marriage?'

'No!' said Liliard. 'He could not, and I would not have it so. I will gladly be handfasted with you; we need not speak of any further hope or expectation. I look no further forward than a year.'

'I do,' said I stoutly.

'So did Hugh,' said she sadly. 'I seem to take this change far harder than the rest of the Columbans. In any case, I would never have changed lightly, but when I think what this change means to you, it comes on me whiles like a stab.'

'What to you is change means to me such bliss as I never dreamed of, such as I could not have conceived possible. Am I the same man who three months ago thought no woman could disturb his plans or his slumbers, who fancied that under all circumstances he would preserve his reason and his prudence and marry some suitable good-looking sensible woman when it appeared to be for his advantage to do so?'

'Why should I feel proud to think that you should have lost your senses about me? but I do – only it may not last Victor.'

'It will last as long as my life.'

'And you are not naturally fickle,' said Liliard thoughtfully, 'but with this love and this anxiety on my mind I am full of apprehensions and vague fears. Pray for me; Victor pray for yourself. Even Hugh has betaken himself to prayer of late, and found comfort in it.'

VIII

WE ARE HANDFASTED

I had a somewhat stormy meeting with the Town Council when I was considered strong enough for the interview, and that was on the day between the Harvest Home festival and the general election. The mode of administering an oath in Columba was by solemn affirmation; among a people who could not read kissing any book, however sacred, was in the ideas of the framers of the constitution, a senseless superstition. I was blamed because I had not told my suspicions with regard to Ninian and my treacherous guide at first, which I had not done because the Council had such an arbitrary mode with their official servants that Ninian might have had no opportunity of proving his innocence. In the second place I was blamed for letting Ninian escape the punishment he deserved and conniving at his escape with Jean Anderson and an amount of booty which the Protector affirmed was as much as all his previous robberies put together. He certainly could not tell either the one or the other, for it was mere guesswork. The Commonwealth confiscated to its own uses all the land which Ninian had acquired, and I believe that these purchases had represented all and more than all that he had got nefariously.

But the Council were disturbed as to whether there had been any accomplices in the affair with Sam Peters; my own suspicions pointed to the only other civil servant in the department of the mines who was his foreman and clerk, but when he was examined he appeared thoroughly to exonerate himself. The slighter business of the violence practised on myself was brought home to four half-Indians who had apparently erred from over zealous obedience to orders from the head of the department. They were each sentenced to three months hard labour on the roads without wages as a caution not to do such things again. I was dismissed without positive blame, but with no thanks, and still less honour, and with no remuneration for the very unpleasant work which had been forced upon me.

It was like a tempest in a teacup to see the little electioneering machinery set in operation for the return of the new Council who were to choose the Protector or President for the next four years. I was not a registered voter nor was Liliard, though widows or even handfasted women who had never been married who were landholders and heads of families had votes. Liliard was a landholder, but after her handfasting expired, she made a gift of her town land to her young sister Marjorie. The result of the election showed that there must have been general dissatisfaction for of the seven retiring members only two were returned, and Protector Elliot by no means at the head of the poll. That position was given to Archibald Keith, who naturally was chosen Protector, and Hugh's satisfaction with this change helped him to bear his own domestic trial. He threw off a hundred photographs of the new Protector on the finest paper he had succeeded in making that would take the chemicals, and that was another triumph.

Hugh's father and mother were not so troubled at his disappointment with Liliard as he thought they might have been and they fully appreciated all the advantages of the new business which I had not only taught him, but had furnished him with the apparatus necessary to carry it out. On the whole the Keith family considered themselves my debtors, and I found a very different feeling in the Council when I was next summoned into their presence and requested to give a written report on the condition of the medical staff and the mining processes, and also to give my views as to the establishment of a printing press and any other matters which I thought would further the interests of the people of Columba.

In this report, I said much the same things as I had in conversation with Master Hepburn; the idea of a hospital for Ebenezer was entertained, and I was requested to make the ground plan of the building, and draw out some regulations, but the printing press and newspaper suggestion was negatived on the same grounds as had influenced the old minister; such an innovation would unsettle the people and combined with Ninian's previous escape with Jean Anderson and their child, and my approaching departure with Liliard, would make them eager to leave this home of peace and plenty and happiness and perhaps be the means of disclosing the passes to enemies who might make a spoil of their beloved plantation.

The last danger I saw no reason to fear for the aegis of Great Britain was stronger for protection than when the settlement was young; but on the other hand if even the Federal Government of the United States threatens the Mormon inhabitants at Salt Lake, would not the more centralised government of Great Britain condemn and abolish the custom of handfasting? It was a much more serious infraction of gospel and common law than the wife's sister business and that has not yet been fully recognised by English law after many efforts at home and in the colonies.

But I could not believe that a printing press and a newspaper could unsettle the minds of the lieges much, nevertheless on the mature deliberation of the Council consideration of this subject was postponed *sine die*. All I could do for the settlement I was glad to do. I left them all my surgical instruments and my few books, but these last not until my own departure.

For now the term was over, and the handfasting of Hugh Keith and Liliard Abercrombie was terminated as solemnly as it had been entered into, and now for a month during which she lived at her mother's house, my delicious season of free courtship began and with it began the education which Liliard was so eager to enter upon which would fit her for the new world in which she had to live.

All we had for schoolbooks were some diamond editions of the poets, and a single Melbourne newspaper, but her quickness of apprehension gave rise to some curious results. I have seen some performers, musicians who read music slowly, who said they could play anything off by heart by the time they could read it correctly, and in the same way Liliard's memory was so wonderful that it was less reading than invention. On half a hint she guessed at the meaning of a sentence, sometimes not at all correctly, but it was always both sense and grammar. In the case of poetry, her guesses were often most felicitous and her ear was never at fault. She never ventured on a false quantity, though she often mistook the words. And how she ploughed through the columns of the Melbourne newspaper, leading articles, news, parliamentary reports and advertisements, with innumerable questions as to places, people, professions and avocations absolutely strange to her but familiar to me, and therefore which she must needs become acquainted with. My term with the Council was over. Hugh did all the photography for the people and Marjorie Abercrombie had learned to help him as Liliard had done. Though I still was willing to go to the sick when I was sent for, I had no other calls on my time, and I felt I had earned a month's holiday after three months of bondage.

Had I ever dreamed of anything so frank and open as this intercourse of declared love? There were none of the drawbacks to my happiness which I had dwelt on to my grandmother when she pressed me to make a choice among her charming circle of nice girls. What a beautiful and original nature was expanding daily under the sunshine of her love for me. Her doubts seemed all thrown aside and her fears lost, she seemed to tread on air as I did. Together we explored the Happy Valley as I called it, the Sleepy Hollow as Liliard called it, in all its length and breadth. We sat under the wall which the first settlers had built, and carried on our studies and our confidences by the side of every little brook that babbled on its way to the Columba river, but that told no tales to other ears. Oh those sacred confidences! Oh those tender vows! Oh those golden September days in the Happy Valley! Harvest was over but the tropical fruitage was in all its glory. There never was such sunshine, there never was such moonlight in the whole world as there was there and then.

Far from thinking that a bride would be a nuisance to travel with, I looked forward to our escape over the ranges and our going through desert and woodland and solitary places and crowded cities with the most bewildering anticipations of mutual pleasure and mutual help. Meantime I felt sure that in the eyes of my compeers in Melbourne, I was as ridiculous a lover as any whom I had ever laughed at. There was little conventional repression exercised, and little of the awkwardness of engaged people felt in Columba. Madame Abercrombie was tolerant and indulgent; we kept a good deal out of the way of other people, except at the social gatherings in the Kirk and on the green, and I could see that there were several other couples apparently as much engrossed with each other as we were.

There was no preparation in the way of trousseau needed in Columba. Every woman could spin and sew and knit, and some could weave, so that after handfasting and after marriage the exercise of her ordinary faculties could keep up her stock of clothes. All Liliard needed was a travelling suit, for at the first civilised place we came to, she should be equipped for the world. She was glad to think she would need to spin no more. And for my part I felt that my beautiful spinster was worth going, not only across a street, but halfway round the world for, and worth perilling my life to get her safely through the stony desert that separated the Columba valley from the troubled world.

My Liliard had completed her twenty-first year and I my twenty-seventh when we were solemnly handfasted in St Matthews Kirk on Monday 8th September 1879. Master Hepburn tied the knot, and he blessed us with as much fervour and faith as if it had been a union for life. We had planned to spend one fortnight in the valley after we were thus given to each other, that I might really have all the experiences possible in the short time I could command, but Liliard and Liliard's family agreed that I must then make my way back to the family and the duties which called me to the ends of the earth. There was provision to make for our toilsome journey and this Madame Abercrombie took on herself. My bride was to feel free from care for the last fortnight. We lived close by the Mother in a house that had belonged to Ninian, and had it all to ourselves. At the end of the fortnight it came to Liliard's turn to tell her tale and for once she was at fault.

'Victor,' she said 'there is nothing but my own life that will come into my head, nothing but the thought that this which seems to us in Sleepy Hollow so natural and so right, would be thought a great sin in all the rest of the world. But it can scarce be a sin, or my heart and yours would not feel at rest. But when I go among the crowd at the Kirk, and see Hugh's eyes resting on me no longer his own, and all the little wonder not at the change, but at the stranger I changed for, it seems as if I could have no words and no notions as to what the words should be about. I cannot speak about ourselves and I can think of nothing else.'

'But you can tell one of your old stories. Other people do often. Recollect the tale of Ralph Abercrombie that took the very heart of me the first day I saw you.'

'No the life has gone out of it to me. You see, I have changed, I am no Palahna. Oh! Victor what would it have been if I had borne a child to Hugh. He had the right to keep the child for it was me that broke the bond, and Hugh would never have parted with it – never! No entreaty from me would have availed. He would have been fixed as yonder mountains that we have to cross tomorrow – and I should have had to turn my back on my bairn for ever – unless – but that trial has been spared to me and to you. Oh no! it could not be the story of fidelity that I could tell now.'

'But you have others, Liliard.'

'Aye, but I should not give them a hash of old things as my parting story,' said she with the old pride of the improvisatrice in her air. 'I would rather give them one of your stories, not the Effie Deans one or that about Laura Collingwood, but you have told me others. Oh Victor, I used to like your stories better – far better than my own – only now my mind is so full of you there seems no room for even them.'

She did not excuse herself from the obligation she was under, though up to the last moment she scarcely knew what she meant to take as her subject, but while she was packing up some of her belongings for departure, she came upon a blue neckerchief into which she had knitted the leading points of *A Tale of Two Cities* which was always my favourite of Dickens's stories, and which from its historic associations had taken the strongest hold of her imagination. With this in her hand she stepped for the last time on the Columban boards. Master Hepburn asked the customary blessing with unusual emotion. If I had thought her beautiful when I saw her there first, if I had admired her fire and her genius then, I was now lost in wonder and delight. Even her mother and brother and sisters thought she was lovelier than ever and to me there was the magical charm of possession. Her expression was tenderer and deeper than before because those wonderful brown eyes sought mine no longer in curiosity, but in confidence and love. The story flowed on with ease and power, the comic parts were all left out, but the story of the Bastille prisoner, the story of the running over the little child in Paris, of the murder of the marquis, the narrative found in the Bastille, the fury of the mob, the hardness of the tribunals, the likeness between Sydney Carton and Charles Darnay on which the story hangs, and which in the end allows the unsuccessful lover to give his life for Lucie's husband, were all given with extraordinary energy and pathos. Where any explanation was needed of the condition of France, it was given briefly and forcibly. During the course of the story, there was breathless attention and many tears, and at the end there were unaccustomed plaudits. It was known that Liliard was to leave the valley. Master Hepburn tried to dismiss the assembly with a fervent benediction, but fairly broke down, and my wife – wife she was – whatever the Columbans thought, hung on his neck for the space of a minute.

Hugh Keith came forward from the others and spoke to us without bitterness but with much feeling. 'It was to be,' he said. 'I can bear it like a man, though perhaps not like a saint or a martyr.'

At early morning we each took our share of our whole present worldly possessions. There was one thing we had to carry that was rather formidable, namely money; I never had such an appreciation of bills of exchange and bank notes as when I reflected that if I took away my Columba earnings in gold, they would shrink marvellously, while if I took them in silver they would be extremely bulky.

The Council had some meetings with regard to my claims on the estate of Ninian who had come by my stolen gold, and who had bought as I have already said a good property which was now forfeited absolutely to the Commonwealth, and in the more favourable disposition of the newly elected representative body towards me, there was little difficulty in settling that matter by giving me the whole amount of gold I had lost. But it was not to be taken in coin but in bullion - the outside world was not to be shown the existence of a civilised nation through this medium, and all my silver coin was called in and an equivalent in pure silver bars given to me. With regard to my camera, it was my gift to Hugh, the books, the Melbourne newspaper and the surgical instruments were presented to the Commonwealth. I wanted to give something to Master Hepburn and presented him with my watch. His son was a watch and clock maker and had much admired it; I bought from him a commoner watch that would serve to keep time on our travels; watches were articles of luxury with the settlers, though clocks were common. We reduced our baggage to the smallest compass, but the necessity of carrying food as well as money and the probability that we should have to carry water, made us somewhat heavily burdened.

Like our first parents on their expulsion from Eden:

Some natural tears she dropped but wiped them soon
The world was all before us where to choose
Our place of rest and Providence our guide
We hand in hand with wandering steps and slow
Through Eden took our solitary way.

BOOK FIVE

BACK TO THE WORLD

I

COMMUNICATION RESTORED

It was no feeblebodied or faint hearted mate whom I had for my companion on the journey, and through the stony desert fleet and strong of limb, and patient and courageous in spirit, she moved by my side with equal step and eager eye. The first glance of the beyond would have appeared to any other person as it did to Hugh, most sterile and uninteresting, but to her it was the highway to all her ambition and all her desire. It was evident that Ninian and Jean Anderson had noted the camping place where my faithless half-breed had robbed and deserted me, the pole which I had stuck up had been burned for fuel, and the ashes and charcoal were still to be seen, as well as the bones of a piece of mutton which they had carried with them, but I had no difficulty in reaching the precise spot, and when we camped there the second night, Liliard's joy was a sight to see. We lighted our kerosene lamp and boiled our coffee for there was no wood or fuel to be had, and we ate our frugal repast with satisfaction. In the solitude of the desert there was no sleep for Liliard; she was in the world, and that was excitement enough to keep her awake all night for joy.

Our trouble came from an unexpected quarter. We had looked forward to drought, and difficulties in hitting on the waterholes or streams, of which Sam Peters had ascertained the localities in his frequent travels, but we were astonished at early morning by a tremendous tropical rain which continued more or less for three days. We could make little way, though at intervals we moved on, but I could not take an observation from the absence of the sun, and so we were forced to trust to the compass for the direction in a general way. Owing to the porous nature of the soil, the rain, when it ceased, left little or no surface water, so that after considerable consumption of provisions, we were little better off with regard to that prime necessary of life. But drenched and draggled as we were, we kept our food and our powder dry, and I never heard Liliard laugh so heartily as she did at our forlorn appearance and our curious makeshifts. All the difficulties and dangers of the march not only brought out her courage, they sharpened her wit; and the one deficiency that I had noted, her want of appreciation of the humorous side of things, appeared no longer in her character. We tried how little we could live on, and now and then by good luck we shot a chance bird or quadruped of unknown species tempted or driven by the rain storm to this unfamiliar place.

But after ten days, things were looking very black with us; we had made but little way, and commons were very short when to our great delight we saw a horseman in the distance. We hoisted what signals of distress were in our power, and he came towards us swiftly, while we too made all the speed we could. He had been looking for stray cattle from a ranch, and had been led out of his usual track by some false information, for which he had been vowing vengeance when we came in sight. He was as rough a specimen of the Western ranchman as could be met with in these latitudes, but if he had been an angel, we could not have been more rejoiced to find him, nor could an angel have been kinder. He put Liliard on his horse, and walked by her side till we reached an outlying hut where we rested for the night, and though the fare was of the coarsest salt beef, and the most stony and husky looking bread that I ever saw, the knowledge that we were now in an inhabited country was full of rest and hope. The next day we travelled to the ranch, and were again hospitably entertained though with little more comfort or cleanliness than before. My Liliard's first experience of the world was certainly of a distinctly retrograde phase of civilisation, but she was not shocked at trifles.

Our onward journey might be taken in a waggon which would leave the ranch two days after our arrival. We were welcome to stay as long as we pleased, but this conveyance would take us to the railwayline leading to San Francisco, and then we would be in communication with the whole civilised world. The ranchman's wife was of mixed breed, and of an absolute ignorance with regard to anything out of her own line but she was kind in her way. Our difficulties with regard to washing appliances were great, and our sufferings from flies, mosquitoes and meaner vermin terrible – or would have been terrible if we had not been so happy.

I had exchanged with the ranchman some of my bullion for Californian gold, but I could not prevail on him to take payment for his hospitality, nor for the ride in the waggon which conveyed to market some of the butter and cheese which his wife made. Every slow step of the bullocks was so much nearer to the goal we aimed at. This was to be the last of the delays in our path. After this all was to be swiftness, fire and life.

When we came to the railwayline and sat down on a bench in front of the rude log station, Liliard looked at the rails with interest and curiosity quite inexplicable to the wondering ranchman who had brought us. When the puffing, snorting engine followed by the train came up, her delight was unbounded. We had previously taken out our tickets so we took our seats, and our luggage with us in the carriage for all classes; rough Western ranchmen and miners and not a woman but herself in the train. We should probably have preferred less democratic arrangements in our honeymoon trip if we had had to choose – but now all was delightful, all was perfect.

When Liliard compared me with these first inhabitants of the world whom she met, she told me she felt how lucky she had been. She kept congratulating herself that the visitor from outside who found his way into the Happy Valley was myself, an educated gentleman of their own kin, who had travelled in many lands, instead of one of these from the ranks of their nearer neighbours which indeed would have been far more probable. In that case however there would not have been awakened in her soul the longing to leave the Happy Valley of Columba.

As we travelled, the face of the country improved, houses and farms, vineyards and gardens, hamlets, villages and towns grew more frequent. Liliard looked from side to side of the carriage, wondered at the swiftness and the smoothness of the travelling, when in fact the railroad was somewhat jerky, and the pace slow. She called my attention now to this, now to that, she asked information, she threw out suppositions. She saw night fall without feeling inclined for sleep, and talked softly to me as to what she should do and how she should behave when she got to the great city when the loud snoring of our fellow travellers gave satisfactory evidence that they were unconscious of our presence. We passed swiftly through several towns which she called little cities before we reached the Queen of the West. At last for the present we had found a resting place. Before we found our hotel, I went to the telegraph office at the railway station and with my darling on my arm, telegraphed:

From Hugh Victor Keith Palace Hotel San Francisco to Dr Archibald Keith Collins Street Melbourne

'Have found the Scottish colony. Am married to Liliard Abercrombie – happiest man in the world.'

'Oh, Victor that is not true,' said Liliard when I read her the message over.

'Is it not; I think it is. Well now for the hotel. Nay, first to a shop; we must get some clothes. But first perhaps to the bank for money and there you must stay in the cab till I come to you.' We whirled through the bustling streets with its motley groups of people of all races under the sun and yet with all the appliances of modern civilisation. I identified myself as the Hugh Victor Keith who had presented a letter of credit on Melbourne five months before, and got what I wanted with wonderfully little delay.

'But the clothes, Victor, will need to be made,' said Liliard.

'Oh no, we can manage things more quickly on such a pinch as this,' said I, and so we went to a great emporium where my first care was to choose for Liliard a rig out from head to heels. There was no difficulty in getting ready-made dresses to fit a woman so beautifully made as my darling, and she left the shop transformed to the outward eye into a fashionably dressed bride. Her glance at the great mirror had startled her. She had never seen herself from head to foot before, and did not know herself. I saw she felt abashed before the sight of grace and fashion which were her very own, and blushed and bowed apologetically to the supposed stranger thus suddenly encountered face to face.

The next visit was to a jeweller's shop, where I bought a brooch and two rings.

When were were again in the cab, I took off the glove into which my bride had struggled, and took off the half ring, and essayed to put on the whole one, with another as a guard.

'Victor,' said she 'this cannot be.'

'It must be' said I. 'I cannot possibly take you with me unless you are my wife. I shall get a licence tonight, and be married tomorrow. It is the first thing that is to be done now we are in a civilised Christian land.'

'No, Victor – no – we are handfasted for a year and a day; if after that time you are willing to marry me, and I am willing to marry you, we will be married then, but not before.'

'My dearest love, do you think it possible if I could change. Are you not happy with me.'

'Happy?' said she. 'Happy! it is just such happiness that it makes me dizzy to think of it but it feels as if it could not last. It is too much for mortal life in this lower world.'

'And will it not be more likely to last if we put it beyond the risk of disturbance.'

'You must give me time to breathe before you press me against my conscience – all the conscience I have. All the experience I have, all the lessons of Madame Keith, all point one way, that the year of probation is a wise thing. Oh! Victor, but for that, my love for you would have been a sin.'

'But Liliard such love as ours can never change.'

'So we think, so many people think that do change, and if it lasts, then we can confirm our union with joy and some assurance. Dear Victor, give me my own way in this,' and her pleading voice and her tears had their usual effect on me.

'Well, so far I will not press it, but the ring you must wear, and you must submit to be called Mrs Keith by everybody, and not look scared at the sound of your own name, as you did at the ranch.'

She submitted to have the ring put on; I wanted to destroy the old one but she said that must not be. If all went well, she meant to keep all her Columban clothes to show to my grandmother, and the old lady should see the half ring too. Liliard had no idea of any concealment of her antecedents from my kindred.

And now for the hotel – for a luxurious bath and a civilised dinner. Liliard whom I shall always call my wife, in spite of the absence of the ceremony, took her place beside me at the public table, and watched all my movements, and took care to do what I did, and to avoid what I did not do whoever might set another example. After dinner we went on foot through the streets.

'Is Melbourne as handsome as this splendid city,' said she, 'and are the streets so busy?'

'Except for the hotels, it is a handsomer city, and except for the magnificence of the harbour, I think it is better situated. But the people here seem faster or perhaps more American than our Victorians, and we have not so many nationalities. You will prefer Melbourne, I am sure.'

'If you prefer it, I will,' said she.

'Now we are not going to spend the evening at the hotel,' said I. 'I must show you the town by gaslight when the display at those shops which are still open shows to most advantage and we must go to a real theatre.'

The spectacular appearance of the drama as presented on the San Francisco boards delighted her much, but the play which was one of modern fashionable life, did not interest her so much as she expected. The hits misfired, she seemed not to understand the language or the circumstances. She had a playbill in her hand, which she could scarcely read, for though she had made great progress in reading in the last six weeks in Columba, it had been from the few books and the Melbourne newspaper, greatly aided by her amazingly good memory. We had bought reading books of a more elementary kind on our walk, for the first thing of all that she had to learn, was to read and write. After our engagement and during our journey I had thrown off the Scotch manner of speaking that I had naturally adopted in Columba, and had practised Liliard in the English use of the vowels, and she was quick and apt in this as in most things. And the amount of talk we had had on that long journey gave her great opportunities for learning to speak in the English style.

II

AN UNWELCOME INTRUDER

In looking over the playbill I saw that there was a new company to appear at the theatre on the arrival of the San Francisco mail from Australia and New Zealand, one too that I had often heard in Melbourne. The mail was expected in hourly and as the company was a good one which sometimes played Shakespeare's best plays, I anticipated a treat for Liliard. While I was speaking on this subject to her between the acts, I saw enter the stalls from above, an old acquaintance who made for me. It was Jack Barnett, whom my grandmother so much disliked, who had been in Melbourne one of the most inveterate playgoers and always deep in the jargon and the secrets of the green room. He always knew when an actor's sudden illness was due to his being drunk, and an actress's to a jealous pique. He knew how much salary each man drew, and how much of the house was pay, and how much dummy orders. He had the first and the most ill-natured account of every quarrel that took place, and knew all the questionable antecedents and all the present scandals of all the members of the profession in Melbourne.

I knew that his father had failed in business and that he had been thrown on his own resources a few months before I had left Melbourne. He was just about the last man I should have wished to see when my wife was new to everything, and not actually formally my wife, especially as she was naturally open as the day, but there was no escape from it. I warned Liliard in an emphatic whisper to be as silent as possible as to our affairs, and as to Columba and its ways, and awaited the approach of my old acquaintance with grim fortitude.

'Victor Hugo!' said he, 'and so you are here when your people almost think you are *non est*. Two mails and not a line from you or a telegram either.'

He looked with curiosity at Liliard, and not with admiration. I was conscious that she was worth looking at anywhere, and that there was a not a handsomer woman in the theatre, on or off the boards.

'I have had a fair excuse for my remissness,' said I. 'Allow me to introduce my wife. Mr Barnett a Melbourne friend.'

He bowed; Liliard bowed a little awkwardly. 'A stunner,' he whispered.

'I have been through a good many adventures,' said I, 'and was out of the way of sending letters, or telegrams either, for many months.'

'But on the whole you have had a high time,' said Barnett looking at Liliard.

'I suppose you are full up now, and will go straight back again.'

'By no means,' said I, 'my travels are to begin. We only arrived in San Francisco today, and I have just telegraphed to my father.'

'Then I have just arrived by the mail a few hours after you. I have come with a coalition company from New Zealand, where we have been astonishing the natives considerable, but the steamer by which we came on, brought me Melbourne letters, and my sister Bell wrote me that the Collins Street folk are altogether put out by not hearing from you. She said you were last heard of from 'Frisco, and said I might come across you and, by Jove, I have not been long about it. We must be fond of the boards, for we put in an early appearance at the theatre, Mrs Keith. But this is a rascally bad company. Don't understand business at all. We will astonish the Browns.'

'Then you are somehow connected with this company that comes from New Zealand.'

'I believe you my boy; I am their agent.'

'Oh, indeed, that is indeed a new line of life for you.'

'Well when the governor came to such howling grief, I had to make tracks for myself somehow, and I fell into this.'

'And how are your sisters?' asked I.

'Oh Eva dropped into a good thing. The Campbells were going to Europe, and when that good-natured Florrie saw that Eva had set her heart on going to complete her musical education, as she called it, but really to give herself a chance to see and be seen, she proposed to the old man to take Miss Barnett too – and it was so.'

'Like Miss Campbell,' said I, 'she is a thoroughly good kind-hearted girl, and generous in all her ways.'

'You used to be spoons on Florrie Campbell yourself, but I'm glad to see you've left the coast clear for me. This party used to be a universal admirer,' continued Barnett addressing Liliard, 'an unconscionable flirt, and as the governor, the old medico, was supposed to be well in there was great pulling of caps about him. But he was not to be caught with chaff – too downy a bird for that, eh! Hugh.'

'I found the real grit at last,' said I, 'something far more to my taste than Miss Campbell, good as she is. My grandmother's great disappointment was that I never would be spoons on her as you elegantly call it.'

'Oh! I recollect. I'll never forget the old lady's face when I asked her to waltz once at your house when you were the head of it. Old Campbell will cut up for a hundred and fifty thou. – and Florrie's the only child. Robert has given up the ghost and a good thing too for all parties.'

'Has he?' said I.

'He'd have made the money spin if he had had the handling of it. The mater was dead before you left Melbourne.'

'Yes the long disease, her life, had ended in February.'

'Oh! and your father got a mourning ring or some such trifle but Florrie is now the heiress, if the old man does not take it into his head to marry again and that is likely enough. See what Victor Hugo has given up for your sake, Mrs Keith. I hope the grandmother will not take it to heart.'

I could see that Liliard felt this to be an unkind speech.

'I am sure not when she sees my wife,' I said.

'I was no way displeased for Eva to be so well provided for, and to have a friend at court but it was a soft thing for Florrie to do when Eva is streets beyond her in accomplishments, not to mention other risks.'

'Where are they now?'

'In Scotland till it gets too cold, then they go to the continent, and wait till the season comes on, when they take a house in London. Eva is in clover for one year at least.'

'And your other sisters?'

'They are knocking about with friends, all except the youngest who is with the pater and mater and going to school. As for Tom – he has gone into the civil service, pro and tem, of course, but I know a trick worth two of that.'

The play recommenced, and Liliard tried to give her undivided attention, but was evidently disturbed. Barnett interposed remarks and criticisms of various merit and told some damaging stories about the actors and actresses – all of whom he knew by name and several by character.

'I hope your party is better,' said Liliard who found it hard to keep silence.

'On the boards certainly they are. I'd be ashamed to shepherd them if they were not, but in other ways there's not much to draw between them,' said he. 'Actors are not a strait-laced set of people; they generally take a back seat as to morals and temper and all that sort of thing. How do you like the performance?'

'It is all so new to me. I like the scenery and the theatre.'

'Do you indeed? Well I think it a very one-horse sort of affair. Not to compare with our Melbourne Theatre Royal, is it Keith?'

'Oh, like Victor you stand up for Melbourne, but it is all so new to me,' and here she stopped short – was she betraying what I asked her to keep secret?

'My wife is from a singularly simple part of this country, but nevertheless I have the greatest confidence in her taste and appreciation of what is excellent, and her own dramatic talents are very great.'

'Oh indeed!' said Barnett. 'In the profession?'

'No, only as an amateur.'

Barnett shrugged his shoulders. 'Amateur theatricals are a sell in general, though the present company may be an exception. How long do you stay here Victor Hugo?'

'Not long, for I want to do my travels now without loss of time,' said I. Barnett's presence in San Francisco was an additional motive for leaving it even sooner than I should otherwise have done.

'And you have lost five months spooning I suppose. Mrs Keith you must let him have a little fling now. And in the first place I must ask Hugh to a little theatrical supper we are going to have the day after tomorrow.'

'And not me?' said she interrogatively.

'No, not you, Mrs Keith, unless you go as a professional.'

'Then I must decline for myself,' said I.

'Absolutely?'

'Absolutely.'

'This is petticoat government truly. How long have you been married Victor Hugo? How long will this last?'

'Don't stay, Victor, on my account,' said my wife fearful she was making some blunder. 'I shall not feel dull at all.'

'I have no wish to go,' said I firmly. 'When I do go anywhere without you, it will need much stronger temptation.'

'What are you going to kill time with tomorrow?' said Barnett.

'We are going on the water – on the sea,' said Liliard with undisguised delight.

'Fond of boating, eh?'

'My wife does not know yet – she comes from inland and has never seen the sea.'

'Mrs Keith will be pretty full up of it before she is done with it,' said Barnett.

'I hope her introduction to it will be propitious,' said I.

'Let me see the play bill again Mrs Keith. What sort of theatres are you used to Mrs Keith?'

'Very primitive,' said she, 'but they give us pleasure.'

I could see that Barnett's curiosity was strongly excited. My wife's beauty was unquestionable, but her accent was unmistakably Scotch.

'What did you do with your camera, Victor Hugo?'

'Made great use of it, and left it behind me to a friend who took much interest in it.'

'I suppose Hugh Keith was a very large order in your quiet parts, Mrs Keith.'

Liliard started; the similarity of names confused her as well as the phraseology. At last she understood that it was of me that Mr Barnett spoke, and that the question related to my importance in her primitive part of the country.

'He knew a great many things that we did not,' said she.

'He could let you in to a wrinkle or two in his profession. Did not the doctors all hate him?'

'Oh no – they learned from him.'

'And what did he learn from you?'

Liliard paused a moment. 'Oh, he learned some new dances.'

'And to conjugate the verb "amo" through all its moods and tenses Mrs Keith. You are not long married I see.'

'No, not a month yet.'

'So I thought from his devotion. You know that will pass off. You cannot always expect him to give up a merry party to stay with you Mrs Keith; the marriage ring does not include all a man's business and amusements.'

'I hope that I will be reasonable at all times,' said Liliard, 'and that he may never feel me any hindrance to his pleasures.'

'I suppose you have dropped no end of money on your travels, Hugh?'

'On the contrary I have earned a good deal.'

'Out of the way of spending, I suppose?'

'Very much so.'

'Well you can drop a good deal in these States; as I hear, everything is horridly dear except travelling. Well, I must leave you for I see a man I ought to talk to.'

And to our delight he left us to speak to some one in the dress circle; we had humbly taken our seats in the stalls.

'I do not like your friend,' said Liliard.

'He is not my friend. I do not like him either, and my grandmother could not bear him.'

'I could not understand half that he said. Is that talk really the sort of English that educated people speak? At the ranch, I knew that there was a great deal of vulgar ungrammatical talk, but this is as puzzling.'

'You will soon learn quite enough of slang for ordinary purposes because the same phrases are used over and over again,' said I.

'Did you notice what he said about Miss Campbell.'

'Yes, but it need not disquiet you. I don't think I should ever have loved Miss Campbell if there had not been any other girl in the world.'

'As for him he thinks only of money,' said Liliard indignantly.

'So your first experience of the world, and curiously enough as it happens of a member of my Melbourne world, is very unfavourable.'

'Oh don't say so! It is only very different – but everything is so different,' and my darling looked round on the brilliantly-lighted theatre, the conventional stage, and the well-dressed crowd with the lovely wonder in her eyes which had struck me so much the first day I saw her. 'Only Victor, I hope and believe you will be the same in the world as out of it.'

III

JACK BARNETT'S ACTIVE CURIOSITY

Our first proceeding on the following day was a reading lesson and a writing lesson in the privacy of our own bedroom. How quick she was of apprehension, and although the stupid first books for the use of children conveyed no idea to her worthy of her mature mind, she found that there was great use in knowing perfectly the short words which occur so often, and which besides so often make parts of longer words. In writing she was more awkward but still her determination to succeed was so strong that she every day seemed to conquer a new difficulty. When we had halted on our march she had often written on the sand or built the letters with stones, and now she appeared to be gathering together all she had learned.

Our second step was to go to the post office for my letters, which were a little reproachful, but still more anxious.

After that we went to the glorious harbour and engaged a boat and took a sail among the shipping. Nowadays, you never can meet with an educated grown-up person who has not seen the sea, and the wonder of the gaping rustic is widely different from the reverential awe with which Liliard gazed on the horizon where the blue sky and the blue ocean met, and on the hundreds of wondrous ships like towns from various lands. She had never even seen a picture of a ship or of a harbour or of the face of the sea with the waves breaking continuously with innumerable whitening lines on the blue expanse. I think the ships impressed Liliard even more than the railway. It seemed a victory over another element, and the Columban traditions about the *Scotia* and the *Berwick Lass* had not prepared her for the magnificent fleet of merchant ships and steamers that lay in the harbour. She wanted to go through a big steamer, and we went on board the Australian mail steamer which I thought would give her double interest, because it had brought me letters with home details and remonstrances, only four weeks old.

When there we met Mr Jack Barnett, who came to see about some theatrical properties which had not yet been sent ashore and he fastened himself on to us rather obstructively. I had quite overlooked this contingency in my selection of a specimen ship. But my surprise was still greater to see my treacherous half-breed Sam Peters busying himself in discharging the steamer. I recollected that it was on the Hongkong steamer that I had met him first, when he made himself out to be a first-rate guide for a sportsman.

I told Liliard of my discovery and left her looking over the ship's side talking to Mr Barnett and the chief officer while I went for my man. He was shuffling off when he saw me, but I stopped him and accused him of his conduct, saying he deserved to be arrested as a thief, and ought to have a long term of imprisonment.

'It done you no harm,' said he. 'You came to good luck over the ranges.'

'Who told you that – your accomplice Ninian?'

'Master Graeme told me that you were a king among the people there, and got him put out.'

'And where is he now?'

'In 'Frisco.'

'And your little game is stopped,' said I.

'Jes so – and all along of you.'

'You were a runaway from Columba,' said I, 'some ten years ago, and surely you made your fair share of the spoils which made Ninian a rich man. You had the toilsome part of the work and if you served others as you served me, there were pickings and stealings besides.'

'You was the first as I made anything out of, and it turned out bad for me,' said Sam, 'and as for what I got to boot for my gold, it all went at euchre, every cent of it. And now Ninian or Graeme as he calls himself says I will be hanged if I show myself over the ranges, for you have left my picture that you took at our first camping place.'

'True I did,' said I, 'but it will be a risky thing for anyone to try after the discovery of Ninian's treachery. What is he doing now?'

'Spekilatin',' said Sam Peters, 'and he has the devil's own luck.'

'And what about Jean Anderson?'

'She lives with him. Do you want to pay them a visit. I could tell you the house, if you would make it worth my while.'

'No,' said I thoughtfully. 'He tried to take my life, and I have no wish to see him again.'

'The woman says you saved her life and speaks up for you at all times, but he hates you. Now I bear you no ill will.'

'Your robbery and desertion of me was next door to murder and I would rather not have seen you either at this time. I don't mean to stay long in San Francisco – I have not a friend in it – but some enemies.'

'It is me that has most cause to complain of you. You have had all the luck and I have all the loss.'

To tell the truth, I felt that as the Commonwealth had restored to me the stolen money, and as the visit to Columba, independent of the great fact of my having won Liliard there, was a thing I would willingly have purchased at ten times the cost, I could scarcely say that I had been injured by Sam Peters, who besides looked poor and downcast. I had not the least doubt that Ninian had made a catspaw of him where he could. Instead therefore of giving information against him, I slipped a gold piece into his hand. He brightened at this pleasanter aspect of things.

'And is that lady your wife?'

'Yes Sam.'

'I will drink her health,' said he and he shuffled off to that part of a passenger steamer where beer and spirits are to be obtained.

My chance meeting with Sam Peters led to other results. Mr Jack Barnett who had apparently taken no notice, and who went from the steamer with us, returned almost immediately and by a judicious tip discovered our connection, and also that a certain Mr Graeme who was to be found in San Francisco knew all about me and my wife. Information about his friends' affairs, especially if they appeared reluctant to give it themselves, was the breath of Barnett's nostrils. Indeed one of his most valuable characteristics as a theatrical agent was his keen sense of the quarrels and jealousies which existed between artistes and which enabled his own people to secure a recruit, or to get rid of a nuisance. So it was quite worth his while to find out Ninian, who now took his father's name of Graeme. Ninian was however not at the place of business he was directed to; he was absent on some mission or other. Barnett, however, discovered through his employer where Graeme lived and he came upon Jean Anderson who was not unfriendly to either Liliard or myself, but who had no motive for silence. He told her that he had seen Hugh Keith at the theatre, and again at the harbour with a very handsome wife and he found Jean pretty communicative both with regard to me, to whom she believed she owed her life, and also with regard to Liliard. He gave her and her husband tickets for the theatre the first night of his own company's performance, and told her where she could find us at the Palace Hotel, where he also was staying, and unluckily within one door of us. Jean therefore came to find us out at the half-hour before dinner when Barnett had supposed we would be sure to be at home, and when he dropped in casually first.

'And so you too have found your way through the desert Liliard,' began our Columban visitor, 'and what think you of San Francisco?'

'Wonderful! it takes away my breath. Oh! the great city and the vast ocean, and the hum of life and the whirl of motion and the coming and going of thousands who know nought and care nought for each other. If it were not for Victor, I should be stunned.'

'It was new to Ninian as to me, but nothing could stun him and so long as he keeps his head, I am not discomposed.'

'And have you made a home here?'

'For the present, but Ninian wants to go to the mines, only he has to make himself known first. Are you going to stay?'

'Not long,' said I. 'Liliard has all the world to see, and little time to see it in. I must ask extension of my year's leave to show it to her.'

'You'll have lots to learn,' said Jean. 'I find I have even when stopping still, but foreign tongues and foreign ways will bewilder you when you go to see all the kingdoms of the world and all the glory of them.'

Here a telegraph messenger brought the reply to my message.

'This is the most wonderful thing of all,' said Liliard.

I read aloud, '*Vale*, son and daughter. Grandmother's love to your wife.'

'Oh, so you have got married,' said Jean looking at the ring on Liliard's hand, and pulling off her glove to show her own. 'You have not lost as much time as we did. Ninian says there is no hurry. He is out of the town now and before that the bairn was ill and we were taken up with him. I'm called Mrs Graeme however, and Ninian got me a ring, for folks don't look respectable here without it. And as for the handfasted one, that I could never part with as long as there was a chance of his coming back to me, and whiles it looked doubtful enough, he threw that into the fire.'

Barnett has his face a little turned from me but I could see from his back that he was listening.

'Well my dear,' said I addressing Liliard, 'are you not glad to get this loving message from Collins Street, Melbourne. My news travelled all through America across the Atlantic to England through Europe, Asia and through Australia, and now the answer has come back by the same route and here we know how they feel. The letters we got yesterday were only addressed to me, but here you are received into the family. Grandmother sends love to my "wife".'

'It is wonderful,' said Liliard, 'but they do not know me, they will be disappointed when they find out what I really am.'

'I have no trouble of that kind to fear, for there is only Ninian to please,' said Jean. 'And Liliard I'm learning to read and write. I suppose you have made a beginning, but you behove to be perfect before you go to his people, for I see that everybody, the very Chinese are learned that much.'

'Of course she made a beginning before we left Columba,' said I laughing, but in my heart a little annoyed, 'and as she knows Shakespeare's plays and Milton's poems by heart, as well as all the literature she came in contact with, she learns with a rapidity that astonishes me and herself.'

'Knows Shakespeare's plays by heart,' said Barnett. 'You might make your fortune Mrs Keith with your face and figure by giving Shakespeare readings like Mrs Scott Siddons or Fanny Kemble.'

'But I must get over my accent first,' said Liliard. 'Our folk were all Scotch, and even English books were read with Scottish pronouncing.'

'That will soon be knocked out of you. There is the memory in the first place, the appearance and the naturally fine voice. Oh I know what takes the public.'

'My wife is not going on the stage, Barnett,' said I. 'None of your theatrical diplomacy here.'

'Not the stage – by no means – but the platform.'

'I'm sure Liliard's well used to that, Victor Keith, and little as I had then cause to like her, I'll say that for her she was just the finest speaker in all Columba. Ninian himself was wild about her, and Hugh Keith might well be proud of her – and he *was* – '

'And he *is*,' said I, 'only my wife's gifts are not for the public.'

'Jean,' said Liliard 'will you come with me to the little dressing room, I want to show you something Victor has got for me in one of these wonderful big shops.'

Why did my darling blush and hesitate as she made this excuse to take Jean out of the hearing of the man who was so eager to know everything? Why did she weep on Jean's bosom, and tell her if she was grateful to me for any good service to herself to be silent as to Columban ways and Columban experiences? 'I cannot marry Victor yet for the handfasting is not over, as yours was. I feel unfit to be his mate till I learn more, and I want to be sure that I can make him happy, but as it is impossible he says for us to live together unless folk think we are married, I consent to appear his wife. It is my doing, not his. He entreated me to marry him at once, and put the thing past recall, but I cannot, Jean, I cannot.' So my darling reported her speech to me, and Jean said she would never say a word, good or bad, to Mr Barnett or anyone on the subject. She thought Liliard was thoroughly in the right in her hesitation, and had not the slightest qualms of conscience as to the necessary deceit. She and Ninian had given themselves out as married people, even though the actual ceremony had not been performed. She was hopeful about their prospects, though she grudged sorely Ninian's leaving all the beautiful property in Columba, but he had taken with him in his flight a very large quantity of silver and even of gold. He was clever and had many plans in his head. I wondered if he planned carrying on the same business that Sam Peters had done on his own account, with the aid of that foreman whom the Commonwealth would not dismiss, in spite of my strong recommendation that they should do so.

While Jean was telling all her news, and comforting Liliard in the best way she could for the trouble she had caused by her indiscreet revelations, I was left with Barnett. I proposed that we should have a drink at the bar, and he, apparently quite satisfied with what he heard, asked no more questions but plunged into his own affairs and as I had said I had plenty of money, he frankly proposed to borrow twenty pounds. I ascertained what were his plans, and determined that if possible we should avoid any route of his, but I made no difficulty about lending the money. Incidentally, I mentioned the strange circumstances of the Columba settlement which left them without a literature, except that only open to a caste, but I said that there I had found friends and kinsmen and that the very woman who had come today was the lineal descendant of an old and faithful servant of our family a hundred and fifty years ago.

Barnett raised his eyebrows at this antiquated tradition with regard to what he had been accustomed to regard as a mushroom Melbourne family. 'And so you made an elopement it appears with a beauty of those southern regions. Any money?' I shook my head. 'I thought,' said he, 'that this might be one way of gaining a little of the ready which you said you had drawn on your travels. But perhaps she has expectations.'

'Not any in the way you mean.' No doubt both she and I had great expectations of our own but they were quite unconnected with money.

'No really? I thought your grandmother would have cut up rough when Florrie Campbell was put out of court, but you had frightened them all by not writing and therefore they are glad to hear you are alive though you have haltered your condition, beg pardon, I meant to say altered.'

Barnett drank freely and all the more pleasantly because it was at my expense. I said goodbye, and returned to comfort my wife, and to bid farewell to Jean. Liliard held the telegram in her hand and kissed it several times. 'They did not touch it,' said she, 'but it is their thought. "Grandmother's love to your wife" – "my son and daughter". How good they are. Oh, Victor will they really be satisfied with me? I am sure your friend, no not your friend, but that Mr Barnett thinks me quite unfit to fill the place you say I have.'

'My darling, it must be more than saying. I cannot stand this awkward position another day. We must be married tomorrow.'

'No Victor, dear Victor – have patience. Let me learn more, see more, think more. I will tell you in a moment when I feel that it will be right, I will not delay or trifle with your feelings or your happiness but these very difficulties show me that we should have some time.'

I protested in vain. Liliard would not yield an inch. She spent the evening over her lesson books and in copying out the beautiful writing of the telegraphic message thirty times over, while I was busy writing home a sort of brief account of some of my adventures. Some I could not trust to paper. I read my letter over to Liliard who said I was absurd in my praise of her, but nevertheless she liked it much. She began to practise writing her own name, Liliard Abercrombie, and shook her head when I said it ought to be Liliard Keith. 'I'll sign just Liliard the first letter I send, and it will be to your grandmother, but oh! I fear it will be months before I dare venture to write.'

How I wished she could have added to my letter, but here alas! my eloquent Liliard would appear to woeful disadvantage. I had to content myself with a verbal message which I wrote down, which I hoped would give the dear ones at home some idea of her goodness. The photographs which I had taken in Columba had all the drawbacks of unusual and unbecoming dress, and besides no photograph could do Liliard justice. It was a face for a portrait painter, who might at his leisure study the play of feature and the variety of expression, but no single aspect could possibly tell what beauty her face was capable of.

She felt the trammels of the new garb, the tight long dress in which she was now arrayed with its tight sleeves and frills at the throat and wrists, the high-heeled shoes, the stiff hat and the gloves, and showed to less advantage in these earlier days when Jack Barnett criticised her, than she did further on in our travels. On the following day I succeeded in getting a tolerable portrait of her at a San Francisco photographer's which I enclosed with my letter. I wrote separate letters to my father, to my grandmother and to Loney. Liliard admired and wondered at my rapidity while I was engaged in writing, but when I read over to her in less than half an hour what it had taken me four hours to write, she meditated for a little and said, 'The voice has some advantage over the pen, Victor, but then I cannot send my voice with all the love and gratitude of my heart in it to your father's house. They may never hear my voice – never – but now if I could only write they would know some little part of what I feel.'

IV

LILIARD'S FORECAST

It would make my narrative too tedious if I were to go into particulars about our travelling and to tell how my wife's large faculties of wonder were constantly aroused. There were many things that surprised her which other travellers notice because there is about American life, especially as seen in a rapid run through the country, a rush and hurry, and an evidence of an almost furious material progress which is unprecedented elsewhere, while the really solid and strong points in the character of the people and the constitutional security of the government are apt to be overlooked. I need not therefore dwell on her surprise at the marvellous hotel and railway accommodation, at the height of the buildings, and the universal use of lifts or elevators, at the lavish use of ice, a thing she had never seen in her life, at the street cars of San Francisco and the endless wire rope for taking them up steep inclines, which appeared to her almost as surprising as the locomotive itself. In fact I felt as if I could not have plunged her out of the eighteenth-century civilisation into the nineteenth on any spot on the globe where the contrast was so marked. She would say to herself softly many times a day 'And so this is the world,' but was always glad to hear me say that in the home to which I was taking her, life was calmer and not so dependent on machinery.

Travelling with such a bride as I had won, untiring in body, eager in spirit, observant where all was new, and thoughtful over all that was old, tender and loving too beyond all my most selfish visions of what I might expect a wife to be, made the whole journey full of interest. Her splendid physique was equal to that of my sister Loney for endurance and Liliard was at the same time much handsomer. If she had not Loney's quick sense of fun and eager eye for the incongruous or the grotesque, she had a larger nature, and far more ambition both for herself and me. Loney was a sort of no-wonderer as so many of our young colonials are. She had scarce patience to take in the whole points of any new object or subject for thought, and in her travels with my father through most interesting places, she had confessed to some weariness at the monotony of sightseeing unless she could meet with new people with whom she could talk and compare notes. There was nothing in the way of the ancient and historic in America to call up what I had thought Liliard's highest capacities for admiration, but her industrial training and her sympathies made her stand in breathless amazement at the wonders of machinery where the human-like arms of the panting iron body which breathed with mighty rhythmic ebb and flow lifted or hauled or whirled or adjusted the things offered to its action by the intelligent reasoning creatures whom it served.

Perhaps not even the railway or the telegraph surprised her so much as a great cotton factory, where she saw the Briareus-like engine set in motion hundreds of thousands of spindles in one department, and in another drive hundreds of shuttles, amid a noise and whirl that was to her deafening and confining. Her first introduction to factory life was in one of the great mills in New York State, where the workmen and workwomen were well-clothed, well-fed and under fairly good conditions for health and happiness, owing to good wages and temperance, but with all her joy at this tedious work being done by this occult power, she could not help contrasting the noise, the dust, the heat, and the closeness of even a well-managed factory, with the whirr of the spinning-wheel and the click of the loom in the Columban cottages, open to the fresh air, with the children running in and out, and the accompaniment of the worker's song.

Everything we saw and heard was talked over at the time and afterwards, and this visit gave rise to a conversation which I set down as a specimen of how much hold things took on Liliard, which any ordinary observer would treat as a matter of course.

'This shows how so many women are left idle in your new ways of saving labour, though these seem busy enough who are here, and when you add to these spinners and weavers, the wonderful sewing machines which are in some ways even cleverer than these panting monsters, for this is more twisting and driving, and not the nice adjustment of shuttle and loop and feed bar; why, they clothe almost all the people of your world! Hugh used to despise the distaff, how much he would learn if he were here!'

'No one in Columba would learn more.'

'The tools here are so wonderful, the beautiful bright polished steel tools of every kind, and the way that they make machinery save labour. No one would go on in the old way even in our Sleepy Hollow if once the new was revealed. Do you think they will be found out?' said she wistfully.

'I am sure of it.'

'But I hope not through us.'

'I hope not, I do not think that even Barnett's active curiosity would take him there, but I have more idea that Ninian will try his old business from the other side, and that tracks will be made that will bring the world in.'

'And the United States – what you call America, though we always called our valley America too – will annex Columba as she has annexed so much before.'

'I think it is only a question of time.'

'And they will disturb all our ways.'

'That too is a question of time; you see that so long as Utah was only a territory, she could do as she pleased about her internal Mormon administration, but if she wants to be a State, she must have the same laws.'

'I don't say our laws are the best,' said Liliard thoughtfully, 'but if our folk like them, why should they not keep to them?'

'What do you think would be the first results of the Americans getting over the ranges?' I asked.

'The first thing that would find their way would be iron and books,' said Liliard slowly and thoughtfully, 'and in time you would see that every child would learn to read. There would be cotton cloth and iron tools poured in far better than any we can make that the folk would pay good prices for, and yet find them cheaper in the end. I can see then that they would have either to grow more stuff such as tobacco and sugar and cotton to pay for them, or to dig more silver and copper out of the mines. The wall would be broken down which our forefathers built with such labour, so that a road might be made to the sea board both to get the new things into Columba that folk want, and to send out the cotton and tobacco and such like things that our now idle hands would have to set about growing, or we would be all the poorer. They would never toil over our poor iron ore when they could get such wonderful iron and steel wares so cheap, and there are many of the tools that would help us even in our small operations.'

'Will they not be as suspicious of the new comers as they were of me – at least as the governing body was?'

'No, I think you did away with that even with the old Council. I think on the contrary that they will be disposed to fancy that people who have so many wonderful contrivances must be wiser and better in all ways than we who have them not.'

'That is the secret of the success of many of our Christian missionaries among savage peoples,' said I.

'Oh, I can see it would make a vast difference if people went in and out freely. There would be more crops of special kinds grown, and there would be more buyers and sellers, or at least more would be bought and sold.'

'Spoken like a book, Liliard – but what about your other ways?'

'The books and the newspapers that would come in would at first have but little effect when there were so few that could read, but the like of my brother Tom and Hugh Keith would not be kept back; they would insist on learning to read, to find out what the goods they wanted could be bought for, and other goods sold for. Hugh pretended to despise things that had nothing to do with practical daily life but he would soon see that he might better himself by being foremost. When two or three had learned, they would have such an advantage over the rest, that there would be a great meeting of the people, and there would be night schools, all over Columba to teach grown men and women too to read and there would be scarce enough of teachers to be found of our own people and strangers would come in to teach.'

'And then after that?'

'Well they would find out that our ways were different from the ways outside, and some folk would no doubt come in and swear allegiance, and begin by appearing to follow our customs and by strictly obeying our laws. There would be handfasting enough no doubt among the men of them, and it would turn out that many of them had left wives and children at home, and maybe that some of them would not stick to the new-fashioned bargain they had made; and there would be scandals and inquiries, and maybe applications for divorce, which is a thing unheard of in Columba. And I should not wonder, that if it appeared to the Council that they would have more power and patronage when there was the whole body of the people to choose from for the servants of the Commonwealth, they might do away first with that provision for deserted children, and going further and further, when there seemed to be a chance of being received into the great republic, that they would give up the handfasting, as you say the Utah people will have to give up the polygamy, which they thought a religious duty, whereas our folk never thought ours more than a wise arrangement.'

'And as to the Sunday and the Kirk?' I asked.

'I don't think that there will be any chance of driving us back to the sort of strictness Madame Keith rebelled against.'

'No,' said I, 'the puritanic Sabbath never took hold anywhere within the tropics, and is being marvellously relaxed in Scotland and New England. But with regard to the Kirk?'

'As the people get richer, and more numerous they will no doubt put up more beautiful churches, and also other buildings which are more suitable for amusement, but then, though no doubt they may be better, there will no longer be the sense of God's blessing on them. I feel that very much now in the theatres.'

'And the concerts sacred and secular?' I said with a smile.

'Oh! don't laugh at me about your sacred concert that I could see nothing sacred in, only that they sang good words over and over again that to me seemed like the vain repetition spoken against in the New Testament, and that no one either singing or listening seemed to feel the meaning of but me. But you know I am hopeless about music. Without words or some idea associated with sounds, music does not impress me.'

'We live in a highly musical society in Melbourne.'

'I am very sorry for it,' said she gravely.

'I must confess that at the concert last night you put me in mind of an old Scotch farmer who came to see Mr Semple on business, whom my aunt Mrs Semple took with her to a concert in Edinburgh which was concluded by some well arranged Scotch airs played with great spirit. He said, "It was very bonny but oh! they were a long time tuning their fiddles." '

'Will people despise me if I do not appreciate what they like? I never despised you for not caring for our Columban music,' said Liliard pleadingly.

'They will not despise you, but they will pity you, as I do a little.'

'I told you always that I was not a fit mate for you,' said Liliard.

'For what, because out of your inner consciousness you drew a prophetic sketch of the reconstruction of Columba. Do you think the Melbourne young ladies could do such a clever thing?'

'No, but with regard to the music, the drawing, the painting, the architecture, everything – I am so ignorant and what is more, I am so hopelessly stupid, it is as if I had not any faculty. When

I hear you talking in a railway carriage to people who have travelled, and comparing notes and each person says how he has been affected and you agree with one or differ from another, I feel as if I belonged to a different world.'

'So you do. Do you know it is easier nowadays for people to learn the jargon of art and even to get into considerable aesthetic altitudes and talk pleasantly about those subjects in which you are deficient than to take just views about human relations and conduct. My dear Liliard, I will be perfectly satisfied with you, even though you never learn to distinguish a water-colour drawing from an oil painting, or the classical from the drawingroom music. But I have hopes of you. Though the Japanese and Chinese can never learn to appreciate Western music, because their own with which they are satisfied and delighted is so exceedingly bad; we are not so far apart. You and I agree about the simple melody of the old "Flowers of the Forest" and "The Bonniest Lass in all the World", and last night I saw you in tears over that lovely ballad which was sung for an encore, though you could not follow the words.'

'I guessed at them. I made them the farewell I heard from Columba from Master Hepburn, from mother and from Hugh,' and her eyes filled with tears.

'You put Hugh last.'

'Because he felt most, not because he was dearest. Oh! Victor I did not think you could be jealous.'

'Jealous! no but you are sure he is comforted.'

'I hope so – but even supposing he is or likely to be, the last look I had of him was very sad. It does not make the least difference in my obligation to leave him, but we should not say when we give pain that it is nothing, or that it will soon be over, or it is all for the best, at least I think not.'

V

KNOWLEDGE OF GOOD AND EVIL

It was on the third night of our stay in New York City as we left the theatre that my darling made her saddest discovery about our great troubled world. I had expected her to find it out before, but somehow she had escaped always as it were by a hairbreadth. But we had to make our way through a crowd, and under the gas, we saw some half dozen bold, faced-painted, showily dressed women, one middle-aged, one a mere child, and the others young, talking loudly with three or four gentlemen and using freely slang and profane and indecent language. They did not fall back as we passed, but stared at me and at my wife steadily and insolently.

'Who are these?' asked she with a curious agitation. 'They make me shudder somehow.'

'Do you not know. Have you no suspicion. Did you read or learn all the *Spectator*?'

'No only parts of it. Are they actresses or singers or what? They look very bold and they speak horribly.'

'My love,' said I in an earnest whisper, 'thank God that your Columban handfasting saves you from such women as these.'

Liliard grew pale as death, though she only half understood it. She asked no further question at the time but waited till we reached our hotel and then in our bedroom she sought for a full explanation.

Before this, I had introduced her to poverty. There are as poor slums in New York as in any old world city; there were many wretched immigrants who had not yet found work or food, there were drunkards male and female and their families; there were lazy vicious fathers and slatternly mothers, and sharp faced thievish children, who looked starved and half-clothed, and she had wanted to empty her purse and mine for their necessities. This however was something of which she had no idea before, and she sat with white face and fixed eyes thinking of it.

'And the children, Victor, the children of these wretched women?'

'They have no children at least so rarely as not to count.'

'Thank God!' she said. 'But no – if there were children, this could not exist. A child might lead its mother back to Heaven from the gates of Hell, and then if there were children to be provided for, it would be as cheap and far more happy to be married. I thought your people sometimes were handfasted without the law allowing it, as in the case of Effie Deans, and that a man could throw his bride off too easily, and allow her to have the burden and something you call shame, but I had no idea that any woman or any man could come to shame like this. For surely the buyer is as bad as the seller.'

'Not in the world's eyes, Liliard.'

'And these are outcasts – pariahs. Is there any good in them?'

'Sometimes, Liliard, sometimes they are true to their friends, and liberal to those in want. Sometimes such a woman will heroically stand to the one man who takes her fancy like Nancy in *Oliver Twist*, but they are pariahs.'

Liliard paused awhile in thought and then asked, 'And if a woman is poor and deserted as your ancestress said her faithful servant Violet was, is she ever tempted to this?'

'Often, too often, I am sorry to say; it is so hard for a woman to maintain herself and her child by honest work.'

'It is a cruel world – a cruel world – Victor, would you mind very much going back to Columba?'

'Now,' said I, 'just at once? If you really want it, I shall consider it, but you recollect you would not accept the sacrifice when I offered it.'

'True,' said Liliard, drawing a long breath and pausing for reflection, 'and it would be cowardly to go out of the world just because things do not please me. Could I do any good do you think? Could I not win back that poor little girl? She was not sixteen, I am sure. Oh! Victor, you say I have the gift of eloquence. Can I do nothing?' And the old eager spirit woke within her, and she walked to and fro in our sleeping apartment with the same rapid stride which had characterised her action when she told of how Ralph Abercrombie gave chase to the Indians, and found his stolen wife and babe.

'Not now, not tonight,' said I, 'but when you know more and have thought more, I am quite sure you can do something to help me with the knottiest problem of the age.'

'Had it not interested you before you saw Columba or me?'

'Deeply Liliard, very deeply.'

'And I might be able to help you – just a little.'

'So I think, but I want to persuade you to one step before we leave America, and that is to be married before I introduce you to my friends and kindred. I do this all the more seriously because in the opinion of the world, there is but little difference made between your position living with me as my wife without a legal bond binding in civilised countries, and that of those wretched women you saw.'

'Victor,' said she with flashing eyes, 'you know there is an infinite difference.'

'So there is – but such is public opinion.'

'If that is public opinion I despise it, and scout it. No, I am more set against marriage than I ever was by this unjust judgment. If we part at the end of our term, I shall find my way back to Columba, unless I find worthier work, but until then I abide by the solemn engagement we entered into. I am a Columban subject bound by Columban laws. You swore fealty to Columba and its laws.'

'But Liliard, supposing our dearest hopes were realised and you gave birth to a child before our legal marriage was entered into and registered, the child would be illegitimate.'

'Well what of that – we would love it all the same.'

'No doubt, but it would have not rights of inheritance. A younger child would take all in case of my death, and my own father would inherit all I had to the prejudice of our son or our daughter born out of wedlock.'

'That is very unjust; all of a piece with the rest of your laws.'

'Not unjust, provided its parents do the right thing and that is so easy to do.'

'Not so easy for me. And besides you can make a will and if you do not, your father is a just man and would not wrong your child or me.'

'And if I were to die suddenly without a will, the law would give you no claim whatever on what I may die possessed of.'

'If you were to die suddenly, it would little matter to me what claim I had or not. It would be my life that I lost.'

'Surely it matters but little the length of probation. We have now been eight weeks handfasted. Do you think it is likely that we will change?'

'I had lived nine months with Hugh before I had a wandering fancy.'

'But you did not love him, you know the difference now.'

'Victor,' said she tenderly 'if you could only see into my heart it would show you what I feel, but there goes more to the obeying of you in this matter than you seem to see. I have no more doubt that you will desert me at the end of the term if you still love me above all women, than I have that the sun will rise tomorrow and I believe that with regard to any child that we may have, that you will deal justly by it, whatever the law may say. But what I have seen this night makes me feel all the surer that the handfasting is right, and when it is all over we will tell the world, and the world that is right and sensible will see that we have been honest, and that I acted up to my education and my lights.'

'People all run in a groove Liliard and those who run counter to public opinion fare very badly.'

'I have heard you say, Victor – I recollect everything you say – that the best and the wisest and the strongest people try to lead public opinion, and not to bend to it. You know you said that our Columban handfasting was a right thing. Does our being outside make it wrong. Is white black and black white on the other side of the mountain range?'

'No, Liliard, but it is inexpedient. All your institutions were so framed as to cause the maximum of advantage with the minimum of evil. Now ours are different. Much as I owe to your laws, I should tremble to advocate them elsewhere.'

'Of two things choose the best, or the better,' said she. 'If there is to be any stand made against the iniquities of the world it is not to be done by crouching under its wheels when it rides roughshod over us all. And if, Victor, you feel when you show me to your people either in Scotland or in Australia that I am not good enough for them, or fit to make you happy if you want to make a second choice, I will not stand in your way.'

'My dear Liliard, I have seen all sorts of women and made choice of you. It is you who have had no free choice and not me.'

'Well then suppose it is for me. I *might* see someone whom I like better. I *might* throw you over as I threw over Hugh, and you will bear it like a man as he did. But you would not bear it like a man if I had married you first.'

'On this point you are absolutely inexorable,' said I. 'You seem to care nothing for what people will say as to our relations.'

'*They say*; *what say they*? *let them say*! That is a good old Scottish motto. I believe in my heart that you and I will be constant till death, aye and maybe beyond it, but nevertheless I will not put it out of our power to draw back. I consent to be called your wife and to be treated as your wife everywhere as I consented to wear this dear marriage ring, but the old half one is round my neck next my heart, as the real bond between us.'

'Palahna!' this was one of my pet names for her, 'you are at heart half a savage. If I were as much of one, I could compel you to my will.'

She saw I was yielding, she smiled again, and then again relapsed into sadness.

'One of the duties you will be engaged in in Melbourne will probably be to join philanthropic and benevolent societies and a very active member you are likely to be, only you must learn to be more yielding than you are to me.'

'Societies!' said she. 'I think I had better be like Harry Wynd and fight for my own hand. There are so many ideas whirling through my head that nobody can understand, and then I will be found so ignorant and stupid that nobody will care to work with me. I think I can only work with you. Oh! this mass of poverty and vice and degradation that we never dreamed of in Columba weighs heavy on me.'

'The fruit of the tree of knowledge of good and evil tastes bitter already.'

'Bitter yes, but unless you taste it, what can you know?' said Liliard, with a flash of her old spirit. 'I told you I felt I had not my fair share of the sorrow of the world, and that made me long to leave my quiet happy home, and how can I have it so long as I have you by my side. Am I to have no trouble of my own except this one difference that keeps life from palling altogether, from growing faint with too much sweet. Victor, I used to tremble with joy to think there was this little battle to keep me humble and diffident of myself – but now I feel as if I took this black plague stain so much to heart that I cannot sit at ease in my own happiness any longer.'

The reader will think me very weak to be over and over again mastered by the woman who was not yet my wife, and probably will be of opinion that if marriage had taken place, I could have exerted my legitimate authority more effectively, but I laid the flattering unction to my soul that her objections were all through excess of love, excess of fidelity; that after all it was a mere legal fiction that she was not my wife; that this was simply an expansion of some of the bolder notions as to marriage that were permeating through society. Except for awkward misrepresentation on the part of others, I rather enjoyed having a peculiar bridal tour, and yet but for the chance of misrepresentation, there would be nothing peculiar to enjoy. The little element of danger and risk had its charms. I was now content to bear with my bride's whim, and to watch the development of her nature, and her gradual adaptation to the manners and customs of a civilisation which had worked all through the English-speaking world with the exception of the lovely valley of Columba.

VI

LILIARD'S FIRST INTRODUCTION INTO SOCIETY

When I was in New York city, I felt bound to visit a fellow student of my father's who was settled there in a very fashionable practice. The fame of the Edinburgh medical school had attracted Henry Burgoyne from his New England home to pursue his studies there. My father and he had been good friends and had corresponded at rare intervals by letters, and more frequently through the means of newspapers and medical journals in which each sent to the other anything that struck him as new or valuable in professional literature. I knew my father had sent him my French contribution on obscure brain disease, and I had a letter of introduction to him. After a little hesitation on Liliard's account, I determined on delivering the letter and standing the consequences. Dr Burgoyne lived in a fashionable Avenue, in a house the like of which is not to be seen in Australia or in England either, both for the spaciousness and number of the rooms, and for the hundred and one arrangements for the convenience of the residents and for saving labour to the domestic helps. Lifts, speaking tubes, washing machines, hot closets for drying – the house all warmed by hot air from the single fire below – electric bells, both for fire and patients, and a telegraph had been succeeded by a telephone laid on from the central station. We had seen many of these appliances at the large hotels, but those were for the convenience of hundreds, whereas this was only a private house. My wife and I had been much struck by the extraordinary display of dress and jewellery in the streets of Philadelphia, where we stayed a week which seemed out of place in the old Quaker city, but New York appeared to us to be in a blaze. In open daylight, ladies wore immense diamonds in their ears and on their wrists, and gentlemen in their shirt fronts – and the costumes were marvellous.

We found the family of Dr Burgoyne in the vortex of fashion, and sons and daughters very much given over to society. Their father led the busy life of a practitioner in great request, and was not much at home, but we thought his welcome to us was the warmest as was natural owing to his knowledge of my father. It had been a disappointment to both parties that my father's year's tour had not taken America in, but my travels had begun in the West, and he would have been offended if I had not gone to claim his acquaintance. Everything that he could do for us in the way of getting access to interesting places, or introduction to notable people, he did, but he was too busy to give us much of his society, and we were much thrown on the hands of Mrs Burgoyne and her daughters.

Now for the first time Liliard could compare herself with other women of education and culture, and the elegant New York belles – pale, slender and with their slightly nasal drawl and with their slow measured movements – contrasted strongly with my pomegranate blossom, as I often called her. Especially about the feet and hands, though Liliard's were in perfectly good proportion to her height and bulk, the descendant of many generations of people who practised all sorts of manual labour and who habitually walked long distances, showed a size and strength reckoned in New York fashionable society as plebeian. I had never agreed with Hawthorne in his depreciation of the colour and roundness of English beauty, and in my eyes the Burgoynes looked washed out and almost emaciated beside my brilliant wife. Somehow they took her at first for half a savage, and me for a semi-civilised Australian. Although their father and mine had studied together, there appeared to be a vast difference between an old New York family like theirs, and a Scotchman who had taken the retrograde step of settling in Australia. All the people who went west lost refinement and social advantages and they could not believe in the civilisation and intelligence of Melbourne.

As for Liliard, the father and mother admired her, but not the young people; even the young men, infinitely preferred their own set of girls, and Liliard saw it as plainly as I did. Her ignorance as to modern light literature, and especially her insensibility to American humour, which, so far as she could understand, she disliked, made them think her uneducated, but especially her not having the key to the *coterie sprache* of New York fashionable society, and no aptitude for picking it up, showed that she was not what they called bright or amusing. While I congratulated myself on the justness and liberality of her judgments and opinions, they were condemning the stupidity that did not reward the pains they took with her for they were willing to patronise, to educate and to polish the girl who might by and by in ignorant colonial society, be supposed to be an American. In all the talk about literary matters in which the eldest Miss Burgoyne dabbled a little herself, Liliard saw evidence of the manner in which women had come to the front. She had of course learned through me that authorship and art were now no longer provinces in which men alone laboured. The Columbans in their narrow library had not a single work from a woman's hand, except Madame Keith's abstract of history which did not profess to be original, and I think that one of the strongest points in favour of Columba as compared with the civilisation the adventurers had left was the great development of the natural gifts of women.

The women's rights question too she heard discussed by people who were not actively concerned in it, for the Burgoynes were perfectly satisfied with their position in the world. American light literature, so far as it is native, is still more in the hands of women than that of England and the list of female novelists and verse writers among the English-speaking races on both sides of the Atlantic filled my wife with astonishment. As the novel and poetry, or as the Germans have it the 'Dichtung' of the people, finds that young girls of all classes are the most eager readers, there is nothing to prevent women from satisfying the popular requirement. Even the popular authors of the other sex, have much more of the sentimental and emotional in their work than the male novelists who form the overwhelming preponderance on the continent.

The Burgoynes thought to dazzle Liliard by the extravagant of New York society as well as to impress her by what they were pleased to call religion, for her ignorance with regard to sects and schools of thought was deplorable. Wherever we had gone, we had attended the churches which were most characteristic of the locality, but during our fortnight's stay in New York we were taken by the eldest Miss Burgoyne to an Episcopal Church of the very highest kind, by the second to the Roman Catholic Cathedral and by Mrs Burgoyne herself to a sort of Gospel service of the neo-evangelical kind.

It was strange how these things impressed my wife. How she took up everything with the quick eager critical apprehension of one who had been educated entirely by the ear, an apprehension which had not been dulled by the hasty perfunctory reading of newspapers and novels, and how what was addressed to the eye in the way of symbol was looked into, and traced back to its origin. When the petition that we should fall into no sin, neither run into any kind of danger first struck on her ear, she said that surely that was praying that life should not be life at all, for without the liability to sin and to danger we should have no power to grow wiser or stronger. True we may ask for more than we could hope to receive, but petition in the Lord's prayer 'Lead us not into temptation but deliver us from evil,' did not go so far as the prayer of the church. Evil we do fall into, and from it we may pray to be delivered. And that the healthful spirit of God's grace should be sent down on His Church, and its duly ordained officers as a great marvel, and not as the normal result of that relation, jarred on her sense of what was reasonable or just. Miss Burgoyne was shocked at this untaught half-savage objecting to the beautiful litany when the wealthiest and most pleasure-loving of New York citizens posed as miserable sinners, only spared all sorts of evils by special mercy, humbly implored. These things seemed to Liliard altogether artificial and factitious, while the ritualism was either too much or too little.

Liliard liked the Catholic service better. Later on, when we were on the Continent she felt the exceeding materialism of the service, and the superstition which was not awe or reverential wonder, but mere ignorant fetishism; but in New York we went to a cathedral service where the poor much resorted, and as the further you get from Rome, the more Catholic and devout is the Church she felt the full force of the best side of Catholicism.

'Though I am far further from my father's creed than my mother's,' said Miss Nettie Burgoyne to my wife one day, 'he is in no way disturbed and she is miserable. We are a disjoined family in religious matters.'

They appeared to us to be a disjoined family in other respects. The girls each received her own visitors, they went out everywhere without their mother, and each chose her own society. One brother was educated to help his father, two others were in offices, and each seemed to move in a set of his own. New York was large enough for a very numerous acquaintance of every variety.

Upon the whole, Liliard's first introduction to society made her more diffident and more embarrassed than she had been before. She received so many hints as to what she should do and should not do, and she was so puzzled as to whether what was required in New York would be required in England and in Melbourne, that I had much ado often to reassure her.

The growth of New York was beyond anything I had imagined; great piles of buildings seemed to rise up before our eyes. In spite of its wealth and its magnificence, there was municipal misgovernment which left the city very dirty, and grasping monopolies which sacrificed the comfort of the inhabitants to the profits of great moneyed corporations. Nowhere did the power of concentrated capital appear to be so shamefully abused.

'I hope Melbourne is not so stunning and so distracting as New

York,' said Liliard to me one day when we were alone. 'I don't think I could settle to anything if it is.'

'Melbourne is smaller and quieter, and more like an English town than an American. The Collins Street house is a much more simple dwelling than Dr Burgoyne's, and the society in which we move is one, and not multiform.'

'Will your people not think me as stupid and backward as the Burgoynes do?'

'Certainly not!' said I. 'And I can assure you that neither Dr nor Mrs Burgoyne think you so. He says you are an original and she says that you are sympathetic.'

'Well I feel for her being so outside her children's pursuits. Our Columban amusements always had the old folks as lookers-on at any rate.'

It was drawing near the end of our fortnight's stay when Liliard had made an engagement with Mrs Burgoyne to go through some of the poorer districts without me. The doctor wanted me to go with him to visit a patient who showed some abnormal symptoms of an attack of fever, and as he was a New York financial magnate, director of several joint stock companies, of one bank, and an insurance company and other smaller concerns, the bulletin of his health was reported daily in the leading journals, and his confidential clerk appeared to have enough of work to answer the innumerable letters of inquiry or condolence. There was no wife or legitimate family, but there was a lady at the head of an establishment in the suburbs, who had been someone else's wife, and her diamonds were larger and finer than those of any lady in the State, and the menage and her equipages were beyond question luxurious. The man however was alarmingly ill, and she was nursing him, but contemporaneously with the illness came a break-up in the particular Insurance Company with which he was identified. This led to inquiries official and private and these brought out some most disgraceful revelations of defalcations and breach of trust in every one of the many directions in which this magnate had carried on his operations. He did not seem to cling to life, which must for the future be dishonoured and impoverished, but all his concern was for the woman on whom he had lavished so much of other people's money, and not for the hundreds of widows and children defrauded of their future provision.

My friend Burgoyne was one of the victims, and as I could see that he lived pretty well up to his income, the loss of the insurance which he had paid for twenty years was a serious one to him. But I was surprised to find that just on the eve of bankruptcy, the company had been extending its operations, and offering large bonuses to agents who could effect new policies, and among others who went in for the high commission, Jack Barnett who had quarrelled with his theatrical company a fortnight after they began to perform in San Francisco, and was out of a billet, was one of the latest recruits. This looked as if he meant to settle in the States if he could get any employment, but I did not see him in New York. Thither however he made his way shortly afterwards, and was full of complaints at the Company smashing before he had made anything out of it. He managed to introduce himself to Dr Burgoyne as a friend of mine. He had heard from my father before he left Melbourne that I was doing to New York to visit his old fellow student, and had asked for a letter of introduction, which might be of service if his theatrical company went so far. Jack was never backward about soliciting anything that might by the merest possibility be of use to him, and my good-natured father, to whom he was not so offensive as to the old lady, had given him a few lines to the American with whom he went through his Edinburgh course so many years before.

Barnett gathered from the various members of the family what they thought of me and my wife and pieced together all the scraps of information in his usual cynical spirit. I had not delivered my letter of introduction till I had been three days in New York which Dr Burgoyne thought a little queer and I had not accepted their invitation to stay in the house but kept to my hotel though we had been a great deal together. The story of the magnate was discussed – and Barnett's questions elicited a good many evidences as to

Liliard's curiosity and extreme concern about the woman who was not his wife, and as to what was to become of her with no legal claims on the generosity of creditors or on her 'husband's' respectable relatives. But by that time, we were on the continent of Europe continuing our travels, and never thinking of any unfriendly questioner following in our wake.

VII

I MEET SOME OLD FRIENDS FROM MELBOURNE

We received our letters in answer to those written in San Francisco in Paris. I settled to take the continent first, both from considerations of climate, and because I wanted my wife to read and write English well before she came into familiar contact with my friends and relatives, and my English agent forwarded the delightful packet to our address. Liliard managed to decipher the trembling lines which my grandmother wrote to her for herself, and prepared to reply to that letter with all the pains she could take. She first dictated a letter which I wrote and then copied it to the best of her ability. It was but a raw schoolgirl hand traced slowly on the paper but the wording was admirable. Loney's long letter with the account of the astonishment of the family at the telegram, and its good wishes and family details could not yet be done justice to in the way of reply, but the dear old lady's affectionate welcome deserved all that my young wife could give back. She was eager for us to make haste home that she might see Hugh's wife and hear with her own ears all the story of the Scottish colony. As for the photograph, she was better pleased with it than with many that had been sent, but it was the romance of the thing that was enclosed in the few words of the telegram, the finding out of the colony that had been the wonder of her youth, and of the bride that had been the desire of her old age all at once, and my exulting confession that I was the happiest man in the world. About that time on that day there was most important public news passing through the telegraph wires. ' "But each one heeds his own she saith" and a few words from San Francisco was more to me, than political revolutions elsewhere,' wrote my grandmother adapting her favourite passage in Jean Ingelow to the subject. She was delighted with the name of my wife, and recalled in her letter the tradition of the devoted maiden who died in the battlefield.

'I hope you will not mind my calling your Hugh Victor,' was part of Liliard's answer, 'for it was by that name he was known in Columba, and I cannot learn any other.'

I need not say that we enjoyed Paris and Fontainebleau to which we made two excursions, and deciphered old tombstones of the de Launays and the Drouins in which I had taken no interest on my former visits. We then moved southwards to Italy, and I thought my wife's taste underwent considerable development. She loved the ancient better than the modern, and all the historical associations with regard to places and to buildings gave them a charm which America could not have. As to natural scenery, she had always been more or less appreciative, and although she expressed her opinions somewhat diffidently as to churches and great public buildings, she could take in the effect of the whole though she might not be skilled in details.

When in Italy, we fell in with Americans, with English people, and even with Australians, and on the last day of our stay in Rome we chanced upon Mr Campbell with his daughter and Miss Barnett. Liliard had now been several months in the world, and could stand criticism better than when we met Jack. Miss Campbell was apparently delighted with her, Mr Campbell was even more demonstrative in his admiration, and Miss Barnett I never had thought clever enough, in spite of her accomplishments, to discover anything for herself as her brother did. She was the most conventional girl in all her opinions and her principles whom I knew, at least in Victoria, though I believe she could be beaten in the Philistine strongholds of Germany and England. She used to take her tone from Miss Campbell at this particular time of her life.

'Well this is a delightful episode in your life,' said Miss Campbell heartily. 'I suppose you will write a book about it Dr Hugh.'

'Quite a romantic episode I should say,' said Miss Barnett.

'Pardon me, scarcely an episode. It forms the main plot of my own particular epic,' said I laughing.

'No but I mean the finding out of relatives and friends at what Papa would call "the back of beyond". That was quite a new experience. Well Mrs Hugh, I envy you one thing the possession of such a grandmother as the old lady.'

'I am very proud of it indeed,' said Liliard. 'She actually sent a telegram to me, and I have had a letter from her which was all kindness. I tried to answer it.'

'It is generally difficult to write to people whom you have not seen,' said Miss Campbell, 'but if Mrs Keith's letters are like her talk, they will make you feel at home at once.'

'I have heard so much of her from Victor that I seem to know her better than any of the Melbourne people.'

'How long are you to stay in Rome, Dr Hugh?' asked Mr Campbell.

'We thought of leaving next Tuesday for Naples.'

'Oh stay another week, and we can go about together. One carriage can hold us all, and we want to see the same things I suppose.'

In spite of Mr Campbell's hundred and fifty thousand pounds he dearly loved to keep down expenses in this way, besides that I think he was a little tired of exclusive female companionship, and wanted a little talk about stock and stations, shares and large concerns, markets and tariffs, with someone who knew men and business. Moreover I had come from America, which was not included in his programme, and as his house of business wanted to push a wool trade in that direction, he wished to obtain as much information on the subject as possible, and only regretted that I was not a business man, and had not been among business men. If Liliard had given me the slightest sign of dissatisfaction, I should have declined, but she evidently wished to make acquaintance with such people as she was likely to associate with in future, while amongst foreign things about which she was as much at home as they were, so I accepted the offer.

Whatever Miss Campbell and Miss Barnett thought of my wife, there was no question that the old gentleman admired her. He was a man on the right side of fifty, and had some questionable antecedents only known to men which were accounted for by the charitable by the fact that he had for twenty years been bound to a wife, a hopeless invalid, who had very lately died.

Though not a perfect husband, he had been a most affectionate father. He had rather spoiled his only son by too much indulgence and too liberal an allowance, and to give Florrie pleasure, he would take much trouble and expend a good deal of money.

It is probable that both Mr Jack Barnett and his sister thought more might come of the companionship than a present easy life and seeing the world without cost, but as yet Eva Barnett had made no way with Mr Campbell, who was more inclined to yawn over her accomplishments than to be fascinated by them. But Liliard had that mixture of courage and distrust, of knowledge and ignorance, of genuine enthusiasm for some things and honest indifference as to others, which combined with her remarkable beauty made her very charming to this middle-aged man. If there had been the least idea in his mind that Liliard was not my wife, he was capable of making a fool of himself about her. In vain did Miss Barnett play and sing, and do both well, and talk art to him; he had no eyes for her while Liliard was present. Miss Campbell was amused at her father's devotion, while Miss Barnett was annoyed at it.

Wherever we travelled, the best seat was always offered to Mrs Keith and whatever was planned, her taste was consulted and her wishes agreed to. This was but natural on my part, and ordinary courtesy on the part of others – a young married woman has always the advantage over unmarried girls – but Miss Barnett tried to work upon her friend's jealousy and to get up a quarrel between her and

Liliard. But Miss Campbell was very unimpressionable as to any grievances of her own, and as Miss Barnett who felt she was only a dependant, could not in conscience say that she felt slighted, she made no progress. So for several weeks we travelled in company, Liliard learning a good deal, but not much asked by any of the party about her old home and her old ways. Her own humility checked curiosity. Miss Campbell and Miss Barnett wanted to hear about courts and drawingrooms, and fashion and society, and millionaires and aristocrats, but the story of an obscure handful of people pent up in a narrow valley could have no interest to them.

The thing which Liliard had dreaded most in this association in travelling was that her lessons might be interrupted, but as we were both early risers, we managed to get them done regularly before the others were about, and now she could read an English newspaper or book without mistakes, and with admirable expression. The foreign languages she let severely alone with regard at least to their literature; the young ladies urged on her to use her opportunities as they did, and her quick ear and strong memory enabled her to pick up more speaking words in Italy and France than either of them did, although they had been taught at school for years.

As we returned, we spent a week at Genoa, which was especially dear to her on account of its being the birthplace of Columbus who was as it were her patron saint. The magnificence of Italian buildings and the poverty of the Italian people struck her much. The contrast between the ugliness and comfort of Columba houses, with the splendour and squalor of Southern Europe struck her in one way, and again the contrast between the keenness of life in the United States with the easy-going, custom-bound Columbans and Italians, was as great in another way. She could conceive of a eclectic sort of life taking the good out of all, but yet in practice people go always to extremes, and there would seem to be as much difficulty in checking the eager pursuit of material progress in the States, as in impressing a sufficient amount of energy and enterprise into the peoples who lack it. In all arrangements for health, liberty, and the pursuit of happiness, Columba appeared to her to take a very high rank compared to larger communities outside. She wondered if the great navigator from his higher point of view, would turn a loving eye from that portion of the new world which he had given to ungrateful Spain and from that which had been settled by the energetic Anglo-Saxon Republic, to the little Commonwealth which lay in the mountain-girt valley.

This is not a book of travels, and but for the relation of the places we saw with my story, and with the development of Liliard's nature, I would not go over the well-worn ground, as I can pretend to no special qualifications which would make my narrative of any value. But we worked back to London, where we intended to stay for some time, as the centre of the busy world, taking a different route through the Tyrol and Germany from that by which we entered Italy, through France and Switzerland. Liliard was interested in German peasant life and university life; the one seemed like Columba in its simplicity, but unlike it in its poverty. The other was unlike anything anywhere, except in her own dreams of plain living and high thinking. Mr Campbell cared little for Germany but was greatly interested in Belgium, for its size perhaps the wealthiest and the most industrious and certainly the most populous country in the world. Business might be done with Belgium, and every business man he met could speak English, which was an additional recommendation. Mr Campbell pressed us strongly to occupy part of the house he had taken for the season in C– Square London. And in order to overcome my scruples, he offered that we should pay part of the expenses.

'To tell the truth Dr Hugh, though I enjoy your company and your wife's very much, I have another reason for asking this. I want to get rid of Eva Barnett, who is like the old man of the sea on my shoulders. I never thought of her doing more than taking the voyage with us, Florrie expected that she would go to study music at the Academy or somewhere, and I would have shelled out to help that which she said was her object, in going to England, but no, she sticks to us like a leech; gone where we go and nowhere else. Now she has relatives in England, an uncle, a county surgeon, and an aunt, a widow living in Manchester, and it is only right and proper that she should visit them. But she has her designs which Florrie is too good to see through, and upon my word if I don't take strong measures, I may get married to her against my will.'

I laughed, and said I did not think that would be very easy, but he said it was no laughing matter.

'Had not you better tell Miss Campbell your suspicions?' said I.

'No I can't bear to let Florrie think how designing women are. She herself is so straightforward and unsuspecting.'

'I see no good purpose to be served by keeping Miss Campbell in ignorance if you are really convinced of the fact.'

'You can see it, can't you, Dr Hugh?'

'Well, I have sometimes suspected it.'

'Does your wife see it?'

'No, I do not think so. It was always the young and the young where she came from.'

'I'm not so old either,' said Mr Campbell firing up at the imputation. 'It is not that, but women old and young, do so look out for money now-a-days, and when a man is "well-in" he is a prize. I'd rather see Florrie well settled first, for of course I mean to marry when I see the right woman, but she is not Eva Barnett. Now if you just agree to this arrangement for as long or as short a time as you please, I can get Florrie to say that her friend ought to do her duty to her own relatives, and once out of the house, I think I can manage to keep her out.'

'Very well,' I said, 'to oblige you I do not mind trying it for a month.'

I know it was no economy for us to pay our share of their large expenses, for our own modest lodging would have been cheaper but still it was an introduction for Liliard to our Anglo-Australian society, where the weight of responsibility would fall on one so good and so capable as Miss Campbell. She liked my wife and wrote my grandmother a very pleasant letter about her originality, and her good looks and pleasant temper. The old lady compared my glowing praise with these more moderate expressions, and drew in her own mind a composite picture. If she could captivate me, and satisfy Florrie Campbell, she herself was more than satisfied.

When Mr Campbell told his daughter that owing to the Keiths sharing the West End house, there would be no room for Miss Barnett, who had better go to see her friends at Knaresborough and Manchester, Miss Campbell was much disturbed. How could she tell her friend that she was not to have all the pleasures and glories of the London season, the theatres, concerts, exhibitions, everything worth coming to Europe for in fact; far better than the foreign travel; where she expected to get mixed up with the wealthy absentees who were always polite to young colonists well-introduced, and might reckon on being invited to a series of brilliant parties. And now it would be Mrs Hugh Keith who would have all these advantages, and Miss Campbell well knew her friend was jealous or envious or contemptuous, or all three together, of the wife whom I picked up in some wild region quite out of the pale of civilisation.

It would be a very hard thing to say, why should not Mr Campbell say it himself, but that he had not courage for and perhaps thought he might be vanquished in the effort or lose his temper and express himself in a way that would be very unbecoming to a young lady, so the poor girl was compelled to mount the breach. She propitiated the foe with gifts in the way of ornaments, both from herself and from her father, and said that of course as their guest for the tour, Mr Campbell would supply the money for her travelling expenses, but as she knew that she must long to see her relatives, this was the best opportunity to do so. Miss Barnett asked how long the Keiths were to stay, and Miss Campbell could give her no certain reply. In the deepest dudgeon, the situation was accepted, and the gifts, and Miss Barnett took the train for Manchester, vowing vengeance, if it ever was within her power. As a Parthian shot when she said goodbye she said she wondered Dr Hugh did not take the first opportunity of seeing his relations, and introducing his wife to his friends, with whom he had spent so many years of his life. Liliard changed colour just a little, for the remark was made before the whole party, but the sensation of relief was so great on Mr Campbell's part, that he got into wild spirits, and wanted to take us everywhere at once. 'Now what do you want to see first Mr Hugh? Crystal Palace, Westminster Abbey, Lord's Cricket ground, St Pauls, picture galleries, or what not.'

'I think,' said Liliard, 'I want to get to the heart of something; buildings and exhibitions and picture galleries we have seen so much of on the continent. I want to see the foundling hospital and hear the singing there, and to see some of the East London charitable work, and the big schools, and the workhouse schools, and mothers' meetings, and hospitals and asylums. I want to know how the poor live in this enormous city.'

'That is a strange sort of choice,' said Mr Campbell.

'You should get acquainted with Miss Mountain,' said Miss Campbell, 'She knows all about such things. I have a letter of introduction to her, and we could go together.'

'Thank you Miss Campbell – but the Foundling – we could see that without anyone's help. And oh! Victor I must if possible hear a debate in parliament, and above all things I want to see the British Museum.'

'The South Kensington is far more fashionable, and the things are much prettier there,' said Miss Campbell.

'It is the British Museum I want to see specially, for Victor tells me that there is a copy kept there of every book published in England.'

'What a deal of rubbish there must be amongst the lot,' said Mr Campbell, who was not much of a reader, and always fancied that it was on account of his own fastidious and accurate taste. It must be a good book that would interest him; he was not going to waste time over anything but the best.

VIII

MR CAMPBELL'S LOSING BET

Liliard was astonished to see the British Museum so very little visited. The few students and country and colonial and foreign sightseers appeared like nothing in these immense halls, but she lingered and lingered and could not be induced to move on as fast as her Australian friends wanted her to do. 'I must go again with Victor or by myself,' said she. 'I feel as if I had seen nothing.'

'I have seen so much that my eyes and head ache,' said Miss Campbell.

'I wonder what sort of confused recollection I shall carry away with me to Melbourne of all the churches, palaces, galleries, theatres and museums we have seen. It all seems to me one blur – one thing running into another. I should have kept a diary; old Mrs Keith advised me to do so and I began one, but really in all the whirl of sightseeing, one is too tired to do all the wonderful things justice, and after I had read over the journal of the first week, I decided not go on with it. It was so bald and so stupid, that if I had read it to the dear old lady, I should have fallen fifty per cent in her estimation. Did you keep a diary, Dr Hugh?'

'A few notes of little value,' said I, 'but my wife's is more worth my grandmother's attention than mine.'

'Yours Mrs Hugh,' said Miss Campbell turning to her with some surprise. 'I have never seen you writing up your diary, and if it is so complete, it takes a great deal of time to keep one.'

'I kept a sort of journal,' said Liliard, 'but no one could read it but myself.'

'Shorthand eh!' said Mr Campbell. 'Is that a lady's accomplishment in Columba?'

'Oh nothing so accurate or scientific as shorthand,' said Liliard laughing. 'I kept my diary in the knitting I used to do in the evenings.'

'Which Eva used to say had neither beauty nor utility to recommend it,' said Miss Campbell.

'That is all Miss Barnett knew on the subject,' said Mr Campbell as if he himself had always been better informed.

'No doubt it seemed so to you also Miss Campbell but it had its use for me. I was taught at school to help my memory in that way.'

'Will you read us a chapter of your diary,' said Mr Campbell whose fancy was much tickled by the idea. 'It certainly would be a capital way of putting down secrets. I suppose Hugh can read your ciphers.'

'No!' said I, 'I am sorry to say I cannot.'

After dinner when Mr Campbell settled in the easy chair in the most comfortable corner of the drawing room, he was in high good humour, for not only had he got rid of Miss Barnett, but he had on this day received an acceptance of his offer for a valuable block of land in one of the best suburbs of Melbourne from an absentee proprietor, out of which he hoped to clear an enormous profit. And to give zest to his enjoyment he had also learned that two other parties were looking after it, one of whom had once got the better of him in a large transaction in cognac. He again asked for a specimen of my wife's notes by the way, and she acceded to the request.

'Shall it be what we saw by ourselves or what we saw together that I should read?'

'What we did not see,' said Miss Campbell. 'That will be new.'

'What we saw together,' said her father. 'That may be new to us.'

'Suppose we have a little of both,' said I.

So Liliard began with her Italian tour before we met the Melbourne travellers and described the meeting, and the few days when we were first together, with here and there a conversation, where it appeared to throw any light on the subject of the narrative.

'Well there are hundreds of books of travel far worse than that,' said Mr Campbell. 'Upon my word Mrs Hugh you are quite a genius. If I were you, Hugh, I'd have that printed. I knew you could talk better than any woman I ever came across, but I never would have thought that you could put down things like that. Let me see the notes as you call them. It looks to me like an antimacassar. Eh, Florrie, is not that what you call it?'

'Yes, father and a very ugly one it is if Mrs Keith will excuse my saying so; because there is no symmetry in the design; of course if this interesting narrative was to go into it somehow, the pattern of the stitches must follow the lead of the idea.'

' 'Pon my soul,' said Mr Campbell, 'this is an extraordinary thing, a very remarkable thing indeed. Do you know you might make your fortune as a sort of shorthand writer or knitter? a parliamentary reporter, eh! No doubt you could. Ladies are going in for these sort of things - you know they are - pushing their way into all sorts of professions, doctors, lawyers and what not, there will be nothing left for us old lords of creation to do in the course of the next fifty years. I used to think that a woman had nothing to do but to be good-looking, and that she would get a husband to do all the rest. That was the way in my younger days, but now even Florrie here would try for the matriculation examination, and got in by a close squeeze, the skin of the teeth. Eh! Florrie, was it not so? and there is nothing strongminded about her either. It was the mere force of example with her, she did as other girls did. Well I saw all along, Mrs Hugh, that you used your eyes and your ears, but I never thought of anything like this.' And he handled the knitting as a savage would handle a book upside - downside - sideways - turned over, and looking through it.

'My ears are far sharper than my eyes,' said Liliard. 'My eyes want a great deal of education yet.'

'But 'pon my word you should really give lessons in this art of yours. Just fancy what a convenience it would be to the poor little beggars at school to take down their lessons like that.'

'What a convenience it would be for them to write it down,' said Liliard laughing. 'It comes to the same thing.'

'But this is quicker and takes less space. Why you had half a book in this piece of knitting.'

'Yes but the knitting contains only the barest of notes. You would scarcely conceive how little is really taken down. It is indeed the shortest of shorthands eked out by the memory of the person who took the notes.'

'It is Liliard's memory, as she says, that is naturally very powerful, and has been trained by constant exercise from childhood. And what she does not recollect, she can supply,' said I.

'No doubt,' said Liliard, 'but that would not do for word-for-word reporting which is required from your shorthand writers.'

'Would it not? Well Mrs Keith I'll make you an offer. You said you wanted to hear a parliamentary debate. I can get admittance to the House of Commons for you and Florrie for Thursday evening. Will you take your knitting needles, and take down what you hear, and let us compare it with the *Times* report next day, and I'll eat my hat if yours is not the best worth listening to.'

'Liliard could not hold out for a long debate, she would get tired,' said I.

'So she would,' said Mr Campbell. 'The shorthand reporters only keep it up for an hour or so at a time, and are relieved, but for an hour or so let it stand good. If your report is as good or better than that of the *Times*, I give you a diamond set. If it is not . . .'

'I'll not give you one,' said Liliard laughing.

'No – no – it is not a bet. I did not mean it as a bet, but I'll eat my hat if it is not better worth listening to than the verbatim report.'

'Poor father, you will be choked – but who is to be the judge?' said Miss Campbell.

'Why myself of course,' said Mr Campbell who had a large idea of his own judgement in all cases, and in this was determined to lose what he did not call a bet.

'Then you will save yourself from an untimely death by absurd extravagance,' said Liliard. 'No, Mr Campbell I do not accept your offer in that shape. If I please you, and another more critical judge, by my report or abstract of a two hours debate you will give me ten pounds for some of the London charities, whichever I think best. If I do not please you you give me nothing. Does that please you Victor?' and she turned to me.

'Better than the other idea of plunder or indigestion for our friend Mr Campbell. But who will be the other judge to protect his interests?'

'I see no need of another judge and I like my own way best,' said Mr Campbell.

We were here interrupted by the entrance of a visitor, a Melbourne man, who was supposed to be an admirer of Miss Campbell, and the old gentleman at once informed him as to the conditions about which we differed. He offered to be associated in the award, and as he was likely to swim with the stream, he was willingly accepted by Mr Campbell.

The next day we went to the Foundling Hospital, and heard the children sing. No music had ever gone to Liliard's heart like this wonderful singing – but yet she felt sad to see the children. 'Are these your children of the State?' she whispered to me as we went out.

'Not so! They are provided for by private charity. A workhouse school will show you the real pauper children. These in the Foundling Hospital are supposed to be better off, but I do not like children being in such great masses under any conditions.'

'Our children were so few that they were like one family,' said Liliard – addressing herself to me.

'I suppose you have nothing so grand as this in your little Columba,' said Mr Campbell who had the common idea that everything that is large and numerous must be grand, and would often boast of the great prisons and charitable institutions of Victoria as one of the signs of its prosperity and enterprise.

'No,' said Liliard, 'and certainly nothing so grand as the music.'

'But it is a very gratifying sight to see the children all dressed alike, so clean, so well-trained, so obedient, and all made fit to earn their living by charity. Although I was brought up a presbyterian I must confess that I like a school where children are taught the English Church Catechism and taught that they *have* betters to honour and behave reverently to; it is a lesson that not only our Melbourne larrikins but our working men and our highly paid and independent servant girls need to learn I'm sure. This is a good place surely for my ten pounds.'

'I don't know,' said Liliard.

'All this row they make about secular teaching deprives us of a cheap police. There is nothing like religion for the masses I read that somewhere, and it sticks to me. I'm no great reader, Mrs Keith, like you, but when I see a thing worth recollecting it sticks to me.'

'Oh! Father, I should never call Mrs Keith a great reader,' said Miss Campbell. 'The surprising thing to me is how much she knows without reading.'

'Well it is the same thing; some people like you Florrie, and your friend Eva Barnett, read constantly, and can give no account of it, and some people like Mrs Hugh and me, use our eyes and our ears and our judgement and make a better show.'

With regard to the workhouse to which Mr Campbell and his daughter did not go with us, Liliard was in no manner of doubt; she was depressed beyond measure by it. She gathered or I gathered for her some statistics from the authorities as to the birth and condition of the children before they were admitted, and some accounts of how they turned out when they went into the world, which were both as unsatisfactory as possible.

'And to think that our deserted or neglected children are our teachers and preachers and masters in every way. These children by no kind of education could become so I think.'

'We cannot tell what might come of them if they were separated from the depressing and demoralising companionship of their fellows. We know that the surroundings here are stifling to ambition. The parish children in Scotland are all boarded out with respectable poor people and show no marked deficiency in intellect or morals. We are all too apt to attach too much to heredity.'

'Of course our children were those of the least worthy,' said Liliard, 'but by training they were made our superiors; and this training was given by the generation of the same class which had preceded them. You saw the homes they had with the teachers were happy ones and they went to school up to twelve years old with the others, and except for the badge on the arm there was no difference to be seen.'

'Out of these three thousand children there are hundreds illegitimate, hundreds orphans and hundreds the children of criminals but the bulk of them are sprung from the inhabitants of that borderland between shiftless pauperism and crime,' said I. 'This hereditary pauperism you cannot have in Columba.'

'In fact we have not pauperism at all,' said Liliard.

'You have not the things that lead to pauperism: public houses, gambling, horse racing, seduction, prostitution, a professional criminal class and terrible ups and downs in people's circumstances.'

'If it is really these things, and not really the closeness of the population which causes so much vice and want,' said she earnestly, 'could not the government put them down? Could you not adopt the best things in our Columba along with the best things in this wonderful England, and shake off half of the horrors that we seem in our West End house to live quite apart from, but that must eat into society, even the highest. If it is not possible in an old country like this, surely in a new country like yours in Victoria something could be done to show the way.'

'Yes, if we could penetrate the mass and its rulers with new ideas, and that is more difficult than you could imagine. Just try such a man as Mr Campbell who is an average Victorian citizen who has had a seat in the legislature, and probably will have it again, and speak to him of the liquor traffic, for instance. Why the bulk of his import trade depends on it; it is his speciality. He would think the colony would be ruined, and what is a more specious and telling argument nowadays, the principles of free trade and the liberty of the subject invaded if you suggested the principle of local option as to the establishment or the prohibition of public houses in a district. Even Sunday closing is an interference between a poor man and his beer which the sellers of beer feel very strongly on his behalf.'

'We never felt it any hardship in Columba.'

'No, you were used to the situation, and there was nobody interested in making a change. Vested interests in any large complex society fight to the death against every social reform.'

'Do you think Mr Campbell would really be so impervious on this subject? He seems to me to be very reasonable and impressible.'

'Oh! Mr Campbell like a good many other people, does not like to contradict a young and good-looking woman, but that is a very different thing from acting on her suggestions.'

'Perhaps you are right,' said Liliard after a little thought.

'It is a more difficult matter than you think, my dear, to regenerate society. You seem to see it in a nutshell in Columba, and you must recollect that you were not contented with it.'

'Ah! that is true Victor, nor would I be contented to go back, at least not till I had observed more, thought more, and done more than I have done or am likely to do for years to come. But outside of Columba, my old ignorant contempt for its ways and its institutions has changed into great love and regret. I used almost to despise Hugh for his complacent satisfaction with everything in the Commonwealth; but as you say, it was a curious political and social experiment on a small scale under the most favourable circumstances.'

'Just so, no such continuous equality of conditions could be possible in a wider field open to all the disturbing elements of different degrees of talent, industry, thrift and opportunity, not to speak of monopoly. Here the social organism is not compact and proportioned, but with great excrescences and devouring hollows, and when you would smooth down here and fill up there, it is as if you tried to stem the ocean with a mop.'

'But do not people take it seriously to heart, I mean many people so as to oppose a good front to the evils they would abate?'

'The people who take it seriously to heart are so divided as to the cause of the evil and the methods of cure, that it is almost impossible for them to act together.'

'We must act together, we two, Victor. We know what other people do not know, we know that these things are not necessary – surely that ought to help us.'

I could only say that I hoped that we might be able to do some little for the right, and that at all events our own union should be complete.

IX

THE RESULT OF LILIARD'S PARLIAMENTARY REPORT

The party to the ladies' gallery of the House of Commons of course consisted only of the two ladies, while we three gentlemen went to another part of the house, and sat down as near to the reporters as we could. I knew my wife had kept up her notes for three hours on the first day of my acquaintance with her, when she feared I might not return from the search for my camera and portmanteau, and wanted to take down the history of the world for a hundred and thirty-four years. But history when it is a making is not quite so interesting as when it is settled down, and one can trace out causes and consequences with some approach to accuracy, and this was only an average debate, where there was no great swordsplay of oratory. She held out for an hour and a half and then stopped, and fearful of weakening her hold on what she had taken down by even listening further, she asked leave to go home, and as Miss Campbell was already tired, and the others had no deep interest in the affair, we all adjourned to the opera as a sort of rest after the debate.

Miss Campbell was very fond of the opera, and her admirer was a connoisseur, though her father thought it was not half so entertaining as a good comedy or farce, and only went to take his daughter. Liliard's face during the opera was a study to me. She wanted so much to get at the soul of the thing through the highly artificial framework. Her musical taste was very slowly developing. She liked the solos and some of the choruses, but her dramatic instinct rebelled against the encores, and the calls before the curtain, and the incongruousness of bawling for silence and telling one's secret thoughts before a score of bystanders on the stage. She thought she could conceive of operas a great deal more realistic than it was. She always protested too against the audible asides in ordinary dramatic performances, and thought the use of them should be restricted to the narrowest limits. And I recollected that at the Columban Kirk, without a scrap of scenery, she had taken part in *As You Like It* somewhat abridged, and appeared to me as real a Rosalind as I had ever seen. The company there too, though without dress or adventitious aid in any way, had simply kept to the impersonated characters, and not stepped forward as the make-believe actors. If there was applause, which was very seldom, the Columban artists never appeared to be conscious of it; they simply stopped till they could be heard; they were not on the watch for it or eager to make the most of it. I was talking to my wife in an undertone on this subject, and drawing comparisons which called up a flush of pleasure on her cheeks between the acts when Mr Campbell had gone to the smoking room and his young friend was making himself agreeable to Miss Campbell. In this great and brilliant crowd we were for the moment as much alone together as in the stony desert outside of the Happy Valley. Miss Campbell and her admirer took no heed of us, and we knew nobody else among that sea of heads.

'Victor,' said she, 'is it a reality? Have I this morning been through the National Gallery with all its stores of pictures and sculpture, in the afternoon in the park with all the wealth and fashion of the Empire displayed before us, then listening to the free discussion of the oldest legislative assembly in the world, and now at the Italian opera which Addison thought so absurd in its beginnings? One would think one of these things might furnish thought for a week or a month, and there are four crowded into a day.'

'The world is really beautiful then, you are not disappointed?'

'It is wonderful, I think that is what I feel most – and it is perplexed.'

'You are living amongst very simple people fortunately. Mr Campbell and his daughter are as straightforward as possible. I always know what he is going to say on any given subject.'

'Do you think so?' said Liliard. 'On the contrary, he rather puzzles me.'

'He is not a clever man by any means, but he is a man who can take a hint. All his business successes I think have been due to his ready adoption of other people's ideas, and fancying them his own. He has no idea how much he owes to his managing clerk, to whom he has at last given a small share of the business, and even now he speaks of himself as Mr Scott's trainer and as the inspirer of all his happiest efforts.'

'I think it was well for us to meet with them as we did, because it gave me confidence for your Melbourne friends. And I always wonder at your not seeing Miss Campbell's merits.'

'I saw them clearly enough, but not so clearly as I do now. I think my love for you makes me think better of all women. But as for Mr Campbell he is so delighted at having found you out to be such a genius; this about the reporting will be a good story for him for all his life, for he will make out that you have done the thing admirably, and whatever you may do hence forward, he will always say he was the first to discover your talents. And that gives him a sort of property in you; neither his daughter nor Miss Barnett could see that you were anything out of the common, but he out of his own powers of observation did.'

I was quite right in my surmise. Partly owing to her own admirable imitation of the tones and gestures of the speakers, and the very fine quality of her voice, and partly because in her abstract she threw out redundances and gathered together the sentences into a point, both Mr Campbell and Mr Marshall agreed that they preferred her report to that of the *Times* and the ten pounds was handed over to her; the first money of her very own she had had in the world. Liliard meant to consult Miss Mountain as to the distribution of her money, for she needed some practical person to appeal to as to the best use to make of it, and she was rather disappointed to find that this excellent lady was distrustful as to all societies, and very chary with her charities. But pending the use to be made of her money, Liliard was invited by Miss Mountain to an evening party of a novel kind, which she thought would be more like the Columban gatherings than anything in London. It was for the inhabitants of the poor quarter which that lady overlooked, and old and young, men and women were to be assembled in a large bare room for an evening's amusement. Tea, coffee and bread and butter were provided, and at first Liliard thought she might use part of her money in this way, but it appeared that there were funds enough already. But could she do anything for their amusement? Those who could sing were to sing, those who could play were to play, picture books and illustrated newspapers were borrowed for them to look over, there was a gyroscope and a microscope and some stereographs.

All these things were out of my wife's line, but when Mr Campbell heard the conversation for he happened to be at home when Miss Mountain returned his daughter's call, he said he was sure that Mrs Keith could tell a story, such as they had never heard before, and that if he was only invited to make one of the party, he would use his influence to make her consent. Miss Mountain gave the invitation to Mr Campbell and his friend Marshall and myself which she had hesitated about doing, because gentlemen as a rule did not care for such gatherings, especially as for the sake of teaching the poor people to amuse each other, she encouraged the lamest artistic attempts and would rather have an indifferent song from one of them than a much better one from an outsider. Liliard's face brightened at this idea. She said she would do her best to entertain the guests for an hour.

'If Mrs Keith takes a piece of knitting with her don't be surprised,' said Mr Campbell. 'We do not want her to lose the thread of her discourse but I guarantee that her contribution will be A1.'

It was drawing near the day fixed for the gathering, and Liliard had settled that her story should be about her ancestor Ralph Abercrombie, with the handfasting omitted, but the marriage and christening on the same day. I had been eager to see how her narrative would affect people so dull and listless as Miss Mountain's protégés were, but I was prevented from attending. I got first a letter and then a telegram from my aunt Mrs Semple demanding my immediate presence in Edinburgh. My cousin Archie was reported first to be seriously and then alarmingly ill; I had been very fond of him, and knew his constitution well, so that his mother wanted my opinion, my advice, and my aid. She hoped that my wife would accompany me, though the family was in such trouble she might find but a poor welcome. Liliard said at once that I should go alone and that she wanted to write to me every day and to get letters. It would be the best possible practice for her. Instead of knitting the events of the day, she could now write them to the person who cared most to hear them.

'And I want you to stand the test of absence, Victor. I believe you will stand all tests but we have never been separated for six hours since we were handfasted.'

Handfasted – that odious word. I sometimes forgot our relations but this brought them back to me. 'My dear, let us go to the registrar's and get married before I go to Scotland. There is no need for the slightest hesitation on either part.'

'Perhaps not,' said Liliard, 'but I am disposed to wait till the time is out and you promised over and over again not to press me.'

I had again to yield and to leave matters in the same unsatisfactory position. However, I had worded my will so carefully that I thought, even in case of my death, there could be no reproach on my memory or her conduct. I accordingly said goodbye for the first time with the idea of staying away for a fortnight or probably longer, and this would perhaps carry my point. Absence would be a good discipline for Liliard; she would weary to join me again, and if I did not come back, but pressed her to come to Scotland, once there, a simple declaration of marriage, the mere going by my name and living as my wife before witnesses was as binding as the most elaborate ceremony. I fancied that was her real objection to going to Scotland, which all her traditionary memories should have drawn her to, but I did not question her too closely, lest I should only put her on her guard.

I found my cousin exceedingly ill, and in the most critical state, and established myself as head nurse and house counsellor for an indefinite period. My aunt was at first so glad to see me myself that she did not disturb herself about my wife, but she soon began to wonder how she got on without me and suggested that I should press her to come to Edinburgh. She united her entreaties with my own, and I thought our difficulty would be got over in this way.

X

LILIARD'S LETTERS

I suppose no husband who cares for his wife receives his first letter from her during an enforced separation without some emotion, and there was so much that was especially interesting in the relations between Liliard and myself, and in the new power of writing that she owed to my instructions, that this first production in that way that had passed through the post office to myself, had a wonderful charm. I used to wonder at the long letters in which some novelists used to frame their narratives in an age which had not such postal facilities as our own, and had often thought that so much time of the actors must have been taken up in writing as would leave very little time for the transactions and conversations they chronicled. But my darling must have sat up half the night to tell me minutely all the events of each day, for she still wrote slowly, and though my shorter hastily-written daily letter was but a poor return for all this wealth of detail as to where she had been what she had seen, and what people had said, she appeared quite satisfied. She said it was such good practice for her that for the future she would give up knitted registers altogether, for a catch-word was as good as a catch-stitch for her memory. A week had passed and this was part of the letter I received from Liliard.

'I had engaged to go with Miss Mountain to take tea with her poor people; that is to say to take charge of a table, and Mr and Miss Campbell were to follow after in time for my story. I did not feel so confident in its success when I saw the dull look of the people I was called on to amuse, but after a little, I caught a gleam of hope. I talked all the time I was making tea and coffee and began to feel interested in a toil-worn woman of about thirty-five called Mrs Ball, terribly seamed and scarred with smallpox, who told me she had buried five children and had only two alive, that her husband had gone to Australia but she had not heard from him since he left her soon after she got better, but perhaps there had been scarcely time. Hearing from Miss Mountain that I had come from America and was going to Australia, she tried to interest me in her husband. She might have been good-looking once, but what between her hard life and the ravages of the dreadful disease, she looked older than our Columbans did at fifty. People thought her lucky to have only two little ones to provide for, but the eldest would have been a great help now if he had only lived. "Many births and many deaths keep people poor," she said, "and the doctors and doctors' stuff cost a mort of money."

'After tea was over, one of the men sang a song in a cracked voice quite as bad as anything in Columba, then Miss Mountain made a little speech, clear and ringing, and much more cheerful than I could have made it, but she is used to these people, and tells me they are brighter and happier than when she first knew them. Then one of the men made a speech, but he sometimes lost himself, and forgot what he had begun his sentence with when he came to the end. All our people were trained to better speaking than that. Then somebody gave a comic recitation that made some of the people laugh, but my friend Mrs Ball and myself saw nothing funny in it. There were some dissolving views shown by a brother of Miss Mountain's, which I thought very curious, with a few words of explanation about each, and then my poor neighbour seemed more interested. At last Miss Mountain introduced me as a friend from America, who was going to tell a story about some of her ancestors.

I missed your eye to encourage me, and just as I stepped on to the platform I saw Mr Campbell, Miss Campbell, Mr Marshall and another gentleman come in. Those whom I had expected to see sat down in front, and I felt more nervous than before, but the stranger took a back seat. I missed not only your presence, but my friend Master Hepburn's blessing; I could only offer up a sort of prayer for myself and I plunged into my story. I suppose it was new to the audience, and therefore pleased them; when I stopped at critical points as I was accustomed to do, I was astonished by their clapping their hands and stamping with their feet, as at the theatre. At first it put me out, but I had to try not to mind it, and go on as usual. I caught the eye of Mrs Ball, and tried to think that there was nobody else there. She followed me with interest; she cried over the abduction and the part about Palahna's baby when she wept over it and prayed for its father's return. She rose off her seat when I came to the finding of the mother and child, she clapped her hands at the putting of the child into his grandmother's arms, and at the close, the wedding and the christening she gave a long sigh of satisfaction. Indeed the whole assembly whom I had thought so stupid, were more impressed than any Columban audience. Partly from the newness of the subject and the speaker, but as Miss Mountain told me, chiefly because of the dramatic effect of a story told without book with a great deal of action. Mr Campbell was loud in applause, and Mr Marshall followed suit, while his daughter had a surprised expression of pleasure in her face. I never saw her look so well before. I do not wonder at your grandmother's admiration for her.

'I had been most kindly invited by Miss Mountain to stay with her a day or two, and to go with her in some house-to-house visiting among the poor. In this way, I am making use of your absence to do what I can best do alone – so I surprised Mr Campbell by saying I could not go home to C– square with him as I wished to accept this kind invitation by which I might see a good use for his ten pounds. He looked disappointed and said he had had other plans. While he spoke to me, the stranger from the back came forward and to my surprise he turned out to be Miss Barnett's brother, the man we neither of us like. He complimented me on my performance in the most extravagant terms, saying I was born for the stage and such-like nonsense, which Mr Campbell seemed half to like, half to shrink from as I did myself.

'I asked him if he had seen his sister lately, and how she was. He said he had landed at Liverpool and visited her before coming to London. Manchester did not agree with her at all, her throat was affected and she had lost her voice, and besides she disliked the whole tone of the place, and especially its society. There was a little tone of pique in what he said, which I had no doubt she had conveyed to him. He was at present Mr Campbell's guest, who apparently thought he would try to make up for his inhospitable conduct to Miss Barnett in this way. I could gather that he had parted from his dramatic company, was not satisfied with the treatment he had received that he had tried something else in New York which Dr Burgoyne had helped him to, but had broken with that too, and was now open to an engagement of any sort.'

Next day's letter was as follows:

'Miss Campbell is the very best girl in the world, my dear Victor, and this she has proved to me today. You used to say that she had no enthusiasm, but I think when you read this letter you will acknowledge that for a worthy object, she forgets herself, altogether and what people will say. I was reading the *Times* while Miss Mountain was engaged with her morning correspondence – which is enormous – before she could go out on her rounds with me, when Miss Campbell came to call on me. She was in a state of great excitement I could see, and I felt rather bewildered. At first she could not speak at all. She went to the door and locked it. "What is the matter Miss Campbell?" said I. She shook her head and her eyes filled with tears.

' "I come as a friend," said she.

' "I am sure of that," said I.

' "And I think you need a friend – you do not know our ways."

' "What . . . what makes you say so today?" I asked with some anxiety.

' "I got a letter this morning," said she.

'"A letter," said I. I had thought Mr Barnett might have said something, but not of a letter.

'"From Miss Barnett," said she.

'"Let me see it," I said.

'"Oh no –" She hesitated a little but on my urging it warmly, she said that perhaps after all it would be the better course and so she gave it to me, it was as follows:

My dear Florrie

I have just discovered a most distressing thing, through my brother who met Dr Hugh Keith, and the girl he passes on us as his wife immediately after their escape from the strange place where she was brought up: not only was she unable to read and write, which I discovered for myself, but she was probably another man's wife before he stole her, and he is quite certain that they have never been married. He was made suspicious at first by her appearance and talk, and by Keith's apparent shyness and hedging as to particulars, and he found some people who had come from the same place, who were first frank, and then being bribed or frightened by the Keiths dumb to all questions, at least the woman was, but her husband or at any rate the man she lived with, for marriage seems to be a quite unnecessary formality in those parts, was more communicative. Do you not recollect that Dr Hugh looked caught when we recognised him, and many little signs that all was not right between them, and a shyness about any of the past life in this out of the way place? I always thought it was very forward in that ignorant woman to put herself on a level with us, but things are so much worse that I write that you may at once break off with both. The Melbourne Keiths will be very much annoyed about this. I write this in bed, for my throat is very troublesome. I have not had a day's health in Manchester.

Ever your most affectionate
Eva Barnett

I read the letter with difficulty, for Miss Barnett's handwriting looks well, but is very hard to make out. Miss Campbell looked at me all the time with a very anxious expression.

' "This is so far true," said I at last, "but I left no husband in Columba. No one has any claim on me there. I was married so far as our Columba laws would allow me to be married to Hugh Victor Keith. Nobody in our little Commonwealth could be married until they had gone through the probation of handfasting for a year and a day. After that they were free to change or to ratify the bond for life."

'Miss Campbell looked as astonished as you did that wonderful day when I told you of our ways, and certainly a little more shocked. "But if these laws are not binding here," said she, "surely Dr Hugh ought to know that you should be remarried according to our laws. You love each other dearly as I see. He should not take advantage of your ignorance, and he must have done so, for I recollect quite well his shyness at first, and he has not taken you to Scotland to see his friends. It was cruel both to you and to us to put you into such a false position. But it can be put right; write to him at once to do you justice, and he need not fear that I will visit his sins upon you. I will visit you and will never breathe a word of the matter; I will contradict Miss Barnett's information. I could even tell lies about it if it is necessary, because I feel quite sure that you are quite innocent of any wrongdoing, though I cannot conceive how so clever a woman as you are could not see that all our social arrangements hang on valid marriage."

'I let her speak, Victor, without defending you. I wanted to find out how a good woman brought up in an atmosphere of prosperity would look on my position, and I saw that her innate sense of right and her kind heart triumphed over all. I then told her the truth, that from the first moment possible, you had urged me to enter into a second lifelong bond, that over and over again you had pressed it with every argument in your power, but that I had held by my country's ways, because I thought them best, and especially because I felt myself ignorant and unworthy.

'"But my dear Liliard," said she calling me for the first time by my Christian name, probably she was puzzled what other name to give me, but there was a kindness in the tones of her voice and in her eyes that went to my heart, "if he were to be so base as to leave you for another, what would become of you? Could you allow him to break off this strange temporary bond, and cast you out into the world? You see I do not dream of your breaking it off – no woman could – but could you bear it being broken off."

'"Better than his keeping to it if he ceased to love me best," said I, "and even at the worst, shall I not have seen the world and satisfied the life long desire of my heart and have I not had a season of such happiness with Victor, as seems to throw all my previous life into the background? What matter for the rest!"

'"Well," said she, "I think the best thing you can do is to take my advice and get married at once. I feel sure that your love will last.

'"When love takes possession of two hearts, I think it assures them of its own immortality. The extraordinary arrangements of your little Commonwealth which you tell me of appear to give far too much countenance to inconstancy."

'"I think it is seeing how good you are, that makes me feel unworthy of Victor," said I, "and it was really my desire that he should have the opportunity of comparing me with others of his own rank brought up in the same way as himself that made me wish to join your party, and that I suppose was a social wrong."

'"Well so far as I am wronged I forgive it, but I do not say that I will forgive it if it can be righted, and you do not right it immediately. Dr Hugh Keith should have asserted his mastership over you. I blame him for that."

'I cannot bear to hear you blamed when you have been so good as to give up your own strong wish, in consideration of what you yourself, and other people too, consider ignorant prejudice and I think that has had more effect on me than any reproach on myself. I promised to think of it, and to write to you all about it, and to let you know. Miss Campbell kissed me and left me, and I had to go with what courage I had to visit the poor. Miss Mountain was full of her own affairs or rather her people's affairs, and did not notice how disturbed I was and whether from excitement or agitation or what not, I was not myself. I had a violent headache when I got home but I have wrapped a wet towel round my head and write this to you.'

On the next day I received this further news, written much worse and with the spelling more imperfect than any previous letter. 'After a restless night, when I turned over matters in my head, I woke with a headache worse than that of the day before and as I think, a good deal of fever but Miss Mountain had arranged a day's work for us, and after reading your kind letter, I felt as if I were revived. I cannot go to Scotland quite yet, though thank Mrs Semple over and over for her invitation. I have had a terrible day. I think I am going to be ill. Miss Mountain was writing letters in her morning room, and I had thrown myself on the sofa in the drawing room after reading your letter, and I was trying to collect my thoughts with a difficulty I never knew before when Mr Campbell came to call upon me. I think I turned pale, though I had been flushed, for it was clear enough that he too knew what you always told me would be fatal to our position in the world; but instead of being distressed like his daughter, he looked triumphant, and as if he would crush us both with pleasure. It was evident that he had got information, not from his daughter who had been honourably secret on the subject, but from our evil genius, Mr Barnett himself, for his first words were: "Well and so Hugh Keith is a scoundrel."

' "No!' said I. "No scoundrel but the most honourable man that breathes in the world."

' "I call it scoundrelly to take a girl from her home, and not give her the rights of a wife."

' "I have all the rights I want," said I. "We are bound by my own country's laws which always give a year's probation which we call handfasting before lifelong marriage."

' "By Jove," said he, "it is a good notion, an amazingly good notion. I did not think there was a Christian country where there was a loop-hole when a man makes a terrible mistake as I did. Never were two people worse mated than Florrie's mother and myself, but there was no escape; and for twenty-three years we had to drag along together. Florrie gets all her spirit from me. Her mother had neither the health nor the strength nor the understanding to be a fit wife for a man who had the world at his feet."

'I thought this a very cruel way of speaking of his poor dead wife. "Our law cuts both ways," said I. "A woman has as much right to rid herself of an unsuitable mate after a year's handfasting as a man has."

' "But she does not do it so often," said Mr Campbell, "for she is at a disadvantage."

' "Not in Columba," said I, "or at any rate not at such a disadvantage as would prevent her from parting where the union brings no happiness."

' "Well," said Mr Campbell, "so it appears that Hugh Keith sees some saviour in this handfasting as you call it and does not compromise his liberty of changing by getting you up to Scotland, very judicious on his part. Ha! ha! ha!"

'I was more distressed by Mr Campbell's amusement than by his daughter's grief. "It is no joke," said I choking back my sobs. "It is a solemn probation. We came together with vows and prayers not lightly."

' "And this is perhaps not your first experiment?" said Mr Campbell.

'I felt as if I would die. "That is between Victor and myself," said I. "No strangers need intermeddle with memories which concern them not."

'Mr Campbell seemed strangely moved. "Mrs Keith, or whatever you choose to be called, I'm glad you are free. You are the finest woman I ever saw in my life, and the cleverest. I have envied that fellow his luck in falling in with a *rara avis* that I don't believe he half values. I'll marry you out of hand, and give you as good an establishment as there is in all Victoria. Tom is gone, poor fellow, and Florrie I think is likely to be settled for herself ere long, and you will be queen in my heart, queen in my house. Ask what you will, and I will give it if it were not the half – but the whole – of my fortune."

'I suppose you wonder why I let the man speak so much, but I was dumb with astonishment, and I think also physically paralysed in a manner, for when I tried to speak, my tongue clave to my mouth. There he was kneeling at my feet as wildly in love as you yourself could be, and clutching at my dress for I held back my hands instinctively as if for life itself. There always had been something in his manner that I did not quite like, but now it was all out. The information which Mr Barnett and his sister had given to make a separation between us and the Campbells for their own purposes, had resulted quite differently from their expectations. Miss Campbell had offered me the services of the most courageous and disinterested friendship, and now her father came with a declaration of love.

' "Do not be absurd, ridiculous, and wicked," said I, when I could find breath to answer. "I have met with the one love of my life in Victor Keith. Even if he should change – which is possible – I never can change."

' "But think of it, Liliard, think of it! I could hurt him and you but I will not. I could tell Florrie and the other Victorians in London and get you tabooed for life in society, blacken you to his parents and the patients, shut all doors against you, but I would not think of such a thing. I can stop Barnett's mouth too. He wants employment. I can give it him on conditions of silence, only do not be so cruel to me. Think what I can give you, jewels, dresses, carriages, everything that your heart can wish. I have lost nothing by the trip but gained by the bargains I have made. I will be worth a million before I die. A million of money! Think of it, Liliard."

'Astonishment now opened my mouth. "If I consent to make a great scandal, and leave off being the reputed wife of Victor Keith to be either your mistress or wife . . ."

' "Wife," said he. "I'd never dream of anything else."

' "Well in that case you would be silent on the lesser scandal that

I, as a Columban, followed my own country's marriage laws which absolutely forbade marriage till after a year and a day's handfasting."

'"Tut! tut!" said he. "If you marry me there will be no scandal at all. A man of my wealth and position can do as he likes. I am rich enough and able to follow my own way. I don't depend on a profession like the Keiths. I could take you into society – the very best of society – and I would worship you. Young men are so selfish, it is the men of mature years who make the most loving and indulgent husbands." I shook my head and I laughed. I could not help laughing at this man of fifty putting himself in competition with my Victor. He felt the laughter to be very cruel.

'"Leave me!" said I. "I have only to move a finger, and Victor will come down from Scotland and marry me out of hand, as he has urged over and over again."

'"It is not such a bad idea," said he. "I think it is a very good idea and as you say the year and day have not elapsed, as you have gone on so far you may keep to it. There need be no hurry in getting married. Let a man have a chance – a man who worships you."

'I think this advice from your middle-aged rival affected me more than all the advice and entreaties and arguments which you and our good friend Miss Campbell had brought forward. I had much to do to dismiss him, and when Miss Mountain came to ask me to accompany her, I was really too ill to go out of the house. I have apparently got a feverish cold, and have gone to bed, in which I have written this which I hope you may be able to read. It is strange to be ill when you are away, but do not hurry back so long as Archie Semple needs you. When I feel better, I think I shall go to Scotland, and there I will do as it seems good to you. I still think my own way is the best, but the way we have got entangled with other people is too strong for us.'

I was distressed at the subject of both these letters and yet satisfied that Liliard could now hold out no longer. I made arrangements to leave my cousin though both his mother and himself were unwilling to part with me. But the next day there was no letter but a telegram from Miss Mountain that the doctor had been sent for, and that my wife was supposed to be taking smallpox and awaited my orders as to treatment. I had tried to have Liliard vaccinated in New York, but it would not take, so that I did not reproach myself as I might have done if I had neglected to do so, and I had thought that she was not likely to take the true disease at the present time. I had therefore to bid goodbye immediately to my cousin and aunt and to hurry to London by the express train and there arranged to have her taken into quiet lodgings where I established myself as her chief nurse and guardian. She knew me when I came up, but as the fever rose she became delirious, and then all her talk was of Columba and her schooldays and her dead father, and her living mother and of Hugh Keith. The last chapter of her life, which she had said had overshadowed all the other, was now completely overshadowed by the disease, and whatever she did or said or thought, appeared to be a sort of struggle in which she was always baffled and defeated. What I said to soothe her was woven with her troubled imaginations, and only seemed to aggravate her sense of discomfiture. We were of course under the strictest taboo, as much isolated in London as we had been in the desert except for the nurse and the visits of the physician whom I called in to consult with me, for my extreme anxiety made me diffident of my own skill. I was more a nurse than a physician in this terrible strait. The eruption did not come out freely, which made the case more alarming, but at last she got relief in that way. Her face was not altogether spared – but much as I prized her beauty, I felt thankful to see that her life might be redeemed by some scars.

When she got the turn she said to me in a faint voice, 'I have been very ill Victor.'

'Very ill, Liliard.'

'Am I going to die?'

'I hope not! I believe not; indeed I feel sure that you will live, you are wonderfully better, and all the symptoms are now favourable.'

'Have I been impatient and troublesome.'

'No more than must be expected – you have been very ill.'

'Did I dream or is it true that it is smallpox? How did I catch it?'

'It appears that though vaccination would not take, that you were liable to infection. Do you recollect taking a wailing child on your knee in a railway carriage the day I left for Scotland. The child was sickening for smallpox.'

'Oh! I am very sorry – I would rather have taken anything else, fever and ague twenty times over.'

'You never would have taken this in Columba,' said I. 'This is one of the contingencies of civilisation that we speak of having fought with and conquered by vaccination.'

'Will you let me see myself?' said Liliard after a long pause.

'No,' said I, 'not yet. You will not be much altered if you give yourself a little time.'

'It is strange that I should have fallen in with the scourge that our people in the Happy Valley thought they had escaped, but nobody can blame you. You tried your best to get me vaccinated but it would not take. You would perhaps have prevented me touching the child, poor little thing; I hope it is better now.'

'I hope so – as you are.'

'Would it not have been like a dream if I had died? Oh! Victor I hope a happy dream to you. We have never quarrelled, never even differed but about the one thing, and that was because we each loved the other so much. And I had such a glorious time with you. Surely it would have been a different Liliard Abercrombie that would have begun life in Heaven than if I had died a year ago.'

'Don't speak of that now.'

'I only want to tell you how happy you have made me.'

'You were troubled in your delirium.'

'Not through you Victor.'

'No not through me; I never appeared to be recollected at all.'

'That's true. If I had only thought of you, trouble and pain would have fled away.'

'The Campbells send every day to Dr –'s to hear how you are.'

'That is kind of Miss Campbell. Has Miss Barnett come back?'

'No, she is still in Manchester with her throat.'

'And he who made so much trouble?'

'He has gone back to America.'

'And oh! in my selfishness I forgot: how is your cousin?'

'Much better; almost well again.'

Liliard fumbled with her clothes, and missed something. 'Where is my handfasting ring. Have I lost it?'

'No, my love, I have it here,' and I took it out of my vest pocket.

'I cannot see yet. I don't believe I could see my ugly face even if you showed me the mirror.'

'It is not ugly,' said I. 'Even being scarred all over could not prevent your being a very handsome woman, and the scars are but trifling.'

'How long have I been ill?'

'A month.'

'I have lost a month; I have learned nothing and I have so much to learn.'

'Only patience my love.'

'Life being difficult,' said she softly, 'seems to bring out the best of people sometimes. Would you have thought Miss Campbell could have been so good as she was that day. She never had a puzzle before, and she just went straight to solve it in the best and the kindest way.'

'Or could you have thought Mr Campbell could have been so bad as he was the following day?' said I laughing.

'Well,' said she, 'I am not so sure about that; I should not wonder that Mr Campbell has done worse things in his life than wanting to marry me when he thought that I had been deceived, and when he thought that I was free. People do not like these offers made to their own but it will not be repeated; you may be sure of that Victor. It was another Liliard Abercrombie whom he admired than this one who lies on a sickbed. But I am tired – will you read to me? I think if you read me something that I know – the Sermon on the Mount or the Last Discourse in St John's Gospel – it will rest and soothe me.'

She lay so still, so subdued, so patient, I could scarcely identify her intellectually with the brilliant woman I had been so proud of; and at present she was sadly changed personally but she would soon be well enough for a private marriage ceremony, and I had determined that she was not to go out of that sickroom under any other conditions than those of my lawful wife. The first thing in the way of occupation she asked for was her knitting and the next thing pencil and paper.

Miss Mountain was her first visitor, and told her how thankful she should be that her life had been spared. Miss Campbell was her second, and as a young girl was more shocked at the change in Liliard's appearance than a middle-aged veteran among sickness and trouble like Miss Mountain could be. She came on the very first day it was pronounced to be safe for her to see Liliard, in order to show that she despised the ill-natured stories of the Barnetts and also, as I thought, to urge our immediate marriage. But she appeared to be scared at the sight of Liliard's face and her subdued manner. Unaccustomed to sickness of that kind, she thought that the patient was dying rather than recovering.

I had a short interview with Miss Campbell, and told her my intentions. She seemed overjoyed, and said that she never could think that I had wilfully wronged Liliard, though appearances were against me. But now she was more than satisfied, since under altered conditions I was willing and eager to keep my word.

'My father said he would come for me,' said Miss Campbell. 'He has been strangely disturbed about Mrs Keith's illness – somewhat reproaching himself, and his listening to Mr Barnett's stories, as exciting her, and making her take the disease harder. For it appears he went the day after I did to Miss Mountain's to remonstrate with her too, and it was all a great deal too much for her. She had her own mistaken ideas about right and wrong, and it must have shocked her to learn how she compromised herself and you.'

I did not much care to let Mr Campbell see Liliard; although I resented his admiration for her, I thought I would find his pity and disappointment worse to bear still. The man himself looked ill, and as if his clothes did not fit him.

'Can I see Mrs Keith for five minutes alone,' said he to me in an undertone. 'I want to make an apology.'

'If she herself makes no objection,' said I.

Liliard did not, but then she did not seem to have spirit to object to anything.

He went in, and as I afterwards heard appeared very much struck as his daughter had been by the change in her appearance. Liliard felt it like a stab in both cases. When other people were so much shocked, it could only be my desire to spare her feelings that made me make light of her disfigurement.

'Will you give me the mirror?' she said. 'No one will let me see myself but you will. I know – the small hand-mirror. It will be quite enough for me to hold.'

He gave it into her trembling hands, and turned aside while she looked into it. 'Oh! I see,' said she, 'it is a woeful wreck. Now is it not a good thing that Victor is not bound to keep his vows made to another Liliard Abercrombie than this is.'

'By Jove,' said Mr Campbell, 'it makes no difference to me. If he draws back, I'll do nothing of the kind. It is your mind and your spirit that I admire, and what's more, the smallpox at its worst will leave you more good looks than most other women have at their best. It does not spoil your eyes, your hair or your figure, and these marks will be to me but as dimples. 'Pon my soul I love you more than ever. That is what I wanted to say to you, and if Hugh Keith shows the white feather, depend upon me.'

'Ring the bell,' said Liliard, 'or call Victor and your daughter.'

He hesitated a little, but her manner was imperative, and in some bewilderment as to her wishes, he summoned us and we both came in. Liliard's face alas was no longer telltale as of old. How I used to watch the colour come and go with every changing emotion but now she could speak and let me know her mind.

'In the presence of these your old friends,' said she, 'I want to tell you that you are perfectly free at the end of a year and a day. Till then dear Victor, you are bound to love and cherish me as you have done, oh so tenderly, since the day we vowed that fidelity to each other. But I always felt unworthy of you and now more than ever.'

'My dear wife,' said I, 'so you have been to me, there is not in my mind the slightest swerving of fidelity and love. You know that from the first I have wanted to conform to the laws outside of Columba, not from any distrust of you or of myself, but because it would lead to misconstruction and misrepresentation, if it was discovered that things were exceptional with us. I will rejoice over this illness of yours if it shows you that let fate do its very worst with you; it makes no difference – none whatever – I want no longer interval. I do not want to wait till you have recovered your beauty, as I believe you will, to put the matter past recall. If you had been scarred and seamed like your poor friend Mrs Ball, so as to be scarcely recognisable, you would still be the first and only love of my heart. What would the whole world be to me without you? Judge by yourself! If any accident maimed or disfigured me would you not cling the closer to me?'

'Surely, surely,' said Liliard slowly, 'that is true enough.'

'And can you credit me with such meanness, such blindness as would be unworthy of yourself? If these good friends will be our witnesses, I shall have the licence and the clergyman tomorrow and have the thing settled.'

'Do so,' said Miss Campbell. 'You have dealt very hardly with our friend Dr Hugh, I don't think you quite understand how cruel your conduct has really been to him.'

'Do so,' said Mr Campbell stoutly and in an undertone, he muttered, 'and the Lord lead me not into temptation again. Hugh Keith speaks well and honestly, and you have no right to thwart his honourable proposal by laying snares for the unwary like myself. You have been for many months what you call handfasted, and have been scarcely a fortnight separated, and I think that is trial enough.'

'It was because I felt myself unworthy,' repeated Liliard, 'and now I am such a wreck.'

'Unworthy?' said Miss Campbell with warmth. 'I think our friend Dr Hugh could not find anywhere in the world anyone more worthy of him or one who would have such perfect sympathy with all his tastes and pursuits.'

'By Jove,' said Mr Campbell. 'I think the disparity is the other way. You have learned to read and write and to speak and behave like an English gentlewoman, and yet have all the gifts of your own outlandish place; you can charm gentle and simple alike with the wonderful way you can tell stories as if they acted themselves through you. And even in this sickbed there is about you that can turn the head of a man old enough to be your father. You have been firm long enough in your overwrought humility; if you keep on any longer we will call it unreasonable obstinacy.'

And as these friends said so it was we were privately married on the day following this conversation by a presbyterian clergyman to whom we told our story, who shook his head over the handfasting as a delusion and a snare, but who rejoiced as he thought to make that wrong right. But somehow Liliard's whole nature was too highly strung, and this which gave me peace, and which I thought would bring tranquillity to her, had not the desired effect and for six weeks after our marriage, she seemed to make little or no progress. As she began to recover, she began to turn her thoughts towards the land of her ancestors, the Scotland which she could now enter without its altering her position, for that was fixed beyond recall and our northern journey seemed to revive her. Under the bracing air of the hills and moors inland, and of the sea breezes on the east coast she recovered her tone and her appetite, and the pilgrimages she made with me to the places sacred in family tradition were of still greater interest than any foreign travel we had had. The wild and rugged grandeur of the Highlands and the pastoral beauty of the Lowlands, each found its way to her heart. And when she stood by the old church at Colbrandspath which looked as if it were the very building in which the masterful Archibald Keith had preached, or ranged with me on the hills and dales of Upper and Nether Keith she filled her mind with memories for the grandmother, more minute and vivid than mine or my father's. She delighted in talking her Columban Scotch to the peasantry, who could scarce believe her to be a true lady, in spite of her clothes, and her bearing, and she astonished some old people with the use of words that they had heard 'long syne' from their grandparents, but never since they had come up to manhood and womanhood. Mrs Semple was disappointed in her at first, and let her see that she was so, for neither Liliard's beauty nor her animation had been recovered when she came. Very much to my annoyance, because it greatly pained Liliard, Mrs Semple bewailed that she had not come up to the North at first with me, when she would have escaped the terrible scourge. But Liliard had not lived with her for a week before she thoroughly won my aunt's heart and Archie's too.

Before I joined my family in Melbourne the six little scars on her face had settled down to a very insignificant position, and somehow I felt that from that sickbed and these troubles she had come out with a still finer expression, that her eyes and her smile were lovelier than ever. There was another gain which I had partly anticipated. She had far more sense of humour, though she was still keenly critical as to its quality. Wit she had always appreciated, but she had learned in mixing with the world to find relief from its pathos and its tragedy by the appreciation of what was grotesque, incongruous and ridiculous. I think that her religious nature too had grown deeper through the long dangerous illness, and still more from the next trial she had to go through, which however had a happy ending. What unknown depths of tenderness were stirred in her heart when she and I looked together on the face of our little one.

It was a year and a day from our first handfasting when we landed in Melbourne. I had gone out alone. I returned rich in the possession of a wife and a child and more proud of my encumbrances than any young father I had ever laughed at in the course of my life. It was a great day in Collins Street, for it was on my grandmother's ninetieth birthday that I brought my Liliard and our little son to my father's house. Liliard knelt with me at the old lady's feet and we received her blessing with hearts full of gratitude for the past, and hope and faith for the future. No one could have been more heartily welcomed into a family than Liliard was, and even when she told the old lady the whole story of our love and of our probation, the grandmother was in no way shocked. Her curiosity was too much aroused and too much gratified for her to make any unkind comments. Liliard delighted in my grandmother's society, and was never weary of hearing her old stories, repaying them with interest from her own recollections and observations and her powers of fertile invention, for she continued to be a wonderful storyteller by word of mouth.

To my wife and to myself, the old lady is now committing all her traditionary knowledge with a sort of faith that in our hands they bid fair to be handed down, though whether young Victoria will care much about it is another question. The Columban ways are to her an unfailing topic of interest, and she expresses herself over and over again as thankful that she had been spared to such a great age for the puzzle of her youth had been solved by my discovery of Columba, and some of the puzzles of her mature years had met with some enlightenment from the experiences of the Scottish Adventurers. She shakes her wise old head however when Liliard says she thinks even out of the Happy Valley there might be wisdom in allowing such a thing as handfasting. 'Oh no, my dear, society is not prepared for it yet, though maybe when you are as old as I am, I'll not say what will happen. But I cannot say a word against the practice in Columba for it has given you to my dear grandson:

And sweeter woman ne'er drew breath
Than my Hugh's wife, his now till death.'

AFTERWORD

How ironic it is that *Handfasted*, Catherine Spence's most optimistic novel, manifesting the characteristic 'hope' she maintained had been inherited from an inveterately speculative father, should have been rejected by a committee of Mrs Grundys in a manner which discouraged the author from continuing with novel writing. In writing about what would now be described as a feminist utopia, Spence was completely at one with the intellectual currents of her time, in particular the gradual liberation of women from political, legal and economic constraints, and the incorporation of idealism with evolutionary theory. The first page of the novel signals the belief in the inevitability of progress, shared by Spence and her protagonist Hugh Keith when he describes the present of 1879 as 'these days when all history is looked upon as evolution'.

Catherine Spence's intellectual development consistently moved away from the restrictions of her Calvinist upbringing, with its pessimistic sense of determinism, towards ideas that promised to liberate man from an apparently inevitable negative destiny. She was drawn to the liberalism of Unitarianism in religious matters, and to Comtean theories of positivism and scientific improvement which suggested that the most fundamental laws of social organisation were laws of evolution. Much of this thinking is summed up in the utopian blueprint for 1988 contained in her *A Week in the Future*, written in 1888.

The utopian impulse seems to be as old as literature itself, and may indeed have a psychological origin; certainly it is a manifestation of an essentially humanist, as opposed to religious, urge for betterment in this world. By the 1880s the utopian dream had taken on a unique form for, armed with the historical evidence of scientific and technological development, as well as a theory of organic progress, at last utopia seemed to have entered the realm of the possible, as opposed to the merely imaginary. To Spence, an idealist as pragmatic as she was optimistic, the urge to speculate in fictional form must have been irresistible. Yet there were a number of factors which distinguished her from many of her fellow utopians.

By the age of fifty-four Spence knew a great deal about the struggle for improvement both in personal and social terms. She was certainly not so naive as to suppose – even in her much-loved adopted State of South Australia which had had the inestimable advantage of idealistic planning rather than the de facto social respectability acquired in the wake of Sydney's convict origins – that a utopian society was possible in her own time. But her optimism never flagged; her whole life was devoted to reformist activity, and she was encouraged by the success of much of it. All her fiction reflects a level-headed devotion to realism which inevitably tempered her idealism.

Thus *Handfasted* was written quite consciously as an experimental speculation on an alternative historical model of social evolution, not as a projection of future development. It is clearly Columba's destiny to be swallowed up by the modern world with all its failings. Spence had the honesty of a genuine experimental scientist, for she concluded that the social superiority of Columba, those things which mean it can be described accurately as utopian, have been won at the expense of higher achievement in the non-utilitarian arts. Immured in their valley in 1745, the Scottish settlers, faced with a grim struggle to survive, re-enact man's evolutionary development in social terms. They must fight for their territory with the Indians, grow their crops, replace their dead with new citizens, build their own houses. Yet because they are men and women of the Enlightenment (conveniently delivered from thraldom to the grim determinism of their minister's Calvinism), they structure their society according to the dictates of reason above all, unimpeded by reliance on Revelation or Old Testament repressiveness. Thus they treaty with the Indians, introduce handfasting, apportion land fairly, do all that seems necessary to maximise the well-being and happiness of their members. Aesthetic and artistic tastes are a luxury in the early days of struggle, and evolution ensures that utilitarian matters continue to govern development. By the time Hugh Keith arrives in Columba in 1879, not only skill in the decorative arts and music has disappeared, but also the taste for them. Only dancing remains, of the recreative arts, and in Columba it has become very much the expression of vigorous physical energy and an opportunity for socially acceptable courting, rather than any expression of civilised refinement. Even the plays and storytellings are not original, but versions gleaned from their remnants of literature and history.

The most telling criticism of Columba is to be found in the character of Liliard Abercrombie. In her, Spence dramatises an inescapable utopian paradox: if man's best nature is manifested in idealistic struggle to improve his lot, the achievement of utopia leaves the noblest natures no scope for the exercise of the highest moral good. Hugh Keith's naive naming of Columba as the Happy Valley should not blind us to the irony of Spence's reference to Samuel Johnson's *Rasselas*, with its paradoxical Happy Valley demonstrating man's persistent discontent even in a utopia of his own making. Johnson's Rasselas and Spence's Liliard point to the human need for more than physical and material well-being.

Handfasted leaves its readers with a sense that the real utopia is perhaps the Melbourne which Hugh Keith leaves and returns to, just as Rasselas and his companions return to their Abyssinia. Spence's sturdy loyalty and affection for Australia, based like Hugh Keith's on a knowledge of the rest of the world gained from travel, made it the measurement of even fictional projections of an ideal society.

There are certainly a number of parallels between the fictional and the real colonies. Spence gives her Columbans a hundred year start on Adelaide, where she arrived as a teenager in 1839. Columba's founding date of 1745 not only allowed a more useful time span to examine social development, but also meant it could be examined in the absence of some of the 19th century's major problems: scientifically-based religious doubt, population pressure, industrial servitude and squalor. Retrograde religious influences are dispensed with by disposing of Presbyterian minister and schoolmaster, and the benign and hopeful New Testament becomes the Columban's spiritual guide. Their rural economy has no need of modern technology. In line with many other 19th-century utopian works, *Handfasted* resurrects the Arcadian dream of rural simplicity in a climate which guarantees plenitude and good health.

In this respect it is similar to William Morris's *News From Nowhere* (1890), and also in its idealising of other aspects of the past. In particular the Scottish past, remembered by both Spence and her mother, is strongly evoked. Scotland is the link between past and present, and between Columba, America, France and Australia. The historical closeness of France and Scotland is subtly evoked in Marguerite de Launay's story with its underlying religious background of Jansenism and its kindred protestant form, Calvinism. Spence herself had acquired a knowledge of French which enabled her to review new French books for the *Adelaide Register*, where she often reminded Australian readers of the social changes going on in Europe but all too often ignored in the colonies which saw relevance for themselves only in the Anglo-Saxon model of England. Spence's utopian ideas must have been influenced by a knowledge of the French theorists and social experimentalists such as Le Play, Comte, and Fourier. Certainly the French nationality of *Handfasted*'s founder Marguerite, and the account of her upbringing, helps provide a richer cultural and historical background to the novel.

Spence's belief in the superiority of the Scots as colonists dictated the nationality of the settlers. Their destination may have been suggested by her knowledge of the Darien Scheme, mentioned in the novel as precursor to the Columban venture. The Darien Scheme consisted of three expeditions of Scottish emigrants who set off for the isthmus of Central America in 1698, only to succumb by 1700 to famine, disease and the depradations of the Spaniards.

The happier move of her own family to South Australia provided Spence with first-hand knowledge of the experience of emigration, and despite more than a decade of struggle for economic independence, the Spence family never appeared to regret the uprooting from their native Scotland. The experience must have affected Spence profoundly, for emigration is undertaken by all the major characters in all her novels, and enables them to transform their alienation into a vital precipitator of personal growth. It also, very often, provides them with a more useful social role than they could have hoped for in the older society they leave behind.

Catherine Spence herself spent all her adult life in the new world, but her mother, Helen Brodie Spence was halfway through her long life when she arrived in Adelaide. Born in 1791, Helen Spence was her daughter's dearly loved companion until her death in 1887, just two years before *Handfasted* was written. Her loss affected Spence profoundly, and it is hardly surprising that she should have written a tribute to Helen Spence in the character of Hugh Keith's grandmother. The portrait would have been recognised instantly by anyone who knew Helen Spence. The real and the fictional woman are the same age, and both married in 1815. Spence's *Autobiography* provides many other correspondences. The account of her parents' families in Scotland, which must have been received from her mother, is virtually reproduced in Hugh Keith's description of his grandmother's background, even to the detail of her father buying the third edition of the Encyclopedia Brittanica in 1797. Other echoes occur, such as Archibald Keith's parish of Colbrandspath sounding very like the parish of Spence's paternal great-grandfather, Cocksburns' Path.

Spence's affection and admiration for her mother is voiced

through Hugh Keith's portrait of his grandmother, whose modernity of outlook makes her a valued companion. She tells her grandson she hopes to live long enough to see women receive the vote, and the outcome of socialism. Spence described her mother in the *Autobiography* as a New Woman without knowing it, her optimistic interest in the new discoveries being made in the world and her patriotic appreciation of her adopted country's advantages putting her in advance of her own times. Affection, however, may have blurred Spence's critical judgment, for the fictional portrait absorbs a disproportionate amount of the novel, and this edition has abbreviated some of the conversations between Hugh Keith and his grandmother. However, the real and the fictional woman provided important living proof for Spence's belief in evolutionary advance. Through conversations with their own grandmothers they have access to 150 years of memory and of history, which provides ample evidence for their optimistic belief in progress. Old Mrs Keith is the sole living link between the 1745 adventurers and the present-day society which provides her with a grand-daughter-in-law in Liliard Abercrombie, for she recalls her own grandmother's eyewitness account of the departure of the Scottish settlers.

The conventions of realism which governed the 19th-century novel suited Catherine Spence's temperamental affinity for biography and autobiography, and in all her fiction there are many real-life sources for both characters and plots. Only in *Handfasted* does Spence employ the first-person form, and in the voices of Hugh Keith and Marguerite de Launay are mingled the tones, attitudes and experiences of Spence herself although they are distinct literary creations. Hugh is the mouthpiece for her vigorous championing of Australia. His travel experiences are drawn from her own first overseas trip in 1865 (although she did not visit America until 1893) when her conviction of colonial superiority was strengthened by a return to Scotland where the narrowness of both physical and intellectual horizons depressed her. In the character of Marguerite, Spence seems to have tapped deeper creative sources than anywhere else in her fiction; the journal constitutes her most powerful and haunting writing. In it Spence has transmuted into fiction the most difficult passage of her own life when, like Marguerite, she painfully emerged from the oppressiveness of the Presbyterian religion into a sense of personal liberation which was never to leave her. For a woman like Marguerite, born at the close of the 18th century, such liberation could only come through extraordinary means. Her odyssey is given tragic dimension by the loss of the two men she loved most in her life, her young lover Paul Durham, and her eldest son Hugh Keith, and the freedom she wins finally as the matriarchal leader of Columba is tempered by the suffering which preceded it.

Madame Keith's journal, with its plangent rhythms, affecting story and the ghostly presence from the past speaking so directly to the beloved son's modern counterpart, provides a timeless portrait of woman's lot: 'It was hard to be a woman; to have no will of one's own and no career: to bear children in sorrow into a world which was all thorns and briars for tender feet, all stabs and blows for loving hearts, was no enviable lot.' Her sorrow and pity are not for herself alone; her powerlessness is most mourned when it limits the help she can offer to others in distress – her own children, the poor and ill of her husband's parish. In a passage added to the original manuscript, Spence has Marguerite Keith articulate her awareness of the most basic lack of freedom for women – economic dependence. Madame Keith's dowry is never her own to command, and she must rely upon the narrow generosity of her husband even to exercise Christian charity to the poor. She sees herself, accurately, as nothing more than her husband's housekeeper and upper servant. It is hardly surprising to find in Columba that women have equal economic opportunities since they are allotted land, the basis of all wealth in a rural economy, equally with the men. What is surprising however, is to find the handfasted Liliard Abercrombie, in 19th-century London, as much an economic vassal as any other middle-class woman of the time, for the £10 she earns through the skill of her 'shorthand' knitting is the first money of her own she has had. What differentiates Liliard from Hugh's ancestress is her sturdy independence of spirit which makes her insist upon handfasting before marriage, with the knowledge that she can always return to her birthplace where she will be guaranteed the opportunity to support herself. Even in the outside world she soon learns that her skills of oratory are marketable.

Madame Keith, on the other hand, reveals superior powers of self-analysis, as she struggles alone against the spiritual aridities of her husband's religion and the bitterness of a loveless marriage apparently made in vain. She discovers the crucial weakness in the Puritanism which offers her so little comfort, and it is an insight which is a revelation of her husband's character as much as her own helpless subjection. A doctrine which destroys self-esteem destroys all potential for self-fulfilment and for good. She says of Pascal's *Pensées*, 'Even this book to which I clung as a relic of the past and of happier days, did not help me. There were some beautiful thoughts in it, but still the idea of human duty that ran through it was that we should hate ourselves in order to please God. I did so want to be loved. If my husband did not love me, if I had lost through submission to my parents the love that might have made my life happy and honourable, why should I not love myself, think of myself kindly and tenderly, make excuses for my own faults which no one else would make, appreciate my own good qualities, compassionate my own sorrows?'

This passage appears where the fiercest criticism of Puritanism is expressed, and the grim picture of the Colbrandspath Sunday is chilling in its protracted and enforced manifestations of piety. It is no wonder Madame Keith recalls with nostalgia and affection the relaxed Sundays of her French childhood, one aspect of European Catholicism which is happily made part of Columba's traditions. Her Jansenist childhood is relieved and made pleasanter than her own sons' Calvinist Sundays are to be. Jansenism, particularly those aspects of it contained in Pascal's *Pensées*, essentially argues the paradoxical necessity for man to use his powers of reasoning to understand that reason cannot be trusted to lead to spiritual truth. Man is a subject full of natural error than cannot be eradicated except through grace. Thus Jansenism, like Calvinism, argues against the direction of the Enlightenment with its emphasis on humanist goals attainable through the empirical application of reason – the direction which led to the development of scientific method and, ultimately, to Darwin's theory drawn from his observations of the animal world. This line of development, which also results in the liberal-thinking Catherine Spence, validates that point of view which suggests Australia is almost uniquely a product of the English Enlightenment. Its origins, like Columba's, are firmly in the 18th century. Both Australia and the fictional Columba offer opportunities for testing rationalist theories unimpeded by superstition institutionally enshrined. Catherine Spence concluded, in her *Autobiography* that 'the doctrine of innate human depravity is one of the most paralysing dogmas that human fear invented or priestcraft encouraged,' and at the age of thirty 'became a convinced Unitarian, and the cloud was lifted from the universe. I think I have been a most cheerful person ever since.' Marguerite Keith's version of a community also given a second chance, an opportunity to jettison the darkness of superstition for the clear light of reason is closely linked to Spence's 'liberation'.

Marguerite names the new society not only after the unjustly neglected discoverer of America, but also after the dove (colombe) of Psalms 55, which poignantly expresses the experience which led her to seek a sanctuary in the New World:

My heart is in anguish within me,
the terrors of death have fallen upon me.
Fear and trembling come upon me,
and horror overwhelms me.
And I say, 'O that I had wings like a dove!
I would fly away and be at rest;
yea, I would wander afar,
I would lodge in the wilderness,
I would haste me to find a shelter
from the raging wind and tempest.'

Marguerite's sufferings and her analysis of her benighted youth provide a background which lifts *Handfasted* out of the ordinary run of utopian novels, for it reveals the psychological origins of reform. This transcends theoretical or theological debate, for it strongly suggests that the urge for improvement is innate, or at least inevitable where lives are involuntarily constricted. Spence makes sure her Columbans are completely ordinary people, driven out of Scotland not by religious zeal, but merely by the urge to live better lives. They accept Madame Keith's ideas of social reform, even handfasting, because the changes are above all rational.

To some extent the Scottish irregular marriages, where a statement of marriage made before witnesses legally binds the parties, was a precedent for Spence's fictional practice of handfasting. But Spence gives a more precise source for the idea of trial marriages. The manuscript of *Handfasted* contains a long footnote, an excerpt from Sir Walter Scott's *The Monastery*, when Henry Wardour encounters Baron Julian Avenel's handfasted union with Catherine. His shocked reaction and strongly worded arguments against the custom are initially shared by Hugh Keith when he encounters the custom. These are Henry Wardour's words: (included in Spence's footnote)

'Then,' said the preacher, 'I tell thee, noble Baron, in brotherly love to thy soul, it is a custome licentious, gross and corrupted, and if persisted in, dangerous, nay damnable. It binds thee to the frailer being while she is the object of desire – it relieves thee when she is most the subject of pity – it gives all to brute sense, and nothing to generous and gentle affection. I say to thee that he who can meditate the breach of such an engagement, abandoning the deluded woman and the helpless offspring, is worse than the birds of prey, for of them the males remain with their mates until the nestling can take wing. Above all I say it is contrary to the pure Christian doctrine which assigns woman to man as the partner of his labour, the soother of his care, his helpmeet in peril, his friend in affliction; not as the toy of his lower hours, or a flower which once cropped, he may throw away at pleasure.'

Walter Scott himself adds a note explaining that the custom arose because of a shortage of priests in remote parts of medieval Scotland, and that it is a custom which has been found in a number of other cultures as well.

Henry Wardour's angry words constitute the case for the traditional opposition to such radical thinking (evidently agreed with by the judges of Spence's manuscript) which must be answered if Spence is to convince us that her Columba is indeed a desirable society, or at least has solved some of the 19th century's most pressing social problems. Madame Keith herself enumerates the advantages of handfasting which develop after it has become settled custom, not merely, as it was initially intended, a way of safeguarding the rights of the Indian women needed for brides in a population overburdened by young males. She points out that it has meant there is no prostitution in Columba, no desertion after seduction, no illegitimacy, no banishment from church privileges, no social ostracism. Apart from prostitution, these had all been suffered by Violet Anderson, whose subsequent life demonstrated her sterling character. In fact handfasting removes all the invidious consequences of the double standard of sexual morality, and places women on an equal footing with men in sexual matters.

The success of handfasting in Columba is due to the community's unique advantages. Where land, food and shelter are to be had in abundance, early marriages and enormous families are the norm. Social conditions in the outside world had made late marriage – with the implied support for prostitution – a necessity. The grim prophecies of Malthus had also provoked much 19th-century anxiety. Spence's social experiment is speculative rather than prophetic, but it did demonstrate that there was no *moral* necessity for women's inferior position. Readers cannot impugn the character of Madame Keith, nor the spiritual struggle which led to the revolutionary practices which were to fulfil her ideals.

The subsequent treatment of unwanted children, 'God's bairns', is as much a reversal of the 19th-century status quo as is handfasting. In making illegitimate children the educated elite of the society,

Spence was not only redressing the bitterly unfair situation whereby the innocent victims of parental irresponsibility are made to pay a lifelong price in social ostracism ('these babies are not really illegitimate – it is the parents who deserve that title, no infant can,' she says in her *Autobiography*), but she is also giving expression to her conviction that environment and not heredity is crucial to character. Recollecting a conversation with Oliver Wendell Holmes, Spence says, 'I objected to the fatalism of heredity as being about as paralysing to effort as the fatalism of Calvinism . . . As a worker among our destitute children, I considered environment the greater factor of the two.' Spence worked tirelessly for much of her adult life to close down orphan institutions, and successfully replaced them with a system of 'boarding-out' children, which made South Australia a model emulated subsequently all over the world. She went on to write a novel about illegitimacy and the effects of heredity and environment (*Gathered In*, 1881).

The Columban experiment, however, proves to have shortcomings, not unlike those disadvantages to 'affirmative action' today. Hugh Keith sums it up in the chapter headed 'Some Short-Comings of the Columban Constitution' when he points out, 'In their eager desire to give perfect freedom in matters of love and marriage to every member of the community, and their determination that the children of separated parents should in no respect suffer, they had erected side by side with the simple representative institutions of a pure democracy, a sort of irresponsible bureaucracy, superior in intelligence, in education and in administrative ability to the people's choice through election.' Legitimacy in fact has become an hereditary barrier to ambition in Columba, for it narrows occupational choice to the manual and practical skills, and thus wastes talent. Liliard is the figure in whom the consequent frustration emerges most strongly and with most justice.

Liliard is the only Columban citizen who wishes to leave and to risk life in the outside world. The rest have kept intact their ancestors' fear and distrust of a world they willingly turned their backs on. But they are also the products of the social system that has evolved in the 150 years since Scotland was left behind. Ambition has been stifled not only by the 'God's bairns' system of promotion to responsible posts, but by the successful achievement of a utopian society. 'With the struggle comes the higher ideal,' says Hugh Keith, as he analyses Columba's weaknesses with Master Hepburn, and explains why Liliard's higher nature craves trial. The nobility of Madame Keith's character is achieved through the suffering of half a lifetime, and it is ironic that the wisdom forged from that suffering should ultimately result in a society content with its own mundane comfort. Catherine Spence articulates these contradictions in a way which makes *Handfasted* a real novel, where intellectual conflict is a continuous process and where character is shown in a dynamic process of development. Far too many other works of the time, utopian in their social idealism, fail to exhibit the genuinely literary qualities of the novel form they borrow. They are, in contrast to *Handfasted*, tracts, manifestoes, handbooks, manuals, but not novels.

Spence has created not only characters who genuinely interest us, but a plot which, in 1879, does not altogether contravene realistic possibility. The love interest, obligatory in the Victorian novel, is given added resonance in the touching vignette of Marguerite de Launay's love for Paul Durham, and its tragic thwarting. Hugh Keith and Liliard Abercrombie's love story is made piquant by the risks they take as a handfasted but not married couple in the outside world. Their happy ending is the ultimate fulfilment of the hopes of Hugh's ancestress.

Already an accomplished novelist by 1879, Spence was not likely to confuse ends and means in this work. It was written for a novel competition, ostensibly to be judged by literary standards. Of course the reasons for its rejection had nothing to do with its literary quality, and only represent a kind of knee-jerk reaction to the radical idealism which Spence had introduced in fictional, and therefore speculative, form. Involved as she was in the painstakingly slow process of real social reform, Spence uses *Handfasted* to articulate and 'accelerate' some of her reformist ideas concerned particularly with the rights of women and children, the formally powerless members of her own society.

But she also incorporates echoes from other literature which helps to place *Handfasted* in a richer imaginative context. Some references are overt, others quite subtle, as in the placing of Upper and Nether Keith near the Lammermoor Hills, a reminder of Scott's tragic story of a forced marriage not unlike Marguerite Keith's. Walter Scott's influence is in fact the most pervasive. Spence's birthplace, Melrose, was within two miles of Scott's Abbotsford, and she had read all of his poetry and fiction before she had entered her teens. He provided her with the idea of handfasting, and even her heroine's name comes from a place in Scott's country known as Liliard's Edge, where a grave contains the remains of a brave Scottish warrior maid, Liliard, who was killed in battle against the English in 1544.

Spence makes interesting use of the truncated literary knowledge of the Columbans. Of course they are ignorant of history and literature since 1745, and the loss of most of their books allows the author to limit strictly their library to a few classics, notably the Bible, Shakespeare, Bunyan, Pope's poems and translations of Homer, and Milton's works. Hugh Keith's account of world history since 1745, and his recounting the works of modern writers such as Dickens and Tennyson, comes as a revelation to Liliard in particular, whose vivid imagination enables her to sympathetically live through these vicarious experiences. What Hugh Keith discovers as he recounts such stories as that of *The Heart of Midlothian* and *A Tale of Two Cities* is that his listeners cannot understand a sexual morality which inevitably makes victims of women, so that prostitution is an almost incomprehensible notion, as is the shame of seduction or illegitimacy. Even the idea of social inequality has to be explained to Liliard. Not only does this provide solid proof of Columba's enlightened ways, it also obliquely and ironically demonstrates that the stuff of fiction is largely taken from what is wrong with the world's social customs and institutions. This in itself explains why Columba has no literature or art of its own. A society that has rid itself of injustice and inequality has also deprived itself of an essential impetus to artistic activity. Spence suggests as well that it has resulted in the loss of religious fervour and of a sense of humour.

19th-century Scots had two writers who gave literary permanence to their language as well as their history, Robert Burns and Walter Scott, both of whom wrote genuinely popular poetry and fiction, much of it an accurate reflection of the proud and independent Scottish rural proletariat. The equivalent writer for the Columbans is Allan Ramsay (1686-1758), Scottish poet and antiquarian notable for his employment of the Scots vernacular. His pastoral play *The Gentle Shepherd* is a favourite with the Columbans, for it is an accurate reflection of both the innocent rustic pursuits of the Scotland their ancestors abandoned, and the equally simple Columban way of life. When asked for some modern Scottish poetry Hugh Keith reads from Robert Burns' *Poems Chiefly in the Scottish Dialect*, 'The Cotter's Saturday Night'. It is another evocation of the piety, simplicity and benevolence of the rural Scots, and like Ramsay's earlier work, is an idealisation of the old ways of peasant Scotland. By 1879 it is as mythical as the classical Arcadia which is the literary model for both writers. Spence's return to Scotland had corrected any lingering idealised memories she may have had. On the other hand, unlike some of her Australian contemporaries who were also writing utopian fiction in the 1870s and 1880s, Spence does not attempt any idealisation of rural Australia either. Her Columba is isolated in space as well as time.

She does, however, suggest another potent literary model for Columba, the paradise of Milton's *Paradise Lost*. Marguerite Keith quotes Satan – 'To be weak is to be indeed miserable' – as she recounts the bitter failure of her marriage, and Milton is again quoted as Liliard and Hugh leave the Happy Valley, their departure being likened to Adam and Eve's sad expulsion from Eden. The subplot of Ninian's corruption by the evil outsider Sam Peters and the theft of the community's wealth suggests a re-enactment of the Fall, and is seen as the beginning of the inevitable absorption of the Edenic Columba into the flawed outside world.

The invocation of these literary idealisations gives an effective resonance to the otherwise somewhat mundane picture of a sturdy commonsense community. Of the Columbans, however, only Liliard has the imagination to apprehend an ideal beyond material well-being. Her favourite stage role is Shakespeare's Rosalind from *As You Like It*, another pastoral Arcady and another heroine who happily abandons it with her lover for the more stirring life of town and court.

More effectively than anything else in *Handfasted*, these literary echoes indicate Spence's own assessment of the utopian possibilities of social organisation her Columba represents. While Columba neither outrages realistic possibilities nor contradicts evolutionary theory, it still belongs to an essentially literary tradition of speculative idealism, and is in no sense a blueprint for actual reform. But Spence's commonsense realism has at least one strongly persuasive effect. While social customs such as handfasting could not reasonably be expected to be adopted by her present-day world, the success of these innovations in Columba speaks volumes for potential human improvement. There is nothing in human nature which forbids the replacement of a faulty society with a better organised one. The Columbans are very ordinary human beings yet they have evolved a set of rules for their society which are equitable and rational, though they seem shockingly radical to their outside contemporaries.

Perhaps what was most threatening of all, at least to those affronted judges in 1879, was *Handfasted*'s depiction of a society where women were in every sense the equal of men. Catherine Spence realised, with a shrewdness and acuteness typical of her, that the *mores* governing sexual behaviour were the basis of female inequality, and all other feminist aims, voting powers, ownership or property, etc., were really only peripheral. She did not even need to suggest an alteration in women's traditional roles. She simply removed the burden of sexual guilt from women and thus freed them from the curse they had borne since Eve's acceptance of the apple from the serpent had branded the female as the cause of the Fall. All her life Spence had been finding ways of repudiating her own Calvinist burden of Original Sin. In *Handfasted* she provides a vision of life without it.

Helen Thomson

Australian Selection

OTHER BOOKS IN THE SERIES

Dal Stivens *Jimmy Brockett*
Ray Parkin *Out of the Smoke*
Frank Huelin *Keep Moving*
William Dick *A Bunch of Ratbags*
Frank Hardy *Legends from Benson's Valley*

JIMMY BROCKETT

Dal Stivens

Fiction – or fact? Jimmy Brockett is that archetypal character – charismatic, ruthless, playing for high stakes in politics, sport, business and the underworld. In the great tradition of Australian con men, he exploits the greed and weakness in others to build his own power.

He toughs his way from the Sydney slums to wealth, fame and influence. Brockett elevates the corruption and brutality in his personal and public life to a level which is bizarre but all too believable.

'. . . a work of importance, a thoroughly Australian work, written with an Australian idiom and tang . . .' Jack Lindsay

A BUNCH OF RATBAGS

William Dick

The bodgies and widgies of the 1950s were treated by the media at the time like monsters. William Dick's novel takes a close look at the human reality.

Born into the extreme poverty and harsh living conditions of Melbourne's western suburbs, Terry Cooke grows through a tough childhood to the apparent glamour of the bodgie gangs.

Terry gradually begins to realize that there is more to life than the gang as the experience goes sour. The novel gives a vivid picture of the locale and fashions of the 50s, but the drama of teenage gang life remains relevant today.

OUT OF THE SMOKE

Ray Parkin

1942, and Japan has struck with all its force at Java, in one of the most bitter sea battles of the second world war. The Australian cruiser *Perth*, one of the two warships remaining in the area, runs into an immense Japanese fleet in the Sunda Strait. *Out of the Smoke* tells not only of the *Perth's* last magnificent fight against such overwhelming odds, but also of a small party of the shipwrecked crew who try to sail a derelict lifeboat to safety – only to land at a port in enemy hands. This outstanding story of courage and endurance is vividly recounted and illustrated by one of the survivors. Ray Parkin's moving and exact honesty makes this a classic tale of war at sea.

'Unique . . . It has a dimension rarely found in stories of action . . . which gives spiritual meaning to physical experience.' Melbourne *Age*

'Here the ferocity of war at sea is experienced at its most intense and bitter.' London *Observer*

KEEP MOVING

Frank Huelin

Keep Moving was the order given by police to the thousands of people like Frank Huelin, who roamed Australia during the 1930s appealing for work and handouts. Pushed from town to town, they jumped trains, slept under bridges or in shanties and, sometimes hilariously, made the best of very little.

The warm communal ethic which developed and the mateship of the road are balanced by the harsh facts of survival. The struggles for rights and dignity during the Great Depression are alarmingly relevant today with more people unemployed than ever before.

Alan Marshall says in his Foreword: 'This is history from one of the men who made it.'

'It works by understatement . . . a gutsy piece of work. I cannot remember a better one about the period.' Melbourne *Age*